Cassandra French's

FINISHING SCHOOL FOR BOYS

Cassandra French's
FINISHING SCHOOL FOR BOYS

ERIC GARCIA

 ReganBooks
Celebrating Ten Bestselling Years
An Imprint of HarperCollins*Publishers*

CASSANDRA FRENCH'S FINISHING SCHOOL FOR BOYS. Copyright © 2004 by Eric Garcia. All rights reserved. Printed in the United States of America. No part of this book may be used or reproduced in any manner whatsoever without written permission except in the case of brief quotations embodied in critical articles and reviews. For information address HarperCollins Publishers Inc., 10 East 53rd Street, New York, NY 10022.

HarperCollins books may be purchased for educational, business, or sales promotional use. For information please write: Special Markets Department, HarperCollins Publishers Inc., 10 East 53rd Street, New York, NY 10022.

FIRST EDITION

Designed by Kris Tobiassen

Printed on acid-free paper

Library of Congress Cataloging-in-Publication Data
Garcia, Eric.
  Cassandra French's finishing school for boys : a novel / Eric Garcia.—1st ed.
     p.   cm.
  ISBN 0-06-073031-5 (acid-free paper)
     1. Dating (Social customs)—Fiction. 2. Single women—Fiction. I. Title.

PS3557.A665C36 2004
813'.5—dc22   2004041873

04 05 06 07 08 RRD/BVG 10 9 8 7 6 5 4 3 2

For the women in my life
(and you know who you are):
Thank you for telling me your hopes,
your fears, your dreams.
After reading this book, you may regret it.

Lesson no. 1

STARK AND
UNRELENTING CANDOR

There was a woman on television the other day who insisted that the best way for us, as humans, to achieve our goals is to grade ourselves, in every aspect of our lives, with stark and unrelenting candor. It's not good enough simply to think about these grades, or to tell them to a friend; according to this woman, who may or may not have been an actual doctor, you've got to write them down at least once a day if you want to make a difference in your life. There's no need, she said, to make any specific proactive plans for these changes to occur. The sheer act of writing them down is, eventually, enough to do the trick. Though I have a strong feeling the woman was a shill for the Bic pen corporation, it's difficult for me to resist what seems like a ridiculously easy method to turn my life toward the better. If all it takes to achieve happiness is a belly flop into the culture of constant self-evaluation, I'm ready to pull on a bikini and call myself a swimmer. To start, I'll give myself a C in metaphor.

GRADES FOR CASSANDRA FRENCH, AGE LATE TWENTIES

(the very latest of the twenties, technically):

Personality: A+, cheery and bright (on a good day); B, moody and pensive (on a low-blood-sugar day); C, morose and sullen (those days when I can't be bothered to strike up the grimace that would net me a B).

Looks: B+, though I hear big hair is coming back into vogue, and I was damned cute in the late eighties, so it may be upgraded to an A- in a short while.

Physical health: A when my mother asks me, B when my friends ask me, C when I'm alone at home, excusing myself from the gym, picking out caramel See's candies to accompany me on lonely video-rental evenings. I guess that's closer to a C-, if we're going for that stark candor stuff.

Mental health: A when my mother asks me, B when my friends ask me, C when I'm alone at home, bloated on aforementioned See's candies and crying from the manipulative movie I rented that's set me back three years in therapy.

Career: This needs to be separated into two sections. Compensation is excellent, A+ all around. I make way more money than should be allowed by law. But in terms of job satisfaction, I'm hovering down near the remedial kids. It might be different if I even had work with which to be unsatisfied. Today, unfortunately, is a day like any other. Today, I have no work to do. Grade: D- with a *see me after class*.

Relationships: Incomplete. Course repeatedly dropped.

There. I feel better already.

In the dark ages before I discovered the joys of working for business affairs here at the studio (said joys: home before six P.M., great clam chowder at the commissary, free admission for myself and six friends to the studio-owned theme park), I put in my time at one of the big Century City law firms catering to the wealthy creative types in town who make and break films and television shows based on their horoscope and mood du jour. The firm had twelve partners, sixteen overzealous associates, and yours truly. That's twenty-eight attorneys eager to litigate tooth and nail over percentages of percentages of profits that would never materialize, and one Cassandra French, who found herself yawning through every deposition. Like an atheist who'd accidentally wandered into a southern Baptist holy-roller convention, I clapped along to the beat but just couldn't see what all the fuss was about.

As in most law firms across America, the partners at Kornfeld, Jannollari, and Winston expected me to account for my time in billable hours, a term derived from the German word *billinbehoren*, meaning roughly "slow death under fluorescent lights." Every billable hour can, in turn, be broken down into ten separate parts (a tenth of an hour, five-tenths of an hour, and so on) which means that my days stuttered by in very small chunks. In the legal world, nothing lasts shorter than six minutes. It's like an electron, unbreakable and unmutable. If you sneeze, that sneeze, technically, takes six minutes to complete itself. On the up side, it makes for fabulous orgasms.

A typical day at Kornfeld would find me running after three cases at once, trying to complete my tasks while still accounting for every minuscule bit of my day. Let's say, for example, that I'd been assigned the task to run down case law involving practical residuals for a U.S. syndicated television show sold to Croatian markets (yes, this is the kind of thing I did for a living; feel free to point and laugh at will). This necessitated a staggering amount of legwork, only a fraction of which could be legitimately accounted for. To wit: Everything in boldface below was considered billable by the firm; that is, they could turn around and charge this time to the client. Everything not in boldface was officially considered a "personal matter."

Tidying office in case someone pops in when I'm not here:—.2 Hours

Checking e-mail for potentially pressing matters I may have missed on my last e-mail check ten minutes ago: ————————.1 Hours

Walking down the hall, being sure to avoid the managing partner's open door: ————————————————.1 Hours

Waiting for the one elevator that works while stopping to chat with the Bagel Lady, who tries, unsuccessfully, to sell me a raisin bagel: ————————————————————.2 Hours

Riding elevator to forty-third-floor library: ——————.1 Hours

Riding it back down to buy raisin bagel from Bagel Lady: ——.1 Hours

Riding elevator to forty-third-floor again: ——————.1 Hours

Trying to convince sweet old staff librarian to let me in with bagel: ————————————————————.1 Hours

Eating bagel outside library while evil staff librarian watches to make sure I've swallowed it all: ————————.2 Hours

Locating, reading, and copying appropriate case law:—.3 Hours

Waiting for scourge-of-the-earth staff librarian to turn her back so I don't have to talk to her or look her in the eye, then darting out of library at full speed: ————————————.1 Hours

Waiting for the one elevator that works:————————.2 Hours

Dropping off research in associate's office, then taking roundabout way back to own office in order to avoid the managing partner, who is standing in my hallway, flirting with my secretary, who is half his age: ————————————————————.3 Hours

The final tally is 2.1 hours, a good chunk of time for what amounted to fifteen minutes of actual work and only .3 billable hours. I was expected to log in 1,800 billable hours a year if I wanted to remain employed, which broke down to 150 hours a month, or 40 hours a week. Based on my usual time-worked to time-billed ratio, I quickly realized that the only way I'd be able to make my hours was to time-travel back to fifth grade and work nonstop from that point onward. But how could I explain to the fifth-grade Cassie French that life wasn't going to turn out exactly as her ten-year-old mind had planned it? How could I break her heart and tell her we won't marry Billy Tillman and have four children named after semiprecious stones (Jade, Opal, Amber, Onyx) and live in a castle on the hill? I have no idea what I'd even say to the fifth-grade Cassandra Susan French, other than, *Don't kiss Aaron Drummer on the bus back from the science museum; his breath smells like cheese and he's going to give you mono.*

Life at the studio is decidedly less stressful. Safe in my office at business affairs, I'm never involved in litigation of any sort, and nearly everything I work on can be put off until tomorrow, or the next day, or the next. I'm almost always home in time to make dinner for the boys, and on those days when I work late, I can usually be expected to knock off a few hours early later that week for a surgical strike at Nordstrom Rack.

Doesn't matter. I've still got no work to do today.

Stan Olsen, one of the senior vice presidents of the business affairs department, has told me that my lack of assigned work has nothing to do with that nasty little loophole on the revised contracts for *Where Did the Time Go?*, the same loophole found and exploited by my former colleagues at Kornfeld, Jannollari, and Winston. That was entirely legal's problem, not ours, and he doesn't blame me a bit. Of course, he stared at my chest the whole time he was absolving me of blame, but I let him gawk for a bit, if only because I do feel a bit guilty about the whole thing. The studio lost $16 million over three stupid little words that, in retrospect, I should have picked up on during final vetting of the contract. Then again, perhaps the studio deserves it for putting out a stinker like *Where Did the Time Go?* in the first place. That was 112 minutes of my life I'll never get back.

I suspect my lack of work is more due to the fact that I won't wear high heels to the office anymore. Stan Olsen told me once that he liked the way my calves looked in high heels, and though I'm not opposed to catching a look or two down the office hallway, I'm not going to torture my feet so some old man with a leg fetish can get his jollies. The next day, I started wearing only flats or sensible pumps, and that's just about when the river of work turned into a stream, then a trickle, and it's been all dry creek bed ever since.

Twenty-nine, highly educated, well compensated, and yet there's nothing to do. In law school, they never warned us we'd be wanting for work. We were pretty much assured that our days would be filled with the opportunity to match wits with the rest of the best and brightest who fell back on law the way our mothers once fell back on teaching.

In law school, though, it was all torts and reasoning. Recitation of facts. There was nothing about how to cope with hours of empty boredom, or how to fold complex origami shapes out of business cards. Not a single one of my professors taught us how to mask our days with fake doctor's appointments or lengthy phone "interviews" with "legal experts" who happen to have the same phone numbers as certain close friends of mine. It was all supposed to be wine and roses and song and decades of intellectual stimulation and financial rewards.

Realization of lifelong expectations: C, but written in pencil. There's time yet.

On my way out of the building (having braved it out until ten fifty-nine and forty-five seconds), I ran into Claire, who was on the lot overseeing one of the shows produced by our television department. She invited me to meet her and Lexi Hart at the Cherry Pan for lunch. I'm not a big Lexi fan, I must admit, but I'm usually willing to tolerate her presence if there's an à la mode at the end of it. We set lunch for noon, which gave me time to run home and feed the boys.

Lunch traffic is always a downer, and by the time I got to the house I was hypoglycemic and in a foul mood. The last thing I wanted to do was cook up something fresh, so I threw a few Hungry Man dinners in the microwave, blasted them for a couple of minutes, and slid the trays down the basement stairs. I understand the importance of the food pyramid and good nutrition, but there are times when it's all I can do to rely on the Tyson family and their frozen godsends.

The boys tucked in good and hard; I could hear them down there, shuffling around in their chains, tearing at the trays, snarfing up the re-heated entrées, licking the plastic for every available morsel. I can't blame them for trying to digest as much food as possible, considering the limited amount of calories I've got them on these days, but the least they could do is keep down the noise. If there's one thing I can't stand in a boy, it's a lack of table manners. I may have to devise a lesson plan to combat this little problem.

I locked the thick basement door, slid on the security bolt, fixed my hair, and headed back out into the rolling gleam of midday L.A. traffic.

The Cherry Pan was relatively busy, but Claire recently dated the head waiter, and even now, after a messy breakup during which she steadfastly refused to speak to him for a full ninety days (she called it the Purge), he always makes sure we get the first table to open up and a complimentary peach cobbler for dessert.

"Afternoon, ladies," he said with a wink as Claire and I stepped in off the street. He was handsome beyond handsome: L.A. handsome, soap-opera handsome, a mop of boyish brown hair tousled over an adorable, kissable face. "Two of you?"

"Three," Claire said. "We've got Lexi today."

The waiter, Alex, nodded and walked away, giving no indication to the others around us that we were about to receive preferential treatment.

"I can't believe he still dotes on you," I said. "The way you broke up with him and all."

Claire nodded as he disappeared into the kitchen. "Hated to do it. Didn't have a choice." Claire, my best friend and a development executive at Fox television, rarely speaks in full sentences when she's on the clock.

"Those puppy dog eyes he gave you . . ."

"Like I said, I didn't have a choice. A sweetie, that one. Like candy."

We were seated five minutes later, and Lexi still hadn't shown up.

This is typical Lexi. Lexi with the teeth too white, Lexi with the thighs too thin, Lexi who can waltz in an hour late for a meeting and get by with a giggle and a wave, as long as the appropriate number of penises are in the room.

"Where does Lexi's stomach go?" I asked Claire once.

"In."

"In where? There's no *in* there. She's practically two dimensional. And if there is a stomach, where's she fit her liver? Or her kidneys?"

"No kidneys."

"No kidneys? Then what cleans her blood?"

"No blood," said Claire. She always has the answers.

Alex led us to a booth in back, and he held my chair as I sat, sliding it under my rump at just the right moment. He smiled that smile and took his leave once again.

"I don't get it," I said to Claire. "Was it the waiter thing? The money? I could understand that."

Claire shook her head. "Waiter thing didn't bother me. I have money."

"Never called?"

"Called just enough."

"Flirted with other women?"

"Only to make me jealous."

I thought for a moment, positive I could come up with the reason why my friend dumped this otherwise yummy boy. I've known Claire for fifteen years; her likes and dislikes are probably easier for me to pick out than my own.

Got it: "Mother issues."

Claire sighed, as if I'd completely lost my mind. "They *all* have mother issues." A moment later, she laid it out. "He was a biter."

"During sex?"

"During sex."

"He bit you?"

"He bit *himself*."

I'm sure I was grinning. "I will never look at peach cobbler the same way again."

Lexi popped up fifteen minutes later in a lime Cynthia Rowley sundress, and Alex lost five big points for mentally licking her from head to toe before seating her next to Claire. Lexi had lost even more weight since the last time I'd seen her, and is now officially thin enough to tread water in a hose.

I read in a magazine once that if you took a Barbie doll and blew it up to human size, the resulting woman would be so thin and yet top-heavy that she'd fall over while trying to walk. Lexi is proof that this is complete and utter bullshit. If you blew up a Barbie doll and introduced her to Lexi, the Barbie doll would run off and join Weight Watchers.

"Cassie!" she shrieked as she reached over the table and grabbed my hands in hers. "Claire didn't tell me you were coming."

"I wasn't."

"Oh, you. You're so clever."

Have I mentioned that the Barbie doll would be a tad smarter? She must be doing something right, though: Lexi's got a beautiful house and yoga studio up near Sunset Plaza where the glitterati pay her money to force their bodies into unnatural positions in the name of health. I've taken exactly six yoga classes in my entire life, and regretted each and every one of them. If the Lord had intended for my knees to wrap behind my neck, he would have given me a man by now to go with it.

For lunch, I had the grilled chicken with fennel, which seemed like the low-carb, low-fat choice, but I nodded and mumbled noncommittally under my breath when Alex asked if I wanted fries on the side. When my food arrived, it was accompanied by a plate of grease-laden potato wedges. Clearly not my fault. I ate every last bite, of course. Everyone knows that once the food has been delivered to the table, it doesn't count.

Claire ordered a Thai chicken wrap. Lexi, the sweetheart, the dear sweet darling, ordered the vegetable plate. I bet she could have ordered a burger or pizza or a bucket of lard and still maintained that figure, but she just had to flaunt her willpower with grilled asparagus and eggplant.

Lunchtime conversation mostly settled around Lexi's most recent shopping experience down in Laguna Niguel, or Claire's last visit to the fifty-year-old psychiatrist with whom she's currently sleeping.

"Isn't that strange?" Lexi asked. "Sleeping with a man who knows so many intimate details about your life?"

"Please," drawled Claire. "Like I tell him the truth."

I popped another fry in my mouth. "That's very progressive of you. Lying to your therapist."

"Only because I'm sleeping with him," she countered. "If we stopped screwing, I could open up."

"So stop screwing," I suggested.

"Eh," shrugged Claire. "He's not that good of a therapist."

"Oooh, oooh," Lexi tittered. "Do you know who I saw at Nordstrom yesterday?"

Claire pouted. "You went to Nordstrom without me?"

"Michelle Pfeiffer."

I oohed and aahed appropriately, even though Michelle's done three films with the studio and I've seen her on the lot about seven hundred times. Lexi's always dropping names like that, and though I could easily counter with my own run-ins with fame, I choose to stay silent. Any lunch with Lexi is full of tongue biting, and if it all seems a bit much, it is. But aside from the nonsense about the celebrities and hangers-on, Lexi's presence is tolerated because she's got the dirt we all want to hear:

Lexi knows where the boys are.

Single in Los Angeles is a much more tiring prospect than Single in San Francisco or Single in New York, if only for the mileage involved. If I lived in a city with a true urban center, I could hop from club to bar to nightspot with just a taxi ride or two, no worries. In L.A., where the hot spots change with the tide and the distances between each locale can run twenty or thirty miles, you'd better go in with a battle plan or it's over before it's begun. Lexi, she of the never-ending legs and smile, runs reconnaissance.

Claire already had out her date book. "Spill."

"Los Feliz is out," Lexi gushed. "Yucatan, Rhumba, it's all last week."

"So what's this week?" I asked. "Better yet, screw this week—what's next week? I like to scope a place before it gets too crowded to move."

"Next week, Hawthorne."

"Eww."

"Exactly. The old *eww* is the new *ooh*."

Claire was doubtful. "Is there a club or a restaurant in particular or just . . . Hawthorne in general?"

"I'm working on it. This is an art, ladies, not a science."

"Hawthorne," I muttered. "Is it going to be all actors? There's no point in doing this if I'm going to be stuck in a corner all night talking about dental crowns and Stella Adler."

"Very few," said Lexi. "Most of the places down there have a cover charge."

Claire grinned. "Vampires have garlic, actors have the cover charge."

"Actually, Cass," said Lexi, flashing her colored-contact baby blues in my direction, "one of the clubs is owned by Stuart Hankin."

Hankin. My heart jumped a bit, and I stared down at my fingernails. "It rings a bell."

"We met his brother at that party on Sunset Plaza. I think he hit on you. The one with the race car."

I shook my head. "A race car? I'm sure I'd remember that."

"Didn't he disappear?" Claire asked. "I thought I heard that."

"Stuart?"

"No, not Stuart. His brother."

"Disappear?" laughed Lexi. "No one disappears anymore. Except maybe on television."

Claire turned to me. "David, maybe? David, Daniel . . . ? I thought it was on the news and everything. This doesn't sound familiar to you?"

I shrugged. Maintained a steady tone. "He probably took a vacation and didn't tell anyone. I agree with Lexi, hon. You're watching too much TV."

"Anyway," Lexi continued, "Stuart owns this bar off Third, some kind of dog theme."

"A dog theme. Sounds right up your alley." Lexi is the proud owner of two rabid Tasmanian devils masquerading as Scottish terriers. They're twenty-six aggregate pounds of terror and tiny teeth, and I have to wear three pairs of socks every time I go to her house to avoid leaving with laceration wounds to my ankles.

Lexi shrugged. "All I know is my sources say it might be the new place to be. And there's only one way to find out."

We made plans to make plans.

I thought I was going to get out of lunch without having to blab about my own life, but just as we threw down three credit cards to pay the bill, Lexi opened up those collagen-injected lips of hers. In the event of a water landing, I bet she could use them as floatation devices. That is, if her breasts fail to inflate first. "So, Cassandra. What's his name?"

"No name. No one to have a name."

"Lonely week?"

"Lonely month." I could play this game if she wanted. "It's a lonely life, Lexi."

"I thought you were dating that production designer."

Claire stepped in. "Cassie has her rules, you know. Break a rule, you're gone."

Lexi leaned in. "Rules?"

"Not many," I said, glaring at Claire for bringing it up in the first place. Next time she brings a new boy around I'll make sure to ask after her athlete's foot. "And they're not rules so much as . . . suggestions."

"Like what?"

I didn't want to get into this with Lexi Hart, not inside the Cherry Pan, but Claire kept elbowing me in the ribs, so I tossed out an easy one. "He has to call the second day after the first date."

"The second day? What's wrong with the first day?"

Claire downed her iced tea and took an extra swig of mine. "Desper-ate."

"Exactly. Second day after shows he's thoughtful but not clingy. Third day is only acceptable if there's an excuse for not calling on the second day."

"But it doesn't matter what kind of excuse," Claire said, filling in the details. "Is that right?"

"Right. If it's the third day, he can get by with the dog ate my phone number, got hurt in a freak circus accident, any of those. Because it shows he's got creativity. Now, if he hasn't called by the fourth day, he needs an actual excuse, preferably with a notarized letter of some type."

Lexi was aghast. "Boys really bring you notarized letters?"

"Not many. Most of them give up at that point and go chase someone with a lower set of standards. Actually, Lexi, didn't you date Peter Hoffman?"

"For a bit. Last January."

"We went out in December. After the third date, he went five days without calling. He begged and pleaded for another chance, but he never came up with the notarized letter and I had to let him go. That must have been when he met you."

Lexi's perfect little jaw clenched oh so tightly. I beamed a wide grin, dabbed at my lips with a napkin, and signed my credit-card slip, suddenly finding myself in a very good mood. Lexi might have teased us all with her vegetable platter, but at least I made her eat a little humble pie.

After work (or lack thereof), and badly in need of a sour apple martini, I braved the Wilshire corridor on the drive back to my little house in Westwood. I never realized how strenuous it could be to avoid Stan Olsen for ten hours a day. Every time he caught a glimpse of me I managed to slip away down another hallway, as if we were playing in some old spy movie. By the time I climbed the front porch of my house and let myself inside, my neck and back were crying out for a massage.

I warmed up some soup I'd frozen earlier in the week and ladled it into the boys' bowls. I had to take away the ceramic ones a few months back because Daniel smashed his against the wall and tried to use the shards to cut away at his nylon. Fortunately, I came home in time to catch him in the act and instruct him as to the proper course of manners when one is staying as a guest in another's house. Since then, I've switched to plastic bowls with Disney characters on the bottom. The boys seem to enjoy it.

I carefully loaded the bowls onto a tray, unlocked the bolt on the basement door, and flipped on the stairwell light. Falling down stairs would be a terrible way to die; the obituary alone would send me into a second death from embarrassment.

"Dinner," I called out. "Soup tonight."

The three of them were quiet, speaking little as they sucked down their meal. Alan, the spoken-word poet from Sherman Oaks, made small noises as he swallowed, cute little mewling sounds like a kitten. He doesn't complain anymore, doesn't whine a bit. What a change I've noticed in him over the past few months.

Afterward, I brought the bowls upstairs, tossed them in the dishwasher, then climbed back down into the basement. Owen was in the corner, trying to get comfortable on his cot. The manacle on his left ankle had become wound up in its own chain, and he was having a bit of difficulty working out the kinks. I stepped in and helped out, and he was instantly grateful.

"Do you mind giving a massage?" I asked him. "My shoulders are killing me."

He nodded and made room for me on the cot, and soon his thick, powerful hands were on my shoulders, my back, my neck, rubbing in all the right places, working out the tension. Back in the old days, when I first enrolled Owen in my Finishing School, I would have been nervous, worried that he would try something dumb, that he'd reach around and strangle me or worse, but the big sweetie is beyond all that now. Six-foot-four, still well muscled even after the low-protein diet I've got him on, and gentle as a mouse. His progress is truly remarkable.

I thanked Owen for the massage, and he gave me a polite kiss on the cheek. I could see an eager glint in his eye. "Tomorrow," he asked softly, "could we watch a film?"

"We'll see," I told him as I tucked him into bed. "If you're good, we can talk about it." Daniel and Alan were already beneath their sheets, and I kissed them each on the forehead before checking their restraints. I turned on the baby monitor, climbed upstairs, shut the basement door softly, and slid the security bolt into place.

Once upstairs, I listened to the single message left on my answering machine:

"Hey Cass, it's Lexi. Great seeing you at lunch and all. Oh my God, I was so bloated by the time I got back to the house." Sure, steamed carrots and a teaspoon of peach cobbler can really come back on a gal. "We set up Friday night at Stuart Hankin's new bar in Hawthorne. It's called the Kennel Club, so it might be in vogue to wear fur. Your choice. Claire will pick you up at eight."

I don't know what enrages me more about Lexi's messages: Her assumption that my social calendar is always available to accept any date and time she suggests, or the fact that she's right.

The boys are down. The monitor is silent. And I'd better knock off for the night if I want to get any sleep. After all, I'm sure to have a hard day of productive, fulfilling nothingness at work tomorrow.

EDITING OUT
THE NEGATIVE

At five-thirty this morning, the phone rang, and, like a moron, I answered it. At five-thirty, there's only one person who could possibly be calling me, and at five-thirty, I'm in no emotional mood to deal with that sort of phone call. But at five-thirty, I'm also in no mental state to discern whether or not I should be answering the phone, so I picked it up and grunted a hello.

"Yeah . . . uh . . ." It was a guy this time, his stutter radiating confusion. Mom had roped some poor early-morning shift worker into doing her dirty work. "Uh . . . is this Cassandra?"

"Yes," I said, instantly annoyed, sitting up in bed and pulling off my aromatherapeutic sleep mask. Don't get me wrong, I love my mother. It's just that on mornings like today, mornings when I'm going to miss out on an extra half hour of much-needed sleep, love isn't quite enough. "What is it?" I snapped.

"Oh. Okay. Right, well, see, I was jogging down San Vicente—"

"And some crazy lady in a cashmere housecoat jumped in front of you."

A pause. He was surprised. "That's right. Hey, that's right. So she stopped me, and—"

"Asked if you had a cell phone because she's not allowed to use hers. I know, I know." It's the same each time, they always want to tell me the story about the woman in the cashmere housecoat. "Can we get on with this, please?"

"Uh, sure. She wants me to tell you . . . uh, hold on . . ."

My mother's voice filled the background, a rapid-fire babble of information I couldn't quite make out, her nasal whine tearing at the phone line. I read somewhere that children are programmed to love the sound of their mother's voice; I must have been out of the womb that day getting a facial.

A minute later, the guy was back on the line. "She wants you to come to her place at noon."

"I can't do noon." At noon, I'll be in the back alley of Cedars Sinai Medical Center buying high-grade morphine from a male RN I met at a sushi-making class in Cheviot Hills.

"She can't do noon," I heard him tell Mom. Another pause, another stream of sinus-blasting instructions. "How about one?"

The thing about Mom is, she doesn't give up. Stubborn isn't just her middle name—Mom is *stubborn's* middle name. I could have put up a fight, but one way or another, she was going to strong-arm me into visiting her at lunchtime. "One is fine," I told him. "Can I go back to sleep now?"

Like a dutiful messenger, he relayed the mostly rhetorical question back to my mother, and, as I hung up, I could hear her instructing the boy, "Tell my beautiful little girl to have sweet dreams."

Relationship with my mother: A- to D+. It all depends on the time of day.

Stan Olsen caught me. Snatched me right up like a cashmere sweater on sale at Bloomie's, and it happened so quick I still don't know exactly how he did it. I had just hung up the phone with Claire, who'd regaled me with yet another installment of her ongoing relationship with her horny-yet-respectable psychiatrist, and was heading out of the office on my way to the back alley of Cedars Sinai where my RN friend Joe was going to slip me the ten vials of high-grade morphine I'd paid for two days ago. Before I'd even stepped two feet from my office, Stan was there, right in front of me, like a tornado popping up in the middle of a clear Kansas day. Only tornadoes don't have thinning hair and bad comb-overs.

"Cassandra," he sighed, half a step away from complete drool. "Cassandra, Cassandra, Cassandra."

"Mr. Olsen."

"Please, you know you can call me Stan."

"I can?"

He smiled and leaned against the wall, as if we both had all the time in the world and wanted nothing more than to spend eternity bullshitting with each other. "I didn't see you at the meeting this morning."

What I should have said:

"That's because I was hunkered down in my office playing on a website that lets you plug in your body measurements to create a little virtual mannequin and then try on the clothes from different stores so you can see how bad you'll look in them. And despite the fact that I spent those two hours staring at an amorphous blob on the screen that was supposed to represent my body in capri pants and then, as a result, wallowing in what can only be classified as a suicidally negative body image, it's probably safe to say that my time was better spent than had I been sitting in a conference room with a hundred other assholes like you staring at my tits while they pretended to take notes about casework on which I'll never see a single minute of time."

What I actually said:

"I was sitting in back."

I tried to slip around to the side, but Stan reacted quickly enough to block my path. Time was running out; Joe's cigarette break ended at twelve-ten, and after that I'd have to wait until next week to get the stolen morphine I'd already laid out $500 for.

"Listen," he said, and I could feel the come-on coming, dripping like grease from every word, "I'm throwing a little get-together at my place this Friday. A lot of vice presidents, mostly, but there's room for a few lucky counsel. If you want to drop by."

I quickly went through my mental social calendar and drew big red X's over every date in the near future. "So sorry," I told him, putting on my best pout as I dredged up Excuse #413. "I've got a friend coming in from out of town."

"Heck," he said, his grin now twice as big, "bring her along. Any friend of Cassie's—"

"Him."

"Hm?"

"Him. Bring *him* along. My friend's a guy."

"Oh," said Stan. I could see those late-night cable-porn fantasies dissolving before his eyes. "Well—"

"Anyway," I continued, "he doesn't have a car out here, so I'm on airport duty, waiting for him to land."

"The whole weekend?"

"Darn airlines. Always keep you guessing."

Honesty: C. I should probably award myself a D or lower here, but I'm taking points for fibbing with aplomb. You can't go through life constantly being honest with everyone around you. The potential conflicts are just too numerous. You know what? I'm giving myself a B. Sometimes the most honest people are the ones who admit how little their honesty counts.

Joe was on time, I was on time, everything worked out peachy. We made the swap behind a Dumpster where they toss out medical waste. It was foul-smelling and icky and generally unwholesome, but I switched out my DKNY sandals for an old pair of Asics and tried to jump over every puddle of mystery moisture in my way.

I tucked the shoe-box-sized container of vials into the trunk of my car, wedging it between the detritus of failed dates: An old picnic basket (dinner at the Hollywood Bowl with a special-effects designer who was too cheap to spring for box seats) and a bundled-up pair of paint-smattered khakis (a messier-than-expected painting party in Van Nuys, wherein all the guests were forced to help a pair of cheapskate newly-weds redecorate for free).

I think you can tell a lot about a person by the things she keeps in her trunk. Aside from the leftover date effluvia and the morphine, I've got a length of rope, two spare pairs of panty hose, a half-empty bottle of chloroform, and a set of jumper cables that I've got next to no idea how to use. This indicates that I'm both ready for any emergency and practical enough to know my limitations.

My cousin Faith stores a forty-eight-piece Clinique makeup set and a battery-operated lighted mirror in the trunk of her Audi so that if she's ever kidnapped at gunpoint and forced into that dark, cramped space, at least she'll go to her maker with a fresh coat of lip gloss and base. I'm not entirely sure what that says about Faith, but it probably says volumes about me that I spent four hours helping her pick out the perfect shade of eye shadow.

My mother, on the other hand, has a spotless trunk; the only thing in the back of her BMW is a six-disc CD changer bolted to the floor. In years past, that changer would have been filled with the best that the Holy Trinity (Barbra, Barry, and Bette) had to offer. These days, it's cleaned out. These days, Mom does all her heavy listening at home.

"It's beeping again."

This is the first thing Mom said after opening her condo door and enveloping me in a tight hug. Have her arms gotten shorter, or has my waistline expanded? Better not to think about it.

"What's beeping?" I asked.

"The anklet. The goddamned anklet."

I looked down at her leg, where a court-ordered electronic monitoring anklet transmits my mother's every move back to a receiver embedded into her kitchen floor, which then relays it to some station downtown. The only noise the anklet made was a soft thunk as the metal casing knocked against her bony tibia. "I don't hear any beeps, Mom."

"Well, not *now*. Before. When I went out."

"And by out, you mean . . . ?"

"To the supermarket. I know my rights, little Miss Lawyer. I heard the judge."

We all heard the judge. The judge was not a happy man when he handed down his sentence. The judge, like the rest of us, was tired, and wanted my mother out of the courtroom as soon as was humanly possible. Their relationship was strained, to say the least. Most of their "conversations" went along the following lines:

JUDGE HATHAWAY: Mrs. French, I'm ready to deliver the sentence.
MOM, ON HER CELL PHONE: That's fine, dear. If you could wait
   just one eensy moment—
JUDGE HATHAWAY: Excuse me?
MOM, STILL OBLIVIOUSLY ON THE PHONE: It's just that I'm
   having the nicest conversation with my colorist right now, and
   I'd hate to lose my train of thought midway through.

This was after eight days of testimony, most of it from victims who were duped out of their hard-earned cash by Ted, my mother's currently-on-the-lam husband and the ringleader of what the prosecution called a telemarketing scam "empire." Don't get me started on Ted. I've already got three forehead creases and two frown lines at the corners of my lips thanks to Ted, and I don't need to work myself any closer to a face-lift worrying myself over that man.

Mom and Ted had been married for only two years when the cops showed up on their front lawn, and Mom, ever the gracious host, invited the nice officers in for blintzes and coffee while Ted scurried out the back door. By the time they had Mom cuffed and inside the patrol car, Ted was long gone. Mom says she has no idea where he went. The D.A. doesn't believe her. I do.

"Judge Hathaway said I could travel up to five hundred feet from my home in order to take care of the basic human needs of living," Mom reminded me. "And I hope you'll agree that food is a basic human need."

She's clearly never met Lexi. "You had some stranger call me at five-thirty in the morning so I could drive halfway across town during my lunch hour and have you tell me that food is a basic human need?"

"What," she asked, "it's so terrible to come have a nice chat with your mother?"

In the sixteen months since she was sentenced to home arrest and electronically tethered to her condominium in West Hollywood, I've seen Mom more often than when she was free to roam the city at will and come knocking on her only child's door at the most inopportune moments imaginable. If I had a boy in bed, Mom was at the door. If I had a *toy* in bed, Mom was at the door. It sounds terrible, but when the judge handed down his sentence, there was a teensy part of me that jumped for joy: Her imprisonment would be my freedom. No longer would I have to fear the dreaded drop-in. I could leave my clothes on the floor for days if I wanted. Weeks, even. The umbilical cord would finally be severed.

That was the theory, at least. Reality hasn't kept pace.

Mom grabbed my hand and pulled me down the hallway, the cashmere housecoat swishing against her bare legs, anklet bouncing up and down beneath her calf. I stumbled along behind, pumping my thighs in order to keep up. She barely clears five feet in height, but Mom's a towheaded fluff of energy, constantly moving in some direction or another. She's always been this way, as far back as I can remember. As a child, I used to stand in the middle of the kitchen and watch her skip about the house, trotting from one room to another like a museum security guard on amphetamines. If you turned on a movie camera in her condo, you'd have to slow down the film to a quarter of normal speed just to see past the blur.

We took the stairs, three flights at a rapid clip, and I nearly tripped over my Linea Paolo sandals as Mom pulled me out of the stairwell and into the bright light of day.

"Listen," she said. "No beeping."

"It doesn't beep unless you go out of range."

Mom held up a finger and dragged me farther along the sidewalk, counting out the distance from her condo as we walked. "A hundred feet . . . a hundred twenty-five . . ."

We passed by two strip malls before arriving at the intersection featuring the Ralph's grocery store frequented by my mother. The parking lot practically crawled with old folks; it was a five-foot-high shag carpet of blue hair. "There it is," she said. "My market."

My lunch break was almost over. I still had to drive home, give the boys their afternoon snack, work the morphine injections, start the VCR, lock up the basement, and fight traffic over the hill back into the valley before two o'clock. If I didn't get to the office by then, I'd be sure to miss the lady who comes around with the banana-nut muffins. Most days I don't give in to temptation and actually buy one, but the lingering smell of her freshly baked treats makes the rest of the workday bearable.

"Is something supposed to happen?" I asked.

"Hush, Cassie. Watch and listen." She checked both ways and stepped off the sidewalk and onto the street, and almost immediately a howling *whoop-whoop-whoop* filled the air, blaring up from some hidden speaker within Mom's anklet. Pedestrians for blocks around slapped hands over their ears; cars screeched to a halt. To call it a banshee howl isn't being kind to banshees.

"You hear that?" she shouted triumphantly over the din. "That's what I'm talking about!"

"That's horrible!" I yelled.

"That," she screamed back, "is three hundred and twenty feet."

It's amazing that something small enough to fit around my mother's puny ankle could make enough noise to scare the horns off a charging rhino. I suddenly had a flash of myself on a talk show telling the sympathetic host in sign language how it took only fourteen seconds for me to be struck deaf. The surrounding pedestrians were beginning to locate the source of the noise. Some were probably having murderous fantasies.

"So you believe me now?"

"Yes, I believe you, I believe you. Just get back on the sidewalk!"

The moment she crossed whatever invisible line the anklet deemed appropriate, the alarm died off, and the normal midday groan of L.A. traffic resumed.

"Three hundred and twenty feet." Mom sighed. "That's not right at all. That's . . ."

"A hundred and eighty feet short."

Mom's warm smile lit the rest of her face. "That's my Cassie Bear," she said, squeezing my cheeks just up to the pain threshold. "Always good with the math."

I pulled my cell phone out of the Philippe Model purse that Claire had brought back for me from her last trip to Paris. It doesn't really go with the outfit I had on today (bone blouse from Express, longish Emporio taupe business skirt, aforementioned Linea Paolo sandals), but the silver leather lining makes me think of strolling along the Champs d'Élysées, and until I find another handbag that reminds me of chocolate croissants and Nutella, I'll be lugging this one around, taste be damned.

"I'll call the courthouse," I told Mom, "see if they can send someone down here to fix it."

She snatched the phone from my hands and popped it back into my purse. "You'll do no such thing. I'm a grown woman, I can take care of myself."

"I know you can. It's just . . . you don't have to bother some stranger on the street when I can—"

"Tut, not another word."

I wasn't going to argue with her any further. The amount of breath it would take to win the battle would be better put to use panting on an elliptical machine at the gym. In any case, it was nearing one-thirty. "So that's it? You had me come down here so I could hear your ankle scream?"

"Actually," she said, "I was hoping you could buy me a mango."

As I was able to cross the street and enter the supermarket without any of my accessories violating local noise-pollution laws, it was easy for me to walk into Ralph's, grab a couple of mangoes off the stack, and throw down a few bucks at the ten-items-or-less line.

By the time I arrived back on the other side of the street, Mom had already located and cornered her next assistant. It was a woman this time, a girl, really, no more than twenty-five, who'd probably been out for a bite to eat when she suddenly found herself trapped by a sixty-inch-high ball of energy. The girl clutched a cell phone to her ear and stood a safe distance away from the crazy lady in the cashmere housecoat.

"Here's what you tell them," Mom instructed her. "You tell them that Judy French's ankle monitor is malfunctioning, and they need to send someone down to my condo right away to fix it. Well, what are you waiting for? Go on, talk."

And the girl, like all the other girls and boys and women and men Mom's sweet-talked over the last sixteen months, repeated the request into her cell phone word for word.

If Judge Hathaway had any idea that by sentencing Mom to three years without the use of a telephone he was effectively sentencing the citizens of Los Angeles to random and sudden confrontations with a slightly crazed ex-telemarketer in a housecoat, I'm sure he would have done us all a favor and let her go free. The time will come, I believe, when His Honor will be taking an early-morning stroll down Beverly Boulevard, and he'll feel a tap on his shoulder, and hear that voice at his back, and before he's even got a chance to cringe or run or both, he'll be dialing whatever number Mom wants him to on his cell and repeating her dialogue verbatim. Most likely, he'll be calling me. Mom is nothing if not consistent.

I'm back at the office now, too late for the muffin lady, but just in time to catch the lingering vestiges of banana-nut scent. They should package that stuff and sell it as cologne. I'd be much more interested in a man who smelled like freshly baked dessert treats than I would in one who smelled like musk. I don't even know what musk is, but I'm pretty sure I can't dunk it in coffee.

The boys were famished by the time I got home. The turkey sandwiches I'd made for them were barely enough to stave off their hunger, so I rationed ten animal crackers for each one, and that seemed to do the trick. It's no good to get a full dose of morphine on an empty stomach. I learned that lesson long ago.

They were anxious for a film. Movie Day is always a big event here at the Finishing School, and I'm proud of how much they've grown to enjoy the process. Sometimes my boys are like little kids, excited about the smallest things, and I can't help but love them all a bit more for it.

Owen was already sitting next to his bed, hands folded in his lap, waiting patiently for me to wheel out the TV/VCR; Alan was doing the same on the other side of the room. But Daniel was still in his cot, blanket pulled up over his head.

"What's wrong with Danny?" I asked.

Owen raised his hand. I nodded, and he said, "I think he's pretty sick. He was tossing all night and talking in his sleep."

I pulled down the covers and rested my palm against Daniel's damp forehead. A quick run upstairs to get the thermometer, which confirmed my guess: moderate fever, probably a flu or cold. This sent me scurrying back into the kitchen like a worried mom to get Tylenol for Daniel and orange juice for the other boys. The air in the basement is recirculated, a veritable theme park for viruses, but I'll be damned if I let some single-celled organism beat me at my own game. As some sports-infected bad date once said over and over, the best defense is a good offense.

"The film today," I said, cueing up the tape to the very beginning, "is called *Pretty Woman*. Does anyone remember seeing this in the theaters?"

Owen's hand shot up; Alan shook his head meekly. Daniel's arm slowly wormed its way through the covers and into the air. "That's fine, that's fine. Hands down. Okay, for the two of you, you'll find that there are some differences in what you may remember from the theater and what you will see today."

"Like with *Casablanca?*" asked Owen.

"Like with *Casablanca*, that's right. I'm glad you remember that. Alan, this will be completely new for you, and I think you'll really like it."

The boys all knew what to do next, and kept stiff upper lips as I injected each of them intramuscularly with 15 mg of morphine. The first few times I tried the injections, I erroneously gave them shots directly into the vein, like I'd seen all the heroin addicts on those TV cop shows do it. As a result, I wound up with drooling, unresponsive students. There are certain times when a drooling boy is exactly what you want, but these are few and far between. The IM approach, I learned after a few quick jaunts on the Internet, reduces the efficacy of the doping aspect but allows the pleasant high to come on nice and mellow without turning the patient into Sling Blade.

In Garry Marshall's version of *Pretty Woman*, the version we've all seen since 1990, Richard Gere plays a jerk of a businessman who buys and sells women as easily as he does large corporations; they've got parts to be used and that's the bottom line. Of course, in the end, through the help of a hooker with a heart of gold played by Julia Roberts, he sees the error of his ways, falls in love, and rides up on his steed to whisk Julia away from a world of degradation at the hands of men like himself. For some reason, this is considered a chick flick. But it also gives boys the idea that they can spend 95 percent of their waking lives as chauvinistic macho assholes so long as they repent by the end of the third act.

In the Cassandra French version of *Pretty Woman*, brought to you via the magic of a $15.99 video-editing program I bought on sale at Best Buy, Richard Gere is much more honest, caring, and forthright.

For example: You may recall the scene in which Mr. Gere bargains for Julia Roberts's time over the weekend, and, after securing her services for $3,000, admits he would have paid much more. That's gone. In its place is the scene, originally much later in the film, where Mr. Gere punches out his slimy, misogynistic business partner (played to a perfect pitch by Jason Alexander, whom I always see in the studio commissary buying tuna salad on rye). With the new edit, it simply seems as if Julia and Richard are enjoying their time together so much that Richard gladly cancels business plans just to be with her and then defends her honor just for kicks. I've made similar cuts and exchanges throughout the course of the movie, each of them exemplifying my main point: Boys don't have to wait half their lives to become good, kind men; women will like them even if they're decent and noble from day one. On a side note, I've also conserved a fair bit of time. The original film was a lengthy hour and a half; mine runs just a shade under sixty minutes.

By the time the show started, the boys were already sinking into their happy places. Alan and Owen were both slumped lower in their seats, staring openly at the film, lips set in a loose grin. Even Daniel was paying attention behind his haze of influenza. Their brains were making the connection, over and over again, that being good to women felt, well . . . good. Look at that Richard Gere—rich, powerful, handsome, and yet he's being so nice to that woman. Chivalry isn't dead. Nice guys don't finish last. Kindness isn't for suckers. The morphine is just a conduit, a way to help these boys reestablish the connection between good deeds and good feelings. A way to teach them all the things they once knew but society had helped them to forget.

I had things to do back at the office, but I couldn't help but sit down next to Owen, take his hand in mine, and watch along for a few minutes. I love the part where Julia Roberts gets revenge on the Beverly Hills shopkeepers, but hate the earlier section when they're so rude to her. Next time, I think I'm going to edit them out, too.

> **Dedication to my boys:** A+. I don't know what I would do without them. No matter what's going wrong in my life—my job, my relationships, my hair—they're a bright spot in every day. One day, they'll be gone, back into the world that made them. That's the goal, after all. All I can hope is that they'll come back now and again and thank me. Then they'll probably ask for another shot of morphine.

It's nearly one in the morning, but I've just gotten back from the bar, and I want to get this all out before a haze of exhaustion, anger, and alcohol wipes it away. The woman on TV who said we should write everything down was very insistent that we stay "in the moment." Reflection, she said, impairs judgment. Or something like that. I'm a bit too bombed to remember correctly.

Claire picked me up at eight, and we headed down into Hawthorne. We had both decided against wearing fur, Lexi's information being shaky on this point. And though my maxim is that it's always better to be overdressed than underdressed, the situation reverses itself if entire animal hides are involved.

On the drive in, Claire launched into another one of her stories about her therapist. This time, they'd been deep into a session exploring Claire's Jungian mandala when the good doctor decided to do a different kind of exploring.

"So there I am on the chair," Claire said, "chopping up my personality into little bits at his request. Suddenly I realize there's a little something-something going on downtown. There he is, on his knees, head up my skirt."

"Which one?" I asked.

"The Garfield and Marks with the straight slit."

"Oooh, that's a tight one. How did he breathe down there?"

"I don't think he could. Two minutes in, I didn't care. But here's the point: We ended up screwing on the sofa, and halfway through, I noticed he wasn't looking at me. So I started watching his eyes. Know what he was looking at?"

"Mirror on the ceiling?"

Claire grinned wryly. "His diploma. The Ph.D. from Berkeley. I think it helped get him off. And then I realized that he's been doing that all along. That's why we only have sex in his office."

"Nowhere else?"

She gave it a moment's thought. "Actually," she said, "we did it at my place once. In the bedroom. But I think he was reading a pillow tag the whole time. Probably imagining it was a textbook."

"At least you know what he's fantasizing about," I pointed out.

"There's that. I've just never been with anyone before who only comes when enlightened."

"Comes When Enlightened," I mused. "That could be his Native American name."

A half hour later, we arrived in Hawthorne, which was about as run-down as I'd remembered it, not so much dirty as it was *chunky*, the way I imagine the insides of my thighs must look to small microbes. With a little liposuction, Hawthorne might be a grand place to make a home. The buildings were short, squat, with thick brick walls that looked like they were held over from the twenties. Mini-malls were in no short supply, but looked untended, as if their owners knew that the regulars would keep coming back one way or the other, but that there wouldn't be many new customers to speak of. It seemed like a city without a lot of self-confidence.

Lexi's information was good, though; the club scene was beginning to hop. Not quite at maximum density levels yet, but all the right (or wrong) signs were there: long lines at club doors, relatively cute bouncers, distinct proliferation of sports utility vehicles at the valet.

The Kennel Club was marked by a small, modest sign next to the door and, remarkably, no line outside.

"*This* is the place she chose?" Claire sighed. "I feel dead already. Check my pulse."

I chose to look on the bright side. "Maybe it's big inside. Maybe they don't believe in all that elitist line bullshit."

"Maybe I'll go across the street."

While I tugged at Claire's purse and convinced her to give it a try, Lexi pulled up in her Beemer and tossed her keys to the valet ten feet away.

"You didn't wear fur!" she pouted.

I checked out Lexi's little green dress, sans fur anywhere on its two square inches of fabric. "Neither did you."

"But I was *going* to."

The club entrance was dark, the walls covered in some sort of felt. Up ahead, a bouncer with deliciously broad shoulders packed beneath a fitted jacket stood in front of a metal door. I dated a bouncer once named Armand, but the relationship didn't take. He was used to being the one who decided which folks were allowed in and which ones weren't, and couldn't get over the fact that when it came to *my* private club, he was the one who had to wait in line behind the velvet rope.

The bouncer nodded as we approached. "Ladies."

We nodded back, but he didn't move to open the door. "Do you have companions this evening?" he asked us.

"Girls night out," Lexi tittered. "Companion-free."

"Not that it's any business of yours," said Claire. I was glad to see she hadn't left the attitude in her other purse. "I assume your job is to look cute and open the door."

The bouncer took it in stride but didn't budge from his spot. "Actually, ma'am, my job is to make sure everyone's got a companion before I let them inside."

"Forced companionship at a nightclub," I said. "A reduction in civil liberties set to a house music beat. I like it."

"Lucky for you," the bouncer continued, "we've still got some loaners left. Follow me."

He led us down a long hallway filled with bright green doors, each with a small, frosted window near the top. I tried peeking inside, but missed the bottom of the window by about three inches. Lexi could have taken a look, what with those runway legs of hers, but she was too busy cozying up to the bouncer to care.

"Didn't you used to work the door at Linus in Silverlake?" she was saying, interlocking his arm with hers, stroking his biceps with her fingernails.

"No, ma'am," he replied, a trace of a southern drawl riding each word. "This is my first job. I'm still in school at UCLA."

I don't know if it was the mention of college or the ma'am that put her off, but Lexi quickly dropped the bouncer's arm and slunk behind me to the back of the pack. She perked up a few moments later and started in about the darling wall treatments, but it was all false bravado. She'll be calling her doctor about Botox injections come tomorrow morning.

"An inch past thirty and already a 'ma'am'," Claire whispered to me. "Where does the time go?"

Such is life in L.A. When you live in a city where casting directors troll the high schools to find the perfect actress to play Grandma Moses, there's no point in sniffling about age. The standards are ridiculous, and you can either visit plastic surgeons, dermatologists, and lifestyle consultants in an exhaustive effort to keep up with the youth culture, or throw all caution to the wind and live life according to the directions on the bottle: Wake up, get one day older, go back to sleep. Rinse and repeat.

"Here we are," said the bouncer, coming to a simple wooden door at the end of the hall. "Our companion holding tank. Each of you can choose whichever one you'd like. Just make sure to bring him back at the end of the night."

"This club is sounding better and better," said Claire. "I don't suppose there's a rent-to-own option?"

I'm pretty sure I smelled our new "companions" before I saw them: the wet, matted hair, the flea-and-tick spray. Yum. As soon as the bouncer opened the door, Lexi was on her toes, jumping and clapping her manicured hands in joy.

"Wuzzles!" she shrieked. "Look at all the little wuzzles!"

The room was filled with dogs of all shapes, sizes, and degrees of affection, each tethered to a short leash attached to the wall. Most of the little buggers launched into spasms of delight as soon as Lexi threw herself into the fray. She scratched behind ears and rubbed rumps and nuzzled snouts as she cooed, "Yes, you smell my doggies. Yes, you do. Yes, you do."

The bouncer made it quite clear that we wouldn't be allowed entrance to the club without a dog tucked under our arm or on a leash. Claire was halfway out the door before I caught her elbow and dragged her back inside. "We're staying," I insisted. "I didn't haul my ass out to Hawthorne to be turned back by a pack of dumb, slobbering animals."

"If I'd wanted dumb, slobbering animals," she said, "I could have stayed on the west side and waited until closing time." But she gave in, trudged back inside, and set to picking out a dog that would match her shoes.

Lexi popped up from the pile of canines with one that looked to be the same make and model of her dogs at home, a ten-pound ball of fluff sans the gnashing of teeth and inevitable blood flow. "I'll take this one," she told the bouncer. "I'm going to name him Snoopy."

It turns out the dog already had an unpronounceable French name, inscribed on a little green metal tag around his neck, but Lexi didn't like it and insisted on calling him Snoopy all night long. The dog didn't seem to mind. He was much more interested in sniffing my crotch than responding to the high-pitched calls of his temporary owner.

Claire chose a miniature pinscher because you can never go wrong with basic black.

"Don't you have anything . . . bigger?" I asked the bouncer. "These are all so froufrou. I'd hate to have someone mistake my companion for a mop."

Frowning as he checked his clipboard, the bouncer took a look around the room. "We've had a lot of single guys coming through here tonight; they always take the larger ones. . . ."

"What about that one?" I asked. A spindly brown tail dragged lazily across the floor; the dog it was attached to preferred to remain in the shadows near the corner of the room. The silhouette was sizable, though, at least two or three times that of the other ankle biters in the pen.

"Oh," the bouncer said sadly. "That's Sanford. You don't want him. In fact, they're thinking about taking him back to the breeder."

"What's wrong with him?" I asked. "Is he sick?"

"No," said the bouncer. "Just moody."

Two minutes later, Sanford and I strolled into the main lounge at the Kennel Club. A proud Rhodesian ridgeback with a mercurial attitude, Sanford's hot-and-cold routine fit my expectations of the night quite nicely.

Claire held her pinscher, Klaus, like a clutch, grasping him around his small, taut waist. The little dog darted his eyes back and forth, looking for a way out. Smart little bugger, that Klaus. Claire's not a dog person. She's not a cat person, either. Come to think of it, she's not even a person person, but that's why we get along so well. Poor Klaus must have come to the realization that, if given the opportunity, Claire would have gladly slam-dunked him into the nearest trash bin. As a result, he made no sudden moves, no loud noises, giving her no immediate reasons to play Globetrotter with his hide.

Lexi and Snoopy made their grand entrance as a commingled ball of fur and breasts, all excitement and panting and yipping.

The club itself was your usual low-wattage affair, well-placed halogens spotlighting certain niches while leaving others in complete darkness. Everyone in the place was leashed to his or her own dog; some were probably brought from home, but most bore the green ID tags of Kennel Club loaners. A gigantic oil painting of four Dobermans playing Connect 4 hung on the rear wall. Bartenders pulled beer from fire-hydrant-shaped taps.

Claire stepped into position next to me as we stood at the entrance to the lounge, surveying our options. She had Klaus stretched across her forearm, lying on his back, and began pressing on his little stomach like a shopper checking the ripeness of a melon. "How will I know when he's got to do his business?"

"Keep pushing on his belly and you'll find out soon enough."

The club wasn't busy by any stretch of the imagination, but the round tables on the outskirts were already taken up by groups straining to talk over all the yipping. While Claire went in search of a booth, Sanford and I chose to take a seat at the long mahogany bar. I perched atop a stool, while Sanford sat dutifully at my feet, scowling at any boy who looked my way. Logically, I had stumbled across the jealous type.

Three or four boys made it past my guard pooch and tried various opening lines, but I wasn't in the mood to give any of them even a courtesy nibble. There was something about the place that was throwing me off. Maybe it was the scent of dog, or the endless techno-jazz loop they were trying to pass off as music, but after a half hour and a couple of sour apple martinis, I was ready to call it a night and head home.

"Sanford!" I heard a voice call out behind me. "Sanford, buddy, you old dog, you. Picked out a winner this time."

Oh great, I thought, *a regular.* Bar's been open two weeks and already this guy knew all the dogs by name. I turned to give him the brush-off like all the others.

And nearly fell off my chair. Hello, handsome. Not only was this guy not bad looking, he was *very* not bad looking. Olive skin, a light dusting of scruff on an otherwise baby-perfect face, a chin that jutted out at just the right angle. Boxer's build, not too thickly muscled, but no lightweight, either. He looked familiar, but I wasn't taking the time to process that; most of my thoughts revolved around coming up with something, anything, to say in return.

"Oh," I grinned stupidly. "You know Sanford?"

The boy sat down on the stool next to me and ruffled the fur behind Sanford's ears. The dog leaned back, into his hand, digging the sudden display of affection. "Me and Sanford go way back," he said, still directing his conversation toward the dog. "They say you're moody, buddy, but I know the truth. You're just picky, that's all. Say, who's your friend?"

I leaned down and whispered loudly into Sanford's ear. "Tell your pal that my name's Cassandra."

"That's a beautiful name," he told the dog. "You think your new friend Cassandra lives around here? I haven't seen her before."

If this guy hadn't already gotten my heart racing, he'd have been dispatched to Loserville long ago. But his smooth features and boyish charm earned him a one-time exemption. "Tell your friend he needs to think of a better pick-up line," I said.

"That's strange, Sanford. I didn't know I was trying to pick her up."

"That's funny, everyone else noticed it."

If dogs could roll their eyes, Sanford would have been fake gagging all over the place. Come on, people, I bet he'd shout. Get a crate.

I gave in first and dropped the Sanford pretext. "If you must know, I live on the west side."

He laughed, and that crinkle at the corner of his dark eyes set me off. Did I know this guy? He certainly seemed familiar, but there's no way a boy like this would have slipped from my files. "You came all the way to beautiful downtown Hawthorne from the west side, huh? You must really like this place."

I waved my hand dismissively about the bar. "Not especially."

"You don't think it's sort of . . . funky?"

"Funky? No. It's just about the saddest excuse for a club I've ever seen."

"Really?"

"Really."

"I rather like it," he said.

"I'm not surprised."

That smile again, that gleam in his eyes. Delicious. "Okay," he said, "I'm all ears. Why is it the saddest excuse for a club you've ever seen?"

"Well, for starters, there's the whole dog aspect."

"But it's called the Kennel Club."

"And how very cute that is. But aside from the health issues—and let me say that the owners must have paid about a million dollars in bribe money to get the health inspectors to sign off on a place where they encourage disease-ridden animals to trot around without hairnets and whizz wherever they feel like it—aside from that, there's the whole 'theme bar' thing, which has pretty much been done to death over the last ten years. I can't tell you how many sensory-integrated, multimedia, mixed-art, fully inclusive, three-dimensional, surround-sound bars I've been to in the last decade, each one worse than the last. Whatever happened to the good local club where you could go and dance and sit at the bar, maybe meet someone nice, have a good time, without having to 'integrate with your surroundings' or 'conceptualize your environment' or 'explore the world of wireless interfacing'? I mean, whatever happened to normal bars and restaurants? Why does everything have to be infused with cilantro? Or, in this case, with dog hair?

"And what's with the drink menu? Look at this. Do I really need to be offered concoctions with 'fun' little names like a Scotch Terrier and Soda or Bloodhound Mary? And let's not even talk about the sweet little doggie biscuits in all the peanut bowls. Just wait until some drunken moron thinks he's tossing back cashews and ends up choking to death on a Snausage. Hello, lawsuit.

"What I wouldn't give for a bar with no theme, with no pretensions, with no plasma screens. Just a shelf of drinks, a few tables, and a jukebox. Maybe a pool table in the corner that no one ever uses. That's what I'm looking for. And that's what I'm never going to find. Not anymore. Not in L.A."

I finished off my little speech, took another slug of my martini, and set the glass on the bar. "There," I said. "That's what's wrong with the Kennel Club."

The guy didn't say anything for a few moments. I guessed he was soaking it all in, trying to come up with some witty comeback he could use to sweep me off my stool and into his bed.

"You're right," he said finally, and walked away.

I looked down at Sanford in confusion, and he stared back up at me with hangdog eyes. It may have been the booze, but I'm pretty sure he shook his head back and forth at the pathetic girl sitting on the stool above him. How had I screwed up so completely and so quickly that even a dog would pity me?

I looked back up, but the guy was gone, having vanished into the crowd to find some other woman who would be less prone to rave like a lunatic on furlough from the asylum.

"Yummy," said Claire as she came up behind me. "Did you make any headway?"

"Hardly. I'm pretty sure I scared him off women for good."

"Were you ranting?"

"Like my mother."

Claire rubbed my back sympathetically. "So he failed the Cassie French litmus test. Better now than later."

"Easy for you to say." I sniffed. "You've got Comes When Enlightened in your back pocket."

"That's not a relationship, honey. That's just relations."

"I don't even have that." I noticed that Claire was no longer carting Klaus beneath her arm. "Where's the pooch?"

"I had to visit the Ladies'," she said, without a trace of guilt. "There was a bathroom attendant. I had no change."

"Klaus was your tip?"

She shrugged. "He fit in the jar."

Snoopy's piercing yip heralded Lexi's arrival. She put her new little companion on the counter, and he trotted over to the bowl of dog treats, his clipped black nails tap-tapping on the bar.

"I knew you'd remember Stuart," Lexi said to me as she picked up a bone and hand-fed it to Snoopy.

"Stuart who?" I asked.

"Stuart Hankin," said Lexi. "The owner. I just saw you two jabbering away like old friends. What a cutie-pie, that one."

As Mom would say: Oy.

I spent the next twenty-five minutes trying to track down the man whose career and club I'd just verbally ambushed, but to no avail. Everyone claimed to have "just seen" Stuart go by, but no one had a lock on his whereabouts.

"Forget about it," Claire advised. "He's just another boy with a club."

"An amazingly cute boy with a club," Lexi pointed out. "An amazingly cute, rich, smart—"

"Thank you, Lexi." Claire waved her off. "She's embarrassed enough, she doesn't need details."

"Forget about it," I said. "I just feel like a tool."

Claire grabbed my hand and held it tight, pulling me away from the bar and what would have been my third drink of the night. "Let's drop off the dogs and get out of here. The music's slow, the drinks are watered down, and I'm pretty damn sure I'm getting mange."

"You two go ahead," Lexi said, scooping Snoopy back into her arms. The little ball of fluff looked quite comfortable nestled between those tanned twigs. "I'm going to hang out with my little Snoops a bit longer. I can't bear to leave him yet."

On the way out of the bar, I felt as if everyone in there was staring at me, whispering, *There's the bitch who said all those mean things to poor, nice Stuart.* I could even feel the dogs glaring me down, eager to attack as a pack and rip out my throat for what I'd done to their master.

"Keep it moving," Claire instructed. "They can smell fear."

"Who, the dogs or the yuppies?"

We were at the valet for only thirty seconds when I heard Stuart's voice behind me, and, for a moment, I was glad we'd found each other. The moment didn't last too long.

"Hey, check it out, there's the girl who wants to tell me how to run my club."

I didn't turn around. A very small part of me chose to believe that if I didn't see him, he couldn't see me, and that I could leave Hawthorne with a shred of dignity intact.

"Says she's all maxed out on theme bars," he continued. Clearly, I was still visible. "That makes a hell of a lot of sense. I'm pretty much maxed out on ignorant bitches."

Claire lashed out before I could mount my own defense, shooting Stuart her best Fox-exec scowl, the one usually reserved for show runners of underperforming sitcoms. "Hey, asshole, go sleep it off and leave her alone. She's had a hard night."

"*She's* had a hard night?" His sibilants were slurring; Stuart had been knocking back the giggle juice. "I'm the one who sunk all his money into a washed-up *theme bar.*"

"Look," I said, finally turning around and into the conversation, "I'm sorry. I didn't get a lot of sleep last night, and I'm hypoglycemic, and I'm in a bad mood. I didn't mean to take it out on you or your stupid bar."

Stuart took a step toward me. I held my ground. "What do you do?" he asked.

"Why does it matter?"

"I figure maybe I can give you pointers on how to run your business. We can be even."

I stuck out my chin and proudly announced, "I'm in-house counsel at a studio. Business affairs."

That shut him up. As his head hung down low, his shoulders slumped into small ski slopes, bouncing rhythmically up and down. At first, I thought he was crying, and I felt even worse than I did before. But then he threw his head back and his mouth opened wide, and it was quite clear he was laughing. At me. *Hard.*

"It's okay, everyone," he called out to the assembled valets who'd been watching the scene unfold. "Show's over. She's just in business affairs."

He leaned in close, and I could smell the whiskey on every ugly word. "When you decide to do something real with your life, come on back and we'll do this again."

By the time the veil of anger and embarrassment had lifted, by the time I was ready to shout back, *Okay, so maybe I don't have a big stupid nightclub like you and maybe I don't spend my days helping sick children go to Disneyland or building rope bridges in developing nations, but I've made my choices in life and I stand by them, even if it does mean I don't have any work to do and spend most of my days hunkered down in my office, surfing the web for good deals on control-top hose*, Stuart was gone, and Claire's car was at the valet.

I don't remember much of the drive back here, other than Claire repeatedly telling me to forget about Stuart Hankin, that the elitist prick wasn't worth the effort, that I was a valued member of an important profession, that the Kennel Club was a stupid idea and would probably go under before next Tuesday.

Claire dropped me off, and I took some time alone before climbing down into the basement to see the boys. I didn't think it would be fair to let my experience at the club sour my attitude with them. So I lit a few candles, poured a glass of red wine, sank into a hot bath, and tried to forget all about stupid Stuart Hankin and his drunken dismissal of my profession and life.

A half hour later, the anger had dissipated into a general haze of uneasiness, and the shame felt more like someone else's, as if I'd watched an old movie on TV and was merely empathizing with the character's mortification.

The boys were already asleep, so I paced the basement for a while, kicking up the small piles of sawdust that have been appearing on the basement floor without explanation for some time now, debating whether or not to wake the boys up so that I could go through the comforting ritual of putting them back to bed again. In the end, I decided to wake only Daniel.

"Danny," I whispered, stroking his cheek softly. I don't know how I didn't see it back in the nightclub, how I didn't figure it out earlier. The tanned, olive skin, the strong jaw, the boyish lips. "Earth to Daniel, come in Daniel."

Slowly, he blinked himself awake, and propped himself up on his elbows. "Are we going to watch another movie?" he asked.

"No, sweetie," I said. "I need to take your temperature, that's all."

He opened his mouth dutifully, and I popped in the thermometer. As we waited for the results, I stroked his jet black hair, brushing the loose strands away from his clammy forehead. Amazing. The same hair, the same eyes; their build was different, sure, but they weren't twins, after all, just siblings.

"A hundred point two," I read. "Not bad." I helped him take a few more Tylenol and sat at the foot of his bed as I sang him to sleep. He was out like a light before the second verse of "The Rainbow Connection." I kept singing until the end.

"I met your brother tonight," I whispered to the sleeping Daniel Hankin. "He's cute, but I think you could probably teach him a thing or two about manners."

Then I climbed upstairs, got out my notebook, slipped beneath my Laura Ashley sheets, and jotted all this down, an act which I'm sure would please the lady from TV, but has only served to make me feel more pathetic than I did an hour ago.

Relationships: F. I'm a realist, so let's face facts: When you're verbally abusive to a strange yet handsome man whose younger brother has been locked up in your basement for half a year, it's pretty safe to say you won't be tossing a bouquet to your bridesmaids at any point in the near future.

Lesson no. 3

PICKING, CHOOSING, APPRECIATING

Jason Kelly is in the building. *The* Jason Kelly. The boy who *People* magazine named Sexiest Man Alive two years running. The boy whose films have grossed over $2 billion worldwide and received fourteen combined Oscar nominations. The boy who's broken more hearts in Hollywood than an entire menagerie of casting agents (or should that be "headshot of casting agents"?). Most important, he's the boy who holds the single-season record for number of appearances in Cassandra French's sporadic late-night, lights-out, blankets-on-the-floor, mattress-stress-test, heavy-duty-vibration sessions.

Oh, yes. *That* Jason Kelly.

He's right next door, in the auxiliary conference room. I know this because I just stood on the back of the sofa in my office and pressed my ear to the air duct like Laverne and Shirley trying to spy on their neighbors and heard his mellow tones filtered through eighteen inches of aluminum piping. Sure, I felt like a fool, and I'd have turned red as a spanked bottom if anyone had walked in and caught me up there, but come on, this is *Jason Kelly* we're talking about. His pecs alone would be considered extenuating circumstances.

The very first time I ever saw him on screen (*Ryder on the Storm,* 1998, Columbia Pictures), my heart stopped for a good ten minutes. I'd be willing to bet I was legally dead. It was just a small part, and the film wasn't that great to begin with, but those bright green eyes of his cut right through me, grabbed ahold of my insides, and squeezed. I walked out of that movie theater bowlegged.

And now he's here. Fifteen feet away, behind a thin veneer of drywall and Sheetrock. Half of me wants to bust through the wall and into the conference room like the Kool-Aid Man and throw myself atop his lean, taut body; the other half of me wants to take the first half out back and give her a good talking to. I'm a professional, for the love of God, and this is a professional atmosphere. I work on a studio lot—I see actors all the time, in bathrooms, in commissaries, in parking lots.

But Jason Kelly is no mere actor. And I'm pretty darn sure he winked at me.

This morning started off like any other: waking up bright and early, shaking off the lingering embarrassment from last night's Kennel Club debacle, feeding the boys their breakfast, starting them on their workbooks, heading out to the gym, stopping off first at Starbucks to get a pick-me-up cappuccino, deciding halfway through that a cruller wouldn't hurt, buying a nonfat mocha latte to wash down the cruller, and finally realizing that it was way too late to start working out now, that I'd just have to double my effort the next time around. In this manner I have officially delayed my workouts sixteen days in a row, which means I'll have to be thirty-two times as efficient when I hit the elliptical machine tomorrow morning. I'm thinking positive.

There was a buzz in the air when I finally got to the office this morning, a bit of adrenaline and anxiety rolled into one, as if everyone was preparing to bungee jump off the top of the building but no one quite knew how to secure the harnesses. Even our mousy little receptionist Cathy (to whom I've given cosmetic advice on at least three occasions, and who, it's clear from her uneven skin tone, has never fully listened to or appreciated my wisdom) had a spring in her step.

"Is something going on?" I asked her.

"I'm not sure," she said. "But everybody seems so happy, I thought

I'd join in." Screw Prozac. Peer pressure must be the new surefire cure for depression.

Then I saw him out of the corner of my eye, a little flash of pearly whites, a curl of chestnut hair, jawbones that could cut glass, and an entourage bigger than the crowd at my last birthday party. They moved through the small office corridors like birds in formation, stopping when Jason stopped, moving again when Jason took the lead. There was laughter, and there was a lot of hugging and kissing, and I wasn't yet any part of it. Travesty.

Slipping into the coffee nook for cover, I poked my head back out and tried to figure out why Jason Kelly would drag his beautiful, talented self up here to dreary business affairs. Most of the time, actors and directors and writers have their agents call us; we don't tend to deal with the talent directly. Maybe he was seeing someone on the twenty-third floor. I wondered who it was: Lorna, the curly-haired freckle face who, rumor has it, slept with four vice presidents and still has yet to be promoted, which means she must be terrible in the sack, or Beth, whose innocent little schoolgirl act doesn't fool anyone except every single boy in the office. They all want to protect her and hug her and give her a good home, when it's perfectly clear that all Beth wants is to screw the rest of us out of a fighting chance. No, none of the women in the office seem quite right for Jason Kelly. None of them except me, of course.

I tiptoed along the hallway, nonchalantly making my way through the office about fifty yards behind Jason and his people. As I perched next to a secretary's cubicle and stared at Jason's cheekbones and the way his lips perk out just the right amount without looking like they've been caught in a vacuum, I felt someone slide up next to me.

It was the Muffin Lady. Seventy-three and going strong, pushing her cart of muffins and bagels down the wide hallway.

"For fuck's sake," she rasped, "he's a hot little piece of ass."

As I fought for breath, the Muffin Lady pulled out a pair of spectacles and dropped them over her eyes. "Oh yeah," she continued, "look at those buns."

"That's Jason Kelly," I told her as soon as I could form words again. "He's an actor."

"I don't care what he does, so long as he does it here."

We watched Jason for a little longer, me and the horny Muffin Lady, as he hugged and kissie-kissed his way through our office. He even got a little face time in with Stan Olsen, and that gave me the opening I needed.

I left the Muffin Lady wallowing in her own fantasies and wiggled toward Stan just as he and Jason were finishing their chat. On the way over, I ran a hand through my hair and licked my lips for extra gloss.

"So I'm doing the points for that Scorsese deal we talked about . . ." I allowed my line of bullshit to trail off as I "noticed" Jason standing nearby. "Oh, I'm so sorry." I believe I may have batted my eyes. So sue me. "I interrupted something."

"Actually," Stan said, "we were in the middle of—"

"Not at all," Jason cut in. "Sam and I were just finishing."

"Stan," my boss corrected. "Stan, not Sam."

But Jason was finished with Stan Olsen; a quick study, he'd already learned that the best conversation with Stan was a completed conversation with Stan.

"I'm Jason," he said, as if I didn't know. As if the entire planet didn't know.

I shook his hand, and the thrill of that momentary contact obliterated whatever I was going to say next. I'm sure it would have been full of wit and charm and grace, but suddenly all I could think about was our future together: the first date, the long walks on the beach, the visits to Jason's villa in Tuscany, whether I should wear a bone or ivory dress to the wedding, and which private schools would be best for our little girl, who would either be named Rebecca (after my grandmother) or Sydney (after the city). As a result, my conversational skills were lacking, and my entire response came out something like, "I'm Cassandra. My mom calls me Cassie Bear for short."

Someone in Jason's entourage of lawyers, managers, agents, and hangers-on snickered, and that little titter brought me crashing back to reality. I released Jason's hand, and, for a moment, I thought he'd join in with the rest of them, and soon they'd all be laughing at me, laughing and pointing, and he'd somehow work the incident into a movie

that would become this big international hit, and someone would let it slip that it was based on a real girl, and at first he'd protect my identity, but eventually my name would come out in the press and Jason would be forced to talk about my rampant stupidity in magazine interviews, and soon the TV talk shows would be hounding me, reporters camped outside my door. I made up my mind then and there to speak to Diane Sawyer and Diane Sawyer only. A girl has to have her standards.

Instead, he simply said, "Nice to meet you, Cassie Bear. My mom still calls me Pumpkin."

That's when I got the wink, and, by the time I recovered, he was gone, down the hall and into the next conversation, and I was left standing in the middle of the office with Stan Olsen.

"Pompous little ass," Stan spit. "Actors, you know? It's all about *them.*"

Usually, at this point, I'd walk away and save myself from any further conversation, but I was still very much knock-kneed and unable to move without falling down. "What's he doing here?" I asked.

"Who, Kelly? He's got a suit against the studio. Typical bullshit."

"He's suing us? Why?"

"Says we fucked him on the deal for *Half-Hearted.* They all say that. They want points, we give them points. Then the day comes along when their solid-gold limousines break down and they need more money for repairs, so suddenly it's our fault. We didn't give them enough points, or they're the wrong type of points, or . . ."

Stan went on listening to himself talk as I thought back through the encyclopedia of contracts that have crossed my desk over the last few years. I'm pretty sure I remember working on the deal for *Half-Hearted,* and I don't recall anything hinky with the paperwork. Every now and then we'll have legal throw something into the fine print just to see whether or not the talent agents and attorneys are doing their jobs, but for the most part, we play clean. *Half-Hearted,* as far as I can remember, was just another movie deal.

"If he's suing us," I asked, "shouldn't he be down in litigation?"

"He was, and they sent him up here. The studio wants to call some of the attorneys who worked on drafting the deal, so under the parole

evidence rule, his lawyers get a crack at them, too. He probably just came in to work the room, get everybody all schmoozed up and on his side before they issue the depo subpoenas. It's pretty standard stuff."

Wait a second, I wanted to scream. *I worked on that deal! They should get a crack at me, too! Where's my subpoena? I want a subpoena!*

"I'm sure they'll work something out," I said instead. "Jason seems reasonable."

Stan laughed. "What'd I just tell you, French? He's an *actor.* Reasonable's not in his vocabulary."

He walked away, shaking his head at my feeblemindedness. I lingered for a while in the hallway, soaking up the eau d'Kelly in the air. I don't care why he's suing the studio or whether or not we win or lose; I just hope he has to come back here a lot before it all gets figured out.

When I got back into my office, I was greeted by a beautiful bouquet of irises and baby's breath in the middle of my desk, and for a fleeting second, I thought it might have been from Jason Kelly himself. Somehow, I reasoned, I'd caught his eye weeks ago, and this whole silly pretext about the lawsuit was just an excuse to meet me.

Then I saw the dog bone attached to the card, and knew it wasn't from any actor. It was from a bar owner.

I was a doggone fool, the card read. It was in a bubbly script, probably the work of some florist, but the trite sentiments were all Stuart Hankin. *If you want to teach this old dog some new tricks (or just hit him with a rolled-up newspaper), give me a call sometime.*

Stuart Hankin. Stupid Stuart Hankin. He has arched eyebrows. Did I write that down the first time I described him? He has arched eyebrows, and his lips are too thin, and the thing about people with thin lips and arched eyebrows is that they can't be trusted. What also can't be trusted is my impression of him as a handsome man. Sure, I might have mentioned something like that at the time, but I was two sheets to the wind, and beer goggling (or martini goggling) is an accepted scientific phenomenon. I read about it in *Cosmo.*

So the flowers are nice, no doubt about it, and it must have taken a little bit of extra work to track me down here at the studio. Plus, I can

respect a man who understands the aesthetic appeal of an iris, but Stuart Hankin, mean and nasty Stuart Hankin, isn't getting any sympathy or forgiveness out of me.

As it is, I've got more pressing matters to attend to at this moment. First I've got to call Claire and tell her who just winked at me. She may die. Then I've got to hightail it back to the sofa, because I think I hear the meeting in the next room winding up. If that's the case, I need to position myself in the office doorway so that Jason gets a good look at me from just the right angle. If the sunlight hits me from behind, I could have a good Grace Kelly thing going. I've got a pair of high heels stashed somewhere in this office, and my calves, I've been told, are shapely enough to catch the eye of the most discerning men. If I can't be the last thing on Jason Kelly's mind before he goes to bed at night, at least I can be the last thing on his mind before he steps into his solid-gold limousine.

Mood: Bummed. Jason and his cohorts left the office way before I ever got a chance to position myself in the doorway and impress them with my silhouetted curves. I was headed to my post with my high heels on when an embarrassing mix of inappropriate footwear and schoolgirl giddiness conspired to bring me crashing to the Berber carpet. By the time I looked up, all I could see was a tasty Jason Kelly derriere moving down the hall.

Balance: D+. I took gymnastics for six years in elementary and middle school; you'd think I could navigate the hazards of your basic legal office. I'm worried about heading down to the commissary for lunch because the servers are mostly older Russians, and Lord knows they're going to score me low on the dismount.

Moments later, as I hoisted myself off the floor, picking bits of carpet from between my teeth, I got a phone call from dear, darling Lexi, she of the toned triceps and sunshine smile.

"Cass, you've got to help me!" I'd never heard her this shaken-up before. I double-checked the Caller ID on my phone; are beauty queens allowed to fluster?

"What's up, Lex? Tanning booth go haywire?"

"It's Jack and Shirley. They've . . . they've been arrested."

Now, I've always told my friends to give me a ring if they ever need legal advice. I figure I went to law school for three years and worked in the legal field for the last five, so the least I can do is parcel out information when and where it's needed. But I'm usually pretty clear on the fact that the extent of my knowledge begins with film and ends with television. Anything else, and I'm just about as useful in a legal setting as is, say, coral.

"I do entertainment law," I reminded her. "If you've got some friends who've been arrested, I could give you the name of the guy who defended Mom. Not that he did such a bang-up job, if you ask me."

She was sobbing on the other end of the line, really letting it out. I wondered if there was snot running down her nose. If there was, I bet it was *pretty* snot. "Jack and Shirley," she repeated. "My wuzzles! They've been taken into custody."

Her wuzzles. Of course. Jack Nicholson and Shirley MacLaine. "The ankle biters?"

"I don't even know how it happened. One minute we were at the dog park, minding our own business, and the next, they were barking and a man was kicking and suddenly the police were there, and . . . Oh, Cass, you've got to come over. I don't know what to do."

"Gee, Lexi, I've got a really full schedule—"

"Puh-lease," she sobbed, whining like a third-grader who'd just been caught passing notes. "Y-you h-have to c-come over. . . ." She dissolved into tears, and my resistance broke. For chrissakes, I'm not a monster.

We met for lunch at an Italian joint up on Sunset Plaza. It was within walking distance of Lexi's house, which she insisted on because she was too rattled to drive. I'd called Claire on the way over, hoping to rope her into this thing as well, but she was heading into a therapy session with Comes When Enlightened.

"I think this time I'm going to suggest doing it with the lights out so he can't see the diplomas," she told me. "See if he freaks."

"Or if he puts on night-vision goggles."

Lexi was already sitting down when I got to the restaurant. Surprise, surprise, her makeup was intact and her hair was perfectly coiffed. She'd even managed to work past her grief to pull on some Forum hip huggers and a pink Hello Kitty T, which drew the stares of all six heterosexual males in the place. When I walked in and sat down next to her, my body did nothing more for them than block their fantastic view.

"Oh, Cass, thank you so much for coming!" Lexi threw her long arms around me and pulled me close. She held the embrace way past the acceptable time frame for the circumstances, but I was powerless to escape. I'm sure the boys staring at us enjoyed the spectacle. Meanwhile, Lexi sniveled and sniffled all over my shoulder.

"Are we sitting shiva, Lexi?"

"What? Who's Shiva?"

As Mom would say: Oy. "Why don't you just let go and tell me what happened?" I took out a legal pad and pen, mostly to make it look as if I was paying way more attention than I intended to.

"Okay," said Lexi, sitting back and taking a deep breath to compose herself before she began. "First, you know the wuzzles."

"Oh, I know the wuzzles." I wrote down *Wuzzles = Evil.*

"And you know they would never hurt a fly. Actually, they do have this one this little rubber toy, it sort of looks like a fly, and they've kind of torn it to pieces over the years, but they'd never hurt a *fly* fly. Anyway, I was planning on taking the wuzzles to this adorable little dog park in Santa Monica. It's got a play set and sand and lots of benches, and they love to run around in there, and it's got this gorgeous view of the ocean, so it's particularly nice to go around sunset, when the light first hits the water. I think Jack, in particular, really likes the park at that time, because he's always a little bit wistful when we go around sunset."

Dog wistful at sunset, I wrote. Check. "Go on. I'm sure there's a point floating around here somewhere."

"So we got to the park around six," she rambled on, "and we were having the best old time. Only I could tell they were feeling a little . . ." She paused, pursed those perfect lips. "What's the word where you feel like you're trapped and can't get out?"

Lunch with Lexi? "Claustrophobic?"

"That's it. They were feeling claustrophobic. So I let them off their leashes, just to give them the run of the place."

"Is it a leash-law park?" I asked.

"Yes, but the sign with the rules is very, very small. You can hardly read it." *Insanity defense*, I wrote, then crossed out the s so it read *inanity defense*. Much better. "Anyway, the wuzzles went off to do their thing, and I started talking to this very nice-looking man, sort of an older but distinguished type, like a Sean Connery only without the accent, and he's telling me about the stock market and I'm telling him about yoga and it's all going really well, and then suddenly I heard the wuzzles barking and this ugly little man started screaming and kicking his leg into the air, and I see Shirley go flying, just totally flying, and so I go running over there as fast as I can.

"That's when I see that the man's not just kicking for no reason—he's kicking Jack and Shirley. And they're doing their best to defend themselves the only way they know how."

"Biting his ankles off?"

"Right. And so of course, I yelled out to them, 'Good doggies! Good doggies, that's some good biting!' "

"Wait a second," I interrupt. "You were encouraging your . . . wuzzles . . . to bite this stranger?"

She was aghast. "Goodness, no. That's how I get them to stop. It's the only thing that works. If I yell 'Stop' or 'Quit it,' they just get scared and latch on harder. They're very sensitive pups. They only respond to positive reinforcement."

I understand positive reinforcement; it's the way I like to train my boys. There's no sense in beating them with magazines or shoving their noses into their own feces; boys and dogs can, with repetition, learn to respond to positive stimuli. I'm glad Lexi's found *something* that stops those little fiends. The last time I went to her place, I nearly had to borrow the Jaws of Life from a local firehouse to pry Shirley MacLaine's choppers from my shin.

"Of course," she continued, "no one could hear me over all the barking, so I just rushed in and gathered them into my arms. Then I gave the guy a good talking to. Kicking a dog like that, and just a little wuzzle, no less. He started screaming at me and said they were biting him first, and that he had no choice, and blah blah blah, but some people are just dog kickers, and they're bad people, and there's nothing you can do about it."

Dog Kickers = Bad People, I wrote. *Wuzzle Kickers = Not Necessarily Such Bad People*. "Is that when the police came?"

She nodded, and the tears welled in her eyes again. "They put the wuzzles in a cage and took them to the pound. They weren't licensed, they said. I didn't know you needed a license. No one ever told me that. They said I could go and visit them today, and a judge would rule if I could have them back or not this Friday."

Oh, did I see where this was going, and oh, did I not want any part of it. "Lexi," I said, "you know I can't officially do legal work for anyone other than the studio. And even then, I'm not a litigator. I don't even do contracts anymore. I just make deals, when they let me."

"I know," she sniffed. "But I thought you could stand next to me at the hearing. Like on *The People's Court*, when the plaintiff has a friend in court, and Judge Wapner asks 'Who are you?' and they're always like, 'I'm her cousin,' and then Judge Wapner asks, 'Do you have anything relevant to add to this case?' and the cousin usually says, 'I'm here as a character witness,' and then Judge Wapner—"

"Okay!" I yelped. "I'll go. I'll go into court with you."

If she didn't annoy me so much, Lexi's genuine smile would have been thanks enough. She wiped the tears from her eyes.

"And you'll drive me to the pound to visit the wuzzles? If I get in a car, I'm afraid I'll wreck it."

Like I need that hanging over my head. "Sure, Lex, I'll drive you. Let's eat first, and then we'll go down there."

Lexi leaned across the table and gave me another hug. "You're the best, Cassie."

"You too, Lex."

And then the skinny bitch ordered the vegetable plate.

The Humane Society of Santa Monica is, I'm sure, quite lovely as Humane Society shelters go, what with their highbrow clientele and all, but it's still the pound, and it still carried the scent not only of doggie doo and antiseptic, but of canine desperation. These critters might not be any brighter than carpet lint, but like every other living thing, they've got some sixth sense that tells them when they've reached the end of the line.

"We're here to see Jack Nicholson and Shirley MacLaine," Lexi told the clerk at the front desk. The woman didn't bat an eye as she checked the register of the dogs in her stead. I expected a whole "who's on first?" routine to break out, but they must get felonious dogs with strange names in there all the time.

"Are you the owner?" The clerk gave Lexi the once-over.

"I'm their mommy," Lexi replied. "And I brought them a few personal items."

She brought them a "few" personal items in the way that there are a "few" people living in China. We cleaned out a local pet store on the way over here; any more purchases, and they would have made Lexi an honorary stockholder.

"No toys in the shelter," said the clerk.

"But they're my wuzzles."

"Oh, they're your wuzzles. That's completely different. That changes everything."

Lexi doesn't have a ticket to board the sarcasm train, so it took a few more minutes of explanation before she was willing to leave the toys in the car. We were led back into the kennels, where a chorus of barking dogs greeted our entrance. There wasn't much difference between the Humane Society and the other night's escapades at the Kennel Club; I wonder if the dogs' water bowls were watered down.

Jack Nicholson and Shirley MacLaine had been placed in the same long run at the back of the main kennel building. Their relative viciousness per pound had earned them a red tag tied to the door of their cage, so as to warn any workers to don protective gear when dealing with them. A pair of electrician's gloves and shin guards hung on a nail next to the run.

To look at them in that kennel, though, you'd never know that they were the canine versions of America's Most Wanted. Shirley lay on her belly, forelegs thrust out in front, her head resting between them on the hard concrete floor. Jack sat at her side, panting quickly, his lips pulling back into a wide doggie smile with each breath. Their fur was matted, already filthy from one night in the slammer. When they saw Lexi, they regained a bit of energy; Jack trotted forward, tail wagging lethargically, and Shirley stumbled to her feet.

"Here you go," said the clerk. "You've got twenty minutes."

Lexi pulled at the chain-link door. "How do I get this open?" she asked.

"You don't. Visitors stay on the outside."

Lexi pouted but knelt down outside the cage and poked her fingers through the open links. The dogs licked at her hands and rubbed their heads against her knuckles.

"Look at this," Lexi said, pulling me down to her level. "They're already getting sick in here. Look how dry their poor little nosies are."

She reached into her purse and pulled out two Wet-Naps. "Here," she said, handing me one of the packets, "you get Jack."

"I get Jack . . . how?"

Lexi unwrapped the wipe and stuck her hands back into the cage. Shirley MacLaine trotted up to her dutifully, and Lexi gently stroked the dog's nose until it was faintly glimmering with artificial perspiration.

"Now you," she said. "Go on, he likes you."

"Likes the *taste* of me, sure." But I sucked it up, because this is what friends do for other friends. I've got to remember to give myself an A for Friendship next time I'm doing the stark and unrelenting candor thing.

Moving as slowly and carefully as possible, I snaked my hands through the chain link and waved the Wet-Nap through the air like a flag of surrender. Jack Nicholson's head immediately spun to the motion, the way I imagine a bull must sight a rippling red sheet. It took all of my willpower not to yank my hands away and run screaming back to the car.

But the furry little Tootsie Roll hopped toward me without a growl, and placed his little head in the palm of my left hand. With my right, I gently dabbed at his nose, which was indeed awfully dry, and I received a grateful lick for my efforts. As a show of goodwill, I reached up and scratched Jack behind his ears. Go figure, he seemed to like it. All was going swimmingly, and I'm pretty sure that for a split second, I considered that I might have been wrong about these little dogs. Maybe they weren't emissaries of the devil after all.

I think that's when the little shit bit me. All I remember is a burst of pain, followed by a furious attack growl that signaled Shirley MacLaine to join in the fray, and soon I was trying to yank my hand back through the fencing as blood flew and the two furry felons laid into my flesh.

Somehow, through the agony, I remembered my training:

"Good doggies!" I yelled at the top of my lungs. "Good doggies! Yes, that's some good biting!"

When I finally got back home, my right hand disinfected and bandaged and still hurting like hell, I found yet another vase of flowers on my doorstep. Startled, I stopped on my front porch and took a look around the house. Had Stuart Hankin been to my home? And if so, did he notice anything amiss? I didn't mind all the flowers; this was another beautiful bouquet, and, in fact, I've got it sitting right next to me as I type this out. But I can't have Stuart poking around my place. It's not as if I'm worried about him getting into the basement; the house is locked up tight, and I've got alarm systems to no end. But brothers know things about each other, and I can't take the chance that Stuart might get some psychic vibe from his sibling and organize an escape. Daniel's training isn't finished. He's not yet the man that he can be. I owe it to him, and to all of the women he will eventually date, to see this thing through to the end.

The bouquet had that same bubbly script on the card; it must have been delivered by the same florist. *No more dog jokes,* it read. *Please give me a call.*

Stuart Hankin's a tenacious thing, I'll give him that much. It's possible, as well, that his arched eyebrows were less convex than I'd first described them, just two little swoops of hair on an otherwise moderately attractive face, but I'm through thinking about him. Stuart Hankin is nothing to me.

I pinched the vase between the thumb and forefinger of my good hand and tried to unlock the front door with the lacerated fingers of my right. I can only hope that my flesh is the equivalent of bad Mexican food, and that Jack Nicholson and Shirley MacLaine come down with a violent case of Cassandra's revenge while squatting in puppy jail. Picturing those two with stomach pains and violent diarrhea makes me feel a bit better, but I'm still hoping the judge is in a bad mood when he decides their fate this Friday. If asked, I will gladly throw the switch myself.

Inside, on the answering machine, were three different voice messages, all from Stuart, each begging my forgiveness. I don't know how he got my home address and phone number, but it doesn't matter. I erased all three messages and headed down to see my boys.

Alan and Owen were playing chess when I came down the basement steps with their afternoon snack of oatmeal and cheese. The chess pieces we use at the Finishing School are little origami shapes I folded myself (thanks, Learning Annex!), because I was worried, back in the early days, about the boys using the hard plastic pieces as weapons. The violence is no longer a concern of mine, but they've grown accustomed to swans instead of knights and lotus blossoms instead of rooks. It's less confrontational this way. There are no battles on the board, just movement and displacement. Very Zen, which is *so* in right now.

Daniel was nowhere to be seen. For a split second, I envisioned his psychic call to Stuart, his escape, their run to the police. The sirens would come next, then the lights and it would all be over. Everything began to swim, and as I whipped around to find a bed on which to collapse, I saw the covers on Daniel's cot shift. The other beds had been stripped of their blankets, and Daniel was buried beneath the entire mound. A light layer of sawdust covered the blanket; where was this stuff coming from?

"Daniel?" I said, regaining my balance and composure as I approached his bed. "What's wrong, honey?"

"C-cold," he chattered. "Wanted more blankets."

He was burning up. I didn't need the thermometer this time around, but popped it in just to get a reading. Hundred and three, definitely getting into dangerous territory. I found a handful of Tylenol and crushed them into a glass of orange juice.

"What happened to your hand?" he asked.

"Shh, don't worry about me. Just drink up."

After he was done with the juice, I covered him back up again; it didn't take long before he was fast asleep. This thing could get bad. I'll need to keep a close watch on it.

"Alan, Owen," I said, "could you two put that game on hold? It's time for me to check your workbooks."

The boys love to be graded; it's something we've all got in common. It helps them to understand their progress, to figure out where they're lacking, and how they can best help themselves in the future.

Alan was first, offering up his workbook like a carefully wrapped present. I sat next to him on his cot and we opened up to the day's assignment. This morning, I'd given them four pages to complete, and I was pleased to see that he'd finished them all.

Today's lesson was in personal fashion, and though both Owen and Daniel had been adequate dressers before they came to the Finishing School, it never hurt to emphasize the basics. Alan was a schlub from day one; the night I picked him up from the parking lot of that bar on Melrose and brought him back here to the basement, he was decked out in eighties-style acid-wash jeans and a bright orange T-shirt that should have been tossed in the trash long before it was ever manufactured.

The first sheet of the day's lessons was simple: Mix and Match. I'd cut out some magazine photographs of pants and glued them down the left side of the page, and then some other photographs of shirts and glued them down the right. The only thing the boys had to do was draw a line from the bottoms on the left to their appropriate tops on the right. Any woman worth her salt could do it blindfolded; most heterosexual men couldn't do it under threat of death. My boys are different, though. My boys have been trained.

I ran a finger along each of Alan's lines and checked off his choices one by one. "Black Dolce slacks to the maroon Prada pullover. Very nice. Front-faded jeans with the yellow button-down and mid-length leather coat. Simple, but good." I ticked off the rest of his answers and put a big A+ at the top of the page. Alan beamed.

The next page was a little more difficult, as I'd added shoes and belts (where appropriate) to the mix. Alan faltered a little here, slipping up with a very simple brown/black combination error, but I gave him the benefit of the doubt and graded that page as a B.

Next we moved on to business wear, and here's where Alan really showed how far he's come, expertly mixing striped ties with checked shirts and crossing out every paisley in the bunch. Let's keep in mind here that when I first saw Alan at an open mike night at some dive bar in Sherman Oaks, he was so poorly dressed that I'd initially written him off entirely as a potential Finishing School candidate. My boys need to start with a modicum of decency and style; I'm not looking to create them, just to mold what's already there. Eventually, though, he worked his way into my heart and I accepted him into the class with open arms.

The final task was an essay, and I had to move the small desk lamp closer to the cot in order to read Alan's scraggly handwriting. "Next time," I told him, "see if you can write a little clearer. Spelling doesn't count, but penmanship does. In its own way, it goes part and parcel with fashion. Handwriting is just another way we present ourselves to the outside world."

I'd thought up this morning's essay question in the shower, and though it wasn't technically a fashion question, it was fashion-related and, in my opinion, spoke to one of the major disconnects between women and their boys:

You arrive at seven P.M. to pick up your date for a night on the town. Expecting to dine at McDonald's and hit a movie, you've worn a combination of jeans and a T-shirt advertising a Hawaiian party thrown by your fraternity during rush week nine years ago. When your date comes to the door, she's wearing three-inch heels, a pleather skirt, a silk blouse, and her best diamonds. The cop-action-buddy-flick movie you've picked out starts at ten P.M. and, if you're late, you'll never get seats. What do you do? See the attached movie schedule for alternate times and/or films, and feel free to use diagrams to illustrate your choices (both fashion and entertainment) for the evening.

"Wait," said Alan as I began to read through his answer. "I'd like to try it again."

"But I haven't even read it yet."

"I know," he said, "but I just thought of a better answer. I'd really love to give it another shot."

Alan's never been one to show much ambition, and that's one of the things I've worked on with him here at the Finishing School. Pleased with his progress, I gave him a new blue book and crayon (pencils and pens were used in an early, failed breakout attempt, and have since been banished from the basement) and he got to work crafting a new answer.

I turned to Owen, whose work was spotless, as always, and as soon as I'd written the final A on the top page, he was eager for me to dig out the gold stars and chocolate bars. Together, we looked for an empty spot on his progress chart to affix his new stickers.

"You've been doing so well, Owen," I said. "I'm very proud of you."

He blushed, and I handed him half a See's chocolate bar, which he immediately opened and consumed. I didn't have to worry about him throwing the candy wrapper on the floor; Owen had long ago passed the basic cleanliness program.

On my way out of the basement, I realized that with all of Owen's success, it's getting difficult to judge his forward progress. There are natural plateaus in any program, of course, but the time may soon come when Owen will have learned all that I can teach him. At some point, like a mama bird pushing her baby out of the nest, I'll have to let him go.

When I first met Owen during the second night of a doubleheader at Dodger Stadium, and in his inebriated state he was under the misguided impression that I would be thrilled to be thrown up against a concrete wall and kissed against my will by a strange man with beer breath and groping hands, I thought his behavior typical of so many of the boys who roam this planet: coarse, unkempt, cruel, and fostering some deep resentment of women.

Today, just shy of fifteen months later, he's barely recognizable as the Neanderthal who once stomped around in Air Jordans. Owen is kind, classy, considerate, empathetic, bright, and fun. He will, I have no doubt, respect the women in his home, his workplace, and the world in general, while still retaining the essence of his sexuality and male bravura. When he finally graduates from Cassandra French's Finishing School for Boys, Owen Carter will be a model citizen and an all-around-perfect friend, husband, and lover. The only thing he won't be anymore is a boy. As soon as he receives his diploma and walks up the basement stairs and out my front door, it is because he will have earned the distinction of being called a man.

I'm getting misty-eyed just thinking about it.

Lesson no. 4

HOW TO HEAR WHAT YOU WANT TO HEAR

Morning. Five forty-five to be exact. Phone call. Guess who.

"*Ja, guten morgen.* Ich vass . . . valking down zee street, und . . . ah, zees lady, *verruckt*, how you say . . ."

Christ, a tourist. Mom had worked her magic on some poor jet-lagged German with a cell phone. "Right, a crazy lady in a housecoat. I know. And she wants you to use your phone to call me. Sir, I'm suggesting to you that you walk away as quickly as possible, save us all a lot of grief."

Silence on the other end of the line. Were my words being plugged into a universal translator? "Du musser says to . . . kamm over et noon. Noon, ist das correkt?"

"Yes, fine," I mumbled. "Tell her it's fine. Now hang up. Go see the sights."

"Sights?"

"Hollywood Boulevard, Mann's Chinese, Disneyland. Go. Run. Get away from that woman, she's insane. She'll kill your children and eat their brains."

"*Das kinder?*" asked the suddenly alarmed voice on the other end.

"Ja, ja!" I yelled. "Like Hansel and Gretel."

That did the trick. The guy took off so fast he didn't even shut off the phone, and I stayed on the line for another minute just to listen to the entire family screaming at one another in German. It's always good to hear Teutonic cuss words before six A.M.; it braces you for anything else that might happen later on that day.

Or almost anything else. Two more surprises were waiting for me at the office.

The first bit hit me early. I wasn't six feet into the lobby of the twenty-third floor when I heard Stuart Hankin's now-familiar voice echo out behind me.

"You haven't returned my calls."

I gave him the slow spin, the one all the stars do in the movies when they're trying to be standoffish and sensual at the same time, but it just came off like I had a crick in my neck. Damn it, how does Sandra Bullock pull that off? By the time I'd swiveled all the way around, Stuart was out of the plush leather love seat and at my side.

"Did you call?" I said coolly. "I didn't notice. I'm terrible about voice mail at the office."

"I left messages at your home, too."

"And how did you get that number?"

"I know people," he said ominously, then quickly added, "at the studio. My cousin works in personnel. He looked up your file for me. Did you get the flowers?"

"Those were from you? I'm allergic, so I just threw them out right away. Didn't even read the dumb card."

"Aha." He smiled. "So you did read it."

"No, I just assume that if you'd written it, it was probably dumb. Or at least sloppy drunk and rambling."

I turned and walked down the hall toward my office. I didn't know if I wanted him to follow me or not. He did. "I deserve that," he said, keeping pace with me. "I said some awful things, things I didn't mean and wouldn't even think on a normal day. I was pretty hammered, and you were the closest target."

"You couldn't have been that hammered," I pointed out. "It didn't take you more than thirty minutes to go from suave to schmuck."

"I was half in the bag when we met at the bar, and the next three drinks after that kinda put me over the edge."

"So that's an excuse?"

"No, not at all." I had to admit, he was playing the apology correctly, and maybe that's why he looked even more handsome in the light of day. Where Daniel was narrow, Stuart was broad. Where he was slack, Stuart was tight. And those arched eyebrows weren't so . . . arched anymore.

He gave me a tight little smile and sat on the edge of a paralegal's desk. "I'll be honest with you. I'm supposed to be this big playboy nightclub owner, and that's the image my investors want me to keep up. Helps with the gossip columns, that sort of thing. But these first few weeks at the club have been tough. I've put a lot of time and money into the place, and it's almost empty every night. The P.R.'s not working, the advertising is for shit, and there's practically no word of mouth." Poor thing couldn't even meet my eye; he stared down at the beige carpet and sighed heavily. "I'd been having all these doubts, wondering if I'd been stupid to go the nightclub route all along, if I just should have listened to my father and opened up a medical building or a warehouse or . . . or just made it a normal, everyday club instead of a dumb theme bar. . . ."

"Oh," I said softly, as I slowly came to understand that I may have pushed all the right buttons at the wrong time. I'd pulled a typical Cassie. Sometimes, I'm almost too psychic for my own good. "And then I went and said all those horrible things about the place—"

"Pretty much confirming every single doubt in my head." Stuart grinned and ran a hand through his thick hair. "Yeah, that's about the way the night went."

My grandmother used to make this horrendous dish out of lentils, peas, beets, organ meat, and a rough grain from the Old Country. It stank like feet. That's pretty much what I felt like when Stuart got through with his story.

"I am so sorry," I said, then repeated myself three more times for good measure. "If I'd had any idea—"

"You didn't," he replied. "And stop apologizing. You were dead-on right. The bar's a disaster, the theme isn't working, and I've already got two lawsuits. One from a guy who slipped on a urine puddle that I'm not entirely sure came from one of the dogs, and the second . . ."

"Choked on a Snausage?"

"Milk Bone. Thank God my bartender knew the Heimlich. So I've just got to accept that the bar is a failure and move on. I'm having a meeting with my major investor Saturday night, and we're going to talk about how to make the place profitable."

Tearing it down and putting up a mini-mall sprang to mind. "Got any ideas?"

"One," he said. "What I'm thinking is that we scrap the dogs and bring in wild ferrets. We'll call it the Unvarnished Tooth."

I didn't want to be critical. Really, I felt guilty enough about the whole Kennel Club mess. So instead of launching into the harangue that immediately came to mind, I just smiled and did my best impression of my mother, who, when confronted with a situation in which she's got nothing positive or constructive to say, goes with the following:

"Neat!"

Stuart couldn't hold it in any longer; he broke down laughing. "No, that wasn't really . . . I was kidding. Oh, God, Cassandra, you must think I'm a complete idiot."

"More of a pervert than an idiot. First the dogs, then ferrets. That kind of thing can make a girl nervous."

"Tell you what," he said, hopping off the desk and stepping a bit closer. I found myself inadvertently closing the distance from my side, as well. Geez, Cassie, desperate much? Step back, girlfriend, let the situation breathe. "Let me make the whole thing up to you."

"I don't know. Showing up at my office like this . . . it's a little forward, don't you think?"

"Immensely forward," he admitted. "Terribly forward. I'm so forward, I could play for the Lakers."

A basketball joke. I didn't entirely get it, but I smiled to let him know I was the kind of girl who *could* get it, if given the chance. "What's on your mind?"

"A redo of the other night."

"Great," I said, "we'll get smashed and criticize each other's life choices. Sounds swell."

At just that moment, Lorna, the office mattress, popped around the corner and veered down the hallway, staring Stuart down and then brushing up against him as she passed by, letting her overpowering perfume finish the job that her suggestive glances had started. I could almost hear her thighs rubbing together, the way that crickets call each other to mate. I hope she gets chafed.

"What on earth was that?" Stuart asked after she passed.

"That was Lorna. Don't worry about her; she just wants to eat your soul. Okay, you're on. Drinks, you and me."

"Great!" he said. "I know the perfect little place. There's no theme, no production design, just a bar and a few tables and a jukebox with crappy music and a pool table that nobody ever uses."

"Sounds perfect. I'll go, on one condition."

"Shoot."

"No animals."

Stuart held up his hands in surrender. "Fair enough. Tell you what—I've got a condition of my own. You help me out with my investor first. Come with me, brainstorm a few ideas while we have drinks. You obviously know what works and what doesn't. If I pass the drinks test, we can have dinner or something afterward."

That's when I heard my father's voice echoing through my head. When I was younger, during those first few years after he passed away, Daddy used to talk to me two or three times a week, reassuring me, helping me through my adolescent battles and traumas. Nowadays he doesn't come around that often; maybe he figures I can handle things on my own. Maybe he's just busy. So when he pipes up, I make sure to listen.

Wait just a second, muffin, I heard him say. *You're a bright girl, the brightest girl I know, but you don't really know anything about restaurant management. This is a major investment this boy is talking about, probably millions of dollars, and you've got no business worming your way into his vocation. He's good-looking and smart and seems genuine, so let's not rush into this too fast. Okay, kiddo?*

"Sure," I told Stuart. "Sounds like a blast."

Sorry, Daddy. I love you more than life itself, but I've got to fly solo on this one.

We made plans for Stuart to pick me up at my place Saturday night at six, which will give me a full day to run errands and spend some quality time with the boys. I feel as if I've been neglecting them lately. Maybe this weekend we'll take one of our virtual trips. Fiji, perhaps, or the Middle East. Tape some travel brochures to the walls, play some world music, bring in food from the kebab joint down the street. It might be just the thing to snap Daniel out of his funk. His fever is still hovering in the 101 range, so perhaps a change of scenery will be just what the doctor ordered. Lord knows the Tylenol isn't doing the trick.

No sooner had I stepped into my office (heart still pumping from the tête-à-tête with Stuart) than I had my second little shock of the day:

Sitting in a cross-legged Lotus position on my sofa was a man wearing a baseball cap, dark sunglasses, and an obviously fake beard. My first thought was that I should run back into the hallway and scream bloody murder. My second was that this stranger was quite limber. I've taken exactly six of Lexi's yoga classes, and the warm-up exercises alone can still make me scream bloody murder.

I stood up on my tippie-toes to extend my five feet, four inches to a more imposing five feet, six inches. "You've got ten seconds to get out of my office before I call security," I said confidently. "Ten . . . nine . . ." I counted all the way down to zero, even threw in a fraction or two at the end, and he still didn't move a muscle.

"That's a nice outfit," said the stranger, and each word sent a special little chill through me. I knew that voice. I knew that timbre. Usually it was filtered through a THX sound system and carried with it the scent of buttered popcorn, but it sounded even sweeter in person.

Thoughts of Stuart Hankin and our meeting in the hallway were wiped clean by a tidal wave of stardom.

"Mr. Kelly?"

He smiled and pulled off the sunglasses and baseball cap, leaving the fake beard affixed to his chin. The emerald eyes were all I needed to see. Jason Kelly was in my office (Hear that, everyone? *Jason Kelly* and *my office* in the same sentence!) and giving me the once-over.

"Sorry about the getup," he said, pulling his legs out of the yoga pretzel and into a long stretch. "I can't go anywhere these days without a hundred people trying to follow me. And half of them are on my payroll."

"Of course," I said, nearly tripping as I stumbled around the room, trying to find a place to sit before I collapsed. Legs weak. Knees buckling. "A disguise. I get it." I managed to make my way behind my desk and into my chair. The only problem was that my legs were covered up, depriving me of a chance to show off my calves. I began bucking my body to the left, scooting the wheeled chair across the carpet, hoping to make my way into the clear so that I could extend my legs and flex them nonchalantly.

I can do this, I told myself. *I can act like an adult and not go blubbering to Jason about how much I love him like some tourist from Minnesota.* Forcing my best professional smile, I said, "Should you be here? Without your attorneys, I mean."

He waved a hand dismissively. "What they don't know . . ."

"Right," I said, suddenly realizing I had nothing else to say. "Sure, great. Right. So . . ." I waited for the end of the world. It didn't come. It never does when you need it to.

Finally, I came up with, "Is there anything I can do for you? Did you leave something in the office yesterday?"

His return grin was just like the one they used on the one sheet for *In the Dust,* the poster that launched a million teenage girls under their bedsheets and into their first sexual awakenings. "Only your phone number."

"Of course. If you need to call the office and you can't get through, sometimes the best thing to do is go through the studio switchboard—"

"No," he said. "*Your* number." He took one of my business cards from their holder on my desk and leaned back into the sofa. "Cassandra French," he read. "Or Cassie Bear to her mother, if I remember correctly. French, huh? Do you speak it?"

I blinked twice, the first time because I was pretty sure I hadn't blinked since I'd walked into the office, and I didn't want to creep him out with some wide-eyed zombie stare, and the second time because I wanted to make sure this was all really happening.

"Do I speak French?" I echoed. "Not . . . not really. It's just my name." Before I knew it, I was off and babbling again. What I wouldn't have given for someone to burst in and suture my mouth closed for everyone's benefit. "It's like I've got this friend named Susie Gardener, but she can't plant anything. I gave her a cactus once for Christmas, and she even managed to kill that. But, see, her name is Gardener, so . . ."

Jason gave me one of those smiles that you give to small children and elderly people when they're clearly off in their own worlds and not coming back. "Too bad you don't speak it. Cannes is great this time of year. You really should go." He pocketed my business card and rubbed his chin. "Listen, I've got some time tonight, how about we go out?"

"Out?" I repeated.

Celebrity conversational skills: D+.

"Or in," he said. "Whatever works for you."

Was he asking me what I think he was asking me? Why on earth would he be interested in taking me out on a date? He could have his pick of pretty much any woman in the Western Hemisphere with a working set of eyeballs.

But that was the thirteen-year-old Cassie French talking, the one who had the size-eight torso on the size-four hips, the one who was gangly and lumpy all at the same time. Sometimes she pops up at the worst moments, and I have to knock her in the head with a dodge ball if I want to get back to business.

My mouth was still on auto-dumb. "Going out is good. Or in. Or both, or . . . Out. Sure, out. Let's go out."

"You know the park on Sunset and Beverly?" he asked. I nodded. Best to keep my mouth shut. Jason donned his sunglasses and baseball cap and opened my office door. "Meet me there at seven. And let's keep this a secret for now. Like you said, I'm not even supposed to be here."

"Scout's honor," I chirped, holding aloft some hand signal that was probably less Girl Scout and more east side Crips.

Then he was gone, and moments later I doubted that he was ever there. But there was an indentation in the couch, an adorable little tush print, proof positive of the visit. I wanted to rush out and buy plaster of paris so I could make a mold of that perfect, movie-star-caliber ass and display it on my wall for all the world to see. It would be an archaeological treasure, revered by millions. I could probably make copies and sell it on QVC.

Instead, I perched on the edge of the sofa, next to the butt groove, and let myself pretend that he was still there, chatting with me about this and that. Politics, maybe. The state of art in modern society. Intelligent conversation with the Hottest Hunk in Hollywood (*Marie Claire*, January of last year). Slowly, I slid my own rump down into his indentation, slipping into what will from this day forward be known as the Jason Seat. The fabric was still warm, and I sat there, joining our tush energies until I could no longer feel his electric presence in the room.

It was all ruined fifteen seconds later when Stan Olsen pounded on the door and galumphed into my office, protruding potbelly leading the way. "Want to call Warners on this licensing deal, French?"

Usually I'd be eager for the work. Now all I wanted was to run to Blockbuster and rent every single one of Jason's movies in preparation for this evening. "I'm pretty busy."

"Looks to me like you're sitting on the couch."

I didn't want to get into it with him. Any protracted argument would ruin my delicious high. The whole thing was already slipping from my memory, like a beautiful dream that drifts into the ether minutes after you wake. If I didn't hold on to the details, it would be lost forever.

"Fine," I snapped. "Put the file on the desk."

Stan Olsen was out of my office five seconds later, and I was back in my happy place: already on my date with Jason, laughing and chatting in some abandoned park as he dispensed with the talk, cupped my face in his hands, and pulled me into a long, deep kiss, his tongue searching out mine, his arms pulling me closer, my back arching as I pulled him atop my suddenly naked body and waited for the moment when we'd become one.

Connection with reality: C. Hey, a girl can dream. There are times when stark and unrelenting candor can really get in the way of a good time. I bet even that woman on TV who came up with this stupid grading program takes a break from the depressing reality of self-evaluation now and again.

But I'd be willing to bet a million dollars she's never had a date with Jason Kelly.

Jason Kelly!

Considering the amount of money that the prosecutors claim Mom and Ted stole from their so-called victims, you'd think she could afford to spruce up her condo a bit. Her design sense has clearly been kidnapped and held captive in the mid to late 1980s, which translates into a lot of abstract art and uncomfortable white furniture. I can't stand walking into her living room because the juxtaposition of mirrored walls forces me to view angles of my body I'm not always prepared to see. A sudden wide shot of your own ass in clingy gym shorts is enough to send anyone into a shame spiral; it's not fair to spring that kind of thing on a gal unannounced.

Note: Since I'm still wound up in stark and unrelenting candor, I should probably point out here that I'm bound to make this whole incident look bad on Mom. I am, after all, sitting in a Starbucks, furiously writing on a legal pad, after having left her condo in what could graciously be called a huff. Some might call it a hissy fit. I prefer huff. So although I'm still seeing every shade of red, I'm going to do my best to be impartial and objective.

Ted is a prick.

His company was called Running Springs Vacations, and they sold midlevel vacation packages over the phone. Nothing wrong with that as far as I can see. They never called people during the dinner hour, and if someone asked to be taken off the call sheet, they'd gladly do so. Neither Mom nor Ted made any of the actual phone calls; they had about fifteen employees who did that sort of thing, mostly high-school kids and elderly folks trying to make a few under-the-table bucks on top of their allowances and Social Security checks. Ted worked the front office, and Mom kept the books. They were registered with the Better Business Bureau. They gave a percentage of their proceeds to charity. They were active in the community. So maybe the company didn't always deliver on what they'd promised; what corporations do? For the life of me, I can't understand why the D.A. chose to go after their little family business. Don't get me wrong; I think Ted's a waste of space. He's loud, brash, the kind of guy who finds it funny to smear guacamole on his chin and pretend he has a skin disease. But that's no reason to try and throw a guy in prison.

Mom's lawyer told me she got lucky with the house arrest. The D.A. could have charged her with obstruction, since Ted escaped while she was serving blintzes to the cops, but chose instead to let her off with a single count of telemarketing fraud. But she steadfastly denied having any knowledge of Ted's whereabouts, nor would she enter a guilty plea. In the end, only Judge Hathaway's mercy saved her from a 2- to 5-year stint in the Big House. That's right, I used the term Big House. That's the kind of outdated terminology that Jason Kelly's girlfriend can use and get away with. If heard by the right people, it might even get printed in the Notable Quotes section of *Entertainment Weekly*.

On the drive over the pass, I nearly got into three accidents. Every guy on the street suddenly became Jason Kelly, and every announcer on the radio was singing his praises. It was all Jason, all the time. It's crazy,

I know, and I'm a fool for getting so caught up in the first place. He probably just wants to hook up for some easy sex, probably saw the infatuation in my eyes that I didn't even try that hard to cover up. If that's his motive, I'm game. A girl in this day and age is allowed to have casual sex with the most famous man in America without her conscious getting in the way. It's written somewhere in the Constitution. Trust me, I went to law school. I had a lot of sex.

But what if his reasons go deeper than that? What if he got a glimpse of Cassandra French, the person? Cassandra French, the dreamer? Cassandra French, the nurturer? Maybe he wants to get to know the real me. The in-depth me. The woman beneath the woman. Shit, I've got to figure out what to wear.

I had barely knocked on the condo door when Mom threw it open and motioned furiously for me to enter, eschewing her usual bear hug. Her hair was a fright, a tousled rat's nest, but for once she was out of the housecoat. The sweatpants and I HEART RUNNING SPRINGS VACATIONS T (it actually said the word *heart*, which was Ted's grand idea of a joke) weren't much better, but it meant she'd probably left the condo and done a little grocery shopping. Hopefully a technician from the court-house had already fixed the electronic monitor and restored her legally mandated five-hundred-foot radius.

"Hey, Mom," I said. "How's the anklet holding up?"

She pulled me inside and slammed the door, but not before looking out into the hallway and checking it for . . . what? Burglars? Mormons?

"What's going on? Is everything okay?"

She put a finger to her lips. "Shhh, Cassie Bear. Shhh."

"Is somebody here?"

Taking me by the hand, Mom led me into the kitchen, where she flipped on the faucet as high as it would go. Evidently, this wasn't enough for her, because a moment later she dragged me into the bath-room. There, she spun the shower knob and both faucet handles, and the white noise of running water echoed throughout the small space. For the grand finale, she flushed the toilet.

"Are you upset about the low-flow meters they put in?" I asked. "Because I know someone who can take those out."

Mom shook her head and pulled my ear down to her lips. "I got a letter," she whispered. "From Ted."

Surprising news, certainly. Bathroom-related, not so much. "Fantastic. So tell me again why we're in here, wasting all this water? You do know we live in the desert, right?"

Mom flushed the toilet once more. "I can't take the chance. They may be bugging us."

"Who?"

"The Feds. You know how they'd love to get their hands on Ted."

The Feds. The so-called "Feds" probably had better things to do than apply bugging devices and wiretaps to my mother's condominium in order to catch a sixty-year-old telemarketing con man on the lam, one who had better odds of keeling over from cholesterol poisoning than he did of wreaking havoc on further innocent victims. But once Mom's got her teeth locked onto a concept, there's no shaking her loose.

"Where is he?" I asked.

"I'm not exactly sure," Mom whispered back, and though she was still keeping her voice low, I could tell that she wanted to shout her joy to the world. Despite the dubious source of her happiness, it was good to see her out of her usual funk. I wanted to tell her about Jason Kelly, to share my own fortune as well, but I'd been sworn to secrecy. It's been only four hours since he left my office, and already I feel like an overstuffed bean-bag chair, bursting at the seams. It's not as if I can't keep a secret, but this is different. If I don't tell someone soon, it's all going to blow in one messy eruption. I just hope he lets me talk about our relationship once the wedding invitations go out.

Grip on sanity: D and slipping.
Amount that I'm bothered by it: Not a damn bit.

The page Mom took out of her pocket was a folded-up magazine advertisement for suntan lotion, the copy written in Spanish. I turned it over, expecting to find some secret message written in the margins, maybe a sonnet of love, and found only an ad for Sambuca.

"Where's the letter?"

"That's it. The whole page." She took the ad back and clutched it to her breast like a schoolgirl getting a mash note from her favorite boy. That's right, I just used the term mash note. Deal with it.

"Mom, it's just an advertisement."

She flushed the toilet again. Christ. The woman is on a fixed income, and her water bill's going to put her in the poorhouse, which is a problem, because I bet the poorhouse is more than five hundred feet from her apartment. "But it came in an envelope with a Colombian postmark." She flapped a ratty-looking envelope in front of my eyes. "See?"

Indeed, three airmail stamps were affixed to the front, just above the space where Mom's name and address had been typed in red ink. Predictably, there was no return address.

"It's Ted," sighed Mom. "I know it's him. See the ad? We used to drink Sambuca together after a hard day at work. It's a message to me. A signal."

"A signal for what? To stock up on Coppertone?"

"To stay strong. That we'll be together one day soon."

I'm all for fantasizing about unattainable goals, but this kind of unrealistic longing had to be nipped in the bud. I weighed my options carefully and chose to go the tough love route.

"If that's really a letter from Ted," I said, "you need to bring it to the police."

Her head rocked back as if I'd slapped her in the face. "Terrible, Cassie Bear! You're being terrible."

"All I'm saying is that if you've got evidence of where Ted might be, the D.A.'s going to want to see it. Maybe if you help them find him, they'll appeal to have your sentence reduced."

"I can't tell them where he is," Mom said. "That would be treason."

Treason. That's really what she called it. "Mom," I said, "let's face facts. You know how I feel about Ted, so I'm not going to pull any punches."

Mom closed the toilet seat and sat on the brown cushioned cover.

See, a brown cushioned toilet seat cover. What am I working with here? "Go ahead," she said coolly, her face a blank mask. Not a good sign. Mom's anger works in reverse; the more passive she seems, the more upset she's becoming. By the time you think she's half asleep, there's a nuclear meltdown in the works. But I'd gotten this thing rolling, so I had no choice but to press on.

"Ted wasn't exactly the catch of the century in the first place," I began. "Now I know I didn't really say much of anything when you told me you were engaged, and despite my initial reservations, I really was delighted to be a bridesmaid at the wedding, chiffon and all." The maid-of-honor gown Mom picked out for me had no sleeves, no shawl, and no way to cover my upper arms. I hate my upper arms. If, in the middle of that wedding, I could have found a surgical scalpel and a bottle of whiskey behind the bar, I would no longer own any upper arms. I would go from shoulders straightaway to elbows and that would be peachy keen with me.

"I was happy for you that day," I continued, "because I figured that you saw something in Ted that I didn't, and that was all I needed to know. And for a few months, I thought everything was going to work out. But then Ted got you into this illicit business of his, put your name on all the papers so you'd be held accountable, and when the shit hit the fan, he tossed you to the cops while he ran away to some beach in South America. You want to talk treason? *That's* treason.

"Now, I'm not even going to go into the bad hairpiece and the rotten sense of humor, but I think it's time you realized that it doesn't matter if Ted's coming back for you or not, because you and Ted don't belong together in the first place. He's not a tenth the man that Daddy was, and I think, deep down, you know it."

I expected her to blow, to go beyond the silence and really lay it out. I'd already steeled myself for a world-class screaming session, in which we could both get out our Ted frustrations and maybe come to some conclusions about their failed relationship. If we managed to squeeze it all in under fifteen minutes or so, we could even eat lunch afterward.

What I got was much worse. "That's fine, honey," she said, patting my hand and rubbing my back, as if I was some mongrel to be appeased. "You let it out."

"Mom, I wasn't kidding."

"I know you weren't, sweetie. There are just some things you'll understand better when you're all grown up."

There. She said it. Twenty-nine years old, and to her, I'm still waddling around the house in diapers and sucking on doorknobs. Long story. "I'm not . . . Look, aren't you even going to argue with me?"

"There's nothing to argue with. You're right, of course. Ted and I aren't perfect together, and I know he's got his faults. Lord, I know it. But you don't abandon your man because of his problems. You stick by him."

"So you're Tammy Wynette all of a sudden."

"Not at all," she said confidently. "Who's Tammy Wynette?"

"The country singer. She sang—look, that's not the point. If you know that Ted's not the guy for you, if he can't measure up to Daddy, then forget about him."

Mom dismissed the comment with a wave of her hand. "Your father had his own problems."

I think that's when the first wave of fury blindsided me. Suddenly, I couldn't breathe all that well. "Don't say that," I blurted out. "Don't talk about him that way."

"What way? I'm just saying he was a man, and men have their faults. No one's perfect, Cassie Bear."

The noise from the shower and the faucets combined with a flash flood of anger, and I nearly walked out there and then. I should have. A quick end would have been the best for all of us. Instead, I turned off the water by slapping at the shower knob, reinjuring my dog-bitten right hand in the process.

"I didn't say Daddy was perfect!" I shouted, even though the roar of the shower and faucets had subsided. If the Feds are indeed bugging the apartment, they've probably got hearing damage now. "I just said he was better than Ted. Better than all of them."

"Honey . . ." Mom started, and I knew from that syrupy, drawn-out whine that she was pitying me. That's right, the convicted felon with an electronic monitoring anklet was pitying an upstanding member of the bar. "I never told you this before, but you're old enough to hear it now. The truth is that your dad and I were having some problems before he got sick. He was a man like any other man—"

I didn't hear any more after that, because I was running out of the bathroom, through the condo, and fumbling with the door lock. I could feel Mom tromping up behind me like the T.rex in *Jurassic Park*, coming to devour me with her jaws of overbearing advice.

"Cassie Bear, wait," she said, but by then I was out into the hallway and jogging as quickly as I could for the stairs. My only goal was to make it past six hundred feet, and then I'd be clear of her. Five hundred for the anklet, an extra hundred for the voice.

I wandered for a while, unwilling and unable to go back to her condo parking lot to retrieve my car. I couldn't stand to be near those lies. Why would she say those things? Was she that brainwashed by Ted? Did his bad hairpiece broadcast subliminal messages meant to bring down happy families? Eventually I stumbled across this Starbucks and staggered inside for a latte. Time, caffeine, and voluminous amounts of whipped cream, I figured, would calm me down.

No such luck, but fuck it all. Mom or no Mom, I've got a date tonight. I need something to wear. I'm going to Barneys.

I'm not one of those women who feels the need to shop every time the going gets rough. In fact, I often prefer to make my purchases when I'm in a good mood; a beautiful pair of shoes enhances a natural high and brings it to a level that's probably illegal in some states. So I didn't want to walk through the front door of Barneys in a funk. It wouldn't be fair to fashion. I needed a buffer.

The more I've thought about it, the more I've come to the decision that Owen is ready to move to the next level of his education at the Finishing School. There's only so much one can learn in a cloistered environment, and though it's going to take a little preparation and equipment, I think we might be ready to take a field trip or two. Fortunately, I had an idea how to find what I needed.

I dialed Stuart's number on my cell and was surprised to hear a woman answer the phone.

"*Allo?*" She had an accent, something European and classy and snobby, and I asked for Stuart straightaway. Why was there a woman answering his phone? Why was she European? Was she an assistant, and, if so, why does a nightclub owner need an assistant, especially a European with a lithe body and pert breasts?

"This is Stuart." I could hear power tools in the background, wood being splintered.

"Hi," I said, trying to hide my annoyance. "It's Cassie French. I hope I didn't catch you at a bad time." What with that European slut walking around naked and all.

"No, no, we're just tearing up the place." I can't say he sounded excited about the whole thing. "What's up? Are we still on for Saturday?"

"Of course. But that's not why I'm calling. I've got a question about those dogs of yours. At the club."

"Did you want to adopt one? Cassie, that would be great! We're trying to find them all some good homes."

"Oh dear God, no," I blurted out, then covered. "My homeowner's association doesn't allow pets. Otherwise, I'd take two. Maybe three. It's just, I heard someone at the club mention that you'd used shock collars to train them not to bark."

"Only on the bigger ones," he said defensively. "And it's just a static shock, nothing damaging."

"Of course. I was just wondering if you remember where you purchased them. See, my aunt has this rottweiler . . ." I launched into some convoluted tale about a barking dog, an angry neighbor, and a court order, and eventually got the name of a reputable pet store before reconfirming our Saturday meeting and letting Stuart get back to the business of tearing down his business.

The pet store was one of those big chains that refuses to sell cats or dogs, but is more than happy to provide any number of other creepies and crawlies. Are there really this many snake and lizard owners running around the United States? And how can I keep them far, far away from me?

"Good afternoon," I said to the only employee in the place, a young girl with purple hair and a diamond stud in the flesh of her nose. The jewelry was so small that for a second I thought it was a fleck of dirt, and I nearly reached out and flicked it away for her. "I'm looking for a shock collar. Something for a really big animal."

"How big?" she asked in a dull monotone.

About six-foot-four and 260 pounds, I thought. "Great Dane. That's a big dog, right?"

"I guess."

"And I'll need it to have a remote control. So I can shock him from a distance if I have to."

The girl led me through the store and down an aisle filled with doggie S&M devices. Harnesses, chains, leashes. Who knew the little buggers were so randy?

She picked up a box and held it out to me. "This one's the top of the line. You're supposed to put it around the dog's neck, so just make sure that those little electrodes go down through the fur and onto the skin. It's got seven different levels of correction, so you can start out with light shocks and go stronger if the dog isn't learning fast enough."

"And I can control it remotely?"

She pointed to the side of the box, where the specs claimed that the remote would work up to a hundred yards away from the collar. It was perfect for my needs, and at $119.95, quite the steal.

I picked up a few more interesting bits of equipment on the way out, and happily tossed all my purchases onto the counter. I was feeling better already.

"Wow," said the clerk, displaying the slightest hint of emotion, "you must have a lot of pets."

"Just three," I said. "But you never know when you're going to find another mutt on the street that you've just got to bring home."

Barneys was a treat, as usual, and I spent an hour in a whirlwind of shopping bliss. Colors, fabrics, and patterns danced before my eyes, mixing and matching themselves in an orgy of fashion, and before I knew it I had dropped nearly a thousand dollars on a black Elie Tahari halter dress, a pair of Gladiola sling backs, and a Dooney & Burke hobo bag with the cutest little braided strap. I wouldn't usually spend that kind of cash on a single outfit, but this is an investment. If Jason Kelly is sufficiently entranced by me and my new clothes, he'll be more likely to take me on a shopping spree to, say, Milan, where I can really do some damage.

Since I'd already blown two hours of my lunch, I headed for home and called in sick. It wasn't as if I had to convince anyone of my level of illness, but I lay down on the bed anyway and dropped my head over the side of the mattress so that when I spoke, I was so nasal it sounded as if I'd shoved gerbils up my nostrils. Cathy, the receptionist, was so overwhelmed by my performance that she offered to bring me her aunt's famous chicken noodle soup when she got off work. I don't even particularly like Cathy, and I'd never trust her with sensitive information, but I nearly busted a lung keeping the secret about my date with Jason. Cathy said she'd pass on the word to Stuart that I'd be in tomorrow.

The instructions for my new PetSafe Big Dog Trainer suggest that the animal to be trained wear the collar for a prolonged period before the actual training sessions begin. This way, the dog accepts the collar as part of his body and doesn't realize that the shocks, when they come, have anything to do with an external source of discomfort. Sounds a little dumb to me, even for a dog, and I've got no doubt that Owen will figure it out pretty darn quick, but hopefully I won't have to shock him at all. If everything goes according to plan, I won't even need to touch the remote once.

Still, I'm a stickler for following the directions on electronic devices. That's something I've tried to teach the boys, as well: when you get a new plaything, read the damned instructions. I can't tell you how many times I've sat idly by as some boy tried to set up home theater equipment, eschewing the packaged directions like they were the unholy writ of Satan himself. They always get something wrong, and it's usually not until they're sweaty and cursing that they check with the instructions and, lo and behold, figure out what they should have done two hours prior. By that time I'm hungry, I'm tired, and I'm sure as hell not putting out.

"Everyone gather around," I said as I entered the basement. "Come over for a special announcement." Daniel was still in bed, and his skin had taken on a sallow tone. Alan helped him struggle to his feet, and together they took their seats on the small plastic chairs we use when it's time for a lesson. Owen began to sit, as well, but I pulled him up to the front of the class.

"Owen, you've been here the longest, and I want you to know I appreciate your cooperation and your willingness to learn."

"Thank you." He smiled warmly.

"No, thank you. I think you might be ready to move on to the next stage of your education with a little field trip. Does that sound like fun?"

"I . . . guess."

"You're not sure?"

He shrugged those thick shoulders and shuffled his feet. "It's just . . . I've gotten comfortable down here. You take such good care of us, and I really like Movie Day."

I wonder: Is he scared of the potential for freedom, or the loss of regular morphine injections? The last thing I want to do is release another addict into the world. I'll have to figure out a way to score some methadone. That's going to kill my weekend.

"That's all very sweet, Owen, honey, but this is just one little trip I'm talking about. I think it's time for you to take the next step. Don't you trust me?"

Owen nodded. Trust exercises are one of the first lessons at the Finishing School.

"Good," I said. I turned to Alan and the shivering Daniel. "You two watch closely, because some day, we'll be doing this same thing for you."

Back to Owen: "Take off your pants."

His fellow classmates looking on, Owen leaned in and, with a little gleam in his eye, asked, "Are we having a sex lesson?"

"Not today." We've had our share of sexuality classes, to be sure. A key component for any boy is learning how to please a woman, and the boys under my watch were, at first, woefully inadequate in this department. Now, after a little assistance and a fair amount of practice at hand-eye-tongue coordination, they can tease and titillate with the best of them. "Take off your pants," I repeated. "Underwear, too."

Owen did as instructed, and soon he was bare-assed and, I could tell from his retracting penis, a bit cold, the poor thing. "This won't take long," I promised.

I'd already made a few modifications to the training collar, shortening the straps and eliminating the cumbersome buckle attachment. Now there was just a series of loops, the battery compartment, and two electricity-conducting brass prongs.

Kneeling down and cupping his testicles in one hand, I wrapped the collar underneath his scrotum, pulling the straps over the top of his penis and fastening it in place. He was already growing harder, so I had to work quickly or I'd end up with a mess on my hands. The prongs met up with his skin at the exact point where his sack was connected to the rest of his body, nestling perfectly within the extra folds of skin. A few extra tugs, and everything was in place.

"There," I said, standing up. "You can put your pants back on now. See how that feels."

Owen tried it out, walking back and forth across the basement floor, as far as his manacles and chains would let him. "It's a little tight."

"The discomfort should go away in a bit. I want you to get used to the feeling, okay? Walk around until you don't notice it anymore. Try it sitting down, standing up, every position you can think of. When we go out on the town, I want you to have forgotten it's even there."

The look on his face was so cute I wanted to kiss him then and there. "We're going out? Like with other people around?"

"That's what a field trip is. Tomorrow night."

"But I've got nothing to wear." Proof positive that, if nothing else, this boy has learned something from me. *I've got nothing to wear.* I nearly cried.

"Not to worry," I said. "I'll find you something."

I whipped out a measuring tape and sized Owen up. There was a dashing Bertoni suit I saw in the men's department at Barneys when I was paying for my purchases, and I might just have to go back tomorrow afternoon and take another swipe at my credit rating.

For now, though, I've got three hours until I have to be at a park in Beverly Hills outfitted in my finest apparel and a liter of bug repellent. I mean, really, a park? I know everyone talks about how Hollywood eats people alive, but I don't think they mean by mosquitoes.

None of it matters. This is Jason Kelly we're talking about, and, like, the board game of my childhood always promised, this is my Dream Date. It's a night I bet I'll remember for the rest of my life.

THE THRILL OF FLIGHT

Stark and unrelenting candor. That's the only reason I'm writing any of this down. The shame, the elation, the mortification, and the excitement of the whole thing. My first instinct is to curl up in bed for two months and let the situation work itself out, but I'm into stark and unrelenting candor for the long haul, and this should certainly prove it beyond a reasonable doubt. No reflection, just recitation.

Common sense: F. F. F. Can I say it again? What's lower than an F? Screw it, I'm giving myself a G.

Get a grip, Cassie. You can do this.

I made it to the park by six fifty-five. Didn't want to seem over-eager, but I didn't want to arrive late, either. I was running behind as it was, because it had taken me forty-five minutes to decide which lingerie to wear underneath my fabulous new outfit: the sexy or the spinster. *Pros for the sexy: They're sexy. Enough said. Pros for the spinster: The bra holds me up, the panties hold me in.* It really came down to a simple question, which was, Will anyone other than myself be seeing said lingerie this evening? In the end, I decided to wear the spinster but bring the sexy tucked inside my purse. Best of both worlds. Of course, knowing what I know now, it would have been less problematic to ditch the entire evening and run off to Canada.

By seven-ten, Jason was nowhere to be seen, and I was beginning to get nervous. As per instructions, I hadn't told anyone about the date, even Claire, so I was comforted by the fact that at least my humiliation would be a private one. To make matters worse, my hand still ached from the wuzzle attack at the animal shelter. I'd managed to disguise the abrasions by a careful application of liquid bandages and Almay cover-up, but the muscles throbbed if I left my hand by my side for too long, so I frequently had to elevate my palm above my shoulder in some sort of half-assed Statue of Liberty impression.

By seven-fifteen and no Jason, I was already thinking of ways to convince myself that the whole thing never happened. Alcohol figured heavily into the equation.

When a yellow cab pulled up next to me at seven-eighteen, I didn't give it a moment's glance. My eyes were glued on the sports cars passing by, the Ferraris and Porsches, anything that looked like a vehicle that a major movie star might drive.

"Forget it," I said, waving the cab away with my bad hand. "I wasn't calling you, I just have to keep my arm elevated."

"Whatever, lady. Are you Cassie Bear?"

This time I pulled off the slow turn with great aplomb (I'd practiced it in the mirror at home), only to find that I was wasting my energy. It wasn't Jason Kelly playing dress-up as some sloppy cabdriver; it was actually a sloppy cabdriver.

"Who wants to know?" I asked.

The cabbie sighed heavily and brushed a thin veneer of nacho cheese dust off his chest. Clearly I was cutting into his precious Cheeto-munching time. "My dispatcher said I'm supposed to pick up somebody goes by the name of Cassie Bear at Will Rogers Park at seven P.M. That you?"

"It's past seven," I pointed out. "You're late."

"Yeah, and I give a crap. Are you Cassie Bear, and are you getting in the cab?"

"Maybe," I said. "Where are we going?"

"You don't know?"

"Not . . . exactly."

The cabbie checked a sheet of paper on the seat next to him. "Heliport," he read.

I got in the cab.

Jason was waiting for me, leaning against the body of his private helicopter as I strolled as casually as possible onto the tarmac. He looked just like he did in *Rangers* ("Two Thumbs Up!," "A Thrill a-Minute!"), with the bombardier jacket and blacked-out specs and the wind kicking his hair into a tousled, adorable mess. Why can't the wind ever kick *my* hair into a tousled, adorable mess?

We exchanged hugs and polite cheek kisses. "You look fantastic," he said. I blushed and looked around; the heliport was completely empty.

"The cab, the heliport . . . We're taking this secretive thing a bit far, aren't we?"

"The paparazzi would love to get their hands on you," he whispered. "Trust me, they rake you over the coals. It's not fun." He took my hand as he led me toward the chopper. That's what I'm calling it now, by the way: a chopper.

Jason fingered the strap of my purse. "Is that a Dooney and Burke?"

Could you die? I nearly did. "Yes, it is," I choked out. "I'm surprised you recognize something like that. A purse, I mean. Most men don't."

He shrugged it off. "Come on, let's get going. I want to get airborne before the sun goes down; the view is better that way."

I'd never been in a helicopter before, but I tried to play it off as if it was all old hat. I took my seat in the first chair I saw, then immediately found and latched the safety belt, as if I'd been doing this sort of thing all my life.

"Um, Cassandra?" Jason was holding back a laugh. "That's the pilot's seat."

"Of course," I said, quickly switching chairs as I tried to hide the blush that was crawling up my neck. "I was just checking the plush . . . ness. Plushness. It's very comfortable."

Jason clambered past me, and, for a split second, his butt was in my face, just within biting distance. A little nibble, that's all a girl can ask for, right? But I refrained, and soon he was sitting in the cushioned seat, checking gauges and knobs and buttons and whatnot.

"Shouldn't you leave that to the pilot?" I asked.

He kept on with the preflight ritual. "You're looking at him."

I must have given a little gasp of surprise, because he laughed and said, "Don't worry, I know what I'm doing. Did you ever see *Rangers?*"

Only about fifteen times. It's one of those eminently re-watchable films, like *The Breakfast Club* or *Top Gun* or, when properly edited, *Pretty Woman.*

"I think so," I lied. "You played a helicopter pilot, right?"

"Chopper pilot, yeah. It took about twenty different meetings, but I finally convinced the studio to let me do my own stunts. At first they didn't want to let me do it, insurance and all that, but then I called Chuck—" Charlie Baker is the head of our studio, the one who decides which movies get made and which stay in development hell "—and took him for a ride out to Catalina. By the time we got back to the mainland, I had the little bastard convinced."

If it's good enough for a multimillionaire studio chief, I figured, it's good enough for me. Jason must have eventually turned the right knobs and pushed the right buttons, because soon the rotors were spinning and we were lifting off the ground.

"Here," Jason shouted over the noise, "put these on."

Headsets. Headsets with an attached microphone and a single metallic bar running down the middle, just the thing to turn my hair into a flattened reverse mohawk. Between that and the wind being kicked up by the rotors, I was bound to spend the rest of this date looking like a reject from Flock of Seagulls.

"How is that?" asked Jason once I'd donned the headgear. His voice came through the speakers on either side of my ears, clear and bright, the noise from the rotors a mild nuisance at best. "They're specially made, from Holland."

"They're very nice," I said into the mouthpiece. "Very . . . Dutch." The chopper was a good fifteen feet off the ground and rising quickly, Jason pulling us into a steep ascent. The ground fell away, the heliport growing smaller and smaller beneath our struts.

"Have you ever been to Holland?" he asked me. I told him I hadn't. "They've got amazing pancakes. When we were shooting *Indifference* in Belgium, I had the studio hire a P.A. to take the train back and forth to Amsterdam every two days and get me those pancakes. Man, I wish I had some right now."

"What about waffles? Isn't Belgium supposed to have great waffles?"

Jason shrugged and pulled the helicopter into a tight bank. "I dunno. I never left the trailer. But I loved those damn pancakes."

I've never been a particularly confident flyer. My father took me on my first airplane flight to visit relatives in Washington State when I was ten, and, even at that young age, I was dimly aware that while the laws of physics were on our side, we were still tempting the fates with our hubris. We must have hit a patch of rough weather on that short flight from L.A. to Seattle, because I remember a lot of bumping, a fair amount of screaming (my own), and Daddy's arms, tight around my shoulders, as he held me close and assured me that everything was going to be all right.

There wasn't any turbulence on the helicopter ride, but there was no Daddy, either; nor were there roasted peanuts or heavily edited movies to distract me from the nothingness below. Helicopters, I also learned, don't have the internal stability of planes. Sitting inside a 747, you could do a pretty good job convincing yourself that you're in a very large bus, tooling down an exceptionally smooth highway. Every time Jason turned the chopper a single degree off its course, the whole structure rotated to compensate for the movement. It was like being on the Tea Cups at Disneyland, only with a small percentage chance added in that the entire ride is going to pop off its moorings and go smashing into Dumbo.

Jason pointed at the sunset splashed across the horizon, moving his hands off the controls to do so. "How about that view, huh?"

Most of my attention was focused on the joystick, and why the pilot felt it more necessary to point out the sights than fly the craft. "Great view," I said hurriedly. "Let's get back to flying now."

"No worries. I'm an old pro. Did you ever see *Rangers?*" He launched into yet another story about that particular film, something about a helicopter duel and a drunken stunt man. It was interesting and all, but I wondered when he was going to stop telling stories and start an actual conversation. Maybe it would be up to me. Boys always like it when you ask about their interests.

"How long have you been flying?" I tried.

"Since I was fifteen. My dad flew in Vietnam, and he taught me how to throw these birds through the air." See, now we were getting somewhere. Fathers teaching their children. I could relate to that. "Speaking of Vietnam," he continued, "did you ever see *Bunker Forty-three?* It was my second film, but in terms of my performance, I really think of it as my first. . . ."

Soon we were out over the coast and heading north toward Santa Monica. Jason and I continued chatting, if you could call it that, about this movie or that movie, as he hung a sharp left that took us right out over the ocean. The island of Catalina was faintly visible in the distance.

"Are we going to Catalina?" I didn't know if I could take another forty minutes of stomach-churning turns and dips.

"Better."

"There's another island out here?"

"Not exactly." He pointed up ahead to a small speck bobbing up and down on the waves. "There. If you squint, you can just make it out."

As a rule, I try to refrain from squinting; it brings on terrible wrinkles and makes my face look like a shar-pei. The speck didn't stay a speck for long, though. Soon a magnificent yacht floated into view. It was easily a hundred feet long, with all the amenities on the top deck that a major-motion-picture star could ask for: pool, Jacuzzi, volleyball court, and, of course, a helipad.

The landing was smooth; my step down off the chopper was not. I tripped over a small metal lip, stumbled, and landed hard in Jason's arms, nearly knocking him to the deck. It wasn't on purpose, I swear it, but it was such an obvious move that he could have kissed me then and there (and I wonder now why he didn't, unless it didn't fit into his master plan), and I wouldn't have resisted.

Instead, he helped me to my feet and led me on a tour around the yacht, which was easily four times the size of my entire house. Strangely enough, it seemed that we were alone on the ship. I asked Jason about it.

"There's a captain," he told me, "but he's under strict orders to stay in his cabin tonight. So far as we're concerned, there's no one else out here. It's just the ocean, the night, and us."

At the time, I bought that cheese hook, line, and sinker. Of course, at the time, I was an idiot.

But I'm getting ahead of myself.

By the time we were done with the tour, the nausea from the helicopter ride had subsided and been replaced with nausea from the rocking boat. It was a different kind of nausea, a special kind of nausea, in which my head felt like it was repeatedly being forced between my legs and then violently swung up again. Not in a fun way, either.

I held it together, though, and smiled my best smile when Jason suggested dinner. He sat me down at a table set up on the prow of the ship and disappeared into the cabin to retrieve our food.

I stared out at the water and wondered what the hell had happened. How did I end up on a luxury yacht in the middle of the Pacific Ocean with one of the world's most famous movie stars? Was it the lip liner I'd worn to work the day we met? It's fabulous lip liner, and the packaging does indicate that it can be helpful in scoring dates, but the piece just didn't seem to fit the puzzle.

He returned from the galley with a covered silver platter balanced on one hand. "I cooked the whole thing myself, so be gentle."

"I'm sure it's fantastic," I said.

"Six years as a waiter, I hope I learned something." He yanked off the cover with a theatrical flourish. "For madam, peanut-butter-and-jelly sandwiches."

Four of them, sliced diagonally. "Crusts removed, I see. Oh, and with a side order of pretzels."

"Only the best for the lady. May I serve you?"

Dinner was more relaxed, and after a few glasses of merlot, Jason opened up about his life outside of the silver screen. Growing up in Virginia horse country, leaving for L.A. when he was just a pup of seventeen, the lean years spent pounding the pavement as an actor before a casting agent saw him in some schlocky horror film playing Corpse #4 and suggested him to Ridley Scott for his next war-torn epic.

"Oh, let's see," he said. "I was a waiter, a personal secretary, I did a little telemarketing."

"You bad man."

"For about three months, I was a gravedigger."

My nose squinched up on its own accord. "Yuck."

"It wasn't so bad, actually. It's just dirt and a tractor. You never see the bodies, unless you get a slider."

"Do I want to know what a slider is?"

"No," he said, "you do not."

We talked a bit more and laughed and drank, and soon I realized I was inebriated, not with wine (although I'd had my fair share), but with Jason. He'd laid off the self-serving chatter and asked me questions about my life, about my goals, about my desires.

"What about the studio?" he asked. "How do you like it there?"

"It's a job," I shrugged. "It's contracts and deals and memos and all those boring things you never have to worry about because you've got agents and lawyers to handle them for you."

"Sure, but then I've got to worry if they're doing their jobs right, too. At the end of the day, the way they act affects my life and reputation. Like this nonsense with *Half-Hearted*—"

He broke off midsentence and reversed direction. "Forget it, I'm not even supposed to be thinking about that deal, let alone talking about it." He grinned. "Especially with the enemy. My lawyers would have about six heart attacks if they knew I was out here with you right now."

No doubt Stan Olsen would be similarly inclined toward cardiac failure. But we'd already taken such lengthy precautions to keep this date a secret, I didn't see the harm in bringing it up. "Who's going to tell?" I asked. "The fish?"

"It's not just that," said Jason, taking my hands in his and rubbing them slowly, up and down, back and forth, the way that the Seminole Indians down in Florida hypnotize alligators (thank you, Discovery Channel). "That's not what I want tonight to be about. It's not about movies or bad contracts or studio double-crossers. It's just you and me out here on this boat, just Jason and Cassandra and the waves, and that's all I want to think about tonight."

Maybe it was the hand rubbing. Maybe it was those eyes. Maybe it was the combination of the names Jason and Cassandra, or the fact that I haven't had a good, proper kiss from anyone not tethered to my basement floor in over ten months. I leaned in and found his lips and didn't let go until I was nearly out of breath.

Without another word between us, we stood and locked arms. I remembered the way to the master bedroom from the earlier tour of the yacht, so I led and Jason followed. My mind was running full speed, but with nonsensical thoughts, years of fantasies and dreams pushing out any degree of reality that threatened to intrude. I didn't even remember that I was wearing my spinster lingerie until the underwire bra and granny panties were off my body and lying at the foot of the bed.

Jason was gentle in all the right places and rough in all the even-more-right places. Say what you will about his acting chops, but he's honed his skills beneath the sheets. And on top of the sheets. And this sort of sideways/roundabout thing we did that had my leg up on the headboard and our bodies twined in a yoga position Lexi could only dream of.

The point is, the sex was good. Screaming hot monkey good. Maybe it was all inflated because of the years of infatuation and months of pent-up frustration, but I could not deny under oath that I was thoroughly pleased and exhausted. The elliptical machine could wait for another week; my cardio quota was full.

Afterward, as we lay on the sweat-soaked sheets and swayed along with the gentle rocking of the boat, I realized that I was no longer nauseated. I'd found the cure for seasickness, and the answer was vigorous sex with Jason Kelly. I thought it best that he learn the healing powers of his manhood.

"Jason," I said softly, "I think you screwed the sick right out of me."

A breezy snore was the only reply. I looked at my watch: It was just past ten. Not the expected bedtime for an international playboy, but with that natural high still running through every limb, I wasn't going to complain. Very little could have upset me just then.

Considering that my ride home was fast asleep and probably working off a little wine, I figured I had an hour or so to kill before he'd wake up and either want to have sex again or fly me back to the mainland. Either way, I wanted to write down some of my thoughts about the evening. Damn it all if that woman on TV hadn't been right about this stark and unrelenting candor. Only half a week in, and already I was privy to the faces Jason Kelly made when he had an orgasm. Another month of self-grading, I figured, and I'd probably wind up running the studio.

No pen in my purse. No pen in the master bedroom. Being careful not to wake Jason, I pulled a sheet around my naked body and tiptoed out into the cabin hallway. I remembered that during the tour he had pointed out an office. He was bound to stock pens and paper in there.

On my way to his study, I passed through the kitchen (or the galley, as we seafaring types like to say), and noticed a bag from Gelson's Market on the counter. Next to it was an unwrapped brown bag, the kind they use at the deli counter when they make their custom sandwiches. *PB&J* had been written on the front, in a handwriting that was decidedly not masculine. *Crusts removed.*

Jason, it seemed, had passed off a Gelson's sandwich as his own. Stranger still, he'd ordered only PB&J. Had he really wanted to impress me, he could have had the deli counter construct a monument to foie gras and truffles and gastronomic excess. Maybe he figured peanut butter would be wackily romantic.

It didn't bother me all that much. After all, it was just one little fib. Boys do it all the time. As long as the lies stay small, I figured in my postcoital bliss, it can't be all that bad. I moved on toward the office, still in search of a pencil.

Jackpot. Ballpoint pens, highlighters, permanent ink galore. I couldn't help but giggle when I found a stack of spiral-bound Jason Kelly Rocks! notebooks, the kind you see stocked at drugstores all over the country for lovesick preteens to purchase and moon over.

Now, before I go into this next part with stark and unrelenting candor, I want to make it clear that I was not snooping. This whole thing was completely accidental, and had I been born with an innate sense of balance, it all would have come out differently.

As I prepared to write down some thoughts about the evening, I leaned back in Jason's desk chair to think, and quickly found myself tipping over. I reached out to grab on to the desk, and latched on to the first thing I hit, which happened to be the center drawer. It slid out as I flew backward, papers flying everywhere, and I went down hard.

Worried that Jason might have been woken by my little accident, I quickly popped up from the floor, rubbed my sore rump, and started shoving papers back into the desk as neatly as possible.

One of the unheralded skills of a good attorney is the ability to pick out salient details from within a greater grouping of useless information. I've got an eagle eye for familiar terms, phrases, and names, and usually my highlighter is on the page before I even realize that I've found gold.

As I was shoving these sheets back into the drawer, a little alarm went off in my head. Two pages back there was a name I recognized somewhere near the top third of a list, written in blue ink. I flipped back through the papers and, yep, there it was, right where I thought: *Lorna Wilcox, Counsel.* Beside her name it said, *Meet on 10th, eight-thirty.*

Lorna! The office mattress. The tenth was two days ago, just this Tuesday. Had she already been out here? Why was her name on one of Jason's papers? And was that his handwriting, or someone else's? Were they having an affair?

Forget about it, I told myself. *It's probably just a contractual matter.*

Jason does business with the studio all the time, and Loose Lorna may be working on a deal of his. No biggie.

I should have put the papers away then and there, but my eyes dropped of their own accord to the next name on the list. *Shauna Kleinberg, Counsel.* Another coworker. Now I knew that the names on these pages had to be business-related, because Shauna was happily married to a contractor, had three kids, and drove a Honda Odyssey minivan. And, if I remembered correctly, she liked only independent films. Shauna Kleinberg was the last person who would abandon her wedding vows for a fling with Jason Kelly.

There was no date or time next to her name, but there was another word: *Married.*

Married? So what? Did that prevent him from doing business with her? Even in Hollywood, that notion didn't seem to fit in.

As I scoured the rest of the page, though, I came across a disturbing trend: All of the names on the list were women, who were either branded as married, engaged, or had dates and times written next to their names. All of them worked for the studio, pretty much evenly divided between legal, business affairs, and litigation. And all of them, from what I recalled, had worked on the contracts for *Half-Hearted.*

It couldn't be, I thought. That's not the Jason Kelly I knew from such films as *Rangers, Indifference,* and *Shaming of the True.* He wouldn't go that far for something as crass as . . . well, money. Would he?

There was a second page stapled onto this first one. I didn't want to look at it, I really didn't, but that damn thirteen-year-old inside my head—the one who'd been telling me the whole time that this was one big fuck over, that Jason was just one of the cool kids who was eventually going to throw pig's blood on me like they did to that poor girl at the end of *Carrie*—made me do it. She twisted my arm behind my back, and I had no choice. I turned the page. Halfway down, I found it:

Cassandra French. Thursday night. Seven P.M.

I don't know how much longer I stayed in that office, sitting in Jason's chair, staring at that list. It must have been at least an hour, because by the time I finally found myself fully dressed and standing over Jason's naked, sleeping body, it was nearing midnight.

"Let's go back," I said, loud enough to wake him up. "I need to get home."

Jason yawned and looked at his watch. "Can't we stay here tonight? We can take the boat back to shore and have breakfast at the marina." It was a pretty good performance, but now I was seeing right through it. Oh yes, the fog had lifted.

"No," I said flatly. "I need to go home now."

He shrugged and hopped out of bed. "You okay?" he asked. "I had a good time."

"It was great. Put on your pants and let's go."

I waited for Jason by the helipad. It gave me time to think. Time to realize that I should put on a happy face, try to seem like the same starstruck Cassie French whom he picked up five hours ago, though I most assuredly was not.

"You sure you're okay?" he asked again as we climbed into the helicopter. "If I did something wrong . . ."

I put my hand on his shoulder and gave him a kiss on the cheek. It sent off a new burst of nausea, but I suppressed it and carried on. "It's nothing. I'm just tired. And I've got to go in tomorrow and work on some contracts."

He believed me. At least, I assume he believed me. Either way, he got in the chopper, which was all that mattered.

During the helicopter ride back home, I kept up a steady stream of nonsense about gardening and techno music and whatever else I could think of to keep my mouth moving while my mind went through the requisite steps. It had been a while since I'd done something like this. I was out of practice.

When we landed at the heliport, Jason offered to call me a cab back to the park.

"Couldn't you bring me back yourself?" I asked. "It's late, and I don't think I should be out there alone."

He didn't take too long thinking it over. Smart man. "Of course. We'll take my car."

Jason's Aston Martin was parked nearby, and I'm sure I would have appreciated the luxurious ride had my mind not been occupied with a thousand other things on the drive. I showed Jason where I'd parked, and he pulled his car up behind mine. He put a hand behind my head and drew me in for another kiss. I kissed back. "I had a great time, Cass," he said as we parted.

"Me, too."

"I'll call you?"

"Sure. Listen, do you think you could walk me to the car? I know it's right there and all, but . . ."

He looked around at the darkness of the park, sizing up, I'm sure, whether or not anyone would see us together. Whether there was anybody around who could see that he was tampering with the legal process by cavorting with a potential defense witness so that she would, if the opportunity arose, perjure herself in his favor.

There was no one in sight. That worked for me, too.

He stepped out of the car and opened my door, then took my hand and led me the twelve feet to my own automobile. "Oh, wait a second," I called as he prepared to leave. "I've got something you really need to see. I think you'll love it."

"Cass, it's late, I should get back—"

"It'll just take a second. Trust me, it's a knockout."

Now he was getting pissed off, but I didn't care. This wouldn't take much longer. I popped my trunk and held up a finger to signal Jason to stay right where he was.

You can tell a lot about a person by what they keep in their trunk. As previously noted, I'm both ready for any emergency and practical enough to know my limitations. It had been over half a year since I'd last done this, but my hands moved with practiced ease.

I could hear Jason stepping closer. "What do you have in there?"

"One second," I singsonged.

Suddenly Jason was behind me, hands on my hips, playfully trying to peer into my trunk. "Come on, I wanna see—"

I spun on him quickly, shoving the chloroform-soaked panty hose against his nose and mouth, holding it tight, letting the chemicals do their job.

CLOSING THE DEAL

Chloroform works fast. Jason fought for about a quarter of a second, and then his eyes lost their focus and his limbs went slack. Suddenly I was buried beneath 180 pounds of sculpted, personally trained muscle.

I squeezed out from beneath Jason's limp body and took a quick look around the park. Still empty, but I had to work quickly. No way to know when someone would saunter by. Jason's upper body had slid off mine and fallen halfway into the trunk, which helped immensely. All I had to do was hoist his legs and give them a good shove, and just like that I had him fully inside. I gagged him with a napkin from the picnic basket, fastened it in place with a few wraps of the panty hose, and pulled his limbs into a hog-tie with the lengths of rope I've had stashed in the trunk since the last time I did all this. With every move, it was all coming back to me.

Jason's car would have to stay where it was; I didn't have time to ditch it in a remote location. I needed to get out of the area, and quickly. I listened to make sure that Jason was breathing properly, double-checked his restraints, and slammed the trunk closed.

The drive home was mercifully short, the traffic thin and most of the lights green. I drove in a sort of trance, in that half-asleep, half-awake dreamland you float through just before you drift off, in which anything real seems fake and vice versa. Halfway home, my cell phone rang, and I nearly ran off the road.

"You'll never guess where I just had sex," Claire blurted out as soon as I answered.

"Claire, this isn't the best time."

"The UCLA stacks."

I hadn't heard Claire this giddy since the day she got to personally call three different sitcom producers and tell them all that their shows had been canceled. "Where are you?" I asked.

"Hold on," she said. "I'll check." There was a pause, then the sound of thick, clunky heels clomping around on creaky floorboards. She must have been wearing her Hilfiger clogs. Not my favorite, I must admit. Claire came back on the line. "Natural history, I think. I don't know the Dewey decimal system all that well."

"You're still in the library?"

"What, you think I'd make you wait until morning to hear about this?"

That made me feel a little guilty. After all, here I was with the man of every girl's dreams in my trunk, and I hadn't even once considered calling Claire since the whole adventure began.

Thoughtfulness while kidnapping major movie star: D.

"Anyway," she continued, "I don't have much time. I think we're going to try and do it near the psychology textbooks next. That'll really get him going."

Comes When Enlightened, it seems, had taken Claire to a ceremony at UCLA in which he was awarded with yet another degree to add to his collection. According to Claire, as soon as he climbed down off the stage, he was by her side and pulling her out of the ballroom and toward the main library.

"I swear," she said, "he threw me up against the stacks with one hand and held that degree tight with the other."

"I'm sorry, hon. Did that upset you?"

"Oh yeah," she drawled. "I hate having multiple orgasms. Ooops, here he comes. Love you."

Just like that, I was alone in my car once again, toting my precious cargo. As I turned down my street, I realized that I was going to need assistance in getting Jason out of the trunk. I can still remember the night I tried to lower an unconscious Owen down the basement stairs without breaking either of our necks. In the end, I used two lengths of plywood, a bungee cord, and a hand truck, and I still nearly gave myself a hernia.

I backed the car into my garage and slid the door closed behind me. I hadn't heard any knocks or screams coming from the trunk on the drive over, so I assumed that Jason was still in dreamland. He wouldn't be for much longer.

Down in the basement, the boys were all asleep. Daniel had kicked off all his covers and removed his clothes, sweating out the fever that was finally beginning to break. Though strong when healthy, he'd be no use to me in his current state. Alan was the smallest of the lot, easily a good thirty pounds lighter than Jason, and he'd only grown weaker with the low-protein diet I had him on.

Owen was the best choice, then, not only because of his relative size and strength, but because this would be, in a way, the first test in the next step of his education. It would be a momentous night for everyone. And me without a scrapbook.

"Owen," I said, shaking his foot lightly to wake him up. He blinked his eyes and gave me a sweet little smile. "I need your help. Stand up, honey."

He dutifully stood and gave his muscles a good stretch. "Are we going out now?"

"Just to the garage," I said. "We're going to have another student join the class."

I checked to make sure that the shock collar was still in place around Owen's testes. It wasn't that I didn't trust him, but I couldn't take the risk. There was too much open space up there, and I wasn't yet fully convinced that Owen was ready to explore it. Tucking the remote control into my pocket, I knelt down and unlocked Owen's manacles with the key dangling from my necklace.

It felt strange to have one of the boys following me up the stairs, especially one who was a good foot taller and wider than me, but I didn't turn around to check on him once. I owed him that much trust. I could feel his massive presence rising up behind me, his shadow dwarfing mine, but to Owen's credit, he didn't make a single move that I didn't first direct.

We both heard the banging on the trunk before we even got into the garage. Jason was awake, and, from the sound of it, a bit miffed. Some boys just can't hold their chloroform.

I positioned Owen right behind the trunk and popped the lid with the key chain remote. The trunk flew open, and a second later the picnic basket that had been inside for months whipped through the air, zipped past Owen's head, and clattered against the garage door.

"Thanks," I called out. "I've been meaning to take that out of there."

Jason had managed to untie the ropes that bound his arms to his legs, but the individual knots holding his hands and feet together were still intact. His eyes bugged out as Owen leaned into the trunk and hefted him out as if he was no more than a stuffed animal, flinging him over one meaty shoulder. Jason screamed through the gag and flailed around, pounding Owen's back with his bound hands.

"Is that bothering you?" I asked Owen.

"A little," he admitted.

I untied the panty hose holding the napkin in Jason's mouth, and all of a sudden the two-time Oscar nominee was screaming bloody murder, really making the worst of the situation.

"You crazy bitch!" he yelled. His lips contorted around those perfect teeth, and his blotch-free skin had turned a cherry red with anger. Between his lovey-dovey routine on the yacht and this display of unbridled rage, it really showed off his range. "What the fuck are you doing? Do you have any idea who you're fucking with?"

That was quite enough of that. He'd already cursed more than I cared to hear. I'm no prude, and I believe that cusswords have their place in any modern conversation, but I don't like to subject my boys to such vulgarity. When they're returned to society, they'll get enough of that in the workplace and on the basketball court.

As Jason continued to rant and rave, I poured the rest of the chloroform onto the napkin and unceremoniously shoved it up against his nose. The effects were nearly instantaneous, and he slumped over Owen's shoulder like a toddler who'd tired himself out after a long day.

"Take him to the basement," I instructed Owen. "Keep an eye on him, and I'll be down in a moment."

As Owen lumbered through the house and down the basement steps, I did a quick search of the garage for the equipment I would need to make this situation bearable. Inside my toolbox I found two combination locks, and in the corner of a tucked-away shelf I located an old set of snow chains (date: a trip to Big Bear with a physics professor who claimed to know how to ski but spent most of the time in the lodge hitting on the fifty-six-year-old proprietress). Locks and tire chains are all fine and good, but it left me woefully short on the basics.

By the time I made it down to the basement, Alan and Daniel had already woken up, scrambled out of bed, and were eager to learn more about their new classmate.

"Is that . . . who I think it is?" Alan asked. "I loved him in *Rangers*."

"We all did," I said, "but he's to be treated like anyone else. He's our guest now, and a new student. I expect you'll all help him through what might be a difficult transition period."

They all nodded dutifully, and I returned my attention to the matter at hand. "Owen, I'll need you to keep a grip on him for about a half hour. If he wakes up, make sure he doesn't get too rambunctious."

"Will do. Could I get a few lengths of rope?"

Together, we reestablished the hog-tie around Jason's hands and feet, and I told the boys I'd be back as quickly as I could. I made sure that the dead bolt on the basement door was locked up tight, and then headed out for West Hollywood.

One of the best things about living in Los Angeles is that we're a twenty-four-hour-a-day city. I've got friends from New York who talk about how Manhattan's so great because you can buy a sandwich and a

DVD player at three in the morning (probably from the same street hustler), but when it comes to sex and the devices that may or may not enhance it, L.A.'s got the market cornered. Especially West Hollywood.

I've had my pick of sex shops over the last few years, and I make it a habit not to frequent any one store for my equipment. A single woman in what is otherwise a predominantly gay sex shop might raise a few tweezed eyebrows if she shows up once too often.

Purple Passion is a store I've noticed many a time while driving down Santa Monica Boulevard, and, from the display window out front, I could tell they'd have exactly what I needed. Moving as quickly as possible, I ducked through the shadows and entered the blacked-out front door.

Inside, it was all fluorescent lighting and bondage gear. Perfect. I made my way down the main aisle, glancing back and forth between gay hard-core tapes and more vanilla offerings until I found what I was looking for. A few male-male couples and some single stragglers wandered the shop with me, but we were all so intent on our own immediate needs that no one bothered to say hello.

"Find what you needed?" asked the young clerk with the cutoff shirt and protruding nipple rings as I tossed my purchases onto the front counter.

"Everything and then some," I said. "You've got a great selection."

The numbing effects of the chloroform on Jason's mind and body were just beginning to wear off as I stepped through the basement door. Owen sat on the floor, his thick arms holding Jason in a headlock. "He's been moving around. And he made a bit of a mess."

One unfortunate effect of chloroform is that it can wreak havoc on the digestive tract, and, true to form, Jason had let go with a good stream of vomit. It ran in a stream down his chin, covering his linen clothes and puddling on the floor by his feet. I'm going to have to flirt extra hard with the guys down at the dry cleaners to get them to pull that stench out of his shirt and pants.

"We'd better do this quickly," I suggested, tossing the bag from Purple Passion onto the basement floor. The boys tore into it like kids on Christmas morning, oohing and aahing over my purchases. They've really become connoisseurs.

Owen graciously offered up his bed, and together we stripped Jason down to his boxers and laid his body atop the mattress. Alan and Daniel held his arms tightly as I pulled out two sets of handcuffs and snapped them into place over his wrists. His hands were silky smooth; when he wakes up, I'm going to find out what kind of moisturizer he uses.

The cuffs I bought were more expensive than some of the other options, but the insides were fitted with padding, which would provide comfort and protection for Jason's million-dollar skin. I certainly didn't want to reduce his bankability due to wrist welts. I attached the other end of each cuff to the metal frame of the cot and gave them a good tug.

"Legs," I instructed, and the boys stretched Jason out good and long. He was beginning to mumble in his sleep as the chloroform dissipated from the pathways in his brain. Something about getting him a Perrier.

I pulled up Jason's pants legs and clamped one manacle around each ankle. "Could you be a dear and work in that chain?" I asked Alan. He pulled out a ten-foot length of half-inch metal chain and snaked it perfectly through the loops at the side of each manacle. I gave it a good spin about the bed frame, then snapped it all in place with a combination lock.

"That should do," I said, standing up and stepping back to get a good look at the setup. Jason was adequately trussed, drawn out spread-eagle across the bed, and, though I would never think of leaving him in that position for too long, I was satisfied that it would do the job for the next twelve hours or so.

Looking at him, lying there helplessly on that cot, I realized what a favor I was about to do for the rest of the world. Here was this boy, who obviously thought he could bandy about his fame and sexuality in order to subjugate women to his will, and I had been given the privilege of teaching him how to become a better man. It's quite the honor, I believe, and, if I succeed, it's very possible that I may one day be spoken of in the same breath as that lady who taught Helen Keller to talk.

In fact, it's precisely because of his fame that Jason's rehabilitation here at the Finishing School will be so sweet. Once he learns all I that I can teach him, once he learns to be a man, he can go back to the rest of the world and say, *Look at me! Look at what I've become! Be like me, and we can make this a better place!*

As for now, though, he's screaming and pulling at his restraints. I can just barely hear the racket through the thick basement door, Jason yanking at his chains and cursing me out. I bet he's keeping the boys awake, poor things. The resistance will pass, though. It always does. Everyone's always nervous on the night before their first big day of school.

BALANCE AND DEXTERITY

Seven A.M. The phone rang. I was just coming out of a terrible night's sleep. "Hello?"

"Cassandra French?" The voice on the other end was no-nonsense, all business. There was no hesitation.

I sat up in bed. "Yes?"

"My name is Lieutenant Holland. I'm with the Los Angeles Police Department."

Propensity for heart attack: B. I eat fairly well, I exercise once every two weeks. I don't smoke. I have no history of heart disease. Still, I don't take well to shocks. One time I took a sweater back to Nordstrom without the receipt, and found that the same Dana Buchman cardigan I'd bought a month prior was now on sale for 20 percent off, and the girl at the counter would let me exchange it only for the new sale price. I nearly fainted.

My first thought was to slam down the phone and run, just get in the car and take off and leave it all behind me. No one would miss me at work. Claire would understand, after a fashion. She might even help me arrange for fugitive travel to foreign lands. Malaysia seemed like a sensible place to go.

My second thought, and the one that eventually slapped the first thought in the cheek and called it names, was to stay cool and collected and deal with the situation like the attorney that I'm supposed to be.

"Good morning, Officer," I said evenly. "What can I do for you?"

He paused for a second before answering. "Ma'am, I'm a bit concerned."

"You are?" I said. "What seems to be the problem?"

Here it comes, I thought, internally prepping my weak alibi. *Jason Kelly? The actor? No, Officer, I was home by myself all last night. Watched a movie on TV. No, I don't remember the name. It had Kevin Bacon in it, I think. Yes, it probably was* Murder in the First. *You're right, Officer, it was definitely an underappreciated film. What excellent taste you have. Are you doing anything tonight?*

"A woman who claims to be your mother just cornered me on the street," said the cop as the first rush of boiling blood pounded into my head, "and wouldn't go away until I agreed to call you on my cell phone and tell you she's sorry about yesterday afternoon. Does this make any sense?"

Deep breaths, Cassie. I didn't want to scream obscenities and hang up on an officer of the law, so I took a moment to calm myself before responding. Eventually, I told him that I didn't know what the woman was talking about, that my mother had died four years ago and was buried at Forest Lawn. "There are so many crazy people out there, Officer," I said. "It's sad, really. This woman probably needs to be institutionalized. I'd suggest a straitjacket if you get the chance."

He apologized for the early call, and I hung up as quickly and politely as possible. I can't deal with Mom right now. Can't deal with her today at all. Too much on my mind, and way too much to do to let myself be caught up in her web of guilt and lies and fantasy.

Releasing. Breathing deeply. Remembering the stupid yoga exercises I learned from Lexi. Damn it all, I forgot about Lexi.

Today at two is the court hearing for Lexi's flesh-eating wuzzles. My hand hasn't even fully healed, yet I'm going into court to act as a character witness for two animals who seem to think I'm haute cuisine. But I made a promise to stand by my friend, and stand by her I shall. That's what friends do, after all. I might not say anything constructive, but I'll be standing.

I'm more excited about tonight's field trip with Owen, the first in his series of lessons outside the confines of the Finishing School. Our outfits have been decided upon, the reservations have been made, and I'm sure it's going to go smashingly well, so long as I can fit the remote control for the electronic scrotum collar into my purse.

After the phone call from the L.A.P.D./Mom, I whipped together breakfast for the boys, making sure to stir up an extra cup of oatmeal for our newest boarder. I didn't remember whether or not Jason Kelly particularly liked oatmeal. The little I can recall about his eating habits came from an article in *Premiere* about two years ago in which he was advocating the raw food movement. As far as I understood it, raw foodies believe in eating nothing that has been cooked above a temperature of 120 degrees or so. The upside to this, as far as I can see, is that it means you're pretty much forced to eat sashimi every night. I could live with that. I don't know if the movement was designed for health reasons or humanitarian ones, but I can't imagine any activists screaming about saving the poor little baby carrots. I'd try to get further information from Jason, but he isn't particularly interested in discussing it with me.

In fact, he wasn't particularly interested in discussing anything with anybody this morning. He wouldn't even let me near him with the oatmeal. Wouldn't give it a single try. Every time I tried to spoon a helping into his mouth, he spit it back out at me. After the third or fourth attempt (I tried airplane into the hangar, train into the tunnel, all the old standards), my shirt and his bed were covered in spittle and grains.

"Don't be a baby," I chided. "Everyone likes oatmeal. Boys?"

Owen and Alan nodded appreciatively as they licked clean their own bowls and held up the empty containers for inspection.

"This isn't the instant kind," I shouted over Jason's howls of protest. "This is real, honest stuff. I made it myself. Raisins and everything. Women like it when you appreciate their cooking, you know."

More thrashing and screaming and threats. He needed a little more time to tire himself out before class could begin, so I sat on an upended box and did my nails. Today I've gone with a color called Kennebunk Port from Opi, a fantastic shade of maroon that will complement both the short-skirt and long-jacket number I'll be wearing for the wuzzles' hearing and the cocktail dress I've chosen for this evening's lesson with Owen.

As I carefully brushed the paint onto my nails, I noticed another one of those infuriating little dust piles beneath the exposed wood beam on the far side of the basement. A quick inspection turned up some minuscule holes, maybe a tenth of an inch wide, as if some microscopic critter was trying to pull a *Shawshank Redemption* on me and tunnel out of the basement. I made a mental note to call in an exterminator.

Eventually, Jason stopped yelling and banging away at his chains and handcuffs. Thank God. It was getting hard to concentrate on my nails with all that racket.

"Listen to me," he said, panting heavily from the exertion. "People will want to know where I am. They'll want to know what happened to me."

I knelt by the side of Jason's bed and stroked his sweaty forehead with a hand towel. "I don't want you to worry about a thing. We know you're very famous, and we're all really big fans." The other boys nodded along earnestly. "But we've all made a promise to treat you like just another student. You don't have to give out autographs if you don't want. That is, once you're allowed to use crayons. Until then, the issue can wait."

Jason tried switching tactics, assuming, perhaps, that I'd be taken in by his charm once again, as I was in my office, on his boat, and in his bed. "Cassandra . . . Cassie." He gave me that megawatt grin, the smile that won Meg Ryan's heart in *Staten Island*. No box office, but a great film. "Cass," he settled on, "let's be realistic. As soon as my staff realizes

I'm missing, they're going to look at my date book and come straight here."

"Which date book would that be?" I asked, pulling out the two sheets of paper I'd found lodged in his office drawer. "This one?"

Jason's eyes went through a convoluted series of motions as I pulled out a lighter, set the whole thing ablaze, and dropped it into the trash. Within a matter of seconds, the list was nothing but smoldering ashes inside a metal garbage can.

Eventually, Jason's eyes popped back into his head. "That's not the only copy," he bluffed. "And I told everyone I knew about our date."

"That's so funny," I replied, "because you were quite insistent that I keep it a secret. Wore that fake beard to the office, sent a cab to pick me up at the park, cleared out the heliport and everything. I know that I sure as heck didn't tell anyone. I've got a feeling you didn't blab, either. You even sent away your staff so the yacht would be empty when I got there. Sounds pretty secretive to me."

"Cassie," he began again, but I cut him off with a palm over his mouth. His lips were dry and cracked. I made a mental note to buy him some high-quality lip balm next time I went out.

"Jason, let's not go through this. I know what you were doing, and why you asked me out."

"Because I liked you?" he mumbled, trying to speak through my hand.

"That's sweet," I replied. "But you don't have to lie to make me feel better. I know you were systematically going through all the unat- tached women at the studio who might have been called for a deposi- tion on the *Half-Hearted* contracts. I know you wanted to get at least one of us on your side so we'd lie on your behalf. I know you slept with me for the sake of two extra points on dollar one gross, and you know what? I'm okay with that now. Do you know why?"

I moved my hand away to hear his response, and he tried out a last bit of bravado. "No, and I don't care. Get me the fuck out of this bed." He deflated at the end, his last words coming out in a punctured- balloon wheeze.

"There you go." I gave him a little pat on the head. "I'm glad you got that out of your system. Now we can get on to the real work. Up, up, let's get him up."

Owen manned Jason's arms as I unlocked the handcuffs from the bed frame. To his credit, Jason didn't even try to struggle. Owen would have crushed him like a bug, and he knew it. As soon as we had Jason upright, his legs still manacled to the frame, I locked the handcuffs to each other, giving him a little room to shake his arms and shoulders about.

"Does that feel a little better?" I asked. Jason grunted, and I motioned for Owen to sit back on his own chair. "The reason I'm okay with all of the things you did—to me, to the women at the studio, to the countless women I'm sure you've been using since you were a teenager—is because all of that is going to change."

Jason avoided my gaze. "Whatever."

"I know you don't believe it now, but it's just your first day. Everyone has a hard time their first day at school. Owen nearly broke the bed, didn't you?"

"Bent the whole thing in half," he said wistfully.

"I remember my mom taking me to kindergarten," I reminisced. "My very first day. She dropped me off, and I clung to her leg, and I cried, just like all the other kids. It took two teacher's aides just to pull me free, but I've always had relatively good upper-body strength for my size. Anyway, by the end of that day, I was clinging to my teacher's leg and crying because I had to go home. I'd come to love it that much, in just one short day, just like I know you'll come to love your time here at the Finishing School.

"That's rule number one, by the way," I added hastily. "If you feel like you want to cry, that's fine. You go right ahead. Daniel cries at least twice a day, don't you, Daniel?"

Buried once more beneath a mound of sheets, Daniel (temperature: 101 degrees) shook the blankets up and down. It was close enough to a nod.

"See? He might even be crying now. Don't stress about that too much, though. Crying for Boys is a course of advanced study. For your first lesson, we're going to start out with something a lot easier, and a heck of a lot more fun."

"A film?" asked Owen.

"A skit!" Alan suggested.

"Better," I said as I pulled five hairbrushes and a portable CD player from a padlocked box beneath the stairs. "We're going to lip-synch."

Cheers all around from the boys. Daniel even managed to stumble out of bed and shuffle over toward the others. It was good to see him up and about. I dispensed the hairbrushes. Jason refused to take his, but I set it on the bed next to him in the hopes that he would eventually join in.

Taking my place at the front of our makeshift classroom, I began the first part of the morning's lesson. "Everyone gets down now and again," I said as sympathetically as possible. "It's human nature, and it's natural. Jason, you're a bit down right now, but I want you to know there's a surefire way to pep yourself right up again. A sudden, random burst of lip-synching can be the answer to many of life's problems. Now Jason, I know that probably sounds a little odd to you, and it's certainly counter to what society's taught you boys about how to cheer your-selves up, but I promise you that three billion women can't be wrong. I've always thought that the world would be a better place if everyone would drop what they were doing and sing along to Madonna now and again."

I ensured that the CD player was plugged in and continued on. "Of course, Madonna's fine in a pinch, but if we're really looking to cure our blues, there's only one style of music that does the trick. Anyone?"

"Motown?" Daniel wheezed.

"Motown," I repeated, tapping Jason on the head with my hair-brush to make sure he was paying attention. "Very good. The Detroit-based Motown label was created in 1959 by Berry Gordy as a way to spotlight his stars by backing them with an array of blues and funk vir-tuosos. Everyone from Marvin Gaye to the Supremes to the Tempta-tions recorded for Mr. Gordy, but there's one recording artist who shines above all the others when it comes time for a true pick-me-up."

Owen didn't wait for me to call on him. "Aretha."

"That's right," I said, pushing Play on the boom box. "The Queen of Soul. Hairbrushes up, everyone."

As the first strains of "Respect" filled the small basement, Owen, Alan, and Daniel pulled their hairbrushes up to their lips to simulate microphones and shuffled into place next to me. "Come on," I called out to Jason. "Join us."

No dice. He just stared straight ahead, refusing to have a good time. In the meantime, we'd formed a straight line, with Owen and me in the middle and Alan and Daniel flanking us on either end. As per tradition, I stepped forward and lip-synched the first verse into my hairbrush microphone.

Behind me, the boys launched into their dance, a sidestep shuffle made slightly more difficult by the manacles and chains around their ankles. Metal clinked against metal as they stepped and hopped in synch with the music.

Owen took the next verse, really getting into the song and making it his own. Crouching down on the guttural notes, his face twisting like Joe Cocker on the high ones. If I didn't know any better, I'd have sworn that heavenly voice was coming from his own mouth.

"Isn't it wonderful?" I called out to the unresponsive Jason. "It's so freeing!" The glory of a good lip-synch is knowing that you're a slave to the music but that you don't have to worry about displaying any actual talent. For a few minutes, you can be Aretha or Madonna or Billy Joel, and let the music flow through you, washing all your worries away. We try to lip-synch at least twice a week at the Finishing School. It does wonders for morale.

The boys and I fell into another choreographed dance sequence as the chorus took over, slapping hands and spinning just as Owen faded back into the line. It's taken the better part of six months to get this routine down; though it's often good to put on a song you barely know and let yourself be drawn into the music, no one just flies into a lip-synch number like "Respect" unrehearsed. Jason was really getting a good show, and it was a shame he wasn't in the mood to appreciate it.

Alan and Daniel took the third and fourth verses respectively, and, though Daniel was sweating away as he stared out at the imaginary audience, he worked that hairbrush like a pro. As the song drew to a close and the music began to fade out, we all cut loose, boogying down to the receding beat. The boys slowly gravitated back to their original back-up singer stances as I stepped out in front and led them in a final bow. The CD was over. The lip-synch was complete.

Silence. Not a single ounce of applause.

"You are all fucking insane," Jason said plainly. "I hope you realize that."

Still with the cursing. "We're not insane," I informed him. "We're happy now. You'd be happy, too, if you joined us." From his stoic reaction, I didn't think he was really grooving with the program. Sometimes it takes a little extra encouragement. "Stay put, I know something that might help."

I nodded to Owen, who stepped behind Jason's cot and wrapped his arms around the actor as I jogged up the stairs and into the kitchen. I returned a moment later with a syringe and a vial of morphine.

"Have you ever used heroin?" I asked.

"What?" He caught a glimpse of the syringe and started to buck.

"Heroin. Horse. I'm sorry, I don't know what they call it in Hollywood these days. Smack?"

"Jesus Christ," he spat, struggling in Owen's arms, "get that shit away from me."

"Or opium? Any opiate, actually? I'm just trying to figure out if you've got a tolerance or not."

He refused to answer, so I started him with 5 mg of morphine. If five minutes passed and there was no reaction, I figured I'd just up the dosage by another 5 mg and reassess.

The shot went in quickly and easily, and Jason's muscles relaxed thirty seconds after I released the plunger. His eyes took on that happy glaze, and just like that he wasn't so belligerent anymore.

"There we are," I said. "All better. Now, let's take the song from the top again. And this time, Jason, I'd like you to help Alan out on the third verse, okay?"

We helped him to his feet, and he managed to stand in place as we shifted our line to accommodate his presence. I knelt down and started up the CD player again, and soon those funky horns were hitting the air.

"Hairbrushes up," I instructed my boys. "This time, let's really make it count."

And I'll be damned if our little Oscar nominee didn't start singing straightaway. Sure, he was singing "Itsy-Bitsy Spider," but he was singing, and that's a start.

I've just come back from the Trial of the Week, and what with stark, unrelenting candor running rampant these days, I've chosen to recap it in the hopes of eventually assigning myself a letter grade for friendship, honesty, and self-sacrifice. How's that for an opening statement?

Though my first instinct after this morning's session with the boys was to call in sick and personally continue Jason's first day of instruction, I realized that I'd have to put in an appearance at work, if only to avoid suspicion. I don't really believe that anyone will put Jason and me together the night of his disappearance, but in case there was some eyewitness I didn't account for, at least there won't be any nosy secretaries corroborating their story by blabbing about how I didn't show up at the office the next day.

I even made a point of finding Stan Olsen and allowing him to ogle my ass as I walked by his office on the way to the coffee nook. "Morning, Stan," I called out, poking my head into his plush suite. He's not even an attorney, but somehow he's worked his way up into senior vice president of business affairs, a position that comes with a corner office and a panoramic view of the entire San Fernando Valley.

"Cassandra, just the girl I was looking for. Come on in."

I stepped inside his office, and turned to shut the door, but it was already closing behind me, seemingly of its own free will.

"Automatic clicker," Stan explained, holding up the remote control that opened and closed his office door so he wouldn't have to get off that bulbous behind. "The boys put it in on Tuesday. Saves time like you wouldn't believe. Sit down, we've got a matter to discuss."

He was going to hit on me again; I could feel it. I started riffling through all my old excuses, trying to remember which ones I'd used on him in the past. The best bet in these situations is to come up with an entirely new pretext, of course, but I think it was Aristotle who said that there are only seven excuses in the world, and the rest are merely variations on a theme.

"I've got to dog-sit," I barked. "All weekend."

"Fascinating," he replied, completely uninterested. He passed me a thin stack of papers. "Here, we received these this morning." I read the first line.

Cassandra Susan French, you are hereby commanded to appear in a civil court of California . . .

"A subpoena," I muttered. At least I'd been right; Jason's plans had been to use me for my eventual testimony. My accuracy didn't make me feel any better about the situation, though.

"For the *Half-Hearted* case. Utter bullshit, but there it is."

"Am I . . . the only one?"

"They pretty much blanketed the whole office. Now, Kelly's lawyers can't get us to testify unless the studio litigators call us first. Best thing to do would be to leave us out of it entirely, but down in litigation, they want to know what we know. I'm supposed to be coordinating the interviews. Are you good around lunch?"

The last thing I wanted was to be talking about Jason to other people, even if it was only about a film contract. It was too soon, and I hadn't fully formulated what I was going to say about our relationship, if anything.

"How about next week sometime?" I countered. "Today's a mess." Stan gave me the go-ahead to check in with litigation on Monday, so I was free to formulate a plan of action over the weekend.

"Oh, and Cassandra?" he called as I stepped out of his office. "Will we be seeing you at the party tonight?"

I was pretty sure I'd already blown him off on that account earlier in the week. "Mr. Olsen, it's not that I don't want to—"

"I know, you're picking up a friend at the airport. But I thought you should know that Arlene Oberst is going to be there. In case you're interested in meeting her. We're very close."

That got my attention. Arlene Oberst is the head of business affairs, not quite on par with the head of the studio or the president of production, but she's the big cheese when it comes to the business side of things. There are as many rumors floating around about Arlene Oberst as there are true stories, and no one's able to get the facts straight; the only thing that's clear is that she's one of the most powerful women at the studio, and it certainly couldn't hurt to get to know her. At the very least, maybe she could find some damned work for me to do.

Owen and I already had reservations at a restaurant in Newport Beach for our first field trip. But a restaurant is so sterile, so cloistered. In many ways, it was too easy of a challenge. The only way to learn how to swim is to jump into the deep end and hope you pop up to the surface.

"You know what," I said, sashaying back into Stan's office, "maybe we could drop by for a bit. If my friend's plane gets in on time."

Stan wrote out directions to his house and slipped them into my hand. I'm pretty sure he tickled my palm with his middle finger, some gesture I vaguely remember being construed as "dirty" in the fifth grade. "See you there," he said. I tried not to vomit.

I scurried back to my office and holed up for a few hours, searching the web for any mention of an Aston Martin abandoned in the middle of Beverly Hills. There was nothing, of course. It's all too soon for anyone to notice something amiss. If I'd dumped a $150,000 convertible downtown, maybe it would have gotten some notice, but Beverly Hills is practically littered with super-luxury cars.

I found a flurry of recent news reports on Jason himself, but they were all fluff pieces that had just hit the newsstands. One interviewer even had the guts to ask a few tough questions, including this little gem:

Q: You've always been a vocal antifur activist.
JK: That's right. I can't idly sit back while there's this kind of cruelty out there in the world.
Q: But you're wearing leather boots right now. And a leather jacket.

JK: See, that's what people don't know, man. Fur keeps the animals
warm. You ever touch leather? Go on, touch it. It's cold, right?
Leather is cold. Take away the fur, the animals freeze to death.
Take away their leather . . . You know, it's not that bad. They
can wear wool or something instead.

Christ, I'd slept with a himbo. I must have known it going in, I suppose, but was blindsided by the shine blasting off his teeth. Now I
understand why men keep following Lexi around.

Speaking of Lexi: I left the office around eleven and headed downtown to the courthouse. After the obligatory metal-detection-and-
grope session, I found Lexi outside of the courtroom, nibbling at her
once-perfect nails. I bet they'll grow back overnight.

"Oh, Cass, thank God you're here." She threw herself on top of me,
sobbing openly. "My wuzzles . . . my poor wuzzles . . ."

I gave her a perfunctory hug, then pushed her back to arm's length.
I might have been recognized by a colleague walking the courthouse
hallways, and the last thing I wanted was to become known as a doggie
Gloria Allred. "Get a grip, Lexi. It's just a hearing; they'll be fine."

"I need you to pull out all the stops," she insisted. "Every legal trick
you know. Confuse the jury."

"Lexi—"

"Throw a monkey wrench into the system!"

"Lexi, stop!" My short burst had the effect of a sucker punch. She
took a sharp breath in and a step back. "First, there is no jury, just a
judge. Second, it's not a trial. It's a hearing. There are no legal tricks for
me to pull, and even if there were, I can't pull them. I'm not here as
your lawyer, remember? I'm here as your friend."

"My friend who knows the law."

"Entertainment law. If the wuzzles book a national commercial,
maybe then we can talk. Otherwise, I'm just going to stand next to you
and try not to look too fat."

"Oh sweetie," cooed Lexi, "don't talk like that. If you feel fat, you
can always stand behind me or something, okay?"

They called the matter before the judge just after one o'clock, and

Lexi dragged me up to the defendant's table. Sitting with the city attorney on the other side of the room was Leonard Shelby, the toadlike man who'd been the victim of the wuzzles' wrath. A short little thing with Coke-bottle glasses and terrible acne, he shuffled in his seat, propping up a comically bandaged leg. There was so much gauze wrapped around his shin it was a wonder he could move the thing at all.

"Looks like he lost a fight with a mummy," I whispered to Lexi, but she was too nervous to smile. She was shivering with anxiety, her limbs quivering as the bailiff called her to the podium. Of course, what with her stunning lack of insulating body fat, it's possible she was just very cold.

The city attorney was decked out in a stylish three-button suit and spit-shined wingtips, and it was gratifying to see a public servant who took his duty toward fashion seriously. All too often those who have been sworn to serve and protect stock their closets with bargain-basement department store castoffs. Lady Justice knows how to wear her toga and blindfold with style; the least we can do is try to keep up.

"Your Honor," said the attorney, standing at the podium and addressing the heavy-jowled judge, "if it pleases the court, we would like to bring the canines in question into the courtroom."

The judge nodded, and the bailiff disappeared behind the lockup doors. Lexi grabbed my hand and squeezed; her bony fingers clenched mine, the skin cold and clammy. I briefly wondered how I'd gotten myself into this. Mostly, I blamed Claire; she's the one who brought Lexi into our little twosome in the first place. Had she never introduced us, I could have passed Lexi walking down the street with her big boobs, long legs, and confident air, and safely hated her from a distance without a single twinge of guilt.

The bailiff returned, pushing a wire cage into the courtroom via a wheeled hand truck, perfectly fitting for the Hannibal Lecters of their species. True to form, though, Jack Nicholson and Shirley MacLaine were in hibernation mode, slumped atop each other like two piles of shag carpeting. A distinct "awwww" rose from the gallery. The fools in the audience didn't know that it was all part of the wuzzles' ruse to lull their victims into a false sense of security.

"Wuzzles!" cried Lexi, bolting across the courtroom and up to the cage. She had her hands halfway inside before the bailiff wrestled her away and back to the defendant's table. The dogs starting barking, Lexi started weeping. Madness.

Judge Olgin banged his gavel, as all good judges must do, and croaked, "I don't have time for this sort of thing. Miss Hart, stay behind your table." He turned to the city attorney. "Let's move this along."

It didn't take long for the lawyer to lay out the facts: Lexi had taken both dogs to a dog park and let them off the leash, at which point they attacked a helpless passerby. As he tried to fight his way out from under them, Ms. Lexi Hart, she of the so-so mind and very sound body, urged her dogs to continue biting the poor victim. Under the California Civil Code, they were requesting that Lexi be charged with an infraction.

"That's just a fine," I whispered to her. "Twenty-five dollars and you're off scot-free."

"Furthermore," the prosecutor continued, "we request that both dogs be labeled as 'potentially dangerous' as provided by Civil Code 31602, which states that any dog which bites a person causing less than a severe injury can be considered—"

"I know what the code says," the judge interrupted. "Is that all?" He turned toward Lexi and motioned for her to take the podium. I pushed her out from behind the table, and she reluctantly stood up, keeping eye contact with her wuzzles the whole time.

Now, justice may be blind, but the judge sure wasn't, and he ogled Lexi with every step she took. I could practically see the drool dripping down the old man's chin. For a moment, I was disgusted, until I realized that if the judge were predisposed to let Lexi off because of her assets, I wouldn't have to stand up as a wuzzle character witness and make a complete ass of myself. Go, Lexi! Go, Lexi's breasts!

"Good afternoon, Your Honor," Lexi said with a bit of hesitation. She looked back at me, and I nodded for her to go on. "My wuzz—my dogs are really quite sweet. They wouldn't hurt a fly. Well, they've got this one toy, it sort of *looks* like a fly—"

I nearly stood up to object, just to stop her from launching into the story again, but the judge mercifully put an end to it first. "Ms. Hart, I have only two questions for you, and then I'll let you and your dogs go home. Okay?"

With the juxtaposition of the words dogs and home, Lexi underwent a radical transformation. Her knee-knocking anxiety transformed into a bubbly, effervescent mess of tears and nonsense syllables, most of them directed at the wuzzles themselves. She eventually managed to regain control and tell the judge that she was ready to answer any and all questions put to her.

"First," asked the judge, who definitely wanted to put something *else* to her, "have you trained these dogs to attack in any way?"

"Goodness, no!" she chirped. "Jack and Shirley get my love, and that's all."

"Second question, and listen closely. When your dogs were biting Mr. Shelby, did you call out . . ." The judge shuffled around a stack of papers on his desk and peered at the top. "Did you call out, 'Get him, doggies. Bite him! Bite that man! Good doggies'?"

"No," Lexi said emphatically. "What I said was, 'Good doggies, good doggies! That's some good biting.' "

Oh, Lexi. How do you not float away, what with your head being lighter than air? I should have seen what was coming next, but I was too enthralled by the disaster in front of me to see the next train hurtling around the corner.

"Why would you tell them something like that?" asked the judge. "You claim you don't incite your animals to violence, but that certainly sounds like a violent statement to me."

Lexi countered, "Not at all, Your Honor. We call it positive reinforcement."

"We?" asked the judge.

"Me and Cassie. She knows all about it." Lexi turned and waved to me, and it took all my strength not to throttle her then and there. I waved back meekly and tried to disappear into the woodwork. We should have been out celebrating her victory with a cappuccino and two rawhide chews by this point; instead, she was quickly moving herself into felony territory, and dragging me along with her.

As I'd expected, Judge Olgin motioned for me to approach the podium. Since I already knew that he was something of a lech, I tried to approximate Lexi's swivel-hipped walk, but halfway there I felt a twinge in my side and had to give it up before I pulled a muscle. I limped the final five feet and announced my name.

"Are these your dogs as well, Ms. French?" asked the judge.

If that were the case, I thought, *I'd ask to be put in prison myself for protective custody.* "No, Your Honor, they're not."

"Then your purpose in this courtroom today is . . . ?"

Lexi pushed me aside. "She's my lawyer."

"What? No I'm not."

The judge sighed. We were losing this thing fast. If I didn't smooth things over, Lexi was going to have to flash the judge in order to buy us more time. "Are you or are you not an attorney?" he asked.

"I am," I admitted. "But not for Ms. Hart. I'm in business affairs." I gave the name of my studio.

The judge nodded in recognition. "Had a bit of a slump recently, didn't you? Took a hit on that World War Two flop last spring. I heard the marketing costs were through the roof."

"Yes, Your Honor." That's L.A. for you; even the civil court judges read *Variety*. "We're . . . going to try harder next time."

"Very well," he said. "Miss Hart seems to think you can shed light on this positive reinforcement theory of hers."

I quickly explained that I'd known Lexi for a couple of years, and that I'd never seen her strike, yell at, or even discipline the dogs in any negative fashion. I said that, as far as I knew, positive reinforcement was indeed a legitimate training technique, though I didn't profess to be an expert on the subject.

As the judge mulled over his response, Lexi leaned in and whispered to me, "Tell him about the other day."

"Are you insane?" I shot back.

The judge cleared his throat. I never signed up for throat-clearing class in law school, but I'm sure it was heavily attended by anyone who aspired toward the bench. "Care to share, ladies?"

Before I could gloss over the situation, Lexi piped up, "Cassie's seen the positive reinforcement firsthand, Your Honor. And I contend . . . is contend the right word?"

"Sure," said Judge Olgin wearily. "Sounds right to me."

"I contend that had Mr. Shelby simply used these positive-reinforcement words like I'd yelled at him to do—instead of kicking my wuzzles, which I notice no one mentioned yet . . ." She glared at the city attorney, who sat there passionless, but who was probably beaming on the inside. "If he'd said the right words, then I contend that the wuzzles would have let go right away and resumed their usual friendly ways. The end."

Lexi elbowed me in the ribs and waggled her eyebrows. Quite proud of her legal wrangling, that little coconut. If the yoga thing doesn't work out, she'll have a great career in constitutional law for complete idiots.

"Go on," Lexi said. "Tell him, Cass."

I kept it short and sweet, regaling the less-than-enthralled court with the tale of our visit to the Santa Monica Animal Shelter to check up on Jack and Shirley after their incarceration. I got right up to the part when I reached into the cage to wipe down Jack Nicholson's nose, and then allowed my voice to trail off.

"Yes?" the judge prompted. "You reached into the cage, wiped his nose, scratched his head, and . . . ?"

Lexi was nodding along eagerly, somehow convinced that this whole story was going to make her look good.

I held my hand aloft, bruised side toward the bench. Judge Olgin leaned forward, squinting to get a better look. "Approach," he commanded, and my feet followed. The judge took my hand in his and inspected it for damage.

I was surprised at how soft Judge Olgin's hands were. Just like Jason's, I thought. I wondered how my newest student was doing back in the basement, and whether or not he was getting along with the other boys during his first day of school. I'd left them with workbook assignments to complete, but Jason was still getting used to the morphine, so I fully expected to come home and find nothing but slobber on the page.

Releasing my hand, Judge Olgin sent me back to the podium,

where I shook my head at a still-smiling Lexi. "I assume," said the judge, "since your hand is still attached to your arm, that the dogs let go at some point."

"That's right, Your Honor," Lexi announced proudly. "And it's all because Cassie said the magic words."

"Good doggies?" asked the judge.

"That's it," beamed Lexi. "See, it's easy. Can we go now?"

The city attorney stood to make a motion, but the judge waved him back down again. "I know what you're going to say, Hank, and I'll do it for you." He returned his attention to Lexi and me, the force of his glare enough to make me cower behind the podium. Lexi, like Old Yeller grinning stupidly down the barrel of a twelve-gauge, stood firm.

"Traditionally," the judge began, "California Civil Code has a 'one free bite' rule. That's not an entirely accurate assessment of the code, but that's how we refer to it. So long as the injuries aren't serious, and the dogs haven't been trained as fighters, we usually just fine the owners, label the dogs as 'potentially dangerous,' and send them on their merry way."

Poor wuzzle-brained Lexi still didn't see it coming. She nodded along with the judge, visions of nuzzling with Jack and Shirley dancing through her vacuous head. I tried to speak up, to tell the judge that the dog bites didn't really hurt, that they were more love nibbles than anything else, but I think he sensed my lie.

"But when two separate incidents are involved," Judge Olgin continued, talking right over my objection, "the code clearly stipulates that the court has a duty to make sure that the animal won't do harm again. In some cases, this can mean forcing the owner to outfit her dogs with muzzles." *Wuzzles with muzzles* sprang into my head. It took everything I had not to burst into peals of laughter.

"It could also mean the removal of the dogs from the premises, or the destruction of the animals, if I so deem it fit."

The key word here was *destruction*. Finally, the dam holding back Lexi's thoughts from the rest of her brain burst beneath the strain, and the full implications of the judge's words fell on her. "No," she choked, short of breath. "Not the wuzzles."

Judge Olgin didn't seem to notice her distress. The only thing holding Lexi up at that point was sheer tension. "I'm going to order the continued impounding of the animals as well as an evaluation by the shelter manager to determine whether or not these dogs pose a threat to the community. One week from today, we'll meet here at the same time for the final hearing."

He slammed his gavel onto its block, and the sudden clap was all that was needed to break what remaining concentration Lexi had left. A soft sigh escaped her lips, her chest heaved outward in one great gasp, and just like that her limbs lost tone as she collapsed to the floor.

Every penis-bearing individual in the courtroom was at the podium in a flash, jumping over chairs and pews to come to Lexi's aid. The city attorney and Mr. Leonard Shelby pushed past each other to lend their support to the fallen vixen. Even Judge Olgin managed to launch himself over the bench and proceed to assert his judicial authority in assisting the poor young girl all by himself. Collectively, the mob of men shoved me out of the way and began to argue over who was going to administer CPR.

Having been rendered completely invisible by the spectacle of Lexi flat on her back, I sighed, collected my things, and showed myself out of the courtroom. Someone would see that Lexi got home safely, I had no doubt about that.

On the drive back from the courthouse, a commercial came over the radio hawking tonight's MTV Movie Awards. Claire had dragged me to one of these overproduced spectacles two years ago when one of her sitcom-turned-movie-stars was nominated for Best Buns. He lost, strangely enough, to a cow. Long story. Bad movie. I paid little attention to the show, instead so wrapped up in the realization that though I was only twenty-seven at the time, I was an entire generation removed from the rest of the audience. I didn't know any of the music, enjoyed few of the film clips, and barely recognized most of the presenters. Exactly when, I wondered, did hip pass me by?

"The MTV Movie Awards!" the radio announcer blared in a voice that sounded like someone had slipped broken glass into his Listerine. "Live from Los Angeles, featuring performances by True Calling, Rachel Ray, Neutral Milk Hotel, and hosted by the one and only Jason Kelly."

Had I just heard what I thought I heard? Fortunately, the MTV folks understand the limitations of their short-attention-spanned audience, and repeated the pertinent information six more times before Jason's own voice came blasting out of my car speakers.

"Hey, this is Jason Kelly, and I'm hosting tonight's MTV Movie Awards. If you don't watch, I'm never gonna talk to you again. And I mean it this time."

I was so fixated on Jason's voice that I failed to notice the red light directly in front of me. I burned through the intersection, swerving around a sedan that shot out the moment his light turned green. Horns blared and I shrieked an apology out my window as I slammed on the gas and escaped the mayhem.

No reason to panic. The commercial was taped, probably weeks ago. Jason was sure to be down in the basement, chained to his bed, just where I'd left him. But the ad had noted that the MTV Movie Awards was a "live" event, presumably meaning that once he pulled a no-show, Jason's absence was going to be noticed much earlier than I'd anticipated. What with being so caught up in Lexi's case and Jason's first day of school, I hadn't made any arrangements. That would have to be rectified.

"How's he doing?" I asked Owen as I climbed down the basement stairs.

"So-so," Owen replied. Jason was curled up in a ball on his cot, the chains from his leg manacles intertwined with his handcuffs. "A little screaming, a little drooling. I don't think he finished his work, though."

I approached Jason tentatively, stepping slowly up to the foot of his bed and rubbing his leg. "Jason, hon? How are you feeling?"

He flinched away from my touch, curling up like a worm on a hook. "Go away," he mumbled. "I'm tired."

"I know," I sympathized. "You had a long night and a rough morning. I understand. But we've got one or two more things to do this afternoon, and I'm going to need your cooperation."

"Fuck off."

Unwilling to be put off by a few casual swearwords, I sat on the edge of the cot and rubbed Jason's back. He tensed at first, but eventually relaxed beneath my hands. I didn't want to ask for Owen's help again; Jason would have to learn to come to me on his own.

As soon as his breathing settled into a regular pattern, I pulled out the hypodermic I'd already filled with morphine and gave Jason a quick shot in the arm with a small, 3 mg dosage. He pulled away at the needle's sting, but rolled over to face me once I was done.

"Why?" he asked, his voice already losing its edge.

"You'll understand eventually," I promised him. "Right now, I need you to write a letter."

Jason's eyes began to fog over; he blinked twice to clear away the cobwebs. "I don't write letters," he murmured. "That's why I have agents."

"I know. But this is a letter *to* your agent. Come on, I'll help you with it."

I set Jason up at the small desk in the corner and propped a ballpoint pen between his long fingers, noting that yet another pile of sawdust had fallen to the edge of the table. As I dictated the words for Jason to write, his hand moved in long, flowing strokes, the morphine slowing him down but not cutting him off. It took a good fifteen minutes to get out eight sentences, but once he was done and I double-checked the work, there was no doubt in my mind that this was the right move.

Jason Kelly is represented by Enterprise, one of the largest agencies in town, a group formed a few years back by nine young turks who splintered off from their own companies to join forces. To hear them tell it, they were on a mission to bring light to the dark side, and make a nice profit in the meantime. The profit has been realized; the redefining of Hollywood ethics is still up in the air.

E. J. Howard, one of the founding members of Enterprise and a long-standing mensch, is Jason's agent. I've dealt with him personally on only one occasion, but I've always been impressed with his relative honesty (it's not fair to grade agents for honesty on the same basis as everyone else; they need their own curve) and willingness to compromise. He's known for having an open mind and an ability to think outside the box.

Let's see how he handles this one.

I locked the boys back in the basement, called my exterminator, got an appointment for next Thursday, and headed out to the Kinko's in Santa Monica. I've got a fax machine at home, but the last thing I wanted was for Jason's letter to be marked with my home phone number. The kind folks at Kinko's let you fax your own letters wherever you like for a low, low price, with relative anonymity. I fed the handwritten note into the fax machine, punched in E. J. Howard's fax number at Enterprise, and hit Send. Moments later, the modern magic of facsimile transmission was beaming the following letter into the Enterprise offices:

E.J., please don't be mad at me. I know it's late notice, but I can't make the show tonight. In fact, I need to take some time off, maybe get away for a while. Mexico, or Southeast Asia. Somewhere without phones, where nobody knows me, where I can figure out who I am and who I should be. Look after my affairs while I'm gone. I'll call you when I'm ready to get back in the game. Tell all my fans that I love them. Jason.

That last bit was a particular bit of genius, I think. When the letter gets out (and E. J. Howard will make sure that at least part of it is leaked to the media), Jason's legions of adoring fans will know that, no matter his personal demons, he's always thinking of them. That way, when he returns in all his triumphant glory, they'll be that much more prone to listen to what he has to say, to witness his changes and want to do likewise.

Satisfied that I'd bought myself at least a few weeks of wiggle room, I headed back home and dished the boys out some lunch. Jason was in a much less argumentative mood this time; he even ate a few animal crackers on top of his soup. I can only hope that someday soon I won't have to use pharmaceuticals in order to secure his cooperation.

Four hours until tonight's big field trip. Owen is clearly anxious about it. I let him know that the venue had been changed from a restaurant to a Hollywood power party, and he took it in stride. "Will there be stars?" he asked me.

"I'm not sure. But there are definitely going to be a lot of lawyers."

I think that might have set him a bit more on edge, but he handled it well. The whole time I was down in the basement, he was pacing the room, back and forth, as far as his manacles would let him go. He smiled nervously at me every time he'd pass by.

"It's going to be fine," I promised him. "If I didn't think you were ready, we wouldn't be doing this."

The big lug wasn't so sure. "I just don't want to let you down."

So I held his hand and stroked his arm and tried to make him feel better. The thing is, I could convince myself and reassure Owen all day and night, but it wouldn't make a lick of difference. Until we actually go through with this little outing, neither of us will really know whether or not Owen's reached that next step in his Finishing School education. As it stands, there's only one way to find out. I do believe, though, that as long as I don't have to electrocute anyone's testicles, everything is going to go just swell.

DEALING WITH HEALING

Friday night. Or Saturday morning. Three A.M., in any case. The back of my head hurts when I touch it. I think there may be a lump there. If I didn't have such an overwhelming dislike of hospitals, I might think about visiting one. As it is, I'm hoping that in the time it takes to write all this down (no reflection, just recitation), the pain will recede and the swelling will subside.

All did not go quite as planned this evening. There were a few, shall we say, hiccups.

The field trip began perfectly. I'd already given Owen the Bertroni suit I'd picked out for him and told him to be ready by seven P.M. There are no clocks in the basement, and all of the boys' watches were long ago confiscated; I feel it doesn't benefit them to be worrying about the date or time of day. But I wanted our field trip to feel as much like a normal date as possible, so I returned Owen's lovely understated Movado Museum Collection, just to be worn this evening and then returned at the end of the night.

I thought it might be fun to start out with a pop quiz, if only to keep Owen on his toes. My BCBG off-shoulder dress was just the right thing for the evening, but I matched it with a pair of hideous green sandals that my mother had purchased for me years ago. I don't know why I've never given them away to charity or some homeless person, but I suspect that deep down, I knew they'd come in handy on a night like tonight. Plus, I'm pretty sure the homeless person would have rejected them flat out.

A hush fell over the boys as I descended the steps, a stunned silence that flattered me to no end. Owen was waiting for me at the bottom of the stairs, resplendent in his Italian suit, the fitted shoulders and tapered waist of the jacket accentuating his muscular physique. His pants were crumpled down around his ankles, the leg manacles blocking their progress.

"You look beautiful," Owen gasped. Five points for coming out with that right away, instead of first asking for help with his pants or making some comment about being late for the party. I sashayed down the stairs and gave him a peck on the cheek. Alan and Daniel glared at us with naked envy, but it was a loving naked envy, so I let it go without comment.

"Here," I said, kneeling down and pulling the manacle key from around my neck, "let me get that."

I unlocked the cuffs from around Owen's legs, and slid the chain from between them. I stopped just before untying him completely, realizing that I was reaching a point of no return. This would be the first time in nearly a year that Owen would be out of the basement for any serious length of time. We'd be in public, surrounded by people on all sides, which meant that he'd be effectively out of my control. Sure, I had the power of the remote-controlled dog collar, but if he started screaming in Stan Olsen's living room, a little shock to the groin wouldn't do the trick. It would all be over. My experiment would be finished long before the results were known.

I banished those thoughts from my mind. Tonight was about opportunities and trust. I owed Owen that much. Seconds later, his legs were free.

"There you go," I said. "You can pick your pants up now."

Owen finished dressing, and the final product was a dashing sight, indeed. He looked like one of those mannequins in the windows of tuxedo shops, all hard muscle and strong lines. I pecked him on the cheek and wrapped my arms around his waist. "What a handsome date I have."

Owen blushed, and I spun away, giving him a good look at my new dress. "Do you like it?" I asked.

"It's fantastic."

"You really think so?" Here was the first little quiz. "Because I can change. I'd really rather know now if there's something wrong."

"No, no," he insisted. "The dress is gorgeous. You're gorgeous." He paused for a moment, just long enough to give me an opening.

"What is it?" I pressed. "You can tell me."

I could almost hear the gears of his mind grinding against one another. The last thing he wanted to do was disappoint me. But his training has been thorough; he couldn't help but help. "It's the shoes," he admitted. "They don't go."

I tried to keep the smile from my lips. "Are you sure?"

"Yeah. I'm sorry. Did I screw up?"

"Not one bit," I chirped, then ran up to the top of the steps, where I'd stashed my real choice in footwear for the evening, a pair of Isaac Mizrahi Perdy Pumps with a three-inch heel.

"That's a great lesson for everyone," I announced as I descended the stairs for a second time, this time properly outfitted across the board. "If your date asks for fashion advice, you tell her she looks beautiful. If she asks a second time, it means she actually wants your opinion, and you should give it to her. Be specific, but be honest. No one wants to go out looking like a fool, and your job is to facilitate that."

Since I knew we wouldn't be back until well past the boys' bedtimes, I walked around the basement delivering standard good-night kisses and stories. Owen stood by my side, and for a moment I felt as if we were a married couple, off for a night on the town while the kids stayed at home with the babysitter.

Jason was back in his funk, curled up in a fetal position on his cot. "I'm supposed to be on TV right now."

"I know, honey. But don't worry, they'll find someone else to take your place."

He grunted, cursed, and turned away, facing the wall so I couldn't even get a good kiss on his cheek. Owen's eyes narrowed to little slits, but I put a restraining hand across his chest.

"Let it go," I told him. "He's new. You were new once, too." *And quite the little chatterbox yourself,* I thought. Owen's tirades would last for hours, his deep voice resonating up from the basement and through the house for those first few, crazy nights. It was because of Owen that I put in the soundproofing. And the security bolts. And all the padlocks.

"He shouldn't talk to you that way."

"He won't," I promised. "Soon enough. Come, we're going to be late."

I checked the boys' restraints, bid them all a final good night, and allowed Owen to lead me up the stairs. Together, we slid on the security bolts and padlocks and made our way to the car.

"Are you comfortable?" I asked Owen as he settled down in the passenger seat.

"Just a little nervous," he admitted. "It's been a long time."

"The world hasn't changed that much," I promised. "Take it easy, have a look out the window, and we'll be there in a jiffy."

Stan's house was up in Bel-Air, but not behind the gates. It was a rambling ranch home clearly built during the eighties, all clean lines and Deco styling. I could almost see Stan pulling off the *Miami Vice* look, jacket sleeves shrugged up his elbows and Day-Glo T-shirt beneath.

The driveway was already filled with the business affairs cars of choice, mostly Mercedes and BMW sedans, with the odd Porsche and Audi thrown in for good measure. Had the Germans known it would be this easy to take over Hollywood, perhaps they would have forgotten about world domination and stuck to chassis design.

Owen hopped out of the car and ran around to open my door. His hands were clammy, cold. "You're going to be fine," I assured him. "Just stay close to me."

We'd no sooner stepped onto the walkway leading up to Stan

Olsen's house when my purse began to vibrate madly. An angry buzz emanated from the bag, like I'd accidentally trapped an Africanized bee inside and the critter wanted out.

"That's not the remote, is it?" worried Owen.

"I don't think so." Then it hit me. My cell phone. I'd turned it to vibrate because I hate it when people answer their phones at parties. I dug into the purse, careful to avoid pushing any of the buttons on Owen's remote, and checked out the Caller ID. It was Claire, on her own cell. I couldn't very well ignore it and continue to call myself her best friend, so I rationalized that I wasn't yet *at* the party, and flipped open the phone.

"Hi, what's up?"

"That BASTARD!" Her scream nearly deafened my left ear. I switched the phone to my right. "BASTARD!" she screamed again, and now I had total hearing loss.

"Claire, get a grip," I said. "What's the problem?"

"The problem is that bastard," she cried, kind enough to lower her volume this time around. "He dumped me."

"Who? Comes When Enlightened?"

"Where are you?" she asked.

Without thinking, I let it out. "Stan Olsen's place. In Bel-Air." I re-gretted it a second later, but the damage was done.

No response from Claire. Was she sobbing on the other end of the line? Too distraught to answer? "Claire," I said, "it's going to be fine, just calm down."

Again, no response. I realized that the line was dead; she must have gone through a tunnel or into a canyon. I flipped the phone closed again and smiled at Owen. "Trouble in paradise," I explained. "Just a friend."

"I hope everything's okay," he said, displaying his awesome talent for empathy.

"She'll be fine." I fixed a loose strand of hair that was dangling down into his eyes. "Let's forget about her and go have a good time. Deal?"

"Deal."

Thirty or forty people milled about the expansive great room of Stan Olsen's house, drinking and laughing, glasses clinking as cool jazz played in the background. Owen stopped in the doorway, and I had to urge him on with a little pat on his rump. "Come on, you can do this."

As we walked through the foyer and into the main part of the house, I took pleasure in watching the eyes of all the other women in the place. They all looked up as we passed by, admiring Owen's physique, his obvious charm, his good graces. It was like a silent wave of applause for my efforts.

I'd seen many of the other party guests before, but knew few of them by name. Studio execs from all up and down the development spectrum mingled with upper-management vice presidents from business affairs and the women they were either married to or currently screwing. I led Owen over to the bar, where a young, attractive woman who'd been hired for the night was serving drinks.

"Sour apple martini," I ordered. "Owen?"

"Diet Coke?" He looked to me for approval, and I nodded.

I looked around for Arlene Oberst, but couldn't find her among the crowd. It was early still. She'd show eventually. What I would do then was anyone's guess, but I figured I'd think of something when the time came.

Ability to think on my feet: B when sober, A with one martini in me, D with two martinis in me.

I'd just have to nurse that one drink until Arlene showed up. We stood near the bar and sipped from our glasses, listening to the chatter of the crowd, most of which seemed to revolve around the news that we'd landed Ranjin Sunn, the hot director of the week, to an overall deal. Owen and I stared at the crowd, unsure of what to do or what to say next. I'd been perfectly clear in my lessons with the boys that awkward silences were to be avoided at all costs on early dates. Of course, I'd also instilled in them a healthy fear of offending the women they were dating by talking *too* much, or saying something remarkably stupid and/or overtly personal, so perhaps I sent one too many mixed signals. I'll have to revise that lesson plan next time around.

"How about those Dodgers?" I said.

"Are they good this year?"

"I don't know," I admitted. "I just know you like baseball, that's all."

"Not really," he said. "I was always more of a football fan."

"But we met at that Dodgers game. Row G, seat twelve."

A waitress floated by with a tray of bruschetta, and Owen and I each took a piece. "A guy I knew from work dragged me there," Owen explained. "I'd never been to a baseball game before, so I thought I'd check it out. He was my ride."

"The one who left you puking in the parking lot?"

"That was him. Charlie."

"It wasn't very nice of him," I said.

Owen put his hand over mine. "If he hadn't left me puking in the parking lot, I never would have come home with you."

The night that Owen and I met at Dodger Stadium started off as a blind date with a friend of a friend of Claire's, a boy who lived in Arcadia and commuted each day to downtown L.A., where he worked as an office manager for one of the big corporate law firms. Claire's friend figured that since I was a lawyer and my date was around lawyers all day, we would hit it off swell, not realizing that about 20 percent of America has now passed the bar, and that we do not necessarily all get along. This guy wasn't even a lawyer; he just liked hanging around lawyers, which was, in its own way, freakier than body piercings or skull tattoos.

Instead of your normal first-date activities like drinks or dinner or coffee, he'd suggested a Dodgers game, and as I'd been in a boy funk for a good half year, I wasn't about to object. It was different, it could be fun, and if it got really bad, I could always leave during the seventh-inning stretch.

Except he left me first. Midway through the second inning, he excused himself, stood up, and walked out. I thought he was going to get drinks, maybe a hot dog, but no, he just up and left the stadium. I figured it out sometime in the fifth inning, right around when the guy sitting behind me said, "He's not coming back, huh?"

I turned to find a winning smile and a pair of massive shoulders, and that was my Owen. He was already three sheets to the wind (with another beer at his feet and ready to go), but with one handshake he was already more interesting than Mr. Whatshisname.

"I don't think so," I responded.

"That's a shame," he said, hopping down over the bench and landing next to me. "Now you've got no one to explain the game to you."

"Is that what I need?" I asked, playing along. "A baseball translator?"

"It can't hurt," said Owen. "Now, that guy there . . . he's the . . . hitter."

"The hitter? Isn't he called the batter?"

"Depends on where you're from," Owen bluffed. "Back east, we call them hitters." I was drawn to him instantly; I like a man who can banter. He was wearing a light cotton button-down and jeans, everything very simple but classically fitted, and the ways that his muscles moved beneath the shirt told me he had power to go with that size.

I played quasi-dumb. "And what about that guy there, in the black, standing behind the catcher?"

"The umpire? He calls strikes. And nonstrikes."

"Balls," I clarified.

"Balls are those little round things they hit. Boy, you really are new to this, aren't you?"

We spent the next two hours not watching the Dodgers lose to the Braves, and the only chink I could find in Owen's delicious armor was the beer. He downed glass after glass, seemingly insatiable. The elderly man walking the stadium and selling the alcohol for $4 a cup would have done well to sit down next to Owen and set up shop with a keg and a funnel. At the very least, it would have saved him countless trips up and down the stadium steps.

Somehow, Owen kept on keeping on, unaffected, as far as I could tell, by the massive quantities of beer in his system. We talked about movies and cooking and the nonsense politics at each of our workplaces, and soon I realized that *this* was the date I was meant to be on. Not with some creepy office manager from Arcadia, but with Owen Carter, an electrician from Woodland Hills who knew how to make me laugh.

When the Braves were finished spanking the Dodgers a good one, the crowd began to clear out. Owen stood, and for the first time I saw a bit of a wobble to his step. By the time I was at his side, the wobble was a stumble, and all of the infirmities usually suffered by one who drinks twelve twenty-ounce beers in three hours came home to roost. Suddenly, there I was on the steps of Dodger Stadium, trying to prop up 260 pounds of boy meat.

We managed to make it up the stairs and into the covered concessions area, where I leaned Owen against a wall. "Do you have a way home?" I asked him.

He managed to nod and mumble something about a friend whom he was supposed to meet in the parking lot.

At this point, I just wanted to give him my phone number and run away before he could do something that would taint my interest in him. I wanted to believe that I'd met a man who was funny, handsome, interesting, intelligent, and all those things I'd been looking for since I turned fifteen.

I turned to Owen, to ask if he had a pen or a business card, something I could write on, and suddenly I felt his hands up against my shoulders, pushing me back, slamming me into the rough concrete wall. I was too stunned to react, and doubly so when he shoved his body up against mine, grinding his leg against my waist, planting his lips over my chin, then moving the whole mess up to my mouth.

The stench of beer and chips was overpowering, and I pushed out with my hands, my arms, anything I could use to get him off me, but I was working against five times more weight than I'd ever tried on the bench-press machine at the gym. I knew I should have listened to that trainer.

The kiss, if you could call an uncoordinated attack with slobbery lips and a wagging tongue a kiss, went on for a good ten seconds, during which I strained and punched and kicked to the best of my ability, all of it futile. Eventually his muscles lost their tone, and his lips slid off mine as he slumped once more against my body. I squirmed out from beneath his mass and he crumpled to the filthy floor, his head squishing a half-full cup of soda on the way down.

I was disgusted. God, I was sickened. I felt like a five-year-old who got to play with the most amazing doll in the world for a few hours—it could sing, it could dance, it could wet itself and clean itself up—and just as I was really learning to love it, a bully snatched it away from me and stomped it into little plastic pieces.

Did I cry? No. Maybe I should have, but something inside me snapped in a different direction, and I held it together. I didn't even curse him out. Owen was still on the floor, giggling over some joke only he could understand, even as he repeatedly tried and failed to stagger to his feet.

I didn't want to look at my ruined toy anymore, and I certainly didn't want him to ever get another glance at me. He didn't deserve it. None of them did. The last fifteen years of failed dates, the boys with wandering hands, the boys whose hands didn't wander enough, the ones who left and the ones who wouldn't let me leave. They didn't deserve to walk into a room with Cassandra French on their arm.

I turned heel and stomped away toward the restrooms. The male-centric contractors who build stadiums never install enough women's bathrooms in sporting facilities, and, true to form, there was a long line for the three available stalls. By the time I did my business, fixed my mascara (okay, perhaps I'd shed a few tears), and headed back into the concessions area, Owen was nowhere to be seen.

Furious with myself, with Owen, with the creep who walked out in the second inning, I'd completely forgotten where I'd parked my car. The lot at Dodger Stadium surrounds the entire ballpark, and I couldn't even remember which entrance I'd come through.

I was checking out Lot 18 for the second time when I heard the sound of heavy vomiting off to my left. This is not usually the kind of thing I investigate further, but for some reason I took a step into the shadows, and found my once-sturdy Owen doubled over, heaving into a growing puddle on the ground.

He saw me, too, and raised a hand in salutation. "Hey, there," he groaned. "Have . . . fun?" A thin stream of yellowed dribble trailed from his lips, the same lips which, half an hour earlier, were pressed against mine.

I'm not sure why I helped him out. Some part of me knew, perhaps, that he was salvageable. He clearly wasn't all bad; he just had a few faults. Everyone's got something wrong with them, something we keep hidden inside; Owen had just shown his hand too early.

As he leaned over to give another heave, I helped steer him to a nearby trash can. At least he wouldn't mess up anybody's shoes this way. Five minutes later, his stomach had been emptied of all its contents, and the only alcohol left was running rampant through his bloodstream.

He was drifting in and out, there one moment and gone the next. I snapped my fingers in front of his lazy eyes. "Where's your ride?" I asked harshly. "You said a friend brought you."

"Left," he grunted. "Didn't want me . . . to puke . . . in his car." For some reason, he found this incredibly amusing, and broke into peals of laughter.

"What about a cab?" I suggested. "Can you take a cab? Where do you live?"

Whatever response he gave was nowhere coherent enough to understand. Even if I'd managed to flag down a cab (a nearly impossible feat at the end of a Dodgers game, when those few trustworthy citizens who knew they'd had too much to drink had already secured every taxi in the L.A. area for their ride home), I didn't think Owen was in any shape to remember his own address. The parking lot was rapidly emptying out, and the sun had just dipped over the horizon. Halogen lights surrounding the lot popped on one by one, illuminating the area in a hospital-white glow.

I knelt down, coming even with Owen's drooping head. His eyes were still swimming, but his legs looked sturdier than before. "Can you walk?" I asked him.

In response, Owen took a few toddler steps backward, nearly trip-ping over his own feet, but righting himself before the big fall. "All right, big boy," I said, curling my arm beneath his, trying to support whatever weight I could. "Let's try and find my car."

Thinking back on it now, I'm pretty sure that my intentions, at that point, were more or less pure. I'd take him to a coffee shop, get some caffeine in him (yes, I was well aware that this would not cure him of drunkenness, but at least he'd be a wide-awake, sloppy drunk), find out his address, and take him home. He'd entertained me and made me feel special for a few hours before turning me off with his Gropey McGroperson routine, so perhaps I owed him that much.

With the parking lots pretty much cleared out, it was easy enough to find my car, sitting all by its lonesome in Lot 22. The more we walked, the more Owen sagged against my frame, and the farther away the car seemed. By the time we reached my parking space, the right side of my body was burning from exertion. I opened the rear door with one hand and pushed Owen inside with the other. He fell like an old redwood, crashing hard onto the leather seats. Those forty-inch legs were still poking out of the door, and for a moment I considered driving home like that, Owen's shoes dragging along the pavement, the metal tips of his laces sending up sparks. In the end, I mustered my strength and folded him up like an accordion, knees into chest, slamming the door on the whole package to keep it in place.

Ten minutes into the drive, I realized that a coffee shop visit wasn't in our future. The boy in the backseat was snoring, deep and loud, and there probably wasn't much I could do short of an air horn to wake him up. Coffee-shop waitresses hate it when you bring sleeping drunks into their restaurants; the passed-out are notoriously bad tippers.

"How's it going back there?" I called out. No response. "Hey, Owen, can't hold your beer?" Still nothing.

I'm not sure what made me do it, but I drove into a residential area, pulled over onto a side street, and parked beneath a sycamore tree. Leaning over the front seat, I took a good look at the boy in the back, lying there peacefully like a kid who'd fallen asleep after a hard day at the park. He was handsome, of course, and strong—nothing new there.

Funny, certainly. Bright, without all the alcohol in him. We'd shared a connection back at the stadium, something I hadn't felt for a boy in quite some time.

He seemed so perfect, I thought to myself. *For once, I thought I had a shot at something special. But in the end, he's just a boy, like all the others. It's their nature. There's no way to change it.*

That's ridiculous, said a deeper, different voice inside my head.

Now, it had been a while since my father and I had spoken. He died when I was thirteen, and though we'd had occasional postmortem conversations through my adolescence, their frequency had dropped off as I grew out of my teens. But that day, he came through loud and clear. As I stared at Owen, something inside me perked up, and I distinctly heard Daddy say:

Help him, Cassie.

"Help him?" I said out loud. "Help him what?"

Help him to become a better man.

"I don't think that's possible, Dad. He is what he is."

Everybody can change. You know that.

"No, I don't. As far as I've seen, everyone pretty much stays the same, which means everyone pretty much sucks."

Don't believe that for a second, muffin. Tell me, what was your major in college?

"Daddy . . ."

Humor me.

"I was a double major. Education and pre-law."

So you've got the tools. You can teach and you can convince. Help this boy, Cassie. He needs you.

"Needs me for what?" I asked, but Daddy had no response. Once again, he was gone without warning.

Despite my reluctance to believe in change, it was hard to deny that what Daddy had said was true. Owen did need my help. From what I'd seen, he was so close, yet so far away, from becoming a real gentleman. Like a beautiful antique chair that had lost its luster over the years, perhaps all Owen needed was a few finishing touches.

The answer came to me fast, a lightning bolt of inspiration, like

Einstein discovering relativity, or Calvin Klein changing the way America viewed denim.

Suddenly, I knew what had to be done. I turned back around and popped the car into gear. My house was still a good half hour away, but to this day, I don't remember one second of the drive. My mind was racing, arguing with itself, working out the plans, the pros and cons, and weighing them against one another. If I'd known about stark and unrelenting candor back then, I would have given myself an A for effort and grace under pressure.

When I pulled into the garage and checked the backseat, I half expected Owen to be awake, wiping his eyes and wondering where the hell he was. That would have ended it all. But he was still out, still snoring away, and an exploratory series of pokes, first to his sternum, then his neck, his cheek, and finally a good shove to his eyelid, convinced me that nothing short of a nuclear blast was going to raise him from slumber.

I left him in the car and let myself into the house, moving quickly from room to room. The bedrooms were no good; each had windows and easy access to the outside world. One interior bathroom had possibilities, but was too small for Owen's large frame. Plus, the wallpaper was beginning to peel, and I'd yet to do anything about it. Embarrassing.

The basement. When I'd moved in three years prior, all of the crap that didn't fit anywhere else in the house was summarily boxed up and shoved downstairs. It was a no-man's-land, dark and dreary, and the few times I deigned to go down there (turn off the water heater for vacation, flip a circuit breaker), I was sure I could hear the squeaking of rats. Not the kind of place I like to be.

Owen would just have to deal. I managed to pull him out of the car and onto the floor of the garage. Luckily for me, he must have been dreaming about walking, because his legs kicked along as I dragged that big body into the house. It took twenty minutes to get him inside and to the top of the basement stairs, and by that time, sweat was pouring from every pore. I was pooped, but nowhere close to finished.

I stepped over his body and flicked on the single naked bulb, illuminating the basement in a pale sixty-watt glow. Boxes were stacked up against the walls, and a single rusted cot, a remnant from the old owners who'd housed exchange students from Indonesia, lay folded in the corner. Careful not to step in any piles of rat droppings or other assorted goo, I tiptoed my way down the steps and unfolded the cot as quickly as possible. The hinges protested, squealing something awful as I pulled them into position, but when I climbed back up the stairs, Owen was still in a beer-induced slumber.

After a few aborted attempts, which involved pushing Owen down the stairs yet holding on to his legs so he wouldn't go tumbling and break his thick neck, I settled on a dubious combination of skateboard, plywood, and hand truck. Utilizing my extensive knowledge of carpentry (one class at the Learning Annex, taken with a boy who professed to love working with his hands; feel free to extrapolate how *that* date ended), I constructed a rickety cart by strapping the hand truck to the skateboard with a bungee cord and propping Owen's body atop the entire contraption.

Setting the plywood down on the basement stairs to form a makeshift ramp, I struggled against Owen's weight, pushing the cart just up to the edge. My plan had been to lower the cart slowly down the steps, moving the plywood along with my legs, but as soon as the hand truck hit the newly formed ramp, Owen's weight pulled the whole thing over the top like a roller coaster reaching full momentum.

"Wait!" I shrieked, leaping for the hand truck and catching the handle just as the whole thing began to give way. I braced myself against the stairway railing and suddenly felt something pull down near my stomach. Fearing a hernia or torn muscle from my underworked abs (no thanks to you, Ab-Erciser!), I let go of the railing and bolted into an upright position. The pain went away, but my quick motion jarred the plywood loose, and with the terrible sound of wood scraping against wood, the entire contraption began to slide uncontrollably down the stairs. I stood behind the hand truck, holding on for dear life, like the pilot of an out-of-control Iditarod team heading for a deadly crevasse.

I may have screamed. I don't recall. The end of the steps rushed up to meet us, the plywood cracked, and my makeshift cart and I went flying into the basement wall. We wound up as a tangled pile of limbs and lumber at the foot of the stairs. Fortunately, though I'd bruised a few ribs and scraped up my elbow something fierce, I was intact and good to go. Owen was still more or less unconscious, though he managed to groan a bit in his sleep.

Did I rest? No. I was a woman with a purpose. Like Marie Curie, only without all the nasty radiation. Panting, sweaty, a bit bloodied, I grabbed Owen beneath his armpits and tugged for all I was worth. Inch by inch, I maneuvered that big body across the basement, dragging him through all manner of refuse and rodent waste. It wasn't my intention to dirty him up like that; in fact, it pained me to do so. But I knew the time for cleaning him up would come later. In the end, I believed, he'd even thank me for dragging him through that rat poop, as long as he didn't come down with typhus.

It took another fifteen minutes to get Owen onto the cot, and ten more to tie him down with the twine I'd found in an old box of craft supplies. Good twine, old-fashioned twine, is hard to come by and worth its weight in gold. When properly made, twine is nearly impossible to break without a cutting tool. I made sure that though Owen was strapped tightly to the cot, none of his limbs would be constricted. I wanted him to be as comfortable as possible. One of the first steps in constructing any classroom is to make sure that the learning environment is one of comfort, ease, and practicality. Do that, and the rest will come naturally. This is one of only two things I learned from an $80,000 undergraduate education. If I tell that to the people who keep bugging me to pay back my loans, I wonder if they'll stop calling me during dinner.

That night, I paid my first visit to the sex stores along Santa Monica Boulevard and purchased my first handcuffs and manacles. I was on pins and needles the whole time, electrified with adrenaline; I had to force myself to refrain from skipping down the aisles. It was a thrill, almost sexual, simply knowing that I was going to be so instrumental in helping this boy reach his full potential. Truth be told, I felt like Oprah, and for Cassandra Susan French, there was no greater feeling in the world.

* * *

My fond reminiscence of our first days together was broken by the sensation of an arm slapping itself around my shoulder, and a column of fetid air tainted with whiskey blown into my face. It was Stan, coming in for a kiss and breathing hard all over me, and I turned away just in time to redirect his lips to my upper cheek.

"Cassie," he cried, loud enough to be heard above the music and conversation. "I knew you'd make it. Picking up a friend at the airport, huh?" He laughed and took another gulp from his rapidly emptying tumbler.

I pulled Owen to an upright position; he towered over Stan by a good eight inches. "Stan, this is Owen. He's from . . . Detroit." No, I don't know why I picked Detroit. I just figured Stan had never been there, what with the urban blight and all.

"Detroit, huh? Never been."

They shook hands; Owen went easy on Stan and didn't squeeze too hard. Stan turned so that his body was wedged between Owen's and mine, and asked, "Maybe later, you and I could talk. Privately."

"Oh," I said deftly. "Um."

I'm not sure in what language "um" means "That sounds great," but Stan took my hesitation as a big old yes and gave me a sly wink before slipping off into the crowd. I hadn't even gotten the chance to ask him if Arlene had arrived yet. It didn't matter; we soon had more pressing issues at hand.

"I need to visit the restroom," I said, grabbing Owen's hand and pulling him away from the bar. My bladder isn't what it used to be; the slightest bit of alcohol sends me scurrying for a toilet these days.

Owen obediently followed me, and with some helpful directions from one of the other guests, we found a bathroom set off from the main area of the house. The other women in the place watched us intently as we went, probably wondering if Owen and I were up to a little backroom shenanigans. Let them wonder; let them dream. They wish they had a boy like him; if they took the time to mold their own, perhaps they could.

149

I positioned Owen in front of the bathroom door. "Stay out here," I told him, "and keep tapping on the door, once every three seconds or so."

"Like this?" He tapped, waited, then tapped again.

"Good. Keep that up. If you stop—"

"I won't," he promised.

The remote control was the first thing out of my purse as soon as I got into the bathroom. As Owen tap-tap-tapped against the door, I pulled down my panty hose and did my business, fingering the buttons of the remote, ready to punch them in rapid succession should the tapping cease for more than a moment.

But Owen didn't let up, evolving the tapping into a funky little beat. I finished up, flushed, and put the remote back in my purse so he wouldn't know I'd been holding it the whole time. I didn't want him to think that I didn't trust him. Trust is very important in any teacher-student setting. That's the other thing I learned from my federally loaned $80,000 undergraduate education. Thanks, Sallie Mae!

We linked arms for our walk back to the party, and no sooner were we mingling than I noticed a tuft of bright red hair bobbing up and down in the distance. It was Arlene, no doubt about it, and now it was just a matter of maneuvering our way through the crowd to reach her side.

Then . . . Hiccup Number One:

We'd barely begun to move when I heard Claire's voice, loud and clear, running through my head. Now, Daddy's voice I was used to. The whispers of my conscience, telling me that the pashmina I'd just bought was way too expensive for my budget, that was another. Claire was a new one on me.

"Cassie French? Has anyone seen Cassie French?"

That was an odd sentence to pop up out of nowhere, I thought. Then her voice rang out again, and I quickly realized it came not from inside my head, but beside my head.

"There you are!" Claire exhaled, and collapsed into my arms, crying out a year's worth of tears. She was all dolled up in a black mini-

mini with matching pumps, dangly diamond earrings, and a face full of saltwater-streaked makeup.

Owen's look of confusion was probably matched only by my own look of fear; Claire and Owen were never supposed to meet, never supposed to know of each other's existence. It was a merging of worlds with which I was not at all comfortable. My heart beat faster. My skin flushed. I felt hot all over. It was menopause, twenty years too soon.

"Claire," I snapped, "what are you doing here?"

She stood upright and wiped away the tears, streaking her makeup even further in the process. "That fucker told me he didn't want to see me anymore."

"I understand, but—"

"You know why, Cassie? You know what he said?"

The best way to make it all go away, I figured, was to play along. "No, why did he break up with you?"

"Because I'm too normal! That's right, too normal. He said that I wasn't a challenge anymore. I didn't *intrigue* him like I used to."

Comes When Enlightened, it seems, was no longer Enlightened by Claire. "Honey, I'm so sorry."

"Don't intrigue him?" she repeated. "My ass sure as hell intrigued him."

People were starting to stare. Out of the corner of my eye, I noticed Arlene Oberst, clad in a matronly but classic floor-length dress, moving in our direction.

"Claire, honey, I'd love to talk, but—"

"And just when I'd finally gotten him to have sex outside the office. Remember when I called you the other night from the library? After that, we broke into a storage room at Barnes and Noble. He took me right on top of a crate of the new Noam Chomsky. Can you believe that?"

I couldn't help myself: "Cunnilingus atop a cunning linguist."

"Tonight," she continued, ignoring me completely, "after dinner, we went back to his place. He's got this amazing walk-in pantry, and these high, sturdy shelves. The perfect height. So we start going at it, him behind me. I've got my face buried in a bag of lima beans, and even though I knew he was reading the ingredients on the cereal boxes the whole time, I didn't care. We were out of that goddamn office, and that was all that mattered to me.

"It wasn't until afterward that he told me I was . . ." She sniffed in deeply, pulling a long string of mucus back up into her nostril. "Normal."

She said *normal* the way that Yankees imagine southerners say the words *New York*. As if it were dirty, wrong. Unclean.

"Honey," I said, "you're anything but normal. You're massively fucked-up."

She swatted a hand in my direction. "Stop. Don't say it if you don't mean it."

"But I do mean it," I swore. "I mean, look—you're here right now, aren't you? Driving halfway across town to crash a party so you can tell me about your psychiatrist slash lover slash ex-boyfriend. That's pretty fucked-up, isn't it?"

She shrugged, smiling despite herself. "I guess so. I was just coming back from his place when I got you on the cell. I called around, got Stan's address, and . . . figured maybe you could . . . I don't know . . ."

She broke down again, crumpling into a deep squat. Not good for the knees, they say. Now the other partygoers were really beginning to take notice, and the last thing I wanted was to scare Arlene away with a weepy willow like Claire. No one wants to talk to the crying girl at a party; believe me on this one. I know.

"Here," I said, pulling her to a row of chairs set against the far wall. "Sit down. Take a few deep breaths."

Claire flopped onto the seat without another moment's thought and leaned into my hips, throwing her arms around my waist for support.

Owen yelped. High and loud, like a dog with a broken tail.

"It's okay," I assured him. "This is Claire. Claire, this is Owen."

Still deep in her grief and anger, Claire reached across my body to shake Owen's hand, and once again, Owen's mouth opened in a wide gasp. Tears sprang to his eyes as he stifled a scream and shook Claire's hand weakly.

It was disconcerting, I thought, that Owen should be so affected by the arrival of one of my friends. Is this the way he expected to act on future dates when other women's girlfriends showed up? "Show a little backbone," I whispered to him. "She'll be gone in a few minutes."

Claire leaned back against my leg, and this time, when Owen slammed the wall with a closed fist, stiffening and biting his lower lip to keep himself from crying out in pain, I felt something rub up against my hip.

"Ooops," Claire said, pulling my Model purse from beneath her shoulder. The side was crushed in. "Sorry. I mushed it all up." I gave the dent a little jab with my index finger, and Owen nearly launched out of the booth. I'm amazed his ears didn't fly straight off the sides of his head.

The remote. Oh, boy.

Owen's eyes pleaded with me to stop the pain, to make it end. He dropped to one knee in agony, and I hurriedly tore open the purse and thrust my hand inside, making sure that Claire couldn't see what I was doing. The graded correction buttons on the remote had been pressed down and held there by the pleather of my purse, and I quickly yanked the device free. Owen's entire body relaxed and slumped to one side, muscles going slack like a hot air balloon rapidly deflating. To his credit, he didn't yell or try to run; he just knelt there on the floor, looking thankful and exhausted all at the same time.

Three of the other partygoers had noticed Owen's difficulty standing and come to his aide. I quickly brushed them away.

"It's okay, it's okay. He dropped a contact, that's all." I made a big show of bending down and picking something up with my fingers. "Aha, here it is!" Without another word, I pulled open Owen's eyelid and poked my finger into his eyeball. He flinched, but held it together.

"All better," I proclaimed. "Thank you, everyone. Go back to the party." As soon as the do-gooders had blended back into the crowd, I kissed Owen's eyelid and apologized, both for the eye poke and the brush with testicular electrocution.

Claire was oblivious, beside herself with grief. "I hate men," she announced. "I know, I know, I'm always the one telling you to give them a chance, but it's official now. Put it on a billboard. Put it on a fucking diploma." She grabbed a glass of someone's discarded wine off a nearby coffee table and downed it in a single chug. "Except for you, of course. What's your name, again?"

Owen had barely recovered to the point of being able to speak. "Owen," he croaked.

"Owen, I'm sure you're a peach. Is he a peach, Cassie?"

"Quite," I said. This was more interaction than Owen needed; Claire was going to ruin the field trip if I didn't work quickly. "Claire, maybe we could continue this conversation by the bar?"

"Don't let me interrupt you two," she said, grabbing a fresh glass of champagne from a passing waiter. "I'll just sit here and drink to the death of mankind. Present company excluded."

"And you could do that even better at the bar. They've got an amazing assortment of ways to get very, very drunk up there. Let's investigate them together."

I apologized to Owen and asked him to give us a few minutes, then dragged Claire away from the great room and back to the bar.

"Where have you been hiding that one?" she asked as soon as we were out of earshot.

"My basement."

"Ha-ha, Miss Funny Lady." She put on her patented pout. "Maybe you've forgotten, but as best friends, you're supposed to tell me everything. At least, everything about the boys you're dating."

"We're not dating," I said, and, word for word, it wasn't a lie. "This is our first night out." Again, technically true, if you don't count the Dodger game ten months ago. "It might be our last night out if you don't give us some room."

Claire ordered up a vodka tonic and leaned against a wall, dropping her head into her hands. "I'm sorry, Cass, I really am. It's just . . . that *fucker*, you know? Using me the whole time, and I didn't even know it."

"I know, honey. But I thought you were just using him for sex, too."

"Oh, please," she drawled, "I wouldn't care if he was using me for sex. He was using me for science. As some kind of experiment. See if he could fuck the crazy out of me. Once I was cured, he didn't want any part of me anymore. That's what hurts."

"So . . . if you were still crazy, he'd take you back."

"In a heartbeat."

"Do you want me to sign an affidavit or something? Because I'll testify that you're a madwoman."

The bartender delivered Claire's vodka tonic, and she threw it back in two big gulps. "You're a sweetie. But I'm done with Comes When Enlightened. He doesn't matter to me anymore. Let him find some other manic-depressive with intimacy issues who'll give him head in the middle of the afternoon."

Claire's words were beginning to slur. "How are you going to get home?" I asked her.

"Not currently my problem." She turned back to the bartender. "Another vodka tonic. This time, hold the tonic."

Owen was still standing in the middle of the throng of business affairs lawyers, and Claire raised her empty glass in his direction. He smiled back nervously. "God, Cass, look at him. A man who looks like that and also knows how to dress? Are you sure he's not gay?"

"Positive."

"Where did you find him?"

"At a Dodgers game." It was clear that the situation wasn't going to get any better, and I couldn't in all good conscience leave her here to drink herself into a stupor. "Listen, Claire, why don't you hang out here for a bit. Let me say a few good-byes, and then we can drive you home. You can come back and pick up your car tomorrow."

She tried to protest, but the bartender came by with her drink, and for a few brief seconds, the memory of her breakup with Comes When Enlightened was washed clear by a wave of fermented grain mash.

As I made my way back into the great room, I noticed that Owen was talking to someone. That was reason enough to panic, but as I drew closer, I realized that his chatty companion was none other than Arlene Oberst. Owen had no way of knowing that he was talking to

Entertainment Weekly's Forty-third Most Powerful Person in Hollywood. The great thing about Owen is that, even if he had known, I don't think it would have changed his conversation one bit.

"I'm back," I said as casually as possible. "Oh, I didn't see you had company."

Owen, the mensch, took the lead. "This is . . . Arlene, right?"

The head of business affairs nodded. "And you must be Cassie. Owen's told me quite a bit about you." Her voice was low, almost scratchy, but in a sensual way. If she ever got bored of being the Forty-third Most Powerful Person in Hollywood, she could have a great career doing phone sex.

I glanced at Owen; he smiled sheepishly. What on earth could he have said? "He has, has he?"

"Well," said Arlene, sighting a colleague across the room, "I'll leave you two alone. Cassie, Owen, it was a pleasure."

"For me, too," I said. "You know, I work on the twenty-third floor—"

And then she was off. I hadn't even gotten a chance to tell her that I was in business affairs, or that I would appreciate it if some of the managers and vice presidents would assign me some work now and again, but perhaps it was for the better. Maybe we'd meet again sometime, and she'd remember me, and we'd get to talking, and she'd comment on my choice of necklace, and soon we'd be best of pals and hang out at the Ivy together, and she'd promote me to senior vice president so I could fire Stan Olsen, and—

Reality stepped in and stomped on my daydream. Claire had stumbled over from the bar and slammed into Owen; he caught her just as she went down to the thick carpeting. "We'd better go," I suggested. I felt terrible that the evening hadn't gone as planned. "I promise you, next time I won't answer the cell phone no matter what. Rain check?"

He smiled and pulled Claire to her feet. "Rain check."

We helped her down the walkway and toward my car, Claire bouncing back and forth between me and Owen like a pinball caught between bumpers.

"You have great arms," she drooled, rubbing her hands up and down Owen's biceps. "But I'm not going to sleep with you."

"O-okay," stuttered Owen, looking to me for help.

"You know why?" Claire continued. "Because Cassie is my friend. And friends don't do that to each other. You hear that? She's my best friend."

"That's right," I said, "which means I can tell you when to shut up."

"Yes, you can."

"Then shut up and get in the backseat."

Claire droned on and on about Comes With Enlightened nearly the whole way home. I was embarrassed, not for me, but for her, because she had no idea that she was revealing intimate details of her life to a man who, up until a few hours prior, had spent the better part of a year in my basement.

"He had a big old curve, too. Right in the middle, his willy just hung a left. If we were doing it sideways, then it really hit the spot, but let's say . . . let's say I was kneeling over his sofa . . ." She trailed off. Owen and I stared out the window, hoping she'd melt from chatty drunk into reflective drunk and give us some peace and quiet.

No go. She leaned forward in her seat and rested her chin on Owen's shoulder, wetting her lips with an outstretched tongue. "Do you have a curve?"

"Claire," I interrupted, "sit down and put on a seat belt."

"I wasn't asking you. I was asking the boy."

I shrugged and nodded to Owen to answer as he saw fit. Unfortunately, taking home drunken girlfriends is often part and parcel of a man's job. He'd have to learn to deal with it sometime.

"I don't think so," he said tentatively. "It sort of just goes . . . up."

Claire nodded slowly, eyebrows raised as if Owen had just delivered a sage bit of wisdom. "Up. I see. And . . . down, too?"

"It's down most of the time," Owen admitted.

"Fascinating," said Claire, before falling backward into the seat and staring out the window. For the remainder of the drive back to her place, she sang television theme songs in a high-pitched voice. By the third rendition of the theme from *Happy Days*, I was almost hoping she'd go back to the penis questions.

Claire lives in a charming little house in Cheviot Hills, just a hop and a skip from her job at Fox. Five-minute commute, tops. She's had offers to jump ship and head up entire TV divisions at other studios, in fact, but has steadfastly refused each time. "It's a quality-of-life issue," she told me once. "For every extra mile I have to drive, that's another twenty grand a year they'd have to pay me. No one's made the offer yet."

Owen helped me drag Claire into her house, and stayed just outside the bedroom door, tapping away, as I undressed my best friend and slipped on a nightgown. The heaviest effects of the vodka were beginning to wear off, but she still had a long night of catalepsy ahead of her. I didn't envy her the morning's hangover.

As I guided her toward the bed, Claire turned and enveloped me in a loping hug, her long arms holding me as tightly as her inebriated state would allow. "I love you, Cassie," she whispered in my ear.

"I know, hon. I love you, too."

Claire pushed away and held me at arm's length. "I'm not just saying that because I'm drunk."

"Of course not."

"But I am drunk."

"Yes," I agreed, "you certainly are. Now climb on into bed."

I tucked her in, fed her three Advil and a glass of water to ward off the worst of what was sure to become a blasting headache, and flipped off the lights. As I turned to leave, Claire put a hand on my arm. "The boy outside," she said. "Owen. He seems sweet."

"He is. Very."

"I'm happy for you. I really am." She meant it, vodka breath and all. "Got any more like him?"

I nearly spilled it all, right then and there. The boys, the basement, the Finishing School. If anyone deserves to know, it's Claire, the woman who's been there for me since Mark Snider took that little tart Debbie Schrager to our high-school homecoming dance when he'd clearly asked me first. I remember it well: Claire sat by my side for two days, rubbing my back as I cried and screamed my heart out. She listened to every pout, moan, and whine. If that wasn't enough, three months later, she scuttled any chance Mark had of getting into college by forging scathing letters of (non) recommendation and sending them to every single one of his top choices. He wound up at a JuCo and, last I heard, is stuck doing customer service for Verizon. All of this, for me. Revenge served cold, sweet, and brutal. This is why Claire has moved so quickly up the executive ladder at Fox.

But by the time I'd made my decision to blab and got my mouth working, Claire was flat on her back and fast asleep. Heck, she wouldn't have remembered a single word of what I told her, anyway. I pulled the covers up to her chin, wiped a bit of drool from the corner of her lip, and took my leave. In the morning, she'll wake up and wonder how she got into her bed. If she's really sharp, she'll look in her closet and wonder who borrowed her Blahniks.

The car trip home was short; traffic was light, even for a weekend night. Owen asked a few questions about Claire, and I answered them as best I could without compromising my relative anonymity. I'm his teacher; I have to keep some sort of distance or the relationship could be tarnished.

We parked in the garage, and I allowed Owen to walk me up to the door, hand in hand.

"I had a great time with you, Cass," he said, playing his slightly outdated part perfectly.

"I had a nice time with you, too," I responded, resisting the urge to call him Bobby Joe.

So we did the basic kiss-at-the-door routine. Short, simple, effective. I may have even raised a leg at the knee. "Usually, here's where you'll either get the signals to come inside or go back home," I said. "But I'm too tired for a lab exercise tonight, so let's just save it for next time."

Owen took it in stride. "Whatever you say."

He followed me inside and over to the basement door, where I popped open the padlock and slid back the security bolt. The stairs were dark, so I flipped on the light and held out a hand. "After you."

The boys all seemed to be asleep, even Jason, who'd kicked his covers into a messy pile that barely covered his upper arms. The basement can get chilly at night, and I didn't want him to catch a cold, so even before locking Owen into his chains, I knelt over Jason's bed and prepared to smooth the blanket over his whole body.

He turned as I approached and mumbled something under his breath. I couldn't tell if he was talking in his sleep or not, but then he opened his eyes and said it again.

"The awards."

"Don't worry about it," I assured him. I'd seen the first few minutes of the program before Owen and I left for the party. "They got that guy from the TV show about the duck to do it instead."

Jason closed his eyes and took a deep breath. "Slappy Anderson?"

"That's the one," I said. "He's pretty funny, if you ask me—"

Jason lunged at me with a violent roar, the blanket over his hands flying away as his flexible left arm, still clamped inside the handcuff, flew over my head and wrapped itself around my neck. Damn that yoga! The viciousness of the attack took me by surprise, and suddenly Jason had me around the throat, choking off my air as he scrabbled for my purse.

Owen was just a few yards away when Jason made his move. It took only a single leap for Owen's long legs to bring him to my rescue, but by then, Jason had what he wanted out of my Philippe Model.

He punched a button on the remote control, and Owen went down hard, crashing to the basement floor as a flood of pain engulfed his nether regions. Little mewling sounds dribbled from between his lips.

"Don't even think about pulling that thing off!" Jason yelled as Owen's hands instinctively reached toward his groin. "That was level five. I've got two more to go." The multitalented Jason Kelly turned his attention back to me. "Open these cuffs. Do it, now."

I tried to reason with him. "Jason, this isn't any way to behave."

He hit the remote again, and Owen's legs shot out ramrod-straight, his feet pounding against the basement floor. "The cuffs," he insisted.

"Or I hit it again. I bet we could castrate the fucker if I left it on long enough."

"Don't! He didn't do anything to you." Jason's look indicated that he knew that even I knew that was bullshit. "Okay, he didn't do anything to you that I didn't tell him to do first."

The distinction was lost on my little movie star. "Are you uncuffing me or do I get to try this thing out at level seven?"

With no other choice, I lifted the key from the chain around my neck and unlocked Jason's left handcuff. As soon as his arm was free, he reared back at the shoulder, and I had just enough time to marvel at his speed before his elbow whipped around and knocked me in the side of the head.

Light exploded in front of my left eye, while my right grew progressively darker. I fell backward, stumbling through the basement, only dimly aware that I was tripping over Owen's prone body and falling flat on my tush. The back of my head slammed into the basement wall, and, for a brief moment, I was back on my play set in my childhood home, swinging on the monkey bars with Daddy, laughing and telling him to catch me when I fell. Daddy slid beneath me just as my arms gave way, and I landed on his chest, giggling as his fingers came up to tickle my armpits.

The scene dissolved as quickly as it had arrived, and by the time my eyes and head began to clear, Jason had my necklace and was three-quarters of the way free from his restraints. He furiously worked the key into the manacle covering his right ankle. "Don't think I'm gonna let you bastards go, either," he told Alan and Daniel, who'd woken up from all the commotion and were stirring off their beds. "You can deal with it when the cops get here, just like these two whack jobs."

I tried to stand up, to talk some sense into him, but a new explosion of pain lanced out from the base of my head, sending me right back to the floor. Owen was struggling to his knees just a few feet away, but keeping his distance. Jason clutched the remote control tightly, a typical boy if ever I've seen one.

With a few more twists of the key, the manacle popped open. Jason was free of his restraints and off his cot, galumphing toward the stairs.

After bounding up the first few steps, he turned and gave us a winning superstar smile. "Jason Kelly," he announced, genetically unable to resist such an Oscar-caliber moment, "is finished on this fucked-up film."

If I've got one shining moment in life, a five-second clip of brilliance, grace, and execution to show to the judges, this is the one I'm picking:

Without even thinking about it, without regard for the firecracker explosions of pain bursting through my head, I plucked a three-inch-heel Isaac Mizrahi Perdy Pump from my right foot, reared back, and winged that thing for all it was worth.

The shoe flew through the air in a graceful arc, twisting over and over itself like the bone in *2001: A Space Odyssey* (moment of confession: I still don't understand the first thing about that movie) and whacked Jason Kelly dead center between the eyes.

His stare went all cross-eyed, like the bit from *Swinging Singles* when his character gets hit on the head with a golf club and falls into the lake. But this was no act; I'd stunned him good and hard.

Suddenly he was doubled over, flying backward into the stairs as Owen launched himself from the floor and into Jason's midsection, pinning him to the wooden steps. The remote flew out of Jason's hand, crashed into the stairs, and even through my haze I could see a wince flash over Owen's face as another bolt of electricity shot through his privates. Then it passed, and the fight was on. I would have cheered, but I was still navigating the art of standing.

It didn't last too long. Owen wrapped Jason's head between his two meaty hands and cracked it back against the steps. Two good shots, and Jason went limp as overcooked broccoli, a third and he was out.

There was heavy breathing. There was a bit of sniffling. Owen wiped away a thin stream of tears. Alan and Daniel looked on, too stunned to do anything.

Without a word between us, Owen dragged Jason's body back to the cot and I refastened the handcuffs and manacles, this time tighter than before to account for his freakish flexibility. Just because he could do a Downward Dog and I could not was no reason why he should get the jump on me in my own house.

Owen laid a hand on my shoulder. "Are you okay?"

"I'm fine," I said, rubbing the growing lump on the back of my head, shaking away the cobwebs. "Pissed, that's all."

"He'll come around," Owen assured me. "I did, right?"

Nothing else needed to be said. Owen quickly stripped to his undershirt and boxers, sat on his cot, and snapped his own manacles in place. Together, we removed the dog collar from around his testicles. Owen had proven himself tonight in a variety of ways; the least I could do was remove the threat of further pain. Rather than take my leave immediately, I climbed onto the bed right behind Owen and laid my head on the pillow next to his. The horizontal position felt extraordinarily good.

The adrenaline rush from the fight wore off quickly. Alan and Daniel were asleep ten minutes after they lay back down, and, before long, Owen's breathing settled into a steady, rhythmic pattern. I lay in bed with him for a while longer, staring up at the ceiling, wondering if I'd done something wrong to deserve this kind of treatment from Jason. All I wanted to do was help him, and he repaid me with anger and violence. It's true what they say on the evening news: Good Samaritans are the always the first in the line of fire.

Charity and willingness to help others: A. I'm so willing to help others it hurts. I'm not saying I'm interested in dying for the world's sins, but it wouldn't be so terrible to be recognized for my generosity. A plaque would suffice. A gift certificate would be even better.

Eventually I crept out of the room and locked the door behind me. I wanted to hold off on the painkillers until I'd gotten out this latest paean to stark and unrelenting candor, but over the last few hours that it's taken me to type this, the dull throb at the base of my head has turned ugly and called in its hoodlum friends to finish the job. Vicodin, and lots of it, is in my future.

After the drugs, I will sleep. And after that, I'll have to figure out what to do about spunky little Jason Kelly. As we say in legal circles, a change of venue might be in order.

CUTTING YOUR LOSSES

Why is it this hard? Why do we have to devote so much time and energy to finding someone who can make us feel complete, who doesn't mind holding back our hair when we're bent over the toilet after a night on the town, who won't complain when we invite our girlfriends over to watch a chick flick, and who might even surprise us with a home-cooked dinner once or twice a week? More to the point: Why have I gone through the last fifteen years of sexual awakening (and sleeping and awakening again) to find that the only way I can keep a man in my house is to strap him to the toilet with chains and twine?

Oh, Jason is in the bathroom. Not entirely of his own free will. I may have forgotten to mention that.

I don't see why the good Lord, in His infinite wisdom, chose to place both men and women on the planet if He was then going to scatter the good ones across the globe so that they'd never have a chance of finding one another. I'll be really pissed off if, on the day I die, God calls me into his office and lets me know that my one true love, my so-called *soul mate*, was a charming man by the name of Wei-Lin Park, a power-grid supervisor in Beijing. We could have been so happy together, raised a gaggle of beautiful Amerasian children, lived full and rich lives well into our nineties, if only I'd made a few little changes, such as moving to China for no apparent reason.

I'll take care of God later. For now, I have to deal with a boy who *thinks* he's God.

This morning started off like any other: with a message from Mom. I'm giving her an A for persistence, which is followed right behind by an A for pestilence. She's relentless, impossible to dodge, like a biblical swarm of locusts swooping down on the unsuspecting Egyptians, leaving them no choice but to hide, quivering, beneath their beds. The locusts, at least, did their own dirty work.

The doorbell rang around eight-thirty. I was still in my night clothes (a Think! T-shirt I'd had since the mid-eighties that hung down past my knees and one of my less attractive but more comfortable set of granny panties), since I'd decided to hold off on visiting the boys until nine. We'd had a hard night, and I thought it best that they have some time alone to think things over.

A column of colorful balloons shot out over my head as I opened the front door, and I ducked just before getting knocked in the nose with Mylar. When the coast was clear, I popped back up to find not a clown, not a jester, but an actual *mime*, white face paint, black clothes, and all, standing at my door.

Moment of confession: I like mimes. I know, it's fashionable these days to make fun of mimes, but I hated them with white-hot passion long before everyone else caught the breeze and have since come around. As a child, I was never frightened of monsters or bogeymen in my room, but I was convinced that the Mummenschanz players were hiding under my bed, just waiting for the right moment to leap out and envelop me in black cotton sheets. But once everyone else started dog-piling on mimes, I guess I had a bit of a backlash. I love the way their little faces squinch up when they're sad and how their smiles stretch out almost to their ears when they're happy. They can climb invisible stairs whenever they feel the need to exercise, or take the invisible escalator when they're tired. For a girl who lives 80 percent of her life embroiled in some daydream or another, a mime represents the professional summit of those who have chosen a world of fantasy.

At eight-thirty in the morning, though, I don't like *anybody*.

The mime waved. I most assuredly did not wave back.

"And you would be . . . ?"

The mime thrust two fingers into the air and grinned in typical mime-y fashion.

"Am I actually expected to play charades?"

The mime nodded.

"At eight-thirty in the morning?"

He nodded again.

"Couldn't you just shoot me and get it over with?"

Not entirely sure how to answer, the mime pretended to pull on an invisible rope, then pushed out at the air around him, as if he were caught in a Plexiglas box. Basic Mime 101 material.

"Is the message from my mother?"

He touched his nose theatrically with one finger while pointing to me with the other. Next gesture: An overblown sad face, bottom lip pouted way out.

"She's sorry about the other day."

Another "on the nose" signal, followed by an elaborate string of facial machinations and limb flailings that could have meant only the one message I've come to expect pretty much every morning for the last nine months. I cut him off halfway through.

"The crazy lady in the housecoat wants me to come to her place today at noon?"

The mime, saddened by the loss of another chance to hone his art, nodded pathetically and slumped off the front porch and into his little mime car, quite predictably a Renault.

As he pulled out of my driveway, summarily ending his theatrical assault on my morning, I fingered the card he'd left on the front stoop. He'd neglected to relay the final part of Mom's message, which read: *Anklet down to 100 feet.* It's a good thing he gave up; I would have slammed the door on him long before I ever guessed the gesture for *anklet*.

It was nearing nine o'clock, and I was painfully aware that if I was going to make nice-nice with Mom and get over to her condo this afternoon, I had a lot of things to set in motion first. For one thing, tonight is my date with Stuart Hankin, the redo of our disastrous first meeting at the Kennel Club, and I haven't picked out a thing to wear. What's the appropriate clothing for an apology date? Basic black, I guess, but I'm woefully short on sackcloth.

As I fretted over what to wear, Daddy's deep voice echoed through my foyer. *Three dates in a row. Not too bad, muffin.*

I laughed out loud. "Some streak. The first was an asshole who was using me to get a better deal with the studio, and the other was electronically tethered to my purse."

Hey, kiddo, a date's a date.

Jason wouldn't even look at me when I went down into the basement. Shame, maybe, or guilt. Both, I hoped. He *should* be embarrassed, after the crap he pulled last night. That was clearly no way to behave in someone else's home, and I hope he took a good portion of the morning to think about what he'd done. The back of my head still throbs when I bend from the hips, which means I won't be able to go to the gym today, so if I can't fit into my jeans next week, I know whom to blame.

After the usual breakfast and compliments on my cooking, I approached Owen and asked if we could speak confidentially.

"Is it about last night?" he asked.

"Yes and no." I led him halfway up the stairs, as far as his manacles would let him go. I'd left the key upstairs, locked inside a kitchen cabinet. No more mistakes, Cassie.

"How comfortable are you with devices?" I asked Owen.

"Devices like . . . what?"

"Gadgets. Doohickeys."

He reminded me that he'd been an electrician by trade when we met. "Gadgets and doohickeys sort of go with the job description."

That was exactly what I'd needed to hear. "Good. Then I think I might have a solution for handling our master thespian."

I fully believe in the school of "Fool me once, shame on you, fool me twice, shame on me, fool me three times and I'm telling Mommy," but Jason Kelly has proven to be a bit of an elusive little chipmunk. His reluctance to even try and understand that I'm attempting to help him is only compounded by the fact that he's as flexible as a Jamaican limbo star. I learned last night that I can't trust my handcuffs and manacles to do the job by themselves. It was clear I was going to need backup. That's where Owen came in.

It didn't take me long to explain what I wanted. A few messily drawn diagrams, a fair amount of erasing, but by ten o'clock, we'd worked out a feasible design. Owen made a list of things he'd need at the hardware store, and I set out to pick them up.

I never realized until today how much fun it can be to shop for things other than clothes and accessories. And shoes. Oh, and gift baskets. But hardware runs a close sixth or seventh. The Home Depot near my house is set up like a darling little department store, with different sections for each category of equipment and some beautifully appointed displays. The clerks were more than eager to help me find the things I needed, and had the most fun trying to guess what I was attempting to build.

"Let's see," mused an older man with a shock of gray hair running right down the middle of an otherwise auburn mane. "Four two-by-fours, fifty-volt transformer, sixteen-millimeter copper wire, rated switch . . . Are you running Malibu lights? No? Okay, wait, don't tell me . . ."

When I got back home, I set Owen up in the small back bathroom, tethering him to the sink with a single manacle and long chain. He needed the unfettered use of his hands for hammering and soldering and whatnot, so I let him go without cuffs. We took the opportunity to moisturize his wrists. They are now kissably smooth.

Owen surveyed the equipment and tools I'd purchased, laid out across the bathroom floor. Unfortunately, there were no cute shopping bags at the Home Depot; it was a horrible brown plastic all the way. That's the one thing that could keep me from really getting into a home-improvement hobby. Perhaps if they made a deal with Tiffany's to sell belt sanders in bright blue boxes with beautiful ribbons, we could work something out.

"Is that everything?" I asked.

"That should do it," he said. "Give me a few hours, and I'll see what I can whip up."

I made it to Mom's place just before noon, after stopping off at Junior's Deli to pick up some brunch platters. Whenever Mom and I get into a fight, the aftermath tends to involve smoked fish. We don't talk about it, we don't hash out our differences, we just eat whitefish and nova and chew ourselves back into a sense of normalcy.

"Cassie Bear!" cheered Mom as she opened the door. I presented her with my peace offering, and Mom took the platter and ushered me inside. She inspected the fish and cream cheese like a sommelier gathering the bouquet of his best wines. "From Junior's, no less."

"Only the best. Even for a mother who sends me a mime at eight in the morning."

"Oh," she said as I followed her into the kitchen, "did they send the mime? They told me it would be between a mime and a man in a gorilla suit, depending on who showed up for work first."

"Well, gorillas are notoriously late." I didn't even want to ask how she'd managed to force some stranger on the street to call a telegram service. "The message said your anklet was down to a hundred feet."

"That was yesterday. It's ninety now."

"Ninety? This doesn't make any sense."

Mom shrugged and schmeared a bagel with cream cheese and lox. "Here, eat."

We sat and ate and specifically refrained from talking about either Ted or Daddy. In fact, we were so definitively *not* talking about Ted or Daddy, it was like they were sitting at the table with us, and we were ignoring them out of spite. We chatted our way around every conversation, speaking slowly so as to avoid accidentally mentioning some phrase or topic that might invoke the taboo conversation. It was exhausting.

Finally, our meal was over. I helped Mom wash the dishes, scrubbing and drying side by side, still dancing around the issue of the other day's fight. "Let's see that anklet," I said once the dishes were back in their cabinets. I fingered the metal bracelet around her leg. "Looks intact."

"It's not the looks, Cassie Bear. It's the sound."

"You really should let me call downtown. They can't expect you to hole up in your apartment forever."

"They came already," Mom said. "I didn't tell you? And of course, the whole thing worked fine. Me and the technician, we took a stroll around the block."

"And . . . nothing?"

"Not a peep. He thought I was crazy. Cute boy, though. Around your age." To my mother, "around your age" means anywhere from thirteen to forty-nine. She's set me up on dates where I've felt like a pedophile, and others where I felt like the victim. "I gave him your number; I hope that was okay."

Not wanting to leave my mother's house in yet another tiff, I told her that it was fine, that I'd be more than happy to date a man whose job it is to ascertain the whereabouts of criminals all day long. "We could throw the most fascinating dinner parties. I'd cook *rumaki*, and he'd make sure our guests don't suddenly go AWOL."

"I do have a great *rumaki* recipe," Mom offered. "If you're interested."

We settled into a predictable pattern of talking about my life, my house, my job. Mom always liked to hear studio gossip, so I threw her a few crumbs I'd picked up at work. Nothing too salacious, but enough to get her going. So long as movie stars were involved, Mom was interested to hear details.

"Speaking of movie stars," she said at one point, "did you see the news on TV this morning? About that actor?"

"What actor?"

"The one from that movie, where he played that guy. You know the one I'm talking about."

My half-guilty conscience guessed for me. "Jason Kelly?"

"That's the one!" chirped Mom. "Wow, you're good."

Everything felt warm. I bounced over to the television, banging my shin against the coffee table. That's going to leave a bruise. "What did they say? What happened?" I punched the On button, and nothing happened. I hit it again, and a third time when I got no response.

"Calm down, Cassie Bear—"

"It won't turn on. . . ."

Mom gently moved my hand from the TV. "It only works with the remote."

"So where's the remote?"

She rocked back, lips pursed as she gave it a good thought. "Now, let's see. I was watching from the sofa—"

"Mom! The remote! Find it." Okay, I was a bit harsh, I understand that, but if there was news about Jason on TV, I needed to see it. "What was the story about?"

Mom's mouth popped into a little "o," the way it always does when she's got some bit of schadenfreude or neighborhood gossip. "Oh, the story. Poor thing's missing."

My heart fell to my feet, passing by my stomach, which was on the express train up to my throat. None of my other boys' disappearances had ever made the news; this was new territory for me. "How do they know?" I asked as calmly as possible.

Mom was searching through her sofa cushions, bent over at the waist, housecoat riding up on her bare thighs. I didn't need to see that right now. No one needed that, ever. "He was supposed to do some show or another—"

"The MTV Movie Awards."

"That's it. He didn't show up."

"But stars bail on projects all the time," I pointed out.

"I guess. You'd know better than me. Wait, I've got something . . . aha!" She pulled a black universal remote from between the cushions and held it aloft for my approval before pointing it at the television and dramatically hitting a button. Nothing. Her smile turned upside down. "Poop. That's the wrong one." She went back to searching.

I was still searching, too: "Did they say anything else?"

"Just that they found his car." The car. Damn it, I knew I should have moved it away from the park. "The window was broken in, so they think there may have been foul play."

Wait a minute, I nearly shouted, *I didn't break his window!* Some vandal roaming the streets of Beverly Hills had just made my life more complicated than it needed to be. If the cops had already gone to the media with the story, then they must have been pretty sure he wasn't just hanging out in rural Mexico like the fax had suggested.

And what about that fax? Why weren't the folks at Enterprise coming forward with the authentic proof that Jason Kelly was alive and roughing it in Aztec country? The lazy shits should have been down there at the precinct, earning their 10 percent.

"I'm sorry, Cassie Bear," Mom said after five more minutes of searching, "I can't imagine where it went. Do you want to go next door to Maude's? Her son bought her one of those flat televisions that are so popular now. She doesn't have cable because she doesn't believe in all those wires, but she gets some okay reception with this one coat hanger—"

"Forget about it," I said. "It's not important." In the time it would take Maude to drill me on my job and attempt to sell me on a date with one of her many ugly nephews, I could hop into a wired café and find the story online.

I promised Mom I'd come back tomorrow with more treats from Junior's and promptly made my way to the Cyberscene Café down the block from her condo. It galls me to pay for web access when I already pay for it at home and get it for free at work, but I wanted facts, and I wanted them fast.

"Where Is Jason Kelly?" There it was, the top story on Yahoo Entertainment news. I burned through the article with world-class speed, relieved to find that the cops seemingly knew next to nothing.

A quick scan of all the other major news sources turned up similar stories, most direct copies off the wire. Jason had last been seen driving away from the Wednesday night premiere of *Thunder Road II* at the Mann Westwood. His Aston Martin was found, vandalized, next to Will Rogers Park in Beverly Hills, Friday afternoon. In between those dates, nothing. A local resident walking her dog had noticed the window smashed in with a rock and had called the police. His no-show at Saturday night's MTV Movie Awards, combined with worries from friends, family, and business associates, led to the cops getting involved. Anyone with information, blah blah blah. All the Reuters news stories were so dry. Journalists just don't give it any oomph these days.

Next to the story was a publicity photo of Jason from *Rangers*, as if there's anyone on earth who doesn't know what Jason Kelly looks like. Put his picture on the side of a milk carton and suddenly you've got a collector's item.

Satisfied that I wouldn't be walking into a police ambush back at the home front, I headed to the house. I called Claire on the way back and eventually got her on the cell; she was driving out to Stan Olsen's house up in Bel-Air with her assistant, who had been kind enough to offer to drop her off at her car.

"I feel like such an idiot, Cassie," she said. "I don't even remember the name of the boy you were out with."

"It's not important," I assured her, leaving out that we were all better off with her lousy memory. "You had a right to be upset."

She told me she was planning on spending the rest of the day shopping and forgetting all about Comes When Enlightened and asked if I wanted to join in the fun.

"I would, hon, but I've got that date tonight. Stuart Hankin."

"Right, the boy from the Kennel Club. Are you going to insult him? Make it two for two?"

"I'll see what I can do."

Back at the house, I found Owen hard at work finishing up our little project. He was sweating through his white cotton shirt, really going at it with the soldering iron I'd bought for him at Home Depot. As I watched him work the tool between the links of a thick chain, the soldering compound softening and melding into something new, something stronger, it suddenly hit me what I'd done.

"Owen," I gaped, "do you realize you could have used that on your manacles?"

He didn't even look up from the job. "I know."

"I've been gone for hours. You could have been out of here at noon."

"I know," he repeated.

"But . . . you stayed."

He wiped a line of sweat away from his forehead. "If I'd have gone, that would have been like skipping school. I'm here to learn, not to screw around."

Instead of shouting out an acceptance speech for Teacher of the Year, I watched as Owen put the finishing touches on the device.

"There," he said, giving the chains a tug. "That should hold."

Giddy with anticipation, and mindful of my six o'clock meeting with Stuart and his investor, I led Owen down to the basement on a re-trieval mission.

"Jaay-son," I singsonged as we danced down the stairs, "we've got a little surprise for you."

He was sitting up on his cot, reading an *Archie* comic. I know it's not the most educational thing in the world, but I like the way that Archie dotes on both Betty and Veronica. That sort of blind devotion is tangential to what I'm trying to teach, but the sentiments are valid. That said, I have gone through and blacked out all of the panels where Reggie spouts off ignorantly or gets into fights for no real reason, as well as those in which Jughead displays a total lack of ambition. There's no reason to spoil the good with the bad, and the boys seem to like the ed-ited versions just fine. I've thought about buying some copies of *Richie Rich*, too, but I'm wary of preaching materialism.

Jason looked up from the comic book. There were dark circles around his eyes, aftereffects from the quick beating Owen had given him last night. He no longer had the same intensity in his gaze that he did in that publicity picture for *Rangers*. There was a defeated look in-stead, a sadness there. I wondered what had caused it. "What do you want?"

I referenced a line from *Rangers*: "Just you, baby. And a beer. In that order." Hey, I didn't say it was a *good* line.

His only response was a sneer. Did I get the quote wrong? No mat-ter. I let Owen work the key into Jason's manacles while I stood back at a safe distance. Though I didn't think he was going to try anything funny with Owen standing right there, last night's events had shaken my confidence.

As Owen worked, Daniel shuffled off the bed and brushed his long bangs away from his eyes. I was glad to see that the color had returned to his skin, and that he was no longer suffering the night sweats. His temperature, taken this morning, was down to a relatively balmy 99.3. "Are we coming, too?"

"Not right now, sweetie. This is just for Jason."

Owen grasped the actor around his midsection with one arm and kept a grip under his left armpit with the other. "Let's just walk straight and steady," I told Jason. "If you try to make a move, Owen's going to start pulling." Which, I didn't have to tell him, would probably result in dislocation of the shoulder or worse. I could tell from Jason's raccoon eyes that he understood perfectly.

Indeed, he was a good little munchkin all the way up the stairs and down the hall, through the back bedroom and into the adjoining bathroom. There are no windows back there and no walls to the outside. It's a completely interior room, which made it perfect for my purposes. I'm still not thrilled with the wallpaper, but maybe someday next week I'll slap on a coat of paint. Do a little sponging, like I saw on TLC. Now that I think about it, that could be both fun and educational. The boys could all help out, learn about interior design. It could be a smashing little lesson plan.

Owen stepped up on the toilet seat and reached up to a box tethered to the high ceiling just in reach of his outstretched fingers. He pulled a long quarter-inch chain from a hole in the bottom of the box and through the holes on Jason's manacles. Owen hopped down and forced Jason to sit on the toilet before looping the metal links through a series of hooks he'd installed in the back wall. The next chain went through Jason's handcuffs, and the whole mess was eventually looped back up into the box and around the pulley system ensconced within. When Owen was done, Jason looked to be securely, but comfortably, tethered to the toilet.

"So . . . what?" said Jason. "You're just going to leave me like this?"

"Until you can learn to get along with the rest of the class, you'll stay back here. We're calling it the Time-Out room."

"How original."

"One feature of the Time-Out room," I continued, "is this wonderful system that Owen and I designed especially for you. Since you're so flexible, I wanted to give you room to move around. Do some yoga if you wanted. I know that's important to you."

Jason took a look at the six-by-ten bathroom, casting, I'm sure, a disparaging glance toward the wallpaper. "I don't see how I'm supposed to do yoga sitting on the crapper."

I clucked my tongue. Boys. "Okay, first, we call it a toilet, not a crapper. Not a john, not a stinkhole, not a shitter. You're not 'dropping off the kids at the pool' or 'going to see a man about a dog' or 'pinching a loaf.' "

"Wow," Jason said, "you know your stuff."

"I go on a lot of bad dates. Second, I think you'll find that you can move around with relative ease if you just give it a try. Go on, see what you can do. Stand up, lie down, asana toward the sun, whatever."

Tentatively, Jason rose from his sitting position and took two steps forward, and the chains around his wrists and legs went with him. A whirr emanated from the box attached to the ceiling as the pulleys released their grip on the metal links and allowed him to move freely about the bathroom.

"Good," I said. "See, it's easy. Owen counterbalanced the whole thing so you can move all around. Try going the other way."

Jason obediently stomped across the bathroom floor, toward the door leading to the bedroom. As he reached the far end, the pulleys began to tug back on the chain, slowing his progress.

"It stops here?" asked Jason.

"I don't know," I said with a wink. "Try and open the door."

Empowered by his newfound freedom of movement, Jason didn't think twice before reaching for the doorknob. I winced in anticipation.

Jason jerked his hand backward as a nasty-sounding buzz from the box heralded the arrival of an electric shock, sent through the metal chains and into Jason's wrists and ankles. He cringed and spun on us, hurt and angry, like a lab rat who's hit the wrong lever for the fifth time.

"I put that in especially for you." Owen grinned.

I must admit, I'd been a little reluctant to let Owen hook the system up to the house's electrical current, but I trusted his skill and inclination. "It won't happen again," I promised Jason, "as long as you don't go too close to the door. Otherwise, you're free to roam about the bathroom."

That was all over an hour ago, and I'm happy to report that I haven't heard a single complaint or wall bang yet. I don't like to separate the boys; I believe that male camaraderie can be a good thing. But sometimes people need their space, and I appreciate the fact that Jason Kelly is used to a lifestyle different from most. I'm trying to accommodate him as best I can. Tomorrow, I may even try to cook a few raw foods for him. How hard could that be?

But tonight I've got plans with Stuart, and very little time to get ready. Grading myself with stark and unrelenting candor might be doing wonders for my personal life, but writing it all down sure sucks up a heck of a lot of time.

Commitment to stark and unrelenting candor: C. But that's only because I'm being frightfully honest about it, which I guess should bump me up to a B. And admitting *that* should push me into A territory.

Have a great time on your date, I can hear Daddy saying. *Try not to kidnap anyone this time.*

Dads. They're so overprotective.

THE IMPORTANCE
OF FLEXIBILITY

It's Friday. As in six days since I last wrote. Seven if you count Saturday, the first day, which some people do and some people don't. Either way, it's been rough. Rough for me, a lot rougher for others. Stark and unrelenting candor to the rescue:

Stuart picked me up in front of my house at precisely six P.M. I'd already popped a tape into the VCR for the boys (*First Wives Club,* unedited, as a cautionary tale) and made sure that Jason was comfortable in the Time-Out room. He was mid-asana when I poked my head in, and I didn't want to interrupt his yoga session, so I blew him a kiss and headed out the front door.

"Looking quite stylish, Ms. French," said Stuart as he opened the passenger door of his convertible. It was a cute little four-door Mercedes, a silver CLK with black leather seats.

"As are you, Mr. Hankin," I replied. We did make quite the dashing couple, me in a Rayure Paris tank and cardigan and Stuart looking sharp in olive slacks and a tan suede shirt open at the neck. He was, if it were possible, even more handsome than I'd remembered. It was a casual handsome, though, as opposed to the studied, feature-specific handsome of Jason Kelly. If Jason was Sinatra, then Stuart was Dean Martin. I guess that would make me Ann-Margret. Keen!

Car conversation was instant and easy. He'd only recently moved out of nearby Brentwood, and we spent some time discussing favorite haunts and restaurants before moving on to television and film and the inevitable discussion du jour:

"Did you see the news about Jason Kelly?"

I sighed and tried to change the subject—"Hey, look at that dog. Wow, that's a big dog!"—but Stuart didn't catch the drift.

"I think it's all a publicity scam," he opined.

Why couldn't the media let this nonstory die on the vine? If Jason stays missing long enough, I bet someone will design a pin to honor his memory that everyone will have to wear to the Oscars. I gave in to the madness. "What, you think he disappeared just to get his name in the papers?"

Stuart nodded. "It happens all the time. When the Kennel Club was starting to go under, I thought about all sorts of ways to draw attention to the place."

"Like setting a fire?"

Stuart's jaw dropped as he feigned shock. "Who told?"

I laughed. "I'm sure Jason Kelly will turn up. He's probably just on vacation." I almost added "in Mexico or Southeast Asia," but stopped myself just in time. Enterprise still hadn't released Jason's fax to the press, and I didn't want to seem as if I'd had any extra knowledge of the situation.

"Have you ever met him?" Stuart asked.

I nearly leapt out of the seat. "Why?" I blurted out. "Why would you ask that?"

"Whoa, settle down, filly. I just thought that through the studio, you might have—"

"Nope," I said too quickly. "Not once. Oh, maybe once, he was walking around the office or something, but I never talked to him. Or had dinner or anything. Nothing like that."

I can see now what a complete and blithering idiot I was being, but at the time I thought I was one smooth kitty. Stuart fixed me with a confused grin and drove on, pulling into the parking lot of the bar where we were going to meet his investor.

The place was up on Sunset in Echo Park, a squat little bar with iron grillwork on the windows, decidedly downmarket in a downmarket area. A single neon sign flashed on and off: THE SHORT STOP. It rang a bell for some reason, but I couldn't place it. I would soon enough.

"You sure know how to impress a gal," I joked, but Stuart wasn't paying attention. He scanned the parking lot.

"I don't see her car yet," he mused.

Her? I had not been aware that there was a *her* in the picture. "Her who?"

"Emmanuelle. My primary investor."

Of *course* her name was Emmanuelle. I hadn't known that Stuart's investor was a woman (I'd pictured a staid businessman in a three-piece suit smoking a Dominican cigar), but it only made perfect the-world-is-out-to-screw-Cassandra-French sense that she was named after a late-night Cinemax program.

"I see," I said as coolly as possible. "Why don't we go inside and wait in there for . . . *Emmanuelle*, is it?" I was getting antsy hanging out in the parking lot; this area of Echo Park was not what real estate agents would call desirable. I held out my hand as if to check for rain. "I feel a drive-by coming on."

As soon as we walked inside, the world came to a screeching halt, and I instantly remembered why the Short Stop sounded familiar. A few months ago I'd gone running to my gynecologist for a mammogram when I thought I'd felt a lump in my breast. Turns out it was a fatty deposit. Yes, even my breasts need to go to the gym. Anyway, while I was sitting there, petrified that I was at the beginning of the end of my life, I picked up a copy of *Los Angeles* magazine and tried to busy myself with the articles. One story was about that month's trend in clubs: hipsters taking over workingman's bars and making them the new hot spots. It was all about irony. Someplace down in Long Beach that had been frequented by dockworkers suddenly became the fresh, happening club for the young and gay set, for example, and a fireman's joint in

Silverlake miraculously transformed into a hangout for moneyed, disaffected Europeans. Needless to say, the dockworkers and firemen packed up their bags and hoses and headed out to search for new bars to settle, but the damage had been done, and a trend was born.

The Short Stop was a cop bar.

Two feet in the door, I froze as an entire squadron of uniformed LAPD beat cops crossed in front of me, laughing and hoisting their beers as they searched for a table. It was like watching a school of barracuda swim past your nose while scuba diving. No sudden movements, Cassie. Breathe in, breathe out.

"Hey, a cop bar." I tried to sound as chipper as possible, even though I practically couldn't see through all the blue. "Neat."

"I know!" he said joyously. "Isn't it great? It's exactly what you wanted."

True to his word, there was no theme, no cheese, no computer terminals set into the walls. Just a bar, some tables, a jukebox in the corner, and a pool table that looked as if it had seen its best days during the years when the LAPD could beat their suspects in peace and no one had video cameras to mess everything up.

"Let's take that table over there," I suggested, leading him to the darkest corner I could find. I banged into at least three of LAPD's finest along the way, each of whom apologized and scooted their chairs aside to let me pass.

I'd barely gotten myself seated before the door opened and a wash of light from outside silhouetted a long, lithe figure with shoulder-length black curls and more legs than I've got body. From a lifetime spent judging myself against other women, I knew instinctively who she was:

"Emmanuelle!" called Stuart, waving a hand in the air. "We're back here."

As she spun toward us, her silhouette began to grow, bulging out from the midsection until it looked as if she was holding a medicine ball at her waist. Then the door closed behind her and the light from outside died out, and I could see that she hadn't brought in any gym equipment.

They say there's no such thing as a little bit pregnant. Maybe not, but there's certainly a thing as a whole heck of a lot pregnant, and it was coming toward us at a rapid waddle.

They did a little kissie-kissie, huggie-huggie, Emmanuelle leaning forward at the hips and lingering a bit too long on the lips. I didn't rise from my seat. She'd easily trumped my Rayure Paris ensemble with what I'm pretty sure was a vintage Givenchy summer maternity dress, and that was reason enough to take on an attitude.

"Cassandra, this is Emmanuelle. Emmanuelle, this is Cassandra, the one I told you about."

The one I told you about! He'd been gabbing about me. Things were looking up.

"Hello," said Emmanuelle. More to the point, she said, "Allo." European, clearly. Probably French. Maybe Swiss. Definitely annoying. I realized that she must have been the one who'd answered Stuart's cell phone that day. We shared an instant bond of dislike.

I mustered all of the available politeness in my body, dredging up cheerleader-level cheeriness unseen for ten years. "So nice to meet you!" It was tiring. I dropped it down a notch. "Will you be staying long, or do you have to go home and lie down?"

"Just a few drinks," said Stuart, "so we can discuss the bar, see if we can come up with some great ideas together."

"Water for me," said Emmanuelle as she effortlessly took a seat, placing herself directly between me and Stuart. I can't imagine how she moved that gracefully with forty pounds of baby and fluids hanging off her waist. When not pregnant, she must walk around *en pointe* all day long. "So, you are the girl who made Stuart wreck the club, yes?"

Stuart cut in: "Now, Manny, wait a sec—"

"Yes," I announced. Staring her down. She wanted to go mad dog? Cassie French can go mad dog. "That was me."

"Do you know how much money we spent on it?"

"I'd say somewhere around three million dollars."

She raised her perfectly plucked eyebrows in salutation; I'd guessed correctly. I felt as if I was in the middle of a Mafia sit-down, and that any second armed assassins would come walking calmly through the front door, guns blazing.

"And do you know," she continued, "what it will cost to redesign?"

"Of course not. I do know that you were never going to make any money back if you left it as it was. The dogs would have eaten up any profit inside the first three months."

"The dogs were my idea." Emmanuelle sniffed.

I grinned. "That doesn't surprise me in the least."

Stuart must have felt the situation getting out of control, because he clapped his hands to draw our attention. "Not that I'd be uninterested in a cat fight between you two ladies, but one of you is about to have a child any moment and the other I still owe a proper date, so if we could put aside our differences for just an hour—"

"No differences," Emmanuelle and I said in unison. Eeek.

"Good. Then let's get to work."

We brainstormed and hashed out plan after plan. I fought the good fight, battling against all the so-called "modern" ideas that floated my way. Emmanuelle lashed herself to her own sinking ship and reacted poorly to every normal concept I suggested.

The meeting was already heading in a downward spiral when Emmanuelle suddenly gave a little gasp and reached for her belly. I thought it was a tactic, a battlefield feint, but then she did it again and I could tell that something going on down there was less than comfortable. Perhaps her unborn child was listening in and had taken my side of the argument.

Stuart was out of his chair immediately, ready to whisk her off to the hospital on piggyback if need be. "Contractions?"

"I think . . . I think it is the fake ones. The . . . what do you call them?"

"Braxton-Hicks?" I offered. I've been an *ER* fan since the second season.

"Yes. There, it's passing."

"Should we call your husband?" I suggested. "I've got a cell."

Emmanuelle choked down a bawl and was up and out of the chair in record pregnant-woman time, somehow making her waddle into an elegant egress from the table. She waded through the throng of cops and disappeared into a bathroom.

"Was she . . . crying?" I asked. "I said something wrong, didn't I? Was it the husband thing?"

Stuart shook his head. "Nothing you could have known about. She wasn't married yet. It's her fiancée's child, and . . . he's not around, that's all."

"Oh, shoot. And there I was, putting my foot in my mouth again. You seem to have that effect on me." I wiped one of Emmanuelle's tears off the table. I had a feeling that if I put it to my tongue, it would taste faintly of champagne. "Did he leave her?"

"Yes and no. We don't know, actually."

"I see." I didn't.

Stuart sighed deeply. Each word pained him. "About seven months ago, my brother Daniel disappeared."

Stunned into stupidity, the only thing I could think to say was, "Like Jason Kelly?"

"I . . . I guess. He was at a house party in the Hollywood Hills, and he'd been smoking a little pot, maybe rolling, too, I'm not sure. Last anybody saw, he was in his car and driving down Laurel Canyon. The police think maybe he crashed into one of the canyons, maybe the car got lost in the underbrush. . . ."

That's not true, of course. Daniel Hankin made it back to my house quite safe and sound that night. He'd been hitting on me at that party for the whole evening, really coming on strong. The Ecstasy tabs he'd taken had this boyishly handsome guy all happy-go-touchy-feely, and though I didn't mind the affection, I wasn't too keen on his patter. He was all flash and cash, a consummate display of style over substance, and when he approached me in a back bedroom (where I'd gone to freshen up) and asked flat-out, "Wanna fuck?," I was completely ready to whack him with my handbag and forget about him forever.

But over the noise of the Afro-Cuban jazz from the speakers in the living room and the crashing waves of shouted conversation, I'd heard Daddy once again, loud and clear.

He's got something, muffin. Check him out.

"You've got to be kidding me," I said out loud.

"Come on," Daniel replied, evidently thinking I was talking to him. "It won't take long."

Trust me on this one, Daddy insisted. *You'll thank me for it later.*

Who was I to argue with the dead? Presumably, they know all. "Okay," I'd told a suddenly surprised Daniel. He must have tried this tactic many a time without much success. "You follow me back to my house, and we'll get you all tied up."

He broke out in a wide smile. Evidently I'd hit upon a kink. "Me likee. Me likee very muchee."

"First, stop talking like that. In fact, don't say anything else. At all. Wait in here, then walk out three minutes after me. If you tell anyone where you're going, it's over."

He'd held up his hands in mock surrender—I'd later see Stuart make this same gesture—and sat down on the bed. "I'll wait here," he said, suddenly calm, almost contrite, like a little boy who knows he's going to get a cookie if he just listens to his mother's instructions. "Whatever you say."

The rest was easy. I still had a full bottle of four-year-old chloroform languishing on a shelf in my storage shed after a stint at learning photography had ended in abject failure. Two minutes in a darkroom, and I got depressed. I tried taking photos only of puppies and smiling kids, but neither did the trick. Every time I went into that darkroom, I felt like I was thirteen again: thick, mopey, heavily confused. I'm a light-sensitive kind of gal, I guess. Fortunately, the teachers let me keep the chemicals when I bailed from the class. Thanks, UCLA Extension!

Daniel parked his Maserati in my garage and eagerly followed me into the bedroom. I allowed his hands to wander all over my body as we walked, partially because I thought it would help get him on the bed, but mostly because it felt good.

I told Daniel to strip down to his skivvies and lie down on my bed, and he complied within seconds.

"Now close your eyes and wait right here," I said, popping out to the shed to grab a chloroform-soaked towel.

"I like it, baby," he said as I came back into the room. "When do I get tied up?"

"Not until I haul your ass down to the basement." I dropped the towel onto his nose and mouth, and he was out even before I pulled it away. Then it was just a matter of dragging him downstairs, securing him to another cot, and introducing him to Owen, who by that time was becoming quite the model student.

The Maserati was a manual transmission, just my luck, so it took me some time and a lot of thrashing of gears to get it up into East L.A., where I'd rented out a storage area just for this type of situation. Okay, so maybe I'd been planning this whole thing ahead of time, just waiting for the right boy to come along. Since Owen had blossomed as a student, I felt as if I needed a new challenge. Like a woman whose child grows up and heads off to school, I'd been thinking for a while about having another young'un around the house. Since then, Daniel has more or less emulated Owen's success, with occasional backslides.

"I'm so sorry about your brother," I told Stuart. Really, I was. Had I known then that I'd hit it off so swimmingly with Stuart, I would have left Daniel to his lechery at that party and plucked some other unsuspecting boy a few days later. "But I don't understand why Emmanuelle was so upset. Were they friends?"

"Of course," Stuart said. "Daniel was Emmanuelle's fiancée. He's the father of her baby."

Geez. You'd think I would have seen that coming. Way to make me feel like a total ass.

Emmanuelle eventually came out of the bathroom, accepted my profuse apologies, sniffled some good-byes, and took off for home to sleep off the false labor. We weren't getting anything productive done, anyway; I had a hard time coming up with bar ideas while I was surrounded by all those police officers. It became doubly difficult when the bartender switched on the local news, which led with a story about Jason's disappearance.

"Could we go somewhere else now?" I asked, downing the rest of my sour apple martini, a drink that I practically had to teach the blue-collar bartender how to make. The alcohol was helping me to forget that I'd accidentally taken in a papa-to-be, strictly against my own stringent rules. And not only was Daniel a family man, but, due to the timing of his enrollment in the Finishing School, he didn't even know he had a baby on the way. It was wrong in so many ways, but there was nothing I could do about it now. Except eat. I was starving. "Maybe a restaurant."

"So I passed the drinks test?"

"Barely. My craving for actual food is strong enough to give you the extra points you need to get over the hump."

I followed him out of the Short Stop and into his car, where we headed back across town to a little Thai restaurant I like on the west side. It's called One in Thai, which I think is supposed to be some sort of joke; I haven't got the heart to tell the owners that their desire for puns exceeds their grasp of English. I know, I know, they speak English better than I speak Thai, but I don't run around Bangkok trying to do stand-up routines, either.

Dinner went as smoothly as I'd dreamed it would. Stuart displayed all of the raw charisma and wittiness I'd only glimpsed in our prior meetings, and by the time our *mee krob* reached the table, I knew we'd be going out again. It wasn't like the schoolgirl crush I'd felt for Jason. There was no irrational heat here, no sudden lust, just a slow burn of heavy interest.

We talked a little about his brother, and how hard it had been for Stuart since Daniel disappeared, but I tried to change the subject as tactfully as possible whenever it came up. It depressed both of us, for wildly different reasons, and I thought it best we keep this date on the cheery side. Still, he persisted.

"He wasn't always the best in school, or . . . well, focused on much of anything. Our dad passed away when we were pretty young and left us a lot of money in trust—"

"Your dad's dead?" I shrieked. "Mine, too!" It was the same little cheer I give Claire when I find out we've both bought the same sweater at Macy's, but Stuart understood my misplaced enthusiasm for his father's passing. It was yet another thing we had in common.

At one point, he asked, "You really like being a lawyer with the studio?"

"Why, are you going to make fun of me again?"

"No, no," he said quickly. "I've learned my lesson. It's just . . . you don't seem to fit in with that crowd."

"And what crowd would that be?"

"You know . . . your basic evil studio hacks."

"Oh, no," I said, "you must have us confused with Disney."

Stuart laughed and sat back in his chair, the collar of his shirt stretching back to give me a good view of his tight upper pecs. I stared at them for quite some time; I think I may have a fetish. "Really, Cassie, what is it? Why do you do it?"

I shrugged. "I don't know. The money's good—"

"You could make it doing something else."

"And it's fun to be able to hang out around celebrities."

Stuart raised an eyebrow. "Do you?"

"No. Not really." I puffed a column of air up through a stray hair that was hanging over my face and gave it a moment's thought. Why on earth *was* I in business affairs? I certainly bitch about it enough; you'd think I'd have some good reasons handy. Finally, I came up with one, and once I started in, the rest came gushing out like water from a hydrant:

"I guess it's just knowing that I can help someone achieve their dreams, you know? Every film we make, every TV show, that's a hundred people working together to make something that didn't exist before, something they just thought up and wanted to show to the world. And I know that I represent the studio, and they're supposed to be the evil moneymen, but the truth is they're the ones with the means to make it all happen. They could take that money and put it in high rises or medical plazas, but they choose to invest in the dreams of others. They're all just trying to entertain us, to make this a better place to live. And if I can find some way to help them do that, then I can wake up in the morning, go to work, and come home feeling good about what I do every day."

I finished up my little rant and slowly raised my eyes; I'd been avoiding his gaze the whole time. Stuart just stared at me, speechless. After a few seconds, it got quite uncomfortable. "What? What is it? Do I have something on my nose?"

"That's about the best reason I've ever heard for doing any job, ever," he said, a grin breaking out over those luscious lips. "Fuck it, I'm going into business affairs, too."

We laughed and ate and talked for three more hours, eventually closing down the joint. The Thai family who owns the restaurant started giving us dirty looks around eleven P.M., so we finished up the last of our food and headed back onto the road.

I was flying high, captivated by Stuart's banter and his willingness to share. We'd known each other only for less than a week, but on the drive back to my house, we found ourselves telling each other things that we hadn't told friends we'd had for years.

"One time," he said, "when I was ten, my parents had this water-bed. And we were supposed to go out to my aunt Ruth's house, but I couldn't stand my aunt Ruth—"

"Did she smell?"

"Big lady, tight hugger."

"Gotcha."

"So, thinking I could use a little diversion, I took this small Swiss Army Knife that my grandmother had bought me for my birthday, and stuck it in the side of the waterbed mattress."

"Niagara Falls?"

"And then some. Their bedroom was up on the third floor, and by the time my parents realized what was happening, we had water damage all up and down the house."

"Did you get grounded?" I asked.

"Nope," he said proudly. "I blamed it on the cat. Said he'd been using the bed as a scratching post."

I hummed in appreciation. "See, I didn't have any pets. No siblings, either, so whatever went wrong was pretty much Cassandra's fault. If I did have a cat, I bet she would have blamed everything on me."

We pulled into my driveway minutes later, and Stuart wasted no time in scurrying around the back of his car to help me out of the pas-senger seat. The single porch light illuminated my front walk in a yel-low wash, but Stuart looked good even beneath its sickly glow.

"So . . . this is my place," I said, looking for something to distract me from the beating of my own heart. Yeah, yeah, I know. Cheese away, Cassie.

"So it is. I recognize it from when I picked you up."

"Right. And the whole stalking-me-with-flowers period in our rela-tionship."

"Ah, yes, the stalking," Stuart said fondly. "Those were the days. . . ."

I allowed myself to inch closer to him. "I had a great time tonight." Memories of last night's mini-lesson with Owen surfaced, and I pushed them back down.

"So did I. We should do it again."

We kissed, nothing big, but it was soft and tender, and he knew just where to suck on my bottom lip to make my head spin, so I wasn't thinking too clearly when I asked, "Do you want to come inside?"

I regretted it instantly, but there it was. That's not the kind of thing that's so easy to take back without looking like either the biggest cock tease in the world or a raving lunatic. The best I could hope for was that Stuart would be tired, or have a big meeting tomorrow, or—

"I'd love to."

Aside from a few visits from Claire, Lexi, and one or two other girl-friends dropping by unannounced, I hadn't invited anyone into my house since the Finishing School project began ten months ago. Not a single male creature, save those who eventually made their way down-stairs, had crossed my threshold. And here I was, acting like a school-girl, flipping my hair and batting my eyes, when I had three boys in my basement and a potentially rabid actor in my bathroom.

"Wait here," I said, blocking the open doorway with my body.

"Excuse me?"

"Right here. On the stoop." No, on second thought, the stoop was too close. Jason was bound to throw a noisy fit when I tried to move him back to the basement. "Better yet, go back to your car."

Stuart cocked his head to one side, like a dog who hasn't quite understood his master's command. "Are you saying . . . Should I leave?"

"No. No no no. Just . . . wait. The house is a mess."

He laughed it off and tried to peek through the door. "Come on, Cassie, all women say that."

I stood up on my tippie-toes, blocking his view. "I'm not all women. Trust me on this one, you don't want to see what I've got in there."

He eventually relented and retreated to his car. I waited outside until he was sitting down in the driver's seat, hands on the steering wheel at ten and two. Ducking inside, I slid the bolt on the front door and hurried down to the basement. The boys, as I'd expected, were fast asleep, but I didn't want to take any chances. As quickly as I could, I shot each one up with 10 mg of morphine. Only Daniel stirred as I gave the injection, but he went right back to sleep with a big old grin on his face.

I bounded up the stairs and toward the back bathroom, freezing halfway there. *Cassie, you moron! You've just put Owen out of commission, and now you'll have to move Jason by yourself.*

To give myself a tad more time, I popped my head out the front door and called out, "Just a few more seconds!" Stuart, inside his car, waved his hand to indicate that even if he didn't totally understand, at least he'd heard me.

Okay, Cassie, I told myself. *You can do this. Jason Kelly is just a boy, not a monster. If you want Stuart to come in tonight, even for a nightcap and nothing else, you've got to get Jason down to that soundproofed basement.*

I searched around for a kitchen towel to soak in chloroform, but all I was able to find during my frantic hunt was a Ralph Lauren hand chamois. Making a silent apology to the gods of Polo, I poured the remainder of my last bottle of chloroform onto its surface and headed for the back bathroom. I gently turned the doorknob, hoping to catch Jason asleep and unaware. But as I pushed against the door, something pushed back.

"Open up, Jason. It's Cassie."

Nothing.

"It doesn't have to be like this," I called out wearily. "I'd really rather do it the easy way, wouldn't you?"

There was no response, and the pressure on the other side of the door stayed constant. I put my shoulder into it, bearing down and pressing out with my legs like I'm supposed to do on the hoist machine at the gym. The door gave way a little bit beneath me, and I redoubled my efforts.

My teeth ground against one another as sweat began to trickle down my forehead. So help me, if my pullover got a stain on it . . . "Jason, this is . . . ridiculous. . . ."

Still no answer, which served only to piss me off more. I launched myself against the door, the wood cracking beneath the attack. It's no wonder I've still got a bruise on my shoulder the size of a cantaloupe.

Another good shove, and the weight behind the door slid back far enough to allow me to slip through the small opening. "For the love of Christ—" I began, and stopped right there.

Jason was on the floor behind the bathroom door, chains wrapped around his arms and legs, his limbs twisted into an impossible yoga position. But the muscle tone was soft, weak. Nonexistent.

"Jason?" I whispered hoarsely, bending down to get a good look at his face, but something told me he wouldn't be looking back. His once-deep green eyes were glassy, the pupils contracted and soulless. That marquee grin had turned to a grimace, his skin had lost its luster, and his cheekbones, the envy of men and women alike, framed a face that had once enthralled the world, but now entertained only those who no longer had any need of their physical bodies.

For a dead man, though, he looked terrific.

Lesson no. 11

FRIENDS AND ENEMIES

Catch and release.

I don't know how long I stood there, gawking at Jason Kelly's dead body, but I do know that all I could think was, *Catch and release, catch and release.* It was not a particularly useful thought, considering I had the corpse of arguably the most famous man in America in my bathroom and a hot date waiting for me outside in his convertible.

Catch and release.

Kneeling down to get a closer look at Jason's body, to make sure I hadn't misdiagnosed his rather terminal condition, I put two fingers against his throat to check his pulse. There was no soothing bump-bump-bump. Then I put two fingers against my own throat and still didn't feel a thing, which meant either we were both dead or I didn't know what the hell I was doing.

Catch and release. Fuck. There would be no release now.

Jason's eyes were still open, staring up at the ceiling where the wallpaper had begun to peel after too many years in a moist environment. Even in death he was judging my decor. I reached out and closed his eyes the way they always do on the medical examiner shows, and it helped my mood immensely. Now Jason looked as if he was just sleeping, albeit in a really uncomfortable position.

The chains from the device that Owen constructed had become tourniquets around Jason's arms and legs. His right leg had become entangled and lodged behind his elbow, and his left arm was somehow tethered to his groin. Picture Pinocchio after a long night of tossing back the schnapps, and that should do the trick.

But there'd be no Blue Fairy flitting in to save Jason Kelly. As I inspected his body, I noticed that the skin around his wrists and ankles was blistered, almost charred.

The electricity. Jason must have been trying to escape via some ancient yoga technique when the chains got pulled too far and triggered the current. Maybe his muscles contracted with the sudden burst of juice, pulling him into an even tighter position, making it impossible to shut off the circuit.

Or maybe he choked on a ham sandwich. Who knows, I wasn't there. The only thing I did know was that I had to think fast and move faster.

First order of business: ditching Stuart. I ran out of the bathroom and locked the door behind me, just in case Jason was pulling an Academy Award–winning performance out of his bag of tricks and only playing dead. As I ran to the front door, I passed a full-length mirror in the hall and skidded to a halt. My hair was a tousled mess, my forehead still shining with sweat. I couldn't let Stuart see me this way, situation be damned. A quick run over to my makeup counter, where I pulled my hair into a semblance of normalcy and puffed on some powder to take down the shine. *There*, I thought, *that ought to do the trick—*

The doorbell rang, and I fell off my makeup stool trying to spin around. Remembering the Lamaze class I attended with Claire when she thought she was two months pregnant and wanted to get an early jump on things, I took a few quick "windowpane" breaths: four short exhales followed by a long inhale. Calming. Soothing. The doorbell rang again, and the hyperventilation returned, Lamaze instantly forgotten.

"Hey, Stuart," I said as casually as possible as I opened the door. I wedged my body into the six-inch space I'd created. "What's up?"

"What's up? I've been waiting out there for a half hour."

"Right. Right, about that . . ." I trailed off, unsure of where to go with it.

Stuart leaned against the doorjamb. "Look, I may have been way off base, but I thought we had a connection. If you're not interested, that's cool, but you've got to tell me—"

"No!" I practically screamed. "I mean yes! I mean . . . that's not it at all. I had a wonderful time, I swear it."

"You just don't want me to come inside."

"I *do* want you to come inside."

"But?"

"But I don't want you to come inside," I admitted. "It's complicated."

Stuart wasted no time in backing down off the front porch, shaking his head in confusion. I'd blown it, and all because of Jason Kelly's stupid yoga classes. Why couldn't he have waited a few more days to electrocute himself?

"Stuart, wait—"

"You know, Cassie," he said, "I'm thirty-three years old, and I've dated a lot of women. Most of the time, I can get a pretty good assessment of them by the time the appetizers show up, and most of the time, I'm not interested."

"Oh," I said. I'd been on the receiving end of enough blow offs to feel the big wind coming.

"You, on the other hand . . . I can't figure you out."

"Is that a good thing or a bad thing?" I asked.

"I don't know yet." He stared me down, and I did my best not to blink. "But I'd like to find out. So if you're saying you don't want me inside—"

"Just tonight. Any other night would be great. With a little advance notice, preferably."

"Then I'll respect your wishes and head on home." He trotted back up the steps and gave me a polite, proper kiss, just a little peck on the side of the cheek. "You have a good night, whatever it is you've got going on in there, and I'll give you a call this week, okay?"

I wanted to throw him down on the porch, then and there, just rip off his clothes and go at it on the naked wood. Damn the neighbors. They throw their parties and play rap music until two in the morning; I should be allowed to howl in ecstasy on my front porch every once in a while. Instead, I nodded and said, "Okay."

Two minutes later he was gone, and five minutes after that I was still standing in my doorway, staring at the spot on the street where his car had been, hating myself for even thinking of sex at a time like this. I'd been lulled into inaction via a deadly cocktail of lust and fear, but the lust had quickly subsided, leaving me petrified and confused.

Jason Kelly was dead. As in *dead* dead. And not the kind of dead like my father or my grandparents, all of whom passed away in hospital beds or nursing facilities and were whisked off to funeral homes before any of us had to confront the specter of their lifeless bodies. This was a special kind of dead, a cadaver dead, an in-my-house sort of dead, which made it all the more real and surreal at the same time.

What was I going to do? I'd never had to dispose of a body before. On the news, they always have stories about hikers or dogs who've accidentally stumbled across bodies dumped in the woods or buried in shallow graves. I couldn't take that kind of chance, plus I had no urge to go tromping through the forest in the middle of the night. I was already upset; I didn't need to be muddy on top of it. What I needed was a plan.

As is often the case, I turned to my first and foremost source of information and inspiration: my DVD rack. Compiled there were hundreds of the greatest films of all time, representing the collective ideas and plotlines of thousands of the most creative minds Hollywood had to offer. One of them must have figured out a solution to my problem. Let's see . . .

Fargo. Steve Buscemi got dumped in a wood chipper. Not going to work. Too messy, and I wouldn't even know where to find that kind of heavy equipment at this time of night.

Casino. The mob buried Joe Pesci in an unmarked grave in the Nevada desert after whacking him heartily with baseball bats. Neat and tidy (except for the whacking part), but while I may have had the energy to drive out to Vegas, I certainly didn't have enough to drive back, too.

Pulp Fiction. The kid who accidentally gets shot in the head by Travolta is crushed inside Sam Jackson's car at a salvage yard owned, strangely enough, by the girl who played Pat on *Saturday Night Live*. I never quite got what she was doing in the movie. Anyway, I don't know anyone who owns a salvage yard, and I'm sure as heck not sacrificing my car in the deal.

I Know What You Did Last Summer. Jennifer Love Hewitt dumps the body of a man she's run over into the ocean. No one finds him, so that's good, but then he comes back to life and kills everyone, so that's bad. Damn.

The rest of my collection was similarly unhelpful. Movie characters always seem to have the means of disposal at their disposal, whereas the only kind of disposal I had was in my kitchen sink, and, unless I could cut Jason up into bite-sized chunks, it wouldn't do me a lick of good. Still, I needed to get moving. Inaction, as my boss Stan Olsen says, only breeds more inaction. God, I just quoted Stan Olsen. I need to wash.

Step one: Get Jason untied. That proved to be slightly harder than I'd first thought. Imagine the biggest shoelace snaggle you've ever seen, then make it metallic and add limbs and joints to the mix. Jason had contorted his body into so many arcane positions that it was difficult to tell which ligaments were supposed to move in which directions. I'm sure, had he been alive and awake, that my unsubtle jostling of his body would have caused a fair amount of pain and injury, but discomfort was one thing he no longer had to worry about.

As I was working the final lengths of chain from around Jason's legs, the phone rang. I checked my Caller ID. It was Claire. I picked up the cordless extension and tucked it under my chin so I could work and talk at the same time.

"Hey, lady," she said as I answered. "How was the hot date?"

"It was fine," I grunted. The chains clanged against one another as I pulled them one by one from Jason's body.

"Just fine? You seem a little out of breath. I'd say that's better than fine."

"It was good," I amended. "Very good."

Claire gasped. "Is he still there? Is that why you can't talk? Oh my God, he's still there. Good for you! Two boys in two nights, I'm proud of you—"

"He's not here, Claire. That's not why—"

The final chain pulled free and Jason's head clonked against the bathroom tile. His body was becoming stiff, difficult to work with as rigor mortis set in.

How was I going to do this on my own? I was barely able to drag Jason into my trunk back at Will Rogers Park; I'd needed Owen to help me cart him around the rest of the house. And it wasn't as if I could count on the safety of my own home or car once I decided what to do with his body. I'd most likely be out in public somewhere, trying to move around nearly two hundred pounds of dead actor. Thank God I hadn't kidnapped Brando.

No, this was precisely the type of situation in which someone else's help would come in immensely handy. This was precisely the type of situation that best friends were made for.

I took a deep breath and spoke into the phone before I could convince myself out of my decision. "Come over."

"What, now?"

"As soon as you can."

Claire could tell that something was wrong. "Did he do something to you? Goddammit, if he hurt you—"

"It's nothing like that," I assured her. "Stuart was a doll. Just . . . just come over."

I waited for her on the sofa in my living room, a formal little area right off the foyer. No one ever sits in there. I don't think anyone's even stepped foot in that room since my housewarming party years ago (gifts: lots of towels, lots of appliances, and a plastic tray filled with plastic pretzels and plastic Cheez Doodles). But I sat on the floral-print Laura Ashley love seat and stared off into the darkness, knowing I was risking everything by allowing Claire into my secret. The way I saw it, though, I didn't have a choice. I couldn't very well leave Jason's body to rot in my back bathroom. There's only so much Glade air freshener you can buy at the grocery store before it starts to look suspicious.

When she knocked on the door, I threw it open and pulled her into a hug. It was primal and childish and just what I needed at the moment. My hands instinctively rubbed the fabric of her pullover. I love to touch cashmere, especially when frightened. If Linus had known about cashmere, he could have ditched the blue blanket long ago.

"Cass, tell me what's going on." Claire was nervous, worried for me.

I released her from my grip. "I will. You'll see everything, I swear. But first I want you to promise that you'll keep an open mind."

"Consider it opened."

"Seriously," I insisted. "No judgments."

Claire took a step back as her eyes opened wide. She'd clearly jumped to some conclusion. "Okay . . . okay, I get it now."

"I don't think you do."

"Look, you know I love you more than anything, and the truth is, if it was ten years ago, maybe a threesome would have sounded pretty good—"

It took me a moment to find the proper words to interrupt. "Jesus, Claire, I don't want to sleep with you!"

"Oh." She smiled sheepishly. "You sure?"

"Quite." Now I felt bad, turning her down like that without giving it any consideration. "It's not that I *wouldn't*—I mean, I hadn't thought of it before, but you are a beautiful woman, and . . ." I shook it off. "That's not why I told you to come over. Stuart already went home. This is something else entirely."

"Fair enough," she said, as eager as I was to put the conversation behind us. "Open mind. Got it."

Our journey to the back bathroom felt like the last mile of the condemned, only I didn't know if I was the priest or the prisoner. Claire was certainly in for a shock, but this was no easy task for me, either.

As soon as I let her into that room, the intricate house of secrets I'd carefully built over the last year was going to come tumbling down around me.

"Look at you," she said as we moved through the back bedroom. "Honey, you're shaking. Come on, now, we can get through this thing together."

My only response was to push open the bathroom door.

"Oh," Claire said calmly. "Now I understand. See, I told you, it's not so bad."

"That's it? That's all you've got?" I couldn't believe she could be so relaxed. Why couldn't I be that relaxed?

"It's a bad wallpaper job, honey. We can get through this."

I realized that she was still staring at the far wall, not down at the floor toward Jason's lifeless body. I took her head in my hands and forced her gaze a bit lower.

Claire screamed and stumbled backward, her calves slamming into the wooden platform bed as she fell onto the mattress. There, *that* was the reaction I'd been going for.

"Not just a wallpaper job, is it?" I said. "Although I was thinking about doing a little sponge painting in there next week. Do you ever watch TLC?"

Claire's mouth opened and closed, making little popping sounds. She couldn't tear her eyes away from Jason's body, but her hips kept scooting backward, legs kicking out from under her as she tried to crawl away.

"Is he . . . is he . . . ?"

"Dead. Yeah."

"Cass, what . . . what happened? Who is he?"

I wasn't sure which question to answer first. The fact that she was wigging out so much was actually making me calmer. Now I know why Mom chills when I go off the handle; it's empowering, in a way, to be the coolest cucumber in the room. "Take a look," I suggested. "Go on, he won't bite."

Claire slowly climbed off the bed and tiptoed up toward the bathroom door. She leaned over Jason's body and knelt down, placing her face a few feet away from his, her legs tensed, ready to leap back at any second in case he jumped up and said boo. We've all seen way too many horror movies.

"You know who he looks like?" asked Claire after a few moments perusal.

I walked into the bathroom and stood behind her. "Jason Kelly?"

"Exactly."

"That's because it is Jason Kelly."

She stood up, hands on her hips. "Shut up, it is not."

"Yeah. It is."

Claire gently nudged Jason's head to one side and then the other with the toe of her Manolo boot. She really doesn't wear those shoes often enough. "God," she said, "it totally looks like him."

I rummaged through Jason's back pockets, pulling out his wallet and dumping the credit cards onto the bathroom counter. Claire pulled a platinum AmEx. There was his name, front and center, just like on the commercials.

She sat down hard, falling to the ground just inches from Jason's outstretched leg. I sat next to her. We stared at Jason.

"Is he really dead?" she asked eventually.

"So far as I can tell. Unless he's just acting."

"No," said Claire, "he's not that good."

Not that good? What was she talking about? "Didn't you see *Rangers*?"

"Sure," said Claire, "everyone's seen it. I think it's a California law."

"So?"

"So what? He was average. I don't know, he doesn't do anything for me."

"Are you insane?" I cried. I grabbed Jason's chin and swung his head toward Claire. "Look at those lips. That nose. Check out the jawline." I flipped his head in the other direction, his stiff neck crackling. "My God, look at that dimple!"

"Eh," Claire shrugged. "I just never got it. He plays the same part in every film."

"Of course he does. He's a movie star!"

"Movie stars used to take chances." She tossed a hand in Jason's direction. "Christ, man, do an indie film now and then."

"When did Cary Grant ever do an indie film?" I asked.

"Okay, maybe not Cary Grant, but . . ."

I turned away from her in a huff. "I can't believe you don't think he's a good actor."

"I'm sorry," she said sincerely. "We'll just have to find a way to move past this."

"Fine," I pouted. "It's done."

"Fine."

Our agreement to disagree didn't solve much of anything. Jason's body was still lying on the bathroom floor. "So . . . what are we going to do with him?"

"What are *we* going to do with him?" said Claire. "I think that's pretty much up to the cops, wouldn't you say?"

"The cops? No no no, we can't call the cops."

"Cassie, there's a very dead, very famous man in your house. I think you'd better start dialing 'nine' and 'one.' If you need me to dial the other 'one,' I'll do it, but that's as far as I'm going with this."

She headed for the phone on the nearby nightstand, but I darted in front of her and blocked her path. "It's not like he just walked in and had a heart attack," I said. "It's a little more complicated than that."

Claire tried to feint to the left and pass me on the right, but I smoked out her trick and raised the stakes by ripping the phone cord out of the wall. At least, I *tried* to rip the phone cord out of the wall. It always works on TV. Instead, I yanked on the plastic cord and the only thing I got for my trouble was a friction burn on my palm. But Claire got the message.

"Did you . . . did you have something to do with his . . . current state?"I nodded slowly as I massaged my injured hand. "Oh, Cass. Oh, Cass."

"It's not like I killed him," I said defensively. "It's sort of a fifty-fifty thing."

"Assisted suicide?"

"Something like that." I led her back into the bathroom, where I pulled aside the shower curtain to reveal the remains of the device Owen and I had designed. Chains, pulleys, and wires lay piled in the tub like a giant mound of pasta.

"I don't even know what I'm looking at," said Claire.

"It was sort of a . . . restraint. For Jason."

"You were restraining him in your guest bathroom?"

"More or less."

"May I ask why?"

"He was bothering the other boys."

"The other boys," Claire echoed.

"Right."

"Do I want to know about them?"

"Probably not just yet," I said. "Let's handle one thing at a time."

I showed Claire the contraption and the marks around Jason's wrists and ankles, and gave her my theory about Jason's twin penchants for yoga and escape. Like a true friend, she didn't even question why he was tied up in the first place; she understood that I'd tell her all in due time.

"Don't you have a basement?" she asked as we fretted over what to do, short-term, with the body. "We could put him in there until we figured out a plan."

Hello, due time.

"Here's the thing about the basement," I began, then stopped. A picture is worth a thousand words and all that. "Follow me."

We left Jason in the bathroom and walked through the house. I really hadn't had a chance to clean up, and there were some dirty dishes piled in the sink when we walked through the kitchen. It was pretty embarrassing. "Now you've got to promise to keep that open mind," I said.

"Cass, my mind's about as fucking open as it's going to get."

"Language," I chided.

"Hey," said Claire, "I haven't freaked out on you yet, have I? Dead actor in the bathroom and everything?"

"Only because you don't like actors in the first place. If I had a dead accountant in there, you'd be screaming bloody murder."

"That's not true," Claire insisted. "I don't like *sitcom* actors. They're a whole different breed. And I don't much care for accountants, so there goes your theory out the window."

We reached the basement door, and Claire ran her fingers over the padlocks and dead bolts. "I don't remember these. When did you go all *Panic Room* on me?"

"They're not to keep anyone out," I explained. "They're to keep people in."

"The . . . boys, I take it?"

"The boys."

I popped open the padlocks, slid back the bolts, and pulled open the door. Claire peered into the darkness beyond, and I flipped on the lights as I led her down the stairs. "Watch your Manolos on the steps," I told her. The footwear was darling but dangerous.

The boys, as I'd expected, were fast asleep. Three mounds rising and falling rhythmically beneath their sheets. "You don't have to worry about waking them up," I said softly. "They're pretty heavily sedated."

Claire moved through the basement as if I'd given her a shot of morphine, too, running her hands slowly across each of the boys' heads and shoulders, perhaps to make sure that they weren't mannequins or wax sculptures.

"That's Alan," I said, following behind her. "He's a sweetheart. Over there is Daniel. Alan's a spoken-word poet. He won some sort of grant a few years back, I think. Daniel . . . well, I don't know what Daniel does, actually. He's just wealthy."

She stopped near Owen's bed and took a good, hard look at his sleeping face. "Isn't this the one from the other night? At the party?"

"Owen. I'm surprised you remember. He really liked you."

"Cass, what do you . . ." She searched for the right word. "What do you *do* with them?"

I noticed that she was staring at the chains and handcuffs. "I know what you're thinking, and it's not a sexual thing. It's nothing like that. Well, we do have a class or two in sexual relations, but it's strictly educational."

Claire blinked and pulled at her cashmere pullover. "I think I'm going to need something to drink."

A bottle of Amaretto and a box of low-fat Fig Newtons later, I was ready to talk and Claire was ready to listen. We sat at the kitchen table, passing the brown glass bottle back and forth between us. I picked up where we'd left off.

"I call it the Finishing School," I began. "For boys who just need a little extra help."

"Help with what?"

"Becoming men."

I explained it all: my selection process, my training techniques, my eventual goals. Claire just sat there and took it all in, asking questions when she needed clarification but otherwise letting me do all the talking. I took her back all the way to that first meeting with Owen at Dodger Stadium and worked my way up to that evening, when I came in and found Jason Kelly in a somewhat less-than-alive state. All in all, it was a two-, maybe three-hour conversation, and by the time I was done, my throat was sore and my voice was hoarse, but I felt better and lighter than I had in years, as if I'd just come off some sort of low-guilt Atkins diet.

Claire, not so much. Her complexion vacillated between a tidy shocked white and a sickened green, but she kept it together and eventually wound up settling on an almost rosy pink that really complemented her outfit.

"I get all that," she said as I finished my story. "The who, the how, the where, whatever. But I gotta tell you, Cass, I still don't get the *why*."

"Is it really that hard to understand?" I asked. "It's just . . . the next logical step."

"The next logical step in what?"

I stood and paced, trying to formulate my thoughts. It had all been clear to me for so long, but I'd never had to convey it to anyone else before. I thought back to my law school days, when our juries professor drilled it into us that people like to be given examples, that it helps them ground abstract concepts in reality. "How much time do you and I spend on the phone, or at lunch, or at clubs, hanging out and bitching about the boys we date?"

"Most of it," Claire admitted. "That's part of the fun."

I shook my head. "No, we *make* it part of the fun, because we do so damned much of it, and if we couldn't laugh about it, we'd break down crying. And that would only be a drop in the bucket next to the tears we've already shed over all the stupid things boys do."

"So . . . ?"

"So what if you could dry those tears before they started? What I'm doing is going one step beyond the complaint. What power is there in crying? None. Why should we spend all our lives whining about someone who doesn't exist when we can take the bull by the horns, so to speak, and mold a male specimen into whatever shape we want? Find a boy who's got most of the qualities we find desirable and iron out the few little defects until he's just about perfect. We do it anyway, right?"

"Speak for yourself," Claire said.

"Oh, really? How about Alex?"

"The waiter?"

"At the Cherry Pan. The one who bit himself during sex. That couldn't have been his only problem."

Claire admitted otherwise, running off a litany of small, entirely fixable problems. "And he didn't have enough ambition. I need a man who wants to move up."

"All perfectly reasonable. So let's say you decided to go long-term with Alex. You would have moved in with him, helped out with his design and fashion sense, maybe urged him to take a few courses at UCLA extension, look into a business school . . ."

I could see the light go on in Claire's upstairs office; she was beginning to slip into the groove. "I did suggest that maybe he should take a few business and cooking courses, think about opening a restaurant of his own."

"See? That's what I'm saying. We change the boys we're with every day, little by little, whether we know it or not."

"So the Finishing School is just a quicker way of doing all that."

"Think of it as an intensive seminar," I suggested. "With live-in dorms."

"And the fact that the boys don't 'enroll' of their own free will?"

"Not the point," I said. "You think if you'd stayed with Alex he would have changed of his own free will? No, you would have pushed and pulled and prodded and maybe he would have left and maybe he would have stayed, but you would have tried one way or the other because that's what everyone does. We try and change the ones we love. I'm just doing it faster."

"And when," Claire asked, "do you plan on letting them go?"

"We call it graduating. It's all on an individual basis. Owen's the closest. He's really made some incredible progress."

I wanted to go on, to tell her about some of the adventures we'd had, about our successes and failures as a class. It was so freeing finally to let it all out that I didn't want to stop. To put it in Lexi-oriented terms: I'd binged for so long that I needed the purge. But Claire, ever the pragmatist, was more interested in the bottom line.

"First things first," she said, standing and pacing the kitchen. I sensed a change in her. She'd accepted my theory, pushed aside her concerns, and moved into studio exec mode, cold and efficient, which is exactly what we needed. "We've got to get rid of that body."

"Agreed."

"Got any thoughts?"

"Not a one."

"How about the ocean?" she suggested. "We could take him out to the pier and dump him over the side."

I rejected the idea as too temporary. "He'll wash up on shore tomorrow afternoon."

"So?"

"So I already faxed that letter to Enterprise," I pointed out. "If they'll just release the damned thing, we can get some time on our side. It'll just look like Jason's gone off to find himself, so long as he stays missing."

"Then we need a long-term solution." She picked up the pace, her heels tap-tapping against the kitchen tile. I noticed that her right stocking had a run in it, but I kept hush-hush about it. No need to upset her any further. "How about burying him out back?"

"No good. What if my landscaper wants to plant a new tree or something?"

Claire said, "So you do your own lawn work from now on."

We both broke down laughing. It felt good. "Anyway," I said, getting serious for a moment, "I don't have a fence back there. We'd be digging for a while, and my neighbors get pretty nosy. Now come on, we're two grown women with God knows how many years of higher education. We've got to think of something—"

"I've got it!" Claire announced.

"Ooh, ooh, tell me."

"Now I don't want you to say no until you've heard the whole thing."

"Deal," I promised.

"We call Lexi—"

"No." I stopped her right there, waving my hands frantically in the hopes of emphasizing my point. "No Lexi."

"But Cass—"

"You want to entrust a dead body to a woman who can't even control two dogs with chicken nuggets for brains?"

Claire sat back down at the table, leaning across it like a detective interrogating me under the glow of a naked bulb. "Do you want to get rid of the corpse?" She used that word specifically to set me on edge. It worked.

"Of course I do."

"And you don't want it to be found."

"Preferably, no."

"That means we've got to put it somewhere no one's going to go stumbling across it. That means private property. Can't do it on your land, and the only thing in my backyard is a Jacuzzi that keeps over-heating."

"They still haven't fixed that?" I asked. "You poor thing. How do you soak?"

"No soaking," sighed Claire. "It's very stressful." We had a moment of silence for her ailing spa. "Now, about Lexi—"

"I'm telling you, it's a mistake to get her involved."

"But she won't be involved, not really. Her parents have that place up in Ojai. They never go up there. No one does. It's thirty acres or something, all undeveloped, all untouched."

I was beginning to understand. Lexi was just a means to an end, like filling out a department-store credit-card application to get the 10 percent discount, but never really using the card itself. "So we just use Lexi for directions."

"And access. She doesn't have to know a thing about Jason. As far as she's concerned, we're just looking for a night in the country."

"But it's almost two A.M."

"Okay, an early morning in the country. It's Lexi, for chrissakes. We're not exactly talking about Sherlock Holmes."

Claire had a point, and I had no other options. Whether I liked it or not, Lexi was about to add her assets to our little circle of trust.

"You told her?" I felt betrayed. I felt sick.

Claire sat in the passenger seat of my car and quickly slipped into defensive mode. "I didn't have a choice. It's the middle of the night, and we're asking to go to her parents' farm in Ojai. What else was I sup-posed to say?"

I was pretty sure I'd brought that potential snag to light back in my kitchen, but there was no use in rehashing old arguments.

"What did you say exactly?" I asked.

"I told her that there had been an accident. That someone had been injured very badly. That, for a number of reasons, we couldn't call the cops and needed to get rid of the body."

"And that's it?"

"Yes," said Claire. Then, softer: "And I may have told her it was Jason Kelly."

"Claire!"

Lexi appeared at the side of the car and opened the rear door. I'd been idling outside her house for ten minutes while Claire was inside giving away all my secrets. Lexi climbed in, and I could see in the rearview mirror that she'd been crying.

"I can't believe he's gone," she sniffled. I nearly told her to look in the trunk; she'd sure as hell believe it then. "All that talent."

"Eh," Claire said. "He really wasn't that—"

"Enough," I snapped. "You're already on my list." I turned around to face Lexi, who'd managed to get control of her sobs. Her mascara had streaked into long sad-clown lines down both cheeks. Better to keep this as friendly as possible, I figured. "Hey, Lex."

"Hey, Cass."

"How you holding up? Okay?"

She shrugged and tugged at the neck of her V-neck chenille sweater. "Between my wuzzles and Jason . . . Is it true? What Claire said? He . . . killed himself?"

Out of the corner of my eye, I caught Claire giving me a single nod. "It's true," I said. Blocked from Lexi's sight by the wide front seat, Claire mimed the taking of some pills and a glass of water. "Overdose," I added. "He went peacefully."

Lexi's eyes lit up with hope. "He did? That's wonderful."

"We should all be so lucky," drawled Claire. She was back to business. "Cass, you drive. Lexi's going to give us directions."

"I didn't know you were coming along, Lex," I said as brightly as possible while shooting Claire the meanest look I had in my repertoire. Oddly enough, it was a look I'd borrowed from Claire.

"You'll never find it without me," Lexi said with pride, aware of her own importance in the scheme. "It's way up in the hills."

The three of us set out along the deserted highways of Southern California, taking advantage of the light traffic to move quickly through the San Fernando and Conejo Valleys. On the way, I told them about Stuart, about our fantastic date and instant connection, and both Claire and Lexi were quite supportive.

"He sounds great, Cass," said Lexi. "And he's such a cutie-pie. We spoke on the phone last week, you know."

A knot of tension suddenly formed in my stomach. Why was Lexi talking to Stuart? She was just the kind of girl to go around stealing the best men without even trying. "Oh yeah?" I said casually. "What about?"

Lexi bounced in the backseat, her hair and boobs flopping around as she clapped her hands. "They're getting rid of all the dogs at the club, and he said I could adopt Snoopy."

"What about Jack and Shirley?" Claire asked.

"When they get out of the pound, Snoopy's going to be their coming-home present. Isn't that exciting? I'm picking him up on Tuesday afternoon, and Cassie's going to use her legal expertise to help me get the wuzzles out on Friday." I was? I didn't argue it, as Lexi was about to help me bury a body and all that. "By Saturday, we'll all be one big, happy family."

Poor Snoopy. I've never seen a schnauzer with a shattered psyche before. Now it's just a matter of time.

They call Ojai an "artists' community," which I'm pretty sure is a code phrase for "hippie commune." Everyone reeks of the same small-town cheeriness you used to find in San Francisco before the techie empire rose and fell.

Lexi directed us up into the hills, down winding roads with few, if any, streetlights. I nearly ran off the road four times trying to negotiate the curves. "What, they don't believe in electric power?"

With every hairpin turn, an audible thump resounded from the trunk. We all tried our best to ignore it, but Lexi burst into fresh fountains of tears each time. The weeping was constant, and really beginning to get on my nerves. The sooner we got out of the car, the better for all of us.

Lexi leaned into the front seat and pointed off to a shadowed driveway. I pulled off the main road, and Lexi jumped out with a set of keys to open a pair of massive wrought-iron gates choked with ivy.

"I didn't know her parents had this kind of money," I said to Claire.

"How do you think she bought the yoga studio and the place up on Sunset Plaza?"

"Hard work?"

"She *stretches* for a living, Cassie."

The property spread out as far as I could see in every direction, which was about fifteen feet with the car lights on. I kept our speed under ten miles an hour so I'd hear any cows on the road before smacking into them.

"This should do," Claire announced after we'd traveled about a half mile on the dirt road. We piled out of the car, swapped our casual but elegant footwear for three pairs of old sneakers, and positioned ourselves around the trunk.

The last time I popped Jason Kelly out of the back of my Infiniti, he was rambunctious and argumentative and a massive pain in the ass. In short, he was alive. Part of me hoped that when I hit the remote control on my key chain, he'd burst out of there ranting and raving, and we'd all have a good laugh and go back to the house, where I could tie him up again, this time without all the electricity and pulleys, like a regular student who was eager to learn.

No dice. The plastic garbage bags in which Claire and I had wrapped his body in didn't move an inch. Lexi approached the trunk cautiously and took a peek inside, running her fingernails across the black plastic. "He's . . . in there?"

"You don't have to help," I told her. "Just sit in the car and we'll take care of it ourselves."

"No," Lexi insisted. "We're in this together."

She extended her arm, palm down, and looked at me and Claire with obvious expectation. Were we supposed to do something? Claire got the hint first, and placed her hand atop Lexi's.

"Come on, Cass," Claire muttered. "Join in."

I sighed and slapped my hand atop the pile, then removed it just as quickly. "Are we done? I'm freezing to death. Let's get moving."

With three of us, it wasn't so hard to carry Jason's body a few hundred feet off the main road and into a copse of oak trees. We propped him up against a nearby stump and took turns digging with the two shovels we'd brought, the cold ground making the work tougher than we'd anticipated. The car's headlights provided our only illumination, our bodies casting long shadows, and for a moment, I felt like Ray Liotta doing heavy work for the Mob in *Goodfellas*.

"Does anyone have any gloves?" Lexi called out, "I think I'm getting splinters from the shovel handle."

It had taken ninety minutes to get to Ojai and at least another ninety minutes to dig a hole deep enough to hide Jason's body from accidental discovery, so by the time we had him lying on the bottom of the makeshift grave, it was well past five, and the sun was beginning to rise.

Lexi was concerned about performing some sort of last rites. "Shouldn't we say a prayer or something?"

"Do you know any prayers?" I asked.

"Just the Our Father."

"Then Our Father away."

As soon as she was done, Claire and I began to dump the dirt back into the hole.

"Wait!" Lexi cried.

Claire slammed the point of her shovel into the dirt and leaned on the handle. "You already said an Our Father, Lex. I think his soul's gonna do just fine."

But Lexi was already running back to the car, calling out over her shoulder, "I'll be back in a second!"

"You see?" I said when she was out of earshot. "I told you we should have left her back in L.A."

"And tried to find this place on our own? We would have been trapped inside the car at the bottom of a mountain by now. Let's just let her go through whatever little ritual she wants, and then we can get—"

Lexi reappeared. "Here we go," she said, waving what looked like a CD jewel case in the air.

"Mix tapes for the dead?" I asked.

"It's a DVD. I thought . . . well, I thought he might want it . . . up in heaven."

She broke down into a new wave of tears, and I took the DVD out of her trembling hand. *Rangers.* I should have guessed. At least she'd chosen the best of the lot.

"This one's for you, Jason Kelly," I said, tossing the DVD on top of the dirt and garbage bags. "Here's hoping they've already upgraded to digital media in the afterlife."

No one knew what to say on the drive back into the city. I piloted the Infiniti expertly around the curves and hills of Ojai and held my own on the freeways, but I had only a small part of my mind on the street. Instead of the road, I was thinking about the road *ahead*, the days to come, and how I would use them to make the world a better place. Jason's unfortunate "event," as I've come to call it, woke me up to the truth behind that tried-and-true aphorism:

Each day is precious. Each day is a gift. If we don't open the wrapping carefully, we might break it and have to return it to the store. And then they're going to ask for a receipt and throw a total shit fit if we've left it at home, and we'll have to call the manager over and give him a good talking-to, and of course eventually he'll relent and tell the clerk to give us full credit, but by then we'll be so upset that we've wasted an hour of our time that we'll end up with a migraine and have to spend the rest of the day in bed, completely defeating the whole idea that each day is supposed to be precious and so forth.

So as I drove I found myself thinking about my boys, about how they'd take the news. Maybe I wouldn't tell them right away. It was bound to be a stressful thing, losing a classmate like that. High schools bring in psychiatrists when a student is killed. I'd taken a course in college based on Kübler Ross's *Death and Dying* in order to fulfill a psych requirement. Perhaps that would come in handy. I'd try to find my notes and see if they applied.

But first, I wanted to sleep. All day, if necessary. I wanted to take a day off from the Finishing School, from the boys, from the hectic work-week, and just lie in bed in sweatpants and a tank, order in spicy shredded pork from the Chinese place down the street, and watch a movie on cable. I knew, if I looked hard enough, that some channel would be showing *Rangers.*

SUBSTITUTIONS AND EXCHANGES

Monday morning at the office was just like any other Monday morning at the office, except for the plainclothes police detectives crawling around the place, asking questions and generally freaking everyone out.

I'd nearly managed to put the previous night's escapades behind me. There was no point in worrying about it anymore; what was done was done, and I wasn't going to score any points by fretting and moralizing over it. Still, it's a bit wiggy to find the L.A.P.D. combing through your office the day after you bury a body up in the hills. Makes you wonder if they've got video cameras in the trees.

The two detectives came in all swagger and spit, stalking around as if they owned the place, clad in off-the-rack suits and horrendous ties. Why did they even try, if they were going to fail that miserably? How could their wives (each had wedding bands, plain and unadorned) let them out of the house looking as if they'd plucked their outfits from the reject bins at the local thrift store? One wore scuffed brown loafers with a black, wrinkled suit, and a sliding-buckle belt that had been in style for about a week in 1988. I mean . . . Where do you even start with that?

I slid up to Cathy in the the lobby and leaned as casually as possible against her desk. "What are they doing here?" I muttered beneath my breath.

"I don't know," she said nervously. "I just hope they leave soon."

She seemed just about as spooked by the detectives as I was, but Cathy's spooked by anything out of the ordinary. I sent her a bouquet of flowers one time as a thank-you present for helping me avoid Stan Olsen during a particularly horny time in his life, and she tossed the whole thing into a locked cabinet by her feet out of fear that bees might be hiding within the tulip petals. Seemed she'd seen some program on Animal Planet, and that was the end of my bouquet. So Cathy's nervousness, by itself, didn't mean a thing.

I'd turned around to leave when she said, "They were in with Lorna all morning."

That stopped me. "In her office?"

"Uh-huh. She came out crying and everything."

The last thing I needed was a double shot of detectives and crying, so I took a quick look around the office to gauge the potential for an early-morning escape. I snuck into my office, grabbed my pashmina, and trotted back around toward the front lobby. "I think I'm going to head out for lunch, Cathy."

She looked at the big industrial clock on the wall. "It's not even ten o'clock."

"If you really want to make it in this town," I said, "you've got to learn to take lunch at any and all times of the day."

I made it to the elevator bank without incident. If I timed it properly, I figured I could go to lunch, check in on the boys, do a little shopping at this boutique I'd been meaning to check out on Ventura Boulevard, and be back in time to let Cathy know I'd be leaving for the day. Keep a running log with the receptionist, make it seem as if you're in and out but always busy, and it never looks like you're avoiding anyone. Casual disappearance is half art, half science.

The elevator doors opened, and Stan Olsen walked out.

Busted.

"Cassandra," he said, throwing a lumpy arm around my shoulder, spinning me back toward the office. "Just the girl I wanted to see."

I tried to duck down and escape, but he had a pretty firm hold on my arm. "Mr. Olsen, I'd love to chat, but—"

"Won't take a second. How would you like to go to Santa Fe with me tomorrow?"

"Santa Fe?"

"Nice city, very hot. Capital of New Mexico."

"That's Albuquerque," I said.

"No, we're going to Santa Fe."

I shook my head. "Albuquerque is the capital of New Mexico."

Stan didn't seem to care. "Studio's trying to make a deal with Ranjin Sunn, but he won't leave the reservation, so we're going to him." Ranjin Sunn was the hot director of the moment, a Native American whose film about drug-running youths on the Indian reservations of the Southwest had won Sundance two years back and sparked a bidding war between studios for his services. We won, I guess.

"Why doesn't he just let his agents handle it?"

"Get this: He doesn't *believe* in them. Wants to handle his own business affairs." Stan barked out a laugh, like a seal with the croup. "We'll rake him over the coals. So, are you in?"

"Oh gosh," I stammered, "I'd love to but . . . I've got a lot of commitments here at the office—"

"They can wait," he said, and released me from his death grip. My shoulder throbbed. "One night, in and out. I'll have the driver swing by your place tomorrow around five in the morning. Flight's at seven. Pack light."

I'm not entirely sure why I was asked when it didn't seem as if I had a choice, but before I could argue further, Stan was gone, and the elevator doors had closed once again, leaving me no possibility for escape. I didn't even have time to start whining or feeling sorry for myself when I heard someone slither up behind me.

"Miss French?"

Police officers have a way of saying the word *miss*, both respectful and derogatory at the same time, as if they're ready and willing to go either way with it depending on how you respond. I chose to play cute and dumb, the Lexi Hart special.

"Oh, hi, Officers," I chirped, giving them my widest smile. "Enjoying your day at the studio?"

Detectives Bishop and Roberts were an evenly matched pair, one slightly older than the other, both a bit paunchy around the midsection and sporting standard-issue close-cropped haircuts and trimmed sideburns. Bishop, the older one with the terrible fashion sense (as opposed to the one with the merely bad fashion sense), said, "We'd like to have a word with you, if you don't mind."

"Not at all," I smiled, and led them back to my office, all the way thinking that if I could find some way to get them down to the garage and into my car, then I might be able to find enough chloroform to—

No, Cassie! It was Dad. *They just want to talk. There's no harm in that.*

Daddy was right, of course. He always is. There'd be no need to go around complicating matters. I sat down behind my desk and offered the sofa to the officers.

"What can you tell us about Jason Kelly?"

"I heard he disappeared," I said truthfully. "At least, that's what the news is saying."

"Uh-huh. And what can you tell us about him personally?"

I shrugged. "Not much, I guess. He came through the office a week or so ago, just saying hi, shaking hands."

"Did you meet him?"

"Sure. Everyone did. Hey, did you guys ever see *Rangers?*"

Detective Roberts smiled patiently. "Other than that first day, did the two of you have any contact with one another?"

The first bells of alarm began to go off in my head. Why were they asking me that? Did they know something, or have they been canvassing the whole office with these questions? I decided to play it safe and deny, deny, deny. I could always come back later and say I was scared or confused. Play the lost-little-girl card.

"I wish," I said, laughing just a bit. "That's every girl's dream, right? To go on a date with Jason Kelly?"

"I wouldn't know, miss," said Bishop. He reached into a manila envelope beneath his arm and pulled out a sheet of paper, then slid it across the desk.

It was a list identical to the one I'd found in Jason's office on the yacht, only typed instead of handwritten. There were no dates and times next to any of the names, but there it was, center page: *Cassandra French, business affairs.*

"We found it on his computer," Bishop explained. "Seems odd, all these women on a list."

"It certainly does." A new flash of anger flared up as I looked down at the sheer numbers of women on the list, women Jason Kelly had either used or was planning on using in order to further his own career. But I held it in check, looked up from the page as innocently as possible, and asked, "What does it all mean?"

"We're not sure," admitted Detective Roberts. "We were hoping, since your name is down there, that you could shed some light on it for us."

So that's why they were talking to me. My name was on the list, just like fifty other women at the studio, and that was it. I relaxed significantly and began to fib in earnest.

"I've got no idea," I said, handing the paper back to Detective Bishop. "Have you checked with some of the others? I know Lorna's on this floor, if you want her office number. . . ."

"We've already spoken with Miss Wilcox."

"Oh. Well, I'm afraid that's all I can suggest." I glanced toward my phone, as if I had more pressing matters to attend to. "Do you have any more questions, or . . . ?"

They stood as one and headed for the door. "We'll let you get back to your work," said Bishop, handing me his business card. "But if you think of anything—"

"I'll be sure to ring-a-ding."

As they stepped out of my office, I couldn't resist one parting shot.

"Officers?" I called. "What makes you so sure he's not just screwing around or off on vacation somewhere?"

The detectives looked at each other, then back to me. Roberts shrugged, handing the decision to Bishop, who said, "Funny you should ask. Mr. Kelly's film agents received a letter last Friday, saying just that very thing."

Aha! Enterprise had finally done their job. "So why the big worry?" I asked.

"We took it to our handwriting experts. They told us it was most likely a forgery. Anyway, if you hear anything . . ."

And with that, they were gone and I was furious. A *forgery*? I wanted to scream after them. A *forgery*? *You dummies, that was a Jason Kelly original!* My sentiments, sure, but his handwriting all the way. If sold in a memorabilia shop, it would be worth hundreds, maybe thousands of dollars. I used to consider handwriting analysis a science; now I lump it in with tarot cards and phrenology.

I didn't have time to be pissed about shoddy detective work; in the long run, it could only help. Plus, I had to get ready to go to New Mexico. I didn't have a thing to wear, I needed reading material for the flight, and, most important, I had to find a babysitter for the boys.

Fortunately, I had just the right woman in mind.

"It's so easy," I promised Claire. "Babysitting is like baking a cake."

"I can't bake a cake, Cassie."

"Then it's like riding a bike."

"I can't ride a—"

"Take something easy, and that's exactly what it's like."

I was heading over to my mother's house. She hadn't bothered me in two days and, sad though it is, that had me worried. I'd be sure to regret it later, but for now I needed to know that she was okay, and not lying in the bathtub with a broken hip trying to reach the telephone that she's not legally allowed to use. On the way, I called Claire on the cell and filled her in on my predicament. "Come on," I nagged, "what's the big worry?"

"You're not seriously asking me that, are you?"

"What, you're still freaked about last night?"

She let out an exasperated yelp. "To be honest, yes. It's not every night that I bury a—"

"Cell phone!" I shrieked.

"Oh. Um . . . It's not every night that I do *you know what* to a *you know who*." Nice turn of a code phrase, Claire. "I still had mud under my fingernails when I woke up this morning. My manicurist is going to kill me."

"That's my whole point," I said. "It's not like I'm asking you to do *you know what* with another *you know who*. You already helped me with the hard stuff. This is easy-peasy."

Claire sighed. "First, you have to promise never to say easy-peasy again."

"Done."

"Second, my parents are in town. Staying in my guest bedroom."

"So?"

"So how can I leave them all alone to come take care of three kidnapped—"

"Cell phone," I reminded her.

"Three *students* in your basement?"

"First of all, they're just boys. They need someone to take care of them. And you don't have to sleep over. Just check in on them every once in a while, bring them food and water. Jesus, Claire, everyone needs food and water. You don't want them to di—you don't want them to *you know what* like the other *you know who*, do you?"

There was silence on the other end of the line. I held firm. Eventually, I knew, she'd either crack or hang up on me.

I wouldn't say Claire warmed to the idea, but after a few more moments, the outer layers of permafrost fell away. "If I do this, and I'm not saying I'm going to do this, but if I do this, it's just this one time. That's it."

Relief flooded over me. "Of course. You'll see, it'll be easy. Like watching someone else's pets."

Perhaps not the best choice of words. She reminded me of the time

Lexi forced her to house-sit for Jack Nicholson and Shirley MacLaine and Claire wound up sleeping on top of the kitchen counter because it was the only place she felt truly safe.

"The boys don't bite," I promised. "And if you want, you can even teach a lesson or two."

"Oh, I . . . I couldn't."

"Of course you could," I insisted. "They'd love it."

"What would I teach?"

I said, "It's up to you. What's the one thing that boys do that piss you off more than anything else?"

"Pee on the toilet seat," she said without hesitation. "It's so incredibly cliché, I know, but it's the truth."

"Perfect. Then you set up a little reward system. Make floating bull's-eye targets. Maybe have them write an essay on the importance of good aim."

"Cassie . . ."

"If I could get out of this, I would. It's not like I want to go flying off to Santa Fe with Stan Olsen, trust me on that. Two days, one night. I'll be back by Wednesday afternoon, and when I get home, I'll buy you dinner. Even better, I'll buy you that pair of Sketchers you're too embarrassed to buy for yourself. I'll—"

"Okay!" Claire shouted into the phone. "I'll do it, I'll be your babysitter."

"Thank you, honey. It means a lot to me."

"But I am *so* raiding your refrigerator."

I rang Mom's doorbell ten minutes later, and waited in the hallway for her to throw open the door and suffocate me with another one of her bear hugs. Instead, all I heard was a muffled, "Who is it?"

"It's me!" I shouted back through the door.

"Cassie?" She sounded as if she was twenty feet away.

"Is something wrong?" I yelled back. "Open up, Mom."

I heard shuffling and the dragging of furniture, chairs clacking and sliding across the tile floor. "Cover your ears, Cassie Bear."

Cover my ears? Why should I cover my—

The anklet alarm cracked through the air, slamming into my head and piercing my sinuses as I slapped my hands over my ears. Mom threw the door open and yanked me inside the house, running as fast as she could, dragging me back toward the kitchen.

Before I could scream above the din, the noise cut out abruptly. "What," I asked, "was *that* about?"

Mom said with a little sigh, "Thirty feet. Give or take an inch."

The dragging of chairs and tables I'd heard was Mom clearing a path to the front door so she could run back and forth unfettered, reducing the amount of time she had to listen to the screaming anklet. "You can't even walk to your front door without the alarm going off?"

"Or the den. Or the second bathroom."

Her two-thousand-square-foot condo had been effectively reduced by half. "That's why you haven't called," I guessed.

Mom nodded. "The only window that looks out over the boulevard is outside my range. I can't get anyone on the street to hear me over the anklet."

Enough was enough. Despite Mom's protests that she could handle the situation herself, I used my cell to call the home-arrest division at Rampart and insist that they send a technician over by the end of the day. When I hung up, Mom was visibly shaken.

"What's wrong?" I asked. "He'll come, they'll fix it, you'll be good as new."

She glanced around the living room and led me into the kitchen, where she turned on the faucet. "Oh no, Mom, not the water again."

"It's a second letter," she confided, reaching underneath the sink to pull out a plastic Baggie inside a Tupperware box. Buried and folded within the bag was yet another page from a magazine, a cereal advertisement with certain words highlighted in pink marker.

"Look," she said, poring over the document like a rabbi pulling hidden meanings from the Torah. "You see here? Ted's highlighted the words *bowl* and *spoon* and *good start to the day*."

"So he's a health fanatic."

"He's trying to tell me something, Cassie Bear."

"And I'm trying to tell you something, too: Forget about it. Forget about Ted and these messages. You need to move on."

Mom just huffed and fingered the advertisement, the glossy paper crinkling beneath her knuckles.

"And you'd better keep that letter under the sink when the cops come to fix your anklet if you don't want them to start asking a lot of questions."

Mom folded the ad back up and returned it to her hiding space. "Look at you, Miss Covert Operations. A week ago you were telling me to turn Ted in."

"Yeah, well . . . Let's just say I've got no love lost for the police these days."

I ran out to the market and brought Mom back provisions to last her for at least another week. We made a light lunch together and sat at the kitchen table, not talking about Ted and not talking about her anklet and not talking about Daddy, and soon we were out of things not to talk about, so we sat on the sofa and watched *Oprah* and waited for her to tell us how to make everything all better.

A five o'clock pick-up time means a three o'clock wake-up time, which means absolutely no beauty sleep and a very crotchety, very miserable Cassandra Susan French. I should have gone to bed earlier than midnight, but I had bags to pack and messages to leave and a babysitter to train.

The boys were not happy to hear that I'd be gone for a few days. Daniel, in particular, took it hard, sniffling and sobbing beneath his blanket. His fever was coming back, too, so that may have had something to do with it, but he just wouldn't stop whining. It was unattractive and unproductive, and it was only after I warned him that his grades might suffer if he continued that he actually sucked it up and put a cork in it. Poor thing.

Claire came over around eight with take-out from the Cajun place I like on Pico, and over po'boys and bread pudding I laid out the basics of babysitting. "Bedtime is flexible, but I like them to go down before ten. They need a good night's sleep if they're going to learn."

She took notes on a pad with the Fox letterhead emblazoned up on top. "Bedtime at ten. Got it."

"And no liquids after nine."

"What are they, gremlins?"

"It's so they don't wet the bed. The chains make it hard to get to the potty in time."

I led Claire down into the basement and formally introduced her to everyone. Shaking hands and hugs and kind words of greeting all around. There was no point in giving her a fake name; Owen already knew who she was from our night out at Stan Olsen's party and would probably tell the others. "I want you all to listen to Claire while I'm gone," I instructed. "Say it after me. Who's in charge?"

"Claire," they said as one.

"I can't hear you. . . ."

"Claire!"

"That's better. You're all going to have so much fun together, and I'll be back in just a few short days."

I thought it would make the transition a little easier on the boys if we all sat down and played a game together, so I pulled Trivial Pursuit down from the linen closet and we had a rousing match of wits and knowledge. Alan, the brain of the group, won quite handily, and I gave him a small piece of chocolate as a reward.

"Could I have some chocolate, too?" Daniel asked.

"I don't know," I said. "It's not really up to me anymore." I looked over to Claire. This was as good a time as any for her to start making decisions.

She pretended to think it over for a while, really making Daniel sweat it out. "Are you going to be good and listen to me while Cassie's away?" He nodded; Owen did, too. "You won't give me a hard time?" No, no, of course not. "Then I think we could all do with a little bit of chocolate."

I knew I'd be leaving my boys in good hands, but unfortunately I couldn't say the same thing about myself.

"You're late, French," said Stan Olsen as I climbed into the back of the studio limo. The sun wasn't even up yet, but here I was dressed and ready to go, and already he was bitching away.

"It's five minutes past."

"I'm just playing around," he chuckled. "Lighten up. Is that what you're wearing?"

Note: I had on a pair of beige suede pants and a Ralph Lauren herringbone blazer with an adorable Sergio Valente top that I got on sale at Barneys. As outfits go, it's a winner. "I was planning on it, yes. Is there a problem with that?"

"Not at all," said Stan. "Usually you wear skirts, that's all."

So you're pissed because you can't stare at my thighs, I thought. Oh yeah, this was going to be a fun trip.

Stan kept up a steady stream of chatter the whole way down to the airport, mostly stories about some studio executive or another who was his "best pal" or tales of his rabid ex-wife Paula, who, according to him, was currently in the process of taking all the money she hadn't gotten around to stealing the first time around.

"Not all women are as sweet as you are, Cassie. You're a treasure, you know that?"

"So I've been told," I muttered. I was trying to busy myself inside my purse, but there's only so many times you can reorganize your dollar bills before it starts to become obvious that you're avoiding conversation.

We made it to the airport by six, zipped through the supposedly stringent security line by six-fifteen, and checked in at the gate a few minutes later. Stan got us an aisle and a window seat back in coach, one empty seat between us, because there were no seats available in business class. When he excused himself to go to the restroom, I begged the ticketing agent behind the counter to put someone in that empty seat. "Preferably someone cute, but I'll really go for anything right now."

The lady looked at me sympathetically and gave my hand a little pat. "He's that bad?"

"Worse."

The Asian woman who eventually sat between us spent half the flight jabbing me in the side with her elbows, but it was sheer heaven compared to sitting shoulder to shoulder with Stan Olsen. I would have even taken a few good shots to the head if it meant avoiding his leg rubbing up against mine.

We rented a Ford Mustang to get from the Albuquerque airport into Santa Fe, where we learned that the reservation where Ranjin Sunn lives is actually in Taos, another hour or so up the mountain. I was already nauseous from Stan's ineptitude at driving the stick-shift rental on the hilly terrain, and I didn't relish another hour of stuttering stop-and-go at sixty miles an hour.

"Why didn't we just get an automatic transmission?" I asked.

"Automatic's for wimps," Stan said as he missed the timing on the clutch for the seven thousandth time that day. "Stick gives you more control over the car."

"Of course," I said, my head whiplashing forward and back. "I can see that now."

The Taos Reservation is set atop one of New Mexico's many mountain ranges, and it's one of those rare places that looks even better in person than it does on the postcards. Clay adobes and pueblo-style homes dot the landscape, which boasts a stunning mixture of browns, greens, and yellows, all of which sounds painfully disco-era seventies but somehow works out there in the desert.

The Taos Pueblo itself is even more iconographic, a perfect rendition of an adobe village replete with handmade wooden ladders leaning against its upper stories, nothing but gravity and friction holding them in place. It's a giant third-grader's fort, all red clay and bright blue paint, with outdoor *horno* ovens and ceremonial *kivas* and little children running around barefoot in the dirt. There's no running water, no electricity, no phone lines. I don't know a single person who could make it out here for more than three days, tops. This is where Ranjin Sunn makes his home.

"I can't believe he wouldn't come to L.A.," Stan bitched as we trekked from the car into the pueblo itself. The heat was already getting to him; dark pit stains rapidly formed and spread across the sleeves of his oxford.

"This is his home. Some people feel more comfortable on their own turf."

Stan kicked at a rock. "Well, it's gonna cost him. I'm already in a hard-ass mood over this deal, and this shit isn't helping. You just keep yourself quiet in there and let him get a good look at you while I do the talking." I don't believe Stan had any idea that what he said could have ever been construed as the least bit insulting. That's Stan—offensive and oblivious.

The contract we'd been sent to Taos to negotiate was a talent development deal encompassing both the film and television departments of our studio, an overall for which Ranjin Sunn stood to make about eight million over the next two years for pretty much sitting on his butt and doing as little or as much work as he felt like. All of this on the basis of one film with great buzz at Sundance and a failed NBC pilot that Claire screened and told me was the most grating, cringe-inducing forty-eight minutes of network television she'd ever seen. "It made my teeth itch," she said, and, though I still don't know exactly what that means, the sentiment was clear.

Ranjin lived with six of his extended family members in the farthest part of the North House, up on what could graciously be called the third floor. As Stan and I approached, the red dust beneath our feet swarming around our legs, a withered old man poked his head out of a window and gave us a warm, toothless smile. I smiled back. Stan Olsen, true to form, did not.

"We're looking for Ranjin!" Stan yelled up at him. "Ran-jin! Di-rec-tor!"

I sighed, "I'm sure he speaks English, Stan."

"You never know with these people."

The old man popped back inside, and a few moments later, a dark brown hand—younger, less wrinkled, with a flashy ring on each finger—poked out of the window and waved us up.

Stan stood back and let me take the lead. "Ladies first." I'm pretty sure he just wanted to look at my ass while I climbed the ladder, but I didn't mind the idea of having his fleshy carcass beneath me to break any possible fall.

The blue door stood open, but the bright sun outside and relative darkness inside made it impossible to see into the room itself. I stood in the doorway, trying to let my eyes adjust to the change in light.

From within, a deep, textured voice rang out: "Welcome to *Hlaumma*. Please, come in." I didn't know what *Hlaumma* meant, but I didn't care. Anyone with the kind of voice that hit me below the belt like that could welcome me practically anywhere short of Bakersfield and I'd be happy to go.

Ranjin Sunn sat on a wooden armchair in the middle of the small, boxy room, gesturing for Stan and me to take a seat on the rickety futon propped up against the far wall. He was older than I expected, shorter, too, and his tanned, almost orange skin mirrored the hues of the pueblo itself.

"It's an honor to meet you," I said as we shook hands. For a diminutive man, his hands were huge, encompassing my little fingers in a firm grip. "I loved *Clay Pots*." Okay, so I'd never seen it, but everyone's allowed at least one lie per meeting. Industry standard.

Ranjin waved a hand dismissively. "That was years ago. I'm interested in the future, not the past."

"And that's why we're here," said Stan, resting his briefcase on his knees and popping it open. He pulled out a sheaf of papers and handed them to Ranjin, who began to leaf through the contract while Stan explained it. "What we've done here is put together a basic overall deal with some modifications that reflect how much the studio values your work and your creativity. Now, if you look on page one, you'll see that the—"

The director dropped the contract back in Stan's lap, instantly shutting him up. Who knew it was that easy? "This is not acceptable," he said.

"We haven't even gone through the first page—"

"Which is itself riddled with problems."

Stan was flustered. I loved it. His tongue darted out to lick his rapidly drying lips, and he flipped through the pages of the contract, stammering out his points. "We can—look, we can fix any of the details, that's not the point of . . . What we're here to do today is go over the big stuff, and the fine print we can hammer out—"

Ranjin extended an arm, and, for a second, I thought he was going to slap the silly right out of Stan. I would have paid serious money to see that, but instead he just laid his oversized palm on Stan's shoulder, calming him down. An old Indian mystic trick, or *Seven Habits of Highly Effective People*? "Let's look on page one together, shall we?"

Stan nodded, calmed and cowed, and we all stared down at the contract. "Right here," Ranjin began, "in the second paragraph, it states that the studio is going to give me an office in one of the bungalows on the lot with two assistants and a parking space."

"That's standard," Stan said defensively. "If you want a bigger office, I can talk to them about it, but that's the same deal they gave to P. T. Anderson after *Boogie Nights*—"

"And I'm sure Mr. Anderson enjoys his parking spot immensely. I, on the other hand, will have no need for it."

Stan was aghast. "You're . . . going to *walk* to the office?"

The director grinned, his teeth a bright, bleached white against his tanned skin. "This is my office," he said, indicating the pueblo. "I will do my work from here."

"But you've got no phones."

Ranjin's eyes narrowed. Perhaps he hadn't considered this problem. "I'll make do," he said.

"I don't know . . ." Stan's jaw clenched tightly. "If you don't have a phone—"

"What about a cell phone?" I interrupted, holding my little Nokia aloft. "I mean, if he doesn't want an office suite or a parking space, I don't think the studio's going to have a problem getting him a nothing little cell."

Ranjin grinned widely. His teeth, white and strong, were flaked with red dust, as if he'd been eating the walls of the adobe and had forgotten to brush. "Yes, a cellular phone. I'll request one of those." That represented about a $100,000 savings for the studio, unless he really abused his free minutes. I'd walked over Stan by suggesting it, but the savings alone had Stan salivating. He wasn't going to have to stick it to Ranjin; the director was sticking it to himself.

"And on page three," Ranjin continued, "let's look under lodging: Should a film be greenlit, the studio will put me in a four- or five-star hotel during shooting and postproduction."

"Of course. Standard per diems each day for food and expenses, as well."

"This is also not necessary. I will do all of my filming here on the reservation and stay in my own home at night."

For Stan, this was only getting better and better. There was no way the studio would ever greenlight a film shot entirely on an Indian reservation, but for our purposes that day, it didn't matter. All it meant was that we were cutting money out of the deal, which, for Stan Olsen, was akin to really good sex.

"Is that all?" Stan asked, fidgeting with the crotch of his pants. "Or is there something else you'd like the studio to not give you?"

Ranjin pulled a pair of wire-framed bifocals from his shirt pocket and studied the contract for a few more moments. "One more thing," he said to Stan.

"Name it."

"Page eighteen, section four, clause B. Residual compensation in foreign television markets . . ."

With that, Ranjin Sunn launched into a four-hour-long tirade on the inequities in the deal and the ways in which each would need to be fixed in order for him even to contemplate signing such a document. He had an eagle eye for details and a sixth sense for bullshit, and since business affairs is pretty much all about trying to hide bullshit from eagles, we were good and properly screwed by the time he was done with us. No wonder this guy has no agents or lawyers; he'd eat them alive.

At the end of Ranjin's filibuster, Stan stood, bleary-eyed and beaten, and excused himself to go to the restroom, which was three floors down and halfway across the pueblo. I stayed with the director, admiring the simple furnishings in the sparse room. It wasn't quite Pottery Barn, but each small table, each stool, had a sense of space within the pueblo itself.

Ranjin leaned back in his chair and watched me watching him. "You don't seem to have much to say, Miss French."

"Who, me? I'm just . . . I usually let Stan do the talking."

"That's a shame. He's competent enough at the job, I can see that. But I'm sure you have some interesting insights of your own."

"Not really. I'm just the muscle."

He smiled warmly. There was intelligence in that smile, as if he knew something I did not, but thought me almost better because of it.

"I think you know what you're doing more than you let on," he said.

"You seem to know your way around a contract yourself."

"It's my business to make art, but my business is also business. You follow?"

I nodded. "I'm just impressed, that's all. Learning about all that from here in the middle of New Mexico."

His deep laugh echoed through the pueblo. I imagined little children down on the reservation stopping their jump rope and games of tag to look up at the adobe in wonder at that resounding chuckle. "Miss French, are you good at keeping secrets?"

"Like you wouldn't believe."

He leaned in close, as if to drop into a whisper, but kept that rich voice steady. "I'm from Chicago."

"Get out!" I shrieked. "You are not."

The director grinned and spread his arms wide, as if to show he had no more tricks up his sleeve. "Born and bred. My father was from Pakistan, actually."

"But you're so attached to the reservation. It seems like . . . like it's a part of you."

"It is now," he said. "But I didn't move out here until five years ago. I was a broker in a commodities firm near Navy Pier for almost a decade."

"What, selling pork bellies?"

"More or less. I was doing research on the web one day and stumbled across a genealogy site. An hour later I learned I was one-eighth

Native American on my mother's side. Taos tribe. I came out here on my next vacation and never went back. Had my brother sell my condo and my car."

I was amazed. "But you seem so . . . comfortable here."

"I am," he said. "Very much so. Back in Chicago, I was quite unhappy. Uneasy in my own skin. I'd wake up each morning hoping the securities exchange had burned to the ground so I'd get a day off work."

"That's a little extreme, isn't it?"

"So was my misery. It wasn't until I set foot on the reservation and began to talk to the family I'd lost even before I was born that I understood where I needed to be."

I felt as if he was trying to tell me something, as if there was some mystical element to my visit that I'd yet to grasp. I leaned forward on the futon, no longer worried whether or not the red clay of the walls rubbed off on my suede pants. After all, my dry cleaner in L.A. really knows what he's doing.

"So it's all about finding your heritage?" I asked.

"For me it was. For others, it's something else. Everyone needs to decide that for themselves." He stood from his seat and sat down next to me on the futon, enveloping my hands in his. "Take the time and find out where you belong, Miss French. How you fit in. For me, it's the reservation. And I don't leave it unless I absolutely have to. I don't want to take the chance that I won't be able to find my way back again."

I wanted to ask him if he knew where it was that I fit in, or if he could perhaps recommend a few places to start. Maybe he even had a couple of brochures lying around. But Stan's thinning hair suddenly appeared at the top of the ladder, and a moment later he hauled his sweaty body into the pueblo.

"Cassandra," he panted, "I think we're done here."

Ranjin sat back on the futon. "I assume I'll hear back from you shortly."

"Of course," Stan said. "I'll go over these notes and we'll see what we can do." I wondered if Ranjin knew that in Hollywood-speak, that meant we'd be getting back to him as soon as we'd first taken care of everything else on our list, including shopping for Christmas presents. I bet he did.

The director didn't show us out; he sat there on the futon as we said our good-byes and climbed down the pueblo ladders. My legs were shaking as I descended. I felt weak, a little off balance. Was it the ladder or was it me? Ranjin Sunn's words haunted me all the way to the car and back to the hotel in Santa Fe, where they were promptly obliterated by the more pressing words of the hotel manager, who informed us that due to a mix-up, there was only one room left in the entire place and that Stan and I would have to share a king-sized bed.

Stan was as much a gentleman as Stan could be, but only because I'd laid down some pretty harsh ground rules before sliding beneath the sheets. I was tired, I missed my boys, and I was thoroughly finished playing the respectful underling. "If I feel a single hand anywhere on my body," I told him, "that hand comes off. I'll do it with a butter knife from room service if I have to, but you'll be Captain Hook before morning."

Stan assured me he had no such intentions. "I wouldn't dream of it."

"If I feel your breath on the back of my neck—"

"My lips come off. I get it, I get it."

True to his word, we slept side by side with no incident. Halfway through the night, I awoke from a dream in which the boys had escaped only to bake me a carrot cake, my absolute favorite. Stan lay next to me, snoring gently, off in his own dreamland (ex-wives burning in fiery torment while he stoked the flames and ate steak served by nubile young secretaries, I have no doubt).

For a moment, I wondered why he hadn't tried to make a move. It couldn't have been my rather lame threats. Perhaps I was no longer attractive to him. Had the dry desert heat screwed with my hair? It was crazy, I know, but suddenly I found myself wondering what would happen if I rolled on top of him and locked my lips on his. Would he kiss back or throw me off? Toss his arms around me and start to thrust or—

Bleech. I respect my body too much to turn it over to the likes of Stan Olsen. I wouldn't have gone through with the carnal act one way or the other, but just then my cell phone, set to vibrate, began buzzing along the nightstand. I hopped out of bed and tiptoed into the bathroom, checking the Caller ID on the way.

Cassandra French, it read, and gave my home number.

I popped the cell phone open, heart beating madly. "What's wrong? Who's hurt?"

"Hey, Cass." Claire sounded giddy. Almost tipsy. "How's the trip?"

"Claire, it's three in the morning. What's wrong?"

"Nothing's wrong," she insisted. "Everything's great. I'm great, the boys are great, everyone's great."

"So you're calling me because . . . ?"

"Where do you keep the twine?"

I could picture the box, sitting in a cabinet inside the garage. I didn't want to judge, not just yet, so I bit my tongue and gave her specific directions on how to find it.

"Great," she said. "And the chains? And maybe a padlock or two?"

"Claire, tell me what's going on."

I could hear a commotion in the background, a distant clanging of metal and pounding of walls. "Nothing I can't handle," she insisted. "I promise you, your boys are just fine. They've been little angels."

I knew there'd be no getting any information out of her tonight. When she wants to keep her mouth shut, Claire clams up so well I'd swear she's half mollusk. "There are some spare chains and locks in a box just above the twine," I told her. "I hope you know what you're doing."

"Thanks, hon," she said, "you're a doll. See you tomorrow."

"Tomorrow," I promised, but by then she was gone.

It took a long time to get back to sleep. Images of Owen and Alan running wild through the basement spun through my mind. Another mental movie: Daniel, shivering and watching from the comfort of his bed as his fellow students broke free of their restraints and slammed into the walls, trying to pound their way out or beat themselves silly trying. I couldn't let it go. What had Claire done (or not done) to my boys? Why had she needed the twine and chains? What was going on in my own house?

But you've got to learn to trust your babysitter, especially when she's your best friend in the whole wide world. I could safely put away my fears because I knew, deep down, that once I got back to the house, I'd find that it was just a false alarm or a silly little prank, and that everything was exactly as I'd left it. Claire's too smart to make any major mistakes, I figured. She wouldn't dare put me, the boys, or the Finishing School in jeopardy.

WHAT GOOD IS
NORMAL, ANYWAY?

When I walked through my front door ten hours later, I found Claire sitting at the kitchen table, wearing my best chenille bathrobe, sipping a cup of tea, and reading my subscription copy of *Entertainment Weekly*.

"Welcome back," she said brightly, folding the magazine in half and coming in for a hug. "You're back early."

"We finished up yesterday," I explained. "How'd they do?"

"The boys? Fantastic. Couldn't have been better helpers. Very cooperative."

I was proud of them, but there was something about Claire's chipper attitude that set me on edge. "What's wrong with you?" I asked.

"Me? Not a thing. Why?"

"I can't put my finger on it. You're . . ." I gave her a once-over, scoping her up and down like any good boy might do at a club. It was something odd about her posture, about the way she was carrying herself, almost as if . . .

"Holy shit!" I cried. "You're happy!"

Claire spun away from me. "No I'm not."

"Yes you are, you big fat liar. You're happy, and I want to know why."

She turned her head, staring at me over her shoulder before turning all the way back around with a big shit-eating grin on her face. "Okay, I am."

"Spill."

"I will. But you've got to promise to keep an open mind."

"Wait, isn't that my line?"

"Promise, Cassie."

I swore up and down that I'd be flexible, and Claire led me over to the basement door and worked the padlock like a pro. I'd been gone less than thirty hours, and already it seemed I had a competent replacement should I have to sit out the season with an injury.

I walked down the basement stairs and at first glance saw nothing out of the ordinary. There were Owen and Alan, playing chess with their origami shapes, and Daniel sitting on his bed, reading a dog-eared copy of an edited *Archie Double Digest*.

And, in the corner, a strange middle-aged man strapped to a chair with twine and chains, a blindfold over his eyes and headphones covering his ears.

Calmly, very calmly, I walked back up the basement steps where Claire was waiting for me at the top, all expectant grins and giggles.

"Well?" she asked.

"The boys look fine," I said as impassively as possible. "May I ask who the older gentleman wearing all the hostage gear might be?"

Claire's eyes practically sparkled. "That's Comes When Enlightened."

"Your psychiatrist-slash-lover-slash-ex-boyfriend?"

She nodded eagerly. "He's our new student."

I didn't even know where to begin correcting her on that sentence. Every word about it was wrong. I believe I may have stuttered and stammered for a good two minutes without getting any actual phrases to form on my lips.

Claire tried to help out. "I know what you're going to say, and you're right. I was just supposed to watch the boys, feed them and help them get to bed, and make sure they were safe, and I did that, I swear it. You saw, they're in great shape. I've even got Daniel's fever down to ninety-nine point five."

"Fantastic. It still doesn't explain why I've got a fifty-year-old therapist in my basement playing hear-no-evil, see-no-evil."

"You're right," Claire said, deflating a bit as she plopped into a kitchen seat and took another sip from my World's Greatest Lap Dancer mug. "Of course you're right. I'll tell you what happened. Tea?"

"No, Claire. No tea. Just the story."

Seemed she'd come over last night to give the boys their dinner when she wound up in a protracted conversation with Owen and Alan about chess, which led into another conversation about psychic abilities, which led into yet another conversation about psychiatry, which, of course, set Claire off thinking about Comes When Enlightened. She left my house in a funk, obsessing about her failed relationship and what she could have done to make it work better.

"I didn't even realize I was driving down to Newport Beach until I was past the San Pedro split on the 405, and by then it was too late." Claire took another sip of her tea. "I don't know why I went to his office first, but I had a feeling he'd be in there."

"What time are we talking about?" I asked.

"Eight, eight-thirty. But he works late a lot, transcribing notes onto his computer." Claire parked in the garage next to his building and headed into his suite of offices. She wasn't surprised to find the door unlocked.

"So I snuck in," she said, "figuring . . . hell, I don't know. Maybe I thought I could reason with him. And we'd talk. And he'd see I'm not so normal after all. And . . ."

"And he'd take you back?" I said.

She nodded pathetically. "It's stupid, I know, but we were doing so well together. So right for each other. I thought there was a chance. Anyway, I made it into the lobby, and that's when I heard him."

"Typing?"

"Grunting. I pushed open the door to his office, just a little, and there he was, on top of some girl with a terrible dye job, just thrusting away. And get this: She was reading to him."

"His diploma?"

"A textbook, I think. Something about Freud. It really got him hot. He kept shouting, 'Tell it to me, baby, tell it to me!' "

"Oh, Claire . . ."

"I couldn't move, Cassie. I stood there, watching the whole thing, his hairy ass pumping up and down. Wondering what neuroses she had that I didn't have. Maybe she was schizo or manic-depressive or something really fucked up like that. I mean, why could he get off by screwing her but not me?"

Claire told me how she eventually let herself out of the office and wandered back to her car, where she sat in the darkness, listened to love songs on KIIS, and cried for all the stupid things she'd ever done with all the stupid boys she'd ever met.

She was just wiping the final tears from her eyes and preparing to leave when the door to the parking garage opened and Comes When Enlightened walked in, heading straight for his car. Claire realized with mounting horror that he was parked directly next to her; if she didn't do something, he'd be bound to see her, and she'd probably die of embarrassment on the spot.

"So I did the only thing I could thing of," she said. "I hit him with my Club."

"The steering-wheel lock?"

"Right over the noggin. I knew that thing would come in handy one day. His back was turned, and he was trying to open his car door. I snuck up behind him and swung and hit him and he went down hard. And he was just lying there, looking so sweet and unconscious and everything, and suddenly, I knew why I'd done it, and what I had to do next."

"And . . . somehow that involved taking him back to my house?"

Claire nodded eagerly and leapt out of her seat. "Exactly! I'm so glad you understand. It just took me a little bit longer to see it all, but now I get the whole Finishing School concept. What you're doing here. What you're trying to accomplish. What *we're* trying to accomplish."

"Whoa," I said, pushing her back into the chair. "Just yesterday, you were quite insistent that there was no we. Now there's a we?"

"Yes, now there's a we."

"Meaning you and me?"

"Well . . ."

As if on cue, the doorbell rang, and, true to form, Lexi didn't wait for anyone to answer. She waltzed through my foyer and into the kitchen, toting a bag of groceries in each hand. "I brought bagels," she called out. "And doughnuts for Owen, because he was so helpful last—" She stopped in the entrance to the kitchen, noticing my presence. It didn't seem to faze her all that much. "Cassie! You're back early. Stuart called, by the way. Last night. I took a message; it's around here somewhere. He is *so* funny!"

Most of my brain knew full well that this whole event was taking place, but a small part of me chose to believe that it was all a dream, and that, at any moment, I was going to wake up next to Stan Olsen in a Santa Fe hotel room. I'd even accept an uninvited caress across my naked thigh if it meant that Lexi's intrusion was but a figment of my imagination.

No go. Considering the fire that was raging inside, I kept myself relatively calm. "Claire, could we have a word? *Now.*"

Lexi brushed by us on her way toward the basement door. "Don't mind me," she called back. "I've just got some breakfast for the boys. They get so hungry." She popped the locks and trotted down the steps, bouncing her tush along in a pair of rolled-up sweatpants that would have made me look as if I'd been incontinent for a week but only managed to accentuate Lexi's natural curvature.

I let a slow burn do all the talking for me. My gaze bored deep into Claire; if her makeup hadn't had SPF 15 in it, she'd be red as a tomato today.

"What choice did I have?" Claire yelped. "How was I supposed to move him all by myself?"

"You could have left him there."

243

"In the parking garage? Cassie, that's barbaric. He could have been mugged. Or beaten."

"So instead you called Lexi, who you *know* I don't trust, and let her into my basement?"

"Someone had to go down and feed them."

I said, "That's what *you* were supposed to be doing."

Claire admitted that she'd been shirking her duties because she didn't want Comes When Enlightened to see her. "I just couldn't face him. God, he was screaming all night and pounding on the wall." That must have been the commotion I'd heard when she called at three in the morning. "I wanted to go down there. I did. But I didn't want to see the look on his face when he saw it was me. Would he be happy? Or repulsed? Or . . ." She shrugged. "So I sent Lexi in."

"Thereby exposing my boys to her corrupting influence."

Claire's hands fell to her slim hips. "Now who's being melodramatic?"

I screamed in frustration. Claire screamed in frustration. Lexi poked her head out of the basement and said, "Could you two keep it down a bit? I'm trying to give the boys a compatibility test from *Tiger Beat*."

"You see," said Claire once Lexi had disappeared back down her rabbit hole, "she's taken right to it. And the boys just love her."

"I bet they do." Bad enough Lexi should busy herself with Stuart Hankin, but now she was messing with my boys. "*Tiger Beat* is not on the approved reading list," I informed Claire. "And doughnuts are not an acceptable breakfast food." The whole thing was spinning out of control. All my hard work, my dedication over the last year, about to be ruined by my best friend and a ninety-eight-pound tart with fake tits and fantastic fashion sense.

"Don't blame me," said Claire. "Lexi's the one who bought the doughnuts."

"And you're the one who let her in here." My heart was pounding, easily up in the cardio range, so at least some good was coming out of this.

"Look," Claire said, coming behind me and massaging my shoulders, "let's just take a step back, okay? Lexi's in, and there's nothing we can do about it now."

I didn't want to admit it, but she was right.

"And, lucky for you, you're staring at the queen of damage control." The other executives at Fox called Claire "the cleaner." When the shit hit the fan, she was always the one who figured out where to find the mops and buckets.

Before Claire could brainstorm a plan of action, Lexi popped her pert little self out of the basement again. "Cass, I think you should probably come down here."

So help me God, if she'd dressed the boys in frilly lace, I was going to kill her. With a growing feeling of despair in the pit of my stomach, I followed her down the basement stairs.

The boys were spread out along the floor, each as far apart from the next as their chains would allow. Owen was laid out on his back, trying to lift his tree-trunk legs high into the air. Alan had already achieved a Lotus Blossom position, and Daniel was halfway into a Downward Dog.

"You've got them doing yoga," I said flatly.

Lexi beamed. "And they're so good at it! Sure, they're a little stiff from lying around all day, but we'll work out those kinks real soon."

I grabbed Lexi by the shoulders and forced her into the corner of the basement. "No more yoga," I whispered harshly.

"I just thought—"

"Yoga's what got us into this mess in the first place. Do you understand me? No. More. Yoga."

Lexi nodded, swallowed hard, and pointed to my head. "What?" I snapped. She pointed again, and this time I realized she wasn't pointing at my head, but above it.

"That's what I wanted you to see. Behind you."

I turned around and looked up. Directly above me was one of the many exposed wood beams that provided structure and support for the basement walls. Only this one was cracked down the center, a long, lightning-bolt fissure running the entire length of the wood. Those familiar small mounds of sawdust lay on the floor beneath it, piled up a good three inches along the wall.

"I think that's the kind of thing you can't fix," said Lexi, running her fingernails along the crack. "Weird. It's like the whole place is falling apart."

Termites. That's what the exterminator said, anyway, and since I didn't go to exterminator college, I wasn't going to argue with him.

"It's pretty bad," he said, picking his nose as he led me on a tour through my infested house. "Up and down through the beams in the basement. Already some pretty bad structural damage down there. Good thing you called when you did, 'cause they're spreading on up here to the rest of the place. One way or the other, it's gonna be a tenter."

A tenter, I learned, is a job that requires erecting a giant Day-Glo carnival tent over the entire house and pumping in toxic fumes strong enough to kill any living things unfortunate enough to be inside. What it meant in practical terms was that the boys and I were going to have to find a temporary place to live.

It was difficult enough moving them out of the basement for the exterminator's visit. I couldn't very well have the boys chained to their beds while the man did his inspection; they might have gotten in his way.

I was on the phone to the pest-control company two shakes after finding the crack in that beam, insisting that they send a technician immediately. They gave me a two-hour window, and I flew into action.

"We're moving the boys," I informed Claire and Lexi. "Each of you grab a set of chains and follow me."

The one good thing about having accomplices is that it increases the teacher:student ratio, a plus in any good school system. Since Comes When Enlightened was still doped up from the massive doses of morphine Claire had administered last night, we left him in the basement while we moved out the other three boys. Like ranchers driving a herd of cattle across the open plains, we roped and hitched our steers up the basement stairs and into the kitchen. Alan and Daniel blinked at the strong sunlight pouring through the windows; it had been months since they'd seen anything other than the glare of a naked one-hundred-watt bulb, and it took their eyes some time to adjust.

"How about the back bathroom?" Claire suggested, but I couldn't in all good conscience leave them in the room where Jason Kelly had his accident. They still hadn't asked about him, and I didn't want them to start now.

Every room in the house posed a potential problem, but in the end Claire came up with a good, if not perfect, solution. I've got to hand it to her; working in TV for so long has forced her to be creative in a pinch, and this time she really came through.

The exterminator completed his walk-through and handed me a lengthy estimate, seemingly based on the number of children he was currently putting through college.

"Forty-five hundred dollars?"

"That's pretty standard for a home of this size," he said. "Maybe your homeowner's insurance covers it. They can cut us a check directly."

I'd already checked. "It doesn't."

"Oh. Then it'll be forty-five hundred dollars up front."

I've never been a good haggler. Somehow, I always manage to wind up paying more than was originally quoted, plus about six pounds of guilt on top of it. "Listen, maybe we could just tent a part of the house, and—"

"You know," he said, moving back through the living room, "I should probably check the yard, too."

I froze. "The yard?"

"Out back. If the termites got into the foundation—"

"They didn't," I blurted out. "I checked."

I couldn't tell if the exterminator was bemused or annoyed. Either way, he wasn't buying it. "If you don't want the whole place to fall down, I should check out the foundation. It'll just take a second."

What was I supposed to do? A collapsed house would do me no good, and probably do serious damage to my wardrobe. I trotted along behind him as he strode toward the sliding glass doors leading to my yard.

Claire and Lexi sat on folding deck chairs, sipping from glasses of lemonade. A pile of laundry lay on the chaise longue next to them, completely covering the sleeping body of Comes When Enlightened. A single shoe poked out from beneath the dirty clothes, and, if you looked carefully, you could see that it led to a leg and a hip. From most angles, though, it was just another soiled garment atop the pile.

Claire looked up, startled, as the exterminator slid back the glass doors. She glanced over to me, alarmed, then back to the pest-control man. "Ummm . . . hi?"

"Don't mind me, ladies," he said. "I'll just be a moment."

He strolled right past Owen, Alan, and Daniel, who stood at the side of the yard, clearly chained to one another with manacles as they meticulously trimmed the hedges with the child-safe scissors I'd pur-chased months ago for use on our weekly art projects. "Afternoon, fel-las." He rounded the corner and disappeared.

Claire mouthed to me: What do we do?

Lexi reached beneath the table and pulled out the bottle of chloro-form we'd brought out for emergency purposes. "There's a little left," she whispered.

No, I mouthed back. Put that away!

Lexi dropped the bottle back under the table. She almost seemed disappointed.

The exterminator reappeared around the other side of the house. "Foundation seems fine from out here," he said. "You might want to clear away some of the dirt, keep at least four inches clear off the ground."

"That's a great idea! Wonderful!" Perhaps I was a bit too enthusias-tic, pushing him from behind as I ushered him back into the house. I could only hope that he'd moved so quickly past the boys that he hadn't seen their chains. "When do we have to tent? Next week? Next month?"

"Friday," he said, jotting down the pertinent information on a work order. "We'll be here at nine."

In a bit of a daze, wondering how on earth I was going to find an acceptable temporary home for the boys and me in just under two days, I walked the exterminator to the front door and saw him out.

"Hey," he said, turning around as he reached the front porch. "How do you get that prison labor to come to your place?"

"Prison labor?"

"The guys with the chains. I could sure use a few cons to help out around my yard on the cheap."

"Of course, right, the prison labor," I ad-libbed. "Um. You just . . . sign up. But there's a really long waiting list."

The exterminator nodded, as if this were the type of bad break that always happened to him. "And I bet you gotta know someone important downtown."

"You've got to know a lot of someones," I agreed. "Well, see you Friday."

I closed the door, perhaps a bit too quickly, but I didn't have time to sit around and make idle chitchat. The boys and I, quite literally, had to get moving.

We gathered up the boys and ushered them back down into the basement. "Garden time is over?" Alan asked.

"For today."

"I liked clipping the hedges," he said. "I could see that as a career. You know, landscape design."

See, the Finishing School is even helpful when it comes to career counseling. Any other time, I would have hugged Alan for showing an interest in a career other than spoken-word poetry, but I didn't have time to pat him on the back. "That's wonderful," I said. "I'll see if I can find a book on the subject. Now let's scoot."

Claire, Lexi, and I set up the cots, locked the boys in, and climbed back up the basement stairs to regroup in the kitchen. Comes When Enlightened was still blindfolded and unconscious, lying beneath the pile of laundry on the chaise longue outside. It had taken all three of us to carry his doughy body up the basement stairs and through the house, and we weren't yet ready to tackle the return trip. So we sat in the kitchen, drinking coffee, working up our nerve and strength.

"I need to be out of here by nine A.M. on Friday," I told the girls. "Which means we'll need to move the boys by tomorrow night. Ideas?"

Claire suggested hotels, motels, abandoned mine shafts, but each option was either too public or too dangerous.

"I've got a basement," Lexi piped up.

I pressed on. "What about a warehouse? There's this storage facility I rent over in east L.A.—"

"I've got a basement," Lexi repeated. It was harder to ignore her the second time around. "It's just like yours. Only furnished. And deco-rated. Not that yours isn't decorated, but, well . . . it's not. Not really. I mean, it looks like maybe you tried, but . . ."

I'd prepared a blistering comeback, a fantastically witty riposte that would have sent Lexi scurrying to her thesaurus and eventually to a therapist, but before I could deliver it, the doorbell rang.

"Keep Lexi in here," I muttered to Claire.

I expected that the exterminator had forgotten some tool or wanted to ask more about my free prison labor, so I pulled the door open without looking through the peephole first.

My first thought was: *Why is the exterminator bringing me flowers? Was I coming on to him without realizing it?* Then the beautiful bouquet moved to one side, and Stuart Hankin emerged from behind it.

"I was at this shop," he said, smiling that wonderfully crooked smile, "and they had these flowers lying around. All over the place. I assumed they were free, so I took a bunch and added some baby's breath and wrapped cellophane around them. Interested?"

I don't know if it was the adrenaline or the surprise or just the ful-fillment of a long week's worth of pent-up frustrations, but I threw my arms around Stuart's neck and pulled him into a long, deep kiss. He laughed into my mouth as we went at it, surprised at my sudden burst of affection.

When we parted, his eyes were wide as Frisbees. "Wow," he said, staggering backward comically. "I'm glad I found the right house."

He took a step to come inside, and I suddenly remembered that Comes When Enlightened was still in the backyard. He might have been buried beneath a pile of laundry, but there was no way of knowing when the morphine was going to wear off. He still had on his handcuffs, blindfold, and headphones, and I couldn't take a chance that he might wake up and start stumbling blindly around the house. Once again, I had to step in Stuart's path and block his entrance to my home.

"You know what?" I suggested. "Let's stay out here. The front porch is so nice this time of day."

"I get it," Stuart said. "Well, I don't get it, but I get it. You don't want me in your house. That's fine, I'm cool with that—"

"That's not it," I promised.

"So let's go out, then. I've got some time right now. Let's grab a late lunch, or an early dinner."

I thought of Comes When Enlightened in the backyard, of the boys, still waiting for their midafternoon snack down in the basement. I couldn't leave Claire and Lexi to do it all by themselves. At the end of the day, a single mom has to learn to fend for herself, and in this case, there was no way I'd be able to get away for at least another few hours.

"I can't right now," I began, "but—"

Stuart held up a hand, stopping me. "That's fine. It's cool, Cassie, it really is." But I could tell from his tone that it was anything *but* fine. "All I want to do is spend some time with you, get to know you—"

"And I want to get to know you, too—"

"But you don't want me to come in, and you don't want to go out. I called you three times since Monday, and didn't get a single call in return." *Three* times? Lexi said he'd called once. Had the little tart been holding out on me?

"Stuart, it's not that simple," I said, fully intending to give him a rousing explanation as soon as I had a few spare hours to think one up. "If you could just wait another day—"

I felt her before I saw her, smelled her before I heard her, but Lexi Hart was in full-on heat. "Hi, there!" she bubbled, bouncing out from behind me, Claire by her side.

I'm sorry, Claire mouthed. I tried.

Stuart was a bit taken aback. He hadn't expected company. "Oh. Hi. It's . . ."

"Lexi. Lexi Hart. Remember, I'm going to adopt little Snoopy from you."

"Who?"

Lexi had forgotten that the dog she called Snoopy had, for most of its life, been named Fripouille. "Oh, you," she laughed, and hopped out the front door, landing right next to Stuart. I noticed that she already had her Prada bag slung across her shoulder. "You want to go get some coffee? We can talk about all your little wuzzles."

Stuart glanced back and forth between me and Lexi's heaving breasts, possibly looking for a definition of wuzzles, but one way or the other hoping to get a bit of extra help in his decision. I sure as hell wasn't going to give him any; this was a test, as far as I was concerned, and an easy one at that.

Stuart failed. "Sure," he said, allowing Lexi to link her arm through his. He stared directly at me and said, "Since Cassie's too busy to go out, coffee sounds great."

Lexi clapped her cheerleader hands and pecked me a good-bye kiss on the cheek. I stood there, mute, unwilling to believe that Stuart had fallen prey to her physical charms. By the time they were down the front walk and driving away, I had no choice but to believe it.

Claire walked up next to me and together we stood in silence as Stuart's car coasted down the block and disappeared around a corner. I should have called the cops and reported a robbery: Lexi had stolen my boy.

Claire was the first to break our silence. "She's a force of nature, Cass. You can't stop her; you can only hope to contain her."

Dumb Stuart Hankin. Stupid Stuart Hankin. Have I mentioned he has arched eyebrows?

Claire and I were struggling to get Comes When Enlightened back down into the basement when I heard a terrible screeching of tires out in front of my house. Was that Stuart? Had he been spooked by Lexi the She-Beast and come running back to my arms for protection?

I was two feet from the foyer when a loud crack exploded through the air and the front door shook madly, as if some giant had come down off his beanstalk and was canvassing the neighborhood selling magazines door to door. I peeked out the peephole to see a battered red convertible screeching away.

"What the hell was that?" Claire asked as she ran into the foyer.

"Some kids," I guessed. "Probably throwing eggs."

"That was a hell of an egg. Open the door, see what it is."

With a bit of trepidation, I pulled the door open just a tad and peered down. There, on the welcome mat, was a large, brass bookend. As I lifted the heavy piece of kitsch for a better look, I realized that I recognized the design: a comically exhausted mouse, trying to push a copy of *War and Peace* into a vertical position.

"What is that?" Claire asked. "A paperweight?"

"A bookend," I sighed. "My bookend, actually." At least, it had been my bookend when I was a child. Now it belonged to my mother, which could have meant only one thing. . . .

I turned the bookend over, and, lo and behold, there it was, a note affixed to the bottom with clear packing tape:

If you find this note, please deliver it to Cassandra Susan French at 3614 Brighton Way, Westwood. Tell her to come see her mother. Have a wonderful day.

"It could have killed someone, Mom. You can't go around throwing ten-pound paperweights out of your window and telling others to do the same."

True to form, she was less than contrite. "You got the note, didn't you? And tell me, Miss Big Idea, what was I supposed to do? How else am I supposed to contact you?"

She had me there. When you can't leave your kitchen and can't use your phone, tossing a brass mouse out of your window might indeed be the next best option.

When I'd arrived at her door fifteen minutes prior, I found it unlocked and slightly ajar. "Mom?" I called. "Are you in there?" There was no response, but the open door had me spooked. I violated the Golden Rule (because I sure don't want Mom popping into my place unannounced) and stepped inside, keeping my arms up in a Krav Maga defense pose I'd learned in a two-hour course taught by a boy who, later that night over coffee, asked me if I'd ever seen any animal sex videos. It's a good thing he knows self defense; if that's his usual first-date line, he'll be blocking a lot of kicks to the groin.

But there were no intruders; there was just Mom, sleeping on a mattress in the middle of her kitchen. A pile of books lay on the corner near the dishwasher, and at least a quarter of her wardrobe was heaped atop the counter. In the sink I found a half-full bottle of shampoo and a disposable razor. Mom had moved her entire apartment into the kitchen.

After waking Mom up and chastising her on her method of communication, I called the sheriff's office once again and ranted at everyone I could find. "She can't leave her goddamned kitchen!" I shouted at some low-level deputy. "Here, listen!"

I pulled Mom out of the kitchen and her anklet started going wild. I held the phone up to her leg and gave it a good ten seconds. When I came back on the line, they'd hung up.

I was furious. With the cops, the judges, sure, but with Mom, as well. "Just go down there!" I insisted. "You walk into the police station with that anklet blaring, they'll fix it right away, I promise you that. At the very least, pick up your phone and use it when you need to. Forget the judge's order; it's ridiculous."

Mom sat down on her mattress and pulled a knitting set from a cutlery drawer. At least she was organized. "I can't, Cassie Bear. Those aren't the rules. The judge was very clear."

There was no point in telling her that in all likelihood the judge was just another lawyer who'd shaken the right hands and massaged the right egos to get his position on the bench. Mom wouldn't care. She was raised in a simpler time, when the letter of the law was the intent of the law. Unlike her daughter, she hadn't gone to law school and been taught that everything, especially words on paper, can be manipulated.

"Promise me this much at least," I said. "If the range gets even shorter and you can't make it to the refrigerator, you'll find some way to give me a call before you eat your own foot."

Mom thought it over for a second. "That's a deal," she said.

We shook on it. Mom going footless was now one less thing that I had to worry about. That only left 499 other little problems, and then I'd be free to sit back, relax, and wait for my life to conform perfectly to my expectations. And really, with everything else that had gone on, I figured: How much worse could it get?

BREAKOUTS, SKIN
AND OTHERWISE

At last count, there were six different boys in my life, each important in his own special way. Owen, Alan, and Daniel were my original trio, the Pep Boys of the basement. Jason Kelly, rest his soul, was an unfortunate bump in the road, and is now an unfortunate bump *beneath* a road. Comes When Enlightened was not, by any stretch of the imagination, my call, but whether I liked it or not, he'd become my responsibility. That was five.

Stuart Hankin made number six. He's the closest thing to an actual man that I've ever dated, and I can't believe I've let him get away three times now. So when Lexi called on my cell as I was driving back from Mom's, you can be sure I opened up with a double shot of espresso-fueled fury.

"How dare you?" I shouted into the phone, and, just for good measure, repeated myself. "How *dare* you?"

Lexi, being Lexi, was oblivious. "How dare I what? Coffee was great, by the way. Stuart is *so* funny. I can't believe how much he talks about you, you lucky thing."

That stopped my impending rant. "He was talking about me?"

"Only like the whole time. I was just glad I was able to get him out of your house before he saw Claire's boy toy."

I ran a STOP sign and didn't care. Had Lexi actually been trying to help, or was this just a cover for stealing the one man in Los Angeles who didn't make me want to run screaming for the hills?

A bit of prying was in order. "So you two just went for coffee?"

"Uh-huh. He didn't stay too long. Said he had to get back to the bar and dropped me off back at your place so I could get my Beemer. I think you should call him, Cass."

I was still upset that he'd chosen Lexi over me. That would be like choosing New Coke over Coke. "I don't see why I should."

"He was really hurt the way you blew him off. I'm telling you, he barely drank his iced latte. I mean, I tried to cover for you, but . . . well, you've screwed up a few times with him."

"You know, Lexi, it's been a little difficult around the house, what with you and Claire taking matters into your own hands—"

"Oh, that reminds me," she interrupted. "For the trial tomorrow, do you think I should wear that red leather number I wore to the Roxy that one time, or something a little sexier?"

"For the last time, it's not a trial. It's a hearing."

"I agree. The red one's perfect. Hey, where did you get all those neat chains and manacles?"

At that point all I wanted to do was get off the phone and check in with the boys, so I didn't give the motive behind her question much thought. I sighed and gave Lexi the name of one of the sex shops I used to frequent up in West Hollywood. "Why?"

"No reason," she said, doing a horrible job at hiding the deception in her voice. "I just thought I might do a little extra legal work on my own, that's all. Ta-ta!"

Yep, there it was again, that all-too-familiar boulder weighing down the pit of my stomach. "What's that supposed to mean?" I said into the phone, only to be answered with a dead line. "Lexi? Lexi?"

She was gone, off to do whatever little scheme she'd cooked up in her half-baked brain. Naturally, I was concerned, as I am every time Lexi decides to take matters into her own hands. Lexi is the Dennis the

Menace of the Nordstrom set: She's got questionable intentions, a little bit of curiosity, and, by the end of the last panel, someone other than her always ends up very, very messy.

Leonard Shelby was not in the courtroom. Scrawny, toadlike, pimpled, bandaged, litigious Leonard Shelby was, as far as the bailiff could tell, nowhere near the entire courthouse. He was not at his home, and he was not in his car. No one knew exactly where he was, but after an hour of phone calls and messengers, it was ascertained that he quite certainly was *not* where he should have been: testifying in the case he'd originally brought against the wuzzles.

The empty chair next to the city attorney announced Leonard Shelby's fate to me as clearly as if Lexi had taken a photograph of him in chains and cuffs and projected it via slides onto the courtroom wall.

I sat next to her at the defendant's table and muttered, "What did you do?"

"This morning?" she muttered back. "I had breakfast at the Corner Bakery. Why, what did you do?"

"Leonard Shelby, Lexi. What did you do to him?"

All I got in response was a wink. She wouldn't give me any more information, and I couldn't very well beat it out of her. There were way too many witnesses around.

Eventually, the court officers decided to proceed with the hearing. The supervisor from the animal shelter was present, and as long as she was ready to testify as to the wuzzles' disposition, the hearing could continue without Leonard Shelby present.

We all stood as the judge, hands in the pockets of his flowing black robe, entered the courtroom. Lexi barely held back her excitement, confident in the belief that without a complainant, the judge would be likely to delay or completely dismiss the case.

Judge Olgin took the bench and nodded to the bailiff, who took the judge's gavel and pounded it three times. *That's odd*, I thought. *I've never seen a bailiff do that before. It's almost as if the judge doesn't have use of his hands. . . .*

The judge turned toward Lexi. "Miss Hart?"

"Yes, Your Honor?" she said, thrusting her chest out so far I was worried her back was going to snap beneath the strain.

Judge Olgin held up two white sausages that were attached to the ends of his arms, and it took me a moment to realize that they were his hands. Heavily bandaged, wrapped in gauze.

"Your dogs say hello."

Without pause, the judge spun back to the city attorney and shelter supervisor. "Is it your expert opinion, Mrs. Fleming, that the two dogs in question are a danger to the community at large?"

The supervisor leaned forward to speak into the microphone, and I got my first good look at her face. At her scratched, bitten, definitely-going-to-scar face.

"It is, Your Honor."

"That was pretty much my impression as well," he said dryly, scratching at his bandages. "Therefore, it is the order of the court that the dogs belonging to Lexi Hart be destroyed at the Santa Monica Animal Shelter no later than tomorrow noon."

The bailiff took up his duties, banged the gavel, and Lexi, true to form, fainted once again. This time, though, no boys came to her rescue. I think any potential saviors might have been worried that she'd show her thanks by introducing them to her wuzzles for their one last meal.

Detectives Bishop and Roberts were in my office again, perched on my sofa like buzzards waiting for something to crawl atop my mahogany-grain desk and expire.

"Detectives," I said cheerily as I entered. "It's a pleasure to see you this afternoon."

The faux friendliness that they'd exuded on Monday was gone, replaced with an equally faux solemnity. It's like they were robots, perfectly programmed to display whatever emotions fit the situation.

"Miss French," said Detective Bishop, who that day had unwisely chosen to mix a navy blue oxford with olive pants. "Where have you been?"

"Santa Fe," I told them honestly. "I got back yesterday morning and took the rest of the day off."

Roberts nodded to Bishop; this must have matched with whatever information they'd gleaned from their investigation. "Can you tell us where you were the night Jason Kelly disappeared?"

"And what night would that be?" Way to think on your feet, Cassie.

"Last Thursday. A week ago."

I'd already checked the television and movie listings, so I broke out big lie number one. "I went out, I think. With a friend."

"And who would this be?"

"Claire Kimball. She works at Fox television." Bishop scribbled a few notes. They'd probably call Claire and check up on me, but we'd already gone over the detailed alibi many times. "We went to the movies to see the new Cameron Diaz."

Detective Roberts was all over that one. "Hey, I saw that. Didn't you love that scene where she gets the ketchup all over her?"

Amateur. As if I hadn't done my homework. "Actually, I'm pretty sure it was hollandaise sauce." Thank you, World Wide Web!

I think I was bumming them out, getting all these things right. I turned it around on them, went all casual. "Can I ask what the problem is, guys?"

Bishop stood up from the sofa and pulled out the chair across from mine. I didn't think anyone had ever actually sat in it before. "We got a guy down at LAX thinks he saw Jason Kelly with a woman on Thursday night at the heliport. Gave a description that sort of fits you."

"Really?" I said. *Steady as she goes, Cassie.* Right, Dad. "And what was that description exactly?"

"About five-five. Shoulder-length brown hair. Nice body."

I was pleased at the "nice body" part, but didn't show it. "So pretty much half the women in Los Angeles. The ones who aren't blonde. Have you tried talking to Lorna Wilcox?"

Bishop was about to talk again, to tell me, I'm pretty sure, that she'd admitted flying out to Jason Kelly's yacht on Wednesday night, and that the cops were now convinced that whoever was with him on

Thursday knew more than she was letting on. But before he could gab too much, his partner was at his side, leaning down and whispering something in his ear. Detective Bishop nodded and stood.

"That's all for right now," Roberts said. "We'll be in touch. And Miss French? Don't go out of the state."

I played it as cool as I could, considering that I needed to pee so badly my legs were crossed in a death grip beneath the desk. Hey, I get nervous, I have to pee. "I'm not going anywhere, Detectives. Come back and see me whenever you like."

As soon as they were gone, I hightailed it to the restroom. Once relieved of my tension and excess fluids, I scurried back to my office to find yet another interloper waiting for me within.

"Come in, Cassandra." It was Stan Olsen, sitting behind my desk. Flipping one of my business cards in his fingers. Inviting *me* into *my* office. What was happening here? I gingerly stepped inside and, when Stan made no move to get up, sat down on the sofa. "Are those police officers hassling you?"

"Not at all," I said. "Just a little friendly chat. They're still fishing around about Jason Kelly."

"Mm-hm," Stan hummed. He hadn't heard a word I said. "Cassie, Arlene Oberst received a call today from Ranjin Sunn."

I was shocked. No one would dare go directly to Arlene, the head of business affairs, for anything short of a full-on, studio-is-about-to-blow-up catastrophe.

"Is everything . . . okay?"

Stan's snake-oil smile did not fill me with confidence. "Oh, it seems everything's more than okay. Why don't you tell me what Ranjin said to Arlene?"

I was atypically at a loss for words. "Why don't I . . . what? How should I know?"

"Well, you two are so buddy-buddy, I figured perhaps you'd discussed going over my head sometime while I was taking a piss on that fucking backwater reservation. That's the only time I can figure you two got together." He leaned further back in the chair, slapping his size-ten loafers atop my desk. "What'd you do, tell him I was no good? Tell him I didn't know what I was talking about?"

"Stan, none of that happened—"

"Did you laugh at me? Hm? I hope you did. I sincerely hope you did." He launched his feet off the table and they came down hard on the floor, popping his body out of the chair. It was a nifty move, but I didn't have time to appreciate it, because suddenly he was in front of me, over me, glaring down with eyes that divulged a lot of self-hatred and doubt and breath that told me he'd been nipping at a bottle or two.

"I don't know what you thought you'd get by screwing me over, Cassandra, but we'll see where it gets you in the long run. You might be Arlene's golden girl now, but in a few weeks that's going to wear off. And as long as you're in this office and under me, you'll always be just another long-legged bitch in a skirt."

He ended this spectacular tirade by thrusting a crumpled-up fax into my shocked face and storming out of the office, trying to slam the door but failing miserably, as one of the detectives must have kicked down the doorstop on their way in. Stan pulled at the door for a few seconds and, unable to mark his exit with a bang, kicked it with the toe of his shoe and stomped off down the hallway.

I sat on the sofa for a while, trying to sort out what had just happened. First, my legs aren't that long. Second, I hadn't said anything to Ranjin Sunn that was out of the ordinary, and I certainly didn't make any overtures toward Arlene Oberst. I don't even say her name out loud, for fear that she'll appear in the office.

Smoothing out the crumpled fax against the edge of my desk, though, I began to understand why Stan Olsen had flown off the handle.

The note was sent directly from Arlene Oberst herself, off her personal fax machine three stories up and straight into Stan's office.

Stan, the memo read. *Ranjin Sunn wants to finalize the deal, but only with a counsel in your office named Cassandra French. Ranjin doesn't want you there, just the girl. You must have pissed him off. Chuck wants Sunn wrapped up as quickly as possible. The French woman has my authority to make the deal. Arlene.*

No wonder Stan was ready to tear my head off. Without any warning, we'd entered Mozart and Salieri territory (moment of confession: Everyone says *Amadeus* is such a funny movie, but I keep falling asleep by the second reel, even when I try to watch it at home. I don't know if it's the plot or the music that lulls me to sleep, but I'm willing to keep trying until I make it at least halfway through). Even if I wasn't Stan's apprentice, I was still very much his junior, and for Arlene to give me deal-making authority when that final word had never been given to Stan was a coup d'état of staggering, mythical proportions.

So mythical, in fact, that when I walked out of my office, still a bit stunned and disoriented, I was met with a wave of applause from my coworkers. The fax, it seems, had made the rounds. I was Lancelot. Stan was the dragon. The villagers rejoiced.

The applause started just like it did at the end of *Bridget Jones's Diary*, a movie I thoroughly enjoyed if only because it taught me a lot of naughty British slang and I got a guilty pleasure out of watching Renée Zellweger eat. First my secretary began to clap, then Cathy up at reception, then two of the paralegals and suddenly the whole place was cheering me on. I still had no idea what I'd done to deserve this, but it didn't matter. I walked out of the office with my head held high, the fax clutched to my chest, and a knowledge that whatever might go down from that point on, whatever calamities would befall me on my journey through this life, at least I had finally found a few powerful people who appreciated my work and understood my value to the studio and the film industry as a whole.

Now, if they could just let me know what the heck I did to earn their respect, I'd be eternally grateful. It might be nice to try to do it again sometime.

When I'd dropped Lexi off at her house after the trial, she was nearly catatonic with grief. I'd offered to come inside, mostly because I wanted to get a look at her basement and see for myself whether or not Mr.

Leonard Shelby was taking an unannounced vacation within, but she was in no shape to be a good hostess.

"You rest," I'd told her. "Lie down, take a Valium, don't think about the hearing."

"The wuzzles," she'd mumbled. "The wuzzles." Those were the only two words she had said the whole drive back to her place.

Three hours later, as I left my office buoyed by a wave of victory and acclaim, Lexi got through to me on my cell.

"You've got to come over," she said earnestly. I was glad to hear that she'd woken up and expanded her vocabulary. "I've got a plan."

A plan. Not the words I want to hear from Lexi. "Lex, I've got a thousand things to do—"

"You owe me, Cass. You owe me big. If I didn't help you figure out a place to bury Jason—"

"Cell phone!" Why do I have to keep reminding these people? But Lexi was right. I'd been hoping she wouldn't bring it up, but she had that trump card in her pocket, and it was hers to play whenever she liked.

I was at her place twenty minutes later. It had been a while since I'd been inside Lexi's house, and now that I knew her money came from Mom and Dad, I was even more resentful of the rotating series of beautiful furnishings and artwork. Every time I go over there, she's got a new sculpture, coffee table, or roof on display. Look, I make a good living, I can't complain, but it's a serious financial decision for me to order a chair from Pottery Barn, wherein I get the feeling that Lexi changes designer dining room sets as often as I do toilet paper.

When Lexi ushered me into her living room, I wasn't too surprised to find Claire waiting for me on the sofa. She raised a tumbler of vodka in salute. "She got you, too, huh?"

"I didn't exactly have a choice."

"Emotional blackmail's a bitch. Welcome to the club. You're just in time, we haven't even read last session's minutes yet."

Lexi buzzed about the house like a Ritalin kid who'd forgotten to take his meds, bouncing from one room to the next, eager to tell us her plan but unable to focus long enough to take the next step into coherency.

I couldn't take it any longer. I had to know whether or not Lexi had snatched Leonard Shelby off the street and hidden him in her house. When Lexi flitted out of the room for the third time, I turned to Claire and quickly said, "Okay, lemme have it. Have you been down to her basement?"

Claire closed her eyes, nodded, and took another sip of her drink. I grabbed the tumbler and downed the rest myself.

"Should I go take a peek?" I asked.

"It's not a pretty sight."

"He's not . . . dead, is he?"

"No, just ugly." Claire walked to the bar and refilled her drink. "I didn't think they even made toupees out of possums."

What kind of monster had I created? Lexi bullet-trained her way through the living room one more time, and, without spilling an ounce of her drink, Claire grabbed Lexi by a bony hip and spun her around.

"Sit down and get on with it already," she said, "you're making us nervous."

Lexi took a seat on the arm of her Atelier love seat and folded her legs beneath her, balancing there like a maharishi who'd forgone the vows of celibacy and poverty.

"We're going to rescue the wuzzles." Her grin was positively maniacal.

Claire and I shared a look of mutual understanding: *Let's get out of this*.

"Lexi," Claire began, "I know how you feel about your dogs, but there's a natural order to things."

"She's right," I added. "I saw it on the Discovery Channel."

"When it's a creature's time to go, it's their time to go."

"But it's *not* their time to go," Lexi whined. "They're healthy, they're active. They've got at least five or six good years ahead of them."

"And on a steady diet of human flesh, maybe even more."

"Exactly!"

Lexi was over the edge, but neither Claire nor I were able to talk her down. She had made up her mind, and was in no mood to truck with dissent. She reminded us, in no uncertain terms, that she'd helped us both out when we were in a jam, and she expected a little assistance in return.

"If it wasn't for me, Jason Kelly would still be in the trunk of your car, Cass, and Comes When Enlightened would be lying on the floor of some parking garage."

"And both," Claire added, "would smell terribly."

In the end, we came to a compromise. What choice did we have? Like it or not, Lexi was a friend, and friends help one another out in a jam, especially when they're guilted into it. It's part of an ancient code, a sacred oral tradition that, as everyone knows, hurts less than an anal one.

The deal was simple: I would help Lexi break the wuzzles out of the shelter, and Lexi would offer up the use of her basement as a temporary home for the Finishing School while my house was being tented. I would stay in the guest room and supervise, because there was no way I was turning my class over to a substitute teacher like Lexi. Usually you worry about the students taking advantage of a substitute; I had very different concerns.

"I'll bring the boys over later tonight," I said, putting down my foot once and for all. "But I'm only dealing with my original three. On the way back from the shelter, you two bring Comes When Enlightened back here yourselves."

After two more vodka tonics, Claire reluctantly agreed to the plan. Lexi was overjoyed. She leapt off the sofa and gave us two kissie-kissies on each cheek. "Thank you guys so much. I knew you'd do it! Stay right here, okay? I've got something for you."

Lexi skipped out of the room. "If she brings us back Leonard Shelby's ears," I said, "I'm first out the door."

"Only if you can push me out of the way, sister."

Lexi returned moments later, two envelope-sized wads of black latex dangling from her outstretched fingers. "Well? Do you like them?"

We peered a little closer. "What are they?" I asked.

"Our outfits, silly!" Lexi pulled down on the bottom of one of the wads, and the material expanded, stretching into a long, thin unitard.

"We're all going to wear them for the wuzzle break. Aren't they just darling?"

Spandex. Of course. Because when you're breaking two demonic dogs out of a death-row animal shelter, it's important to make sure you look as fat as possible for the security cameras.

Our first mistake was taking the bus. None of us had even been on L.A. public transportation before, let alone during the commission of a felony, but Lexi felt it crucial that we not bring any of our cars to the "jailbreak." Instead, Lexi and Claire had both left their cars at my house in Westwood. We piled into my Infiniti and I drove everyone down to the Park-n-Ride, where we stared at the bus map for a while before figuring out which one would bring us closest to the Santa Monica Animal Shelter. Eventually, we located a stop that would deposit us four blocks from our destination.

"You mean they don't just drop you off at the door?" Lexi was dismayed. "That's horrible, making people walk all that way. How can they do business like that?"

"Some people can't afford cars, Lex," I said.

"Right," mumbled Claire. "And other people own cars but choose not to take them because they're idiots."

"And thus public transportation continues to operate."

Lexi did have a point, though: The system is woefully inadequate, especially when you're trying to remain incognito. Three girls in black designer spandex unitards (at least she'd gone all out and bought us Donna Karan) with blue jeans and sneakers, accessorized to the hilt, don't exactly fit in with the basic L.A. bus crowd. I'm not saying that the people who take the bus are bad, or unworthy, or anything like that. I'm just saying they have so many other things to worry about that basic fashion choices are far down on their to-do list. For some of them, hygiene seemed to be hovering down at the bottom, as well.

Between the three of us, we had a large burlap sack, a bolt cutter, a box of Organic Greenery Dog Treats, six gardening gloves, a nylon pet carrier, and more gauze and bandages than they use ringside at a boxing match.

"Just in case," Lexi had said as she tossed the gauze into the bag. "Sometimes the wuzzles get a little rambunctious." I thought it best not to point out that their rambunctiousness was what had gotten them into this mess in the first place, and that perhaps the state knew what it was doing when it sentenced them to death. That kind of negative talk would just send Lexi into another downward spiral, and if she passed out again, I fully planned to leave her on the seat and let the bus dispatcher deal with her in the morning.

So we tried to avoid eye contact with the other passengers and sat in the back of the bus like a bitchy clique of schoolgirls, whispering among ourselves. We got out at Cloverfield and slinked our way through four darkened blocks as nonchalantly as possible, considering the fact that we were dressed like the girls from Robert Palmer's infamous "Addicted to Love" video.

(Moment of confession: I always wanted to be the Asian girl in that video; she looked as if she was having more fun than the others, and I'm pretty sure she and Bob were getting it on.)

The shelter was eerily quiet. It was only ten at night, but presumably the dogs were all tuckered out from a long day of yapping and yipping.

"How do we get inside?" I asked Lexi.

She thought it over for a second or two. "Try the front door, I guess."

Claire sighed and pulled the bolt cutters from the burlap sack. "Amateurs. Follow me."

We trotted after Claire as she led us around the back of the building, toward a high chain-link fence. She immediately set to work clipping the metallic wires, snipping out a hole big enough for everyone to fit through. "Make it a little wider," I suggested. I was going on three weeks with no gym time. Claire worked quickly and expertly, and I was impressed with her skill.

"Have you done this before?" I asked.

"Remember sophomore year at Berkeley when a bunch of radical environmentalists broke into the research lab and tried to let all the monkeys go free?"

It had been in all the papers. The monkeys, freed from their confines, refused to leave the lab and instead holed up in their cages and threw feces at anyone who tried to take them out. "You were involved in that? I don't remember you ever caring much about the environment."

"I didn't. But I'd met some cute guy at a kegger, he went on and on about the poor stupid monkeys, and I helped him break in just to get him to shut up and sleep with me."

"Did it work?"

"Unfortunately. He was lousy in bed, and it took two weeks to get the smell of monkey shit out of my hair."

She clipped the last remaining link, and a Fox-exec-sized hole fell away from the fence. "Now forget you ever heard that story and let's get this over with."

The inside of the animal shelter was just as quiet as the outside, and we tiptoed through like seasoned cat burglars, the cute little Keds that Lexi had bought for us silencing our steps.

I remembered the way to the wuzzles' kennel from the last time we visited them. There was no lock on the door leading to the dog runs, so I grabbed the handle and pulled it open as softly and slowly as I could. Carefully, quietly, I poked my head inside.

A hundred barking dogs leapt to their scruffy feet, howling and yipping in a deafening cavalcade of excitement and fear.

"Wuzzles!" Lexi cried, and ran down the middle of the kennel toward her dogs at the far end. Claire and I sighed and shook our heads; we didn't have much time before the barking pissed off some neighbor and brought a caretaker or the cops into the shelter. We jogged after Lexi.

She was already down on her hands and knees outside Jack and Shirley's run, caressing their doomed heads, smushing her lips through the fencing and letting them get in a good lick. "Bolt cutters," she said firmly, holding out her hand like a doctor in the middle of surgery.

Claire played the dutiful nurse and soon Dr. Lexi Hart was hard at work, grunting and sweating as she worked the tool into the lock, straining to snap it open.

"Wait a second," I said, taking a better look at the door to the run. "That's not locked. None of these are. They're just closed so the dogs can't get out." It's not like the critters were going to figure out how to open the doors but wind up stymied by a complicated Master Lock. The workers hadn't bothered to spring for expensive locks, so it was just a simple matter of lift and pull.

Protecting my shins with the burlap sack, I reached out and popped the chain holding the kennel door in place. It swung open easily, and Jack Nicholson and Shirley MacLaine burst out of their run and into Lexi's arms, knocking her down and licking her all over. I'd never seen Lexi that genuinely happy before. She cried and laughed and hugged the evil little furballs so tightly I thought their eyes were going to pop out.

Alas, they did not.

The chorus of barking dogs had been warming up for a good four minutes, but now they were really launching into the overture. We needed to get out, and quickly. I tossed Lexi the nylon pet carrier, and she coaxed the wuzzles inside.

"Hold up," Claire said as we prepared to leave. "This won't work."

Lexi turned around. "What won't?"

"The whole scheme. We've got a plot hole we didn't count on." Claire had slipped into exec-speak without even realizing it. She's been doing that a lot more recently. "Tomorrow morning, they come in here to take your dogs down the green mile, and the run is empty, right?"

"Right." Lexi pressed her face against the mesh pet carrier. "Because the wuzzle-puzzles are home with me!"

I figured out where Claire was going with this. "So where's the first place they go looking for them?"

Do you ever get the feeling that you're talking to a wall, and that the wall just isn't getting it? Lexi stared at us, uncomprehending.

"They go to your house," Claire explained. "And two days later, Jack and Shirley are right back here on death row."

That got through to her. Lexi clutched the bag to her chest. "No! They can't take them away again. I won't let them!"

Hugging her around the shoulders, Claire calmed Lexi down a notch. "Take it easy. All we need to do is make it look like this was a bigger job than just a wuzzle break."

That's why I love Claire. She doesn't just think fast; she thinks deviously. "I'll get the left," I offered. "You get the right."

Lexi asked, "What do I do?"

"Stand still. And don't scream."

We started at the back of the kennel and moved our way to the front, popping open run after run. As I yanked open the doors, dogs of all shapes, sizes, and temperaments bolted between my legs, barking with excitement, licking my jeans, and humping everything in sight. I bet that's what Studio 54 was like in the good old days.

Lexi barely contained herself; she wanted to pet and squeeze every single one of the little beasts. Scratching behind their ears, rubbing their bellies, she was in heaven, and would have been perfectly content to stay there all night, but we didn't have that kind of time. Soon all the dogs were free from their cages and scampering around the locked kennel, a knee-high ocean of matted fur and slobber.

"What the hell's goin' on in there?" A man's voice, from outside the kennel area. "Shut up already!"

"Security," Claire whispered. "Crap."

Lexi began to shake; she could sense the whole plan coming apart, and I knew she was way more concerned for her wuzzles than she was for the humans involved in this situation.

"Back here," I said, urging them to follow me to the kennel door. "Follow my lead."

We crouched against the wall of the kennel, just behind the space where the door would open. Soon enough, a beam of light played through the frosted-glass window, illuminating the sea of pups raging through the kennel.

"Goddamn!" The security guard unwisely flung open the door, and a wave of dogs bowled him over, knocking him to the ground. I grabbed Lexi with one hand and Claire with the other and we ran along with the pack, woofing and barking at the tops of our lungs as we streamed over the downed guard, out of the shelter, and into the yard. Like a team of trained border collies herding sheep, Claire and I drove the dogs toward the cut-out gap in the fence. Within moments, a hundred canines were loosed upon the streets of Santa Monica, scattering wildly in every direction like a pack of shoppers released upon Macy's at six A.M. the day after Thanksgiving. The dogs may have been slobbering a bit less.

We ran until we reached the bus stop at the corner of Cloverfield and Pico. No one had followed us out of the animal shelter; the security guard, if he noticed us at all, was probably too busy rounding up the two or three dogs who'd been too dumb to follow the rest of the pack.

We had to wait fifteen minutes at the bus stop to catch the right ride back to my car, during which time Lexi whispered sweet nothings into the pet carrier, and we did our best to ignore her. All around us we could hear barks and screams as the freed mob of dogs continued their mad romp about the once-peaceful beach community.

The bus ride was uneventful, as was the trip back to my place. Lexi transferred the pet carrier from my car into hers, and was preparing to take off back for her home when I stopped her. "Hey, lady, we had a deal in place."

"Oh, right," she said. "I was hoping to get home and feed the wuzzles a good meal."

"And you can do that with an extra houseguest."

The three of us marched down into the basement together. The boys were fast asleep, but Comes When Enlightened began to wake when we stood him up from the chair. The blindfold was still wrapped around his eyes, and the earplugs I'd switched out for his headphones earlier that afternoon remained in place. He couldn't see or hear us, but put up little resistance when we unlocked him from the chair and led him to the stairs.

"Be gentle with him," Claire urged us. "He's got a bad left knee."
"Will do."
"Oh, and watch his head when you take him under the doorway. Sensitive scalp."

I'd never heard my best friend speak in such tender tones about a boy before. She'd even been cynical about her middle-school crushes. "You really like him, don't you?"

Almost ashamed to admit it, Claire nodded. She took Comes When Enlightened's hand in hers and, instinctively, he gripped it tightly. There's no way he could have known that it was Claire's hand he was holding, but I think he was eager for some kind of reassuring contact.

Lexi and I each took an elbow, and we led him up the stairs and into the garage, where Lexi had left her car. We piled Comes When Enlightened into the backseat, and Claire climbed in next to him and put a comforting arm around his shoulder. He relaxed appreciably, and she snuggled closer. I closed the door and stared through the window as Claire let her head rest against her ex-therapist's shoulder. I had to admit that, even with the blindfold and earplugs and chains and cuffs, he and Claire had the potential to make a lovely couple. If I got to give the maid-of-honor speech at their wedding, I vowed to stay away from ball-and-chain jokes.

As soon as they were gone, I began a quick sweep about the house, putting together a suitcase of the clothes I'd need over the next week or so: A few days of work, business skirts and modest dresses. Check. Nightclothes. Check. A couple of racier numbers in case I decided to hit the town over the weekend. Check. Oh, and what if Arlene Oberst needed me out in Taos to make the deal with Ranjin Sunn before I could get back into my house? Better remember to bring desert-appropriate shoes.

When I was all done, I piled the three suitcases and one hanging bag into the trunk of my car. I stalled for a little longer, tidying up the house so I wouldn't be too mortified when the termite technicians came through, but I knew that eventually I would have to get the next phase of the evening started. It was time to relocate the Finishing School.

CATCH AND RELEASE

I woke the boys as gently as possible, shaking each one by the foot and applying gentle caresses to their hair. "I know it's late," I said, once I had their full attention, "and I'm sorry to throw this at you so suddenly, but we're all going to have a little field trip tonight. Isn't that wonderful?" Chipper, I'd decided, was the way to play this. There was no need to freak any of them out.

Daniel raised his hand unsteadily. "I don't feel so well," he said. "Everything's real hot."

I ran a quick Florence Nightingale with my thermometer, expecting to get the usual 100, maybe 101 or so, and nearly fell over when, in the dim light of the basement, I read the digital readout: 105.4.

I didn't know what to do. For the first time since taking the responsibility over these boys, I felt paralyzed with indecision. Daniel needed medical attention immediately, that much was clear. I'd been feeding him orange juice and Tylenol for two weeks, but obviously it hadn't been enough to stave off his illness. I've seen them throw fever patients in ice baths on TV, but the ice machine on my refrigerator was broken and in my panicked state I'd forgotten about the 7-Eleven three blocks down.

The only thing I could think of was that we needed to get to the emergency room. That meant forms and paperwork and nosy nurses asking questions. That meant medical insurance. That meant Social Security numbers. That meant, in short, danger.

But what choice did I have? I couldn't very well leave him to the ravages of fever and disease. Daniel hadn't done anything to deserve that. I was his caretaker. I was his teacher. And right now, I had a responsibility. Like a mother tending to her sick child, it was time to put my own selfish needs on hold for once.

Plans switched around in a heartbeat. "Okay, everybody stand in line. Come on, we don't have all night."

The boys shuffled into place, and I went about unhooking their cuffs and chains, giving little thought to the fact that I was leaving the boys free and open.

"Where's Jason?" asked Owen. "And the new guy, the one with the blindfold? Shouldn't they be down here?"

I froze, just for a split second, then geared back up to speed. "Let's not worry about the others," I said. "Stay focused, okay? We've got a big night ahead of us."

UCLA Medical Center is one of the premiere teaching hospitals in the nation. Experts from all around the country conduct incredible, life-saving research within its numerous hallways, and the best surgeons and doctors in the world regularly cure and heal even the most deadly of wounds and infections on a daily, even hourly, basis.

It doesn't keep them from being massive pains in the ass, though.

I'd assumed that they'd rush Daniel right inside, given the fact that he looked like a zombie and you could probably sauté fish on his scalp, but no go. They seemed to think that gunshot wounds and some sort of blunt trauma classified as a higher rating on the triage scale.

"Ma'am, could you please let the gentleman speak for himself?" The nurse at the front desk, a woman who must have been in her sixties but was trying to beat back the clock with poorly applied makeup and hair products, kept trying to sneak the admission form to Daniel, and I kept grabbing it back from her.

"He's not in his right mind," I explained. "He's got a high fever which, if you listened to me, you would know is the reason why we're here in the first place. We'll be paying by cash, so that shouldn't be a problem. So, if you'd just let me have the forms, I'll be happy to fill them out for him."

"Are you family?"

"Yes," I said flatly. "I'm his mother."

"You're his mother."

I smiled back. "Prove that I'm not."

Eventually she let me have the admission form, and I marched back to the waiting area of the emergency room. Owen, Daniel, and Alan shuffled along behind me, because they had no choice. After all, we were bound together with fishing line.

It seemed the most rational choice. Rather than bulky chains that would clank and generally call attention to us, I'd wrapped a length of near-invisible one-hundred-pound fishing line around all of our ankles, binding us together like a happy little chain gang. The box that the line came in said that it wouldn't snap even under the strain of a five-hundred-pound marlin, so I imagined that it should do a fine job keeping the boys where I could see them. I don't really have any idea how much pressure a five-hundred-pound marlin can exert, but I figured it had to be quite a bit, or there would be a lot more ugly fishing trophies on the walls of seafood restaurants.

Daniel was tethered to my left ankle, Owen to my right. Alan was on the far end, his leg strapped to Owen's. We all took our seats on the uncomfortable plastic emergency-room chairs as I filled out the forms, lying where I needed to lie but being completely honest about Daniel's condition. Daniel was moderately helpful, answering whatever questions he could through his haze, but I had to fudge a little on some of the answers.

I was halfway through the section where they ask about prior diseases when my cell phone rang. I figured it was Lexi or Claire calling to find out why I hadn't yet shown up at the house, but when I checked my Caller ID, I saw something there I hadn't seen in nearly a year: *Judy French.*

Mom was calling me. That meant one of two things: Either she was breaking the law of the land and violating everything she ever believed in by doing so, or she was about to eat her foot. Either way, I figured it would be best to answer.

"Mom," I said, "what's going on? Is your foot still on your leg?"

"I'm doing it, Cassie," I heard her say. Road noise filled the background.

"Doing what, Mom?" Eating her foot?

"I'm going to Bolivia!" She was giddy, shouting into her phone. "Can you believe it? I got another letter in the mail today from Ted, and he sent me a plane ticket and a map. I'm going to go find him, Cassie. We're going to have a life together."

This was all too much for me to take. Maybe the cell phone was blurring her words, making me hear things she wasn't actually saying. "Where are you right now?" I asked.

"Olympic and Spalding," she said. "Heading for the 405."

I pleaded with her to take a detour to the UCLA Medical Center emergency room. "It's right up Westwood Boulevard, five minutes out of your way." I couldn't believe she was leaving, just like that. Just yesterday, she was prisoner in her own kitchen, a pathetic shell of a woman relying on me to bring her the basic necessities of life, and now she was going off to hang with Ted in some Third World jungle? "You can't leave without saying good-bye."

It didn't take much convincing. She was inside the emergency room ten minutes later, and the first thing I noticed as she bounded inside was that she was wearing one of her old outfits, a stylish little boutique pants-and-jacket set that she'd bought in the pre-incarceration days. It was the first time since she was banished to her house that I'd seen her in anything other than a housecoat or schlumpy T-shirt. She looked terrific.

The second thing I noticed was that the only sounds her ankle made when she walked were the sounds that everyone's ankle makes when they walk, which is to say: nothing. There was no screaming anklet noise because there was no screaming anklet. Her leg was unadorned and, since she'd spent the last nine months or so on her sofa anyway, she didn't even have any nasty tan lines.

"Cassie Bear!" she cried as I stood from the waiting room chair and we clenched in a tight embrace. Daniel and Owen's legs came along with me as I staggered away from the bank of chairs, but the boys didn't seem to mind; they just slid down in their seats to give me some extra slack.

"Mom," I said, once we'd both separated and stopped the tears from flowing, "what happened to your anklet?"

"Did you know the damn thing comes off with one hit of a screwdriver? It's a wonder there aren't more criminals running around this country with that kind of shoddy craftsmanship."

"But aren't you worried about . . . well, you know, what the judge said?"

Mom reached out and stroked my hair with the back of her hand, the way she used to when I was a child. It was always reassuring to both of us. "Honey, I'm going to Bolivia. That means I'm leaving the country, and I don't know when I'm ever coming back. I think the judge is going to be more upset about that than he will be about me breaking the anklet."

I nodded and wiped away a few more tears. I'd complained about Mom and her visits for so long that I never realized how important it was to me to have her nearby. It was selfish, I suppose, but now it was all about to come to an end. "Are you sure about this?" I asked her. "About Ted?"

Mom laughed, and that's when I noticed the third thing about her: She was happy. Almost, dare I say, optimistic. It had been a long time since Mom had a smile on her face that wasn't, in some way, tinged with regret or cynicism. Whatever her fate was going to be, she was ready for it and eager to meet the challenge. Sure, I don't like Ted, and I can't for the life of me understand what Mom sees in him, but how can you argue with happiness?

In fact, everyone around me seemed happy. Claire had found joy, however improbable, with Comes When Enlightened. Lexi had her wuzzles back. Where did I fit into this sudden explosion of cheer?

"It's not about Ted," Mom assured me. "It's about me, making my own decisions. If I keep letting other people decide what I'm going to do with my life, then there's no point in going on. It doesn't matter if we're talking about Judge Hathaway or your father or my friends—"

"Or your daughter."

Mom smiled warmly. "Or your mother. That's all I ever wanted for you, Cassie Bear. That you're happy, certainly, but that your happiness comes from the choices you've made." She leaned in closer and whispered in my ear. "For starters, you should check out the nice-looking fellow sitting next to you. I think he's been giving you the eye."

I smiled down at Owen and he smiled back; Mom was impressed. "See," she nudged, "you've hit it off already."

We hugged again and made promises to call and e-mail and do all of the things that we could without the cops coming down on us. She figured she had about twenty-four hours before the sheriff's department realized that the electronic monitor was no longer functioning, but by then she'd be way out of their reach.

"Go," I told her. "Before I start crying again."

She handed me the keys to her condo. "Sell it if you want. If I ever do come back, I'm getting a place on the beach. I bet the people there are more willing to deliver messages from a crazy lady in a house-coat."

And then Mom was gone, out the emergency room doors and into her car, taking off down the 405 for LAX and the wilds of South America. I hope she was able to grab some penicillin on the way out.

I'd barely turned back around when Nurse Ratched appeared in front of me, all fake smiles and real scowls. "We can take him in now."

"Okay," I said, addressing my boys as I wiped away the last of the tears. "Let's all help Danny inside."

The nurse stepped in front of me. "Just the patient. The rest of you can wait out here."

"But I'm—"

"His mother. I know." She didn't seem to be going for it. "If you want him to be seen by a doctor, you're going to have to follow the rules like everyone else and wait out here."

Daniel hadn't been out of either my sight or my basement for over half a year, and now this nurse was asking me to give up complete control. That was patently ridiculous.

You listening to yourself, Cass? It was Daddy, and he made a valid point. *It's about decisions, just like Mom said. Everyone needs the chance to make his own.*

A lot of people talk about epiphanies they've experienced in the lobbies and waiting rooms of hospitals. Usually there's a loved one dying on some gurney or a sick infant in the neonatal ICU; things tend to pull into focus when the Grim Reaper's just about to come off his lunch break. For me, it was less traumatic but just as real.

I looked over to Daniel, who could barely keep his head upright. It was clear that he needed medical attention quickly, and though his illness surely wasn't life-threatening, I suddenly realized what had to be done.

"Could you turn around for a moment?" I asked the nurse, going all sweetie-pie on her. "Just a little eensy second?"

She sighed but gave in and executed a grudging 180. I quickly knelt down, pulled a pair of wire cutters from my purse, and snipped the fishing line tethering me to Daniel. Just like that, he was free. No graduation ceremony, no diploma. One snip, and it was done.

I didn't say a word. What Daniel did, what he said—it wasn't up to me anymore. I just gave him a kiss on the cheek, a pat on the back, and the nurse led him away, through the swinging double doors and out of my control.

"Now what?" asked Owen.

"Now we wait," I said, taking my seat once again on the hard plastic chairs. "That's all we can do."

We leafed through year-old copies of *Cosmo* and *In Style*, and when I noticed that Owen kept glancing over at the stack of *Sports Illustrateds*, I suggested that he pick up a copy.

"Really?" he asked, surprised. "Usually you don't like us to read that stuff."

"Read what you want," I said. It felt good, actually, knowing that I no longer had to make decisions for other people. Maybe I'd find some time to make decisions about my own life. "If you want to check out the swimsuit issue, be my guest."

Owen plucked a magazine from the top of the stack. "Actually, I was sort of hoping to check out the NFL preview. See who the good teams are going to be this year."

I didn't have the heart to tell him that the NFL was already ten weeks into its schedule. I said, "That sounds great."

So Owen opened up the *Sports Illustrated* and Alan looked on from one side as I peeked at it from the other. And I'll tell you, I learned a valuable lesson sitting there in that hospital waiting room:

Some football players have *terrific* butts.

The doctor woke me up. "Miss Hankin? Miss Hankin?"

Was I dreaming that Stuart and I had gotten married? If so, I didn't want to wake up. I shifted in the seat and tried to drift back into the dream, but there it was again. "Miss Hankin? Your husband's doing just fine."

I blinked, and the white-coated doctor was in front of me. His name tag looked like it said Dr. Bastard, and I thought, *That's not a very confidence-inspiring name for a doctor*, but I blinked again, my contacts shifted into place, and I read it right: Dr. Bastian.

"Your husband's fever is down," he said, "and he should be able to go home soon. We've got him on some IV antibiotics and fluids, but it's all under control."

I looked at my watch. It was nearly five in the morning. Owen and Alan were both passed out next to me. "Can we see him?" I asked.

"I don't think that would be a problem," he said. "In fact, he's been asking for you."

Considering that he had a needle and tube stuck into his wrist, Daniel looked pretty good. His skin was pink, his eyes were relatively bright. He sipped at a cup of apple juice as I wet his lips down with ice chips.

"I told them we were married," he whispered to me once the doctor had left the four of us alone in the room.

"I noticed that."

"But I didn't tell them anything else."

What a trooper, huh? From trust-fund brat to team player in half a year. "That's not important right now," I told him. "The only thing that matters is that you feel better."

They released him two hours later with a prescription for antibiotics, and we all climbed into my Infiniti. I'd snipped the rest of the fishing line, freeing our legs from their tethers, which made it a heck of a lot easier to drive. The sun had just risen into the L.A. sky, and we headed down Sunset toward Lexi's house.

Claire and Lexi were in a state of near-panic. "Where were you?" they cried as I pulled into the garage and unloaded my passengers. "We kept calling your cell phone. All night, no answer."

I'd gotten the calls at the hospital but had chosen to ignore them. I wanted the time alone with my boys; after all, I'd be losing them to the real world soon enough. Was it too much to ask for a few uninterrupted hours of quality time?

I told them that we'd been at the hospital but that everybody was fine. "We just need to get some sleep."

"You poor thing," said Lexi, taking me by the hand and ushering me into the house as the boys trotted behind. "You look terrible. Oh my God, look at your eyes. Claire, look at her eyes."

"They look fine to me," said Claire.

"No they're not," Lexi insisted. "They're all baggy and puffy. And that skirt is horrible. You just get right on in the back bedroom and get some sleep, and I'll take care of the boys for you." She potched me on the tush to send me on my way and turned to Owen, Alan, and Daniel. "If you three would be so good as to follow me down to the basement . . ."

I was already halfway to the back bedroom when I turned back around. "Wait," I said. "They don't go down to the basement. Not anymore."

"But that's where I've got that mean wuzzle kicker," Lexi said. "And Comes When Enlightened."

"I know that, and we'll figure out how to deal with them later. But the boys . . ." I stopped myself and readjusted my thinking. I wasn't yet ready to call them *men*, but there had to be a middle ground. "The guys sleep on beds tonight. In bedrooms, like anyone else."

"Cass," Lexi began, "you're tired, and you're clearly a little out of it. So I can take over—"

"No, Lexi," I said firmly, getting right up into her face and laying down the law, "you can't take over. There's nothing to take over anymore. Now you find the guys some beds and some sheets, and we'll discuss it in the morning."

Claire was by my side. "Cassie, honey, it *is* the morning."

"Oh," I said. "Right. Well, then we'll discuss it in the afternoon. We all need our sleep."

But sleep didn't come as quickly as I'd hoped. I lay on the queen-sized bed in Lexi's guest bedroom, staring up at the ceiling, wondering how on earth I was going to solve all of my problems. If I just let the guys go, run off into the wild, they'd eventually be questioned by the police. I had no doubts that they'd be able to keep quiet, to blindly repeat whatever story we concocted together, but the combined disappearance and reappearance of three guys at the same time would set off an investigation. Worse still, they'd all met Jason Kelly, and, if threatened, could testify that he'd been a guest in my basement. And what about Detectives Bishop and Roberts? They'd specifically told me not to leave the state, but if I wanted to take advantage of the opportunity Ranjin Sunn had provided for me at work, I'd have to find a way into New Mexico before the week was out. And, of course, I still had to find a way to get Stuart Hankin back, but it was clear that as long as everything in my life was mixed up and confused, the two of us would continue to drift apart faster than we could race back together again.

Stark and unrelenting candor had been a dismal failure. It didn't matter how many letter grades I had assigned to myself; my life clearly had not turned itself toward the better. This could only mean one depressing thing: Popular culture had lied to me. There were no easy fixes or shotgun solutions. The woman on TV was dead wrong, and all of the books I'd read and shows I'd watched about making it on my own via the power of positive thinking were just so much Silly Putty in the cracks of the dam. Eventually, despite my best efforts to the contrary, it was all bound to come crashing down.

Sweet dreams.

I awoke to a tongue up my nostril. I'm not sure if there's any sexy way to get a tongue up the nostril, but if there is, this certainly wasn't it. The tongue was cold, slimy, and bore the distinct odor of dog's breath, and it got in six or seven good licks before I shrieked and sat up in bed, tossing poor little Snoopy off my chest and onto the mattress.

"Look at how much he loves you!" Lexi cried. "Yes, you do! You love Cassie, don't you, even though she's a mean old grouch? Well, we've got something to cheer her up, don't we? Yes we do!"

My eyelids weighed eighty pounds apiece, but I managed to pry them open. Lexi was in a skimpy little shorts outfit. So, I noticed with dismay, was Snoopy.

"What time is it?" I asked.

"Just past six," Lexi said.

"A.M.?"

"No, six at night, silly. You slept for almost twelve hours." She turned her attention back to Snoopy. "And we've had so much fun during that time, haven't we? Yes we have! Yes we have!"

Though I'd been asleep for half a day, it felt as if I'd just laid my head on the pillow. I pivoted and hung my legs off the bed. "Where is everyone?" I asked.

"Claire went to work. The boys are in the den."

"Are they awake?"

"I don't know," Lexi admitted. "I haven't checked on them in a while." She grabbed my arm and hoisted me out of bed; considering I outweigh her by thirty pounds, it was pretty impressive. "Come on, Snoops, let's go see if Cassie's boys are still asleep!"

Snoopy and I followed Lexi through her house. I realized, with no small degree of joy, that the wuzzles weren't chasing after me and biting me to death.

"Hey, Lexi," I said, "where did Jack and Shirley go?"

She scooped Snoopy and his short-shorts off the floor and snuggled him close. "Snoopy and the wuzzles haven't learned to get along like good brothers and sisters yet," she said, stroking Snoopy's fur, "so I've set up a schedule. From nine until twelve, it's wuzzle time. Then from twelve until three, it's Snoopy time again. Then from—"

"I get it," I said, making sure to remember which times were safe and wuzzle-free and which were not. "But I don't remember Snoopy being here this morning."

Lexi led me toward the den. "He wasn't. Stuart brought him by around ten. You were already sleeping."

Stuart! He'd been near Lexi again. What had she told him about me? What kind of fibs had she been spreading? "Why didn't you wake me?" I asked.

"You'd just gone to bed. And don't worry about it. You can talk to him all you want."

"How? How am I supposed to do that, Lexi, when every time I try to talk to him, somehow you manage to get your boobs in the way?"

With a game-show hostess smile and a bump of her hip, Lexi popped open the door of her den. I stepped inside.

The boys were there. Owen, Alan, and Daniel lay side by side on a king-sized fold-out bed, sitting up and watching an old *Three Stooges* show on TV.

"Hey, guys," I said as I entered. "How's it going?"

Owen and Alan smiled tightly and returned to watching their show, but Daniel couldn't meet my gaze. "What's up?" I asked him. "Are you feeling okay? Lexi, did you give him the antibiotic?"

"He's fine," Lexi assured me. "His fever's below a hundred."

But he still wouldn't look at me. I snapped my fingers in front of his eyes, hoping to get some kind of response, but all he would do was glance over at the closed closet door.

"Do you . . . want me to look in the closet?" I asked. Daniel shrugged.

Lexi urged me on, shaking with excitement almost as rapidly as Snoopy. "Go on, check it out. I think you'll be proud of me."

My arm suddenly weighed a thousand pounds, but I powered through the pain and grabbed the door handle. Half knowing and half fearing what was inside that closet, I closed my eyes, took a deep breath, and pulled the door ajar.

That was just over twelve hours ago. It's taken me that long to write all of this down. I may no longer believe in the power of stark and unrelenting candor, but I figure it can't hurt to have all my bases covered, just in case.

I shut the door on Stuart Hankin as quickly as I'd opened it. Like Comes When Enlightened, he'd been strapped to a chair (a classic Eames, which was a nice choice) and deprived of all the basic senses. No wonder Daniel had been so horrified; his brother was tied up in the closet like some fairy-tale interloper.

I was ready to explode. Mount Cassandra had reached her final stage of dormancy. I stormed out of the room, dragging Lexi behind me and slamming the door so the guys wouldn't have to hear us go at it.

"What the fuck are you doing?" I yelled, then took my volume down a notch. "You know how much I like Stuart!"

Lexi tried to squirm out from beneath my grasp. "Cass, that hurts."

"How could you do this to me, Lexi? Just when we had a chance of making something happen?"

I pushed Lexi away, and she staggered away, bouncing off the far wall before coming back at me. "He kicked the wuzzles!"

"Oh, not this shit again—"

"He dropped off Snoopy and I invited him inside. I figured maybe I'd see if he wanted to go to coffee, talk about you—see, I was doing it for you—and then Snoopy and the wuzzles got into a fight and he tried to separate them and they started biting him, and . . . well, now he's in the closet. But it's a good thing, Cass! He can join the school. We can teach him to be nice. Isn't that what you want? A nice man?"

"What I want, Lexi, is Stuart. Just as he is. No more school, no more students."

Lexi folded her arms across her chest. They barely reached. "Well, I'm afraid that's not possible. Stuart's already been enrolled in the class, and he's going to have to go through a rigorous course of study. If you won't continue the Finishing School, then I will."

I didn't know what to say. Didn't know what to do. Short of kicking Lexi in the shins and running for the hills, I had no answers.

It wasn't Daddy who came to me then, but the thirteen-year-old Cassandra Susan French, the one who's usually so damned negative about everything. This time, though, she had a new take on things.

You can do it, she said, and instantly I knew what she meant. *You can solve everything with one simple move.*

Holy shit, she was right. Maybe she had small boobs and a big butt, and perhaps she had to shave her upper lip or the dark hairs up there would make her look like Juan Valdez, but that pubescent Cassandra Susan French knew how to make things right.

So I did it. I didn't think, I just acted.

"Hey, Lexi," I said, pushing away the anger and lacing my tone with honey. "I've got such a great idea."

Like one of her prized wuzzles, Lexi was beautiful, vicious, and easily distracted. "You do? Does it involve shopping?"

"Of course it does," I said. "Why don't you follow me down to the basement, and we'll talk about it?"

THE NEW CLASS

It's been nearly half a year since I finished that last journal entry, each and every phrase practically swollen with stark and unrelenting candor. Now that I've reread it, I feel I should apologize to myself for being such a pain in the you know what, but that's what stark and unrelenting candor is all about. Still, I did whine an awful lot.

Sorry so long and all that, but it's been a busy time here at the French household. In fact, I've just now gotten back from the grand opening of Stuart's new club, a fabulous new place up on the west side called Gratis. It's hip and trendy and now. *The only theme*, goes our motto, *is no theme*. That tends to confuse some of the more obtuse customers, but they drink a lot, and Stuart says that's where most of his profit margin comes from, so hurrah for the dumb.

I sat with Stuart and Claire at a large VIP table set up in the back, across from Daniel and his new wife, Emmanuelle. She's such a dear, and I've really grown to love her accent. Now that I know she's not after my Stuart, we get along just wonderfully. Their baby, a little girl named Sophie, just turned six months old the other day, and Daniel and Emmanuelle threw a little party at their place in the Palisades, just a small get-together for friends and family. The Spielberg/Capshaws were there. Kate is *so* sweet. I brought the baby a Winnie-the-Pooh pasta set made out of actual bone china. I don't even think six-month-old babies can eat pasta, but when Sophie's ready to go al dente, she'll be doing it in style.

We sat at our VIP table and talked about film and music and the decline of good continental food, laughing and chatting well into the night. At one point, as we prepared to hit the dance floor, Emmanuelle excused herself to go to the ladies' room.

"I'll come, too," I said, standing with her. It had been a while since we'd been out together; she stayed home with Sophie most nights, but couldn't miss the grand opening of her brother-in-law's club.

Emmanuelle took her time in the stall. "My bladder . . . it's a wreck since I had the baby."

"Don't worry about it," I told her. "My bladder's a wreck and I haven't even thought about a baby."

"You've got time, Cassie, don't worry about it." She flushed and emerged from the stall looking as radiant as ever. We both washed up and brought out our compacts. I'd made sure that Stuart's architects and builders understood that the ladies' lounge was a high priority; as a result, the bathrooms at Gratis had scored entire articles in *Los Angeles* magazine and *Architectural Digest*.

As we reapplied our eye shadow, Emmanuelle turned to me and said, "Cass, could I ask you something?"

"Anything. So long as it's after 1994. Before that, it's all a blur."

"Why doesn't Daniel ever talk about that Lexi woman?"

I rested my eyeliner on the marble counter. "You know, Manny—" that's what I call her now "—that was a time in his life we can never really understand. You've got to remember that he was in her basement for like six, seven months. Ever since she took him from that party in the hills. Who knows what she did to him, or to the other men she had down there."

"And you never knew?" she asked. "Not even an inkling?"

"Not even a smidgen. We were close, but . . . Lexi was an odd duck." I put away the eyeliner and went for my blush. "You heard where she buried Jason Kelly's body, right?"

"On her parents' farm, I heard."

"Uh-huh. With a DVD of *Rangers* on top of it."

Emmanuelle shivered. "All I can say is thank God that Owen guy got loose and led the police back to her house before something happened to Danny. Or Stuart."

Stuart was quite forthcoming with the police, detailing for them how Lexi had smashed him over the head with a glass vase and strapped him to a chair inside a den closet. His story was corroborated by a Mr. Leonard Shelby, who'd been involved in a lawsuit against Lexi when he was kidnapped from a park near his home, and a psychiatrist from Newport Beach who'd just broken off a relationship with one of Lexi's best friends when he was nabbed in his office parking garage. The three men who'd been held in Lexi's custody the longest were relatively silent, but corroborated with the tales told by the others.

I still get e-mails from the boys now and again, keeping tabs on their lives as they incorporate what they learned into their day-to-day existence. Owen has resumed his life as an electrician, picking up where he'd left off before his almost yearlong interruption. He's got season tickets to the Dodgers now, but stays away from the beer stands. Alan gave up on pursuing the life of a spoken-word poet and applied to a few postgraduate programs, eventually relocating to Ithaca, New York, where he's in a five-year postdoc in landscape architecture. He still attends open-mike nights at the local bars and wows undergraduate coeds with his tales of life in Los Angeles. Daniel, we now know, came home to find his fiancée two hours from giving birth to a child he hadn't even known existed.

Once the detectives found Jason Kelly's body on a farm owned by Lexi's parents up in the artists' community of Ojai, the case was all but solved. Six different men had fingered Lexi for the job, and all of the physical evidence—chains and manacles in her basement, receipts from S & M shops on Santa Monica Boulevard—pointed to her as the sole culprit.

The only problem was that Lexi Hart was nowhere to be found. She'd gone on the lam, the cops guessed, when the first of her captives escaped, and no one had seen her since. After six months of dead ends and empty leads, the case, though still technically active, was considered all but closed.

Strangely enough, Lexi disappeared the same week my mother went AWOL from her house arrest, even though the authorities didn't realize she'd gone missing until months after the fact. Mom's parole officer, having not heard from her for weeks, reported her to the sheriff's office, who claimed that their devices showed her electronic anklet was still working and inside the condo. When the police broke down the door to her apartment, they were attacked by two small, black, fluffy dogs, one of whom was wearing the anklet around his neck. Someone had been coming into the building unseen and feeding the dogs by sliding food beneath the front door and then running away as quickly as possible. The dogs were taken into custody by the sheriff's office, and eventually adopted by a lieutenant in the K-9 division, who turned them into expert drug-sniffing wuzzles. The last I heard, they'd made a one-million-dollar bust down off the Long Beach pier and received a key to the city made out of rawhide.

Emmanuelle and I left the restroom fully made up and ready to boogie down. "It may take Daniel a while to want to talk about his experiences," I explained to her. "He may never come around. You just have to be prepared for that."

She nodded her head, the long hair flowing in and out of her face. "I'd give anything for Danny," she said. Then, leaning in closer, she added, "Before he . . . went away, he was wild. Not . . . tame, yes?"

"Some women like that."

"I did, I think. But that is an emotion for schoolgirls, not for women. Once I became pregnant, I thought perhaps I could change him. Make him learn how to be a proper husband. A good father. But since he has returned . . . he is everything I ever wanted. Respectful. Caring. Kind." Emmanuelle was nearly crying. "To me, he is almost perfect."

We locked elbows and walked arm in arm out onto the dance floor. Claire was already out there, chatting it up with a handsome fellow in a brown vest. I was glad to see she was getting back into the groove of things after her relationship with Comes When Enlightened fizzled out for the second time. She dumped him this time around. Told him that while she might not have been crazy enough for him, he was more than screwy enough for the both of them.

Stuart, Claire, Daniel, Emmanuelle, and I danced well into the night, meeting new people and hearing new stories. Everyone had read about Lexi in the papers, and a few people wanted to meet the infamous girls who'd been friends with her, but, for the most part, Claire and I blended in with the rest of the crowd and had a smashing good time.

I came home around two A.M. to find a case of Veuve Clicquot, my favorite champagne, waiting for me on my doorstep. There was a note attached:

Ranjin Sunn's deal has been signed and delivered, all thanks to you. We expect even more from you in the future. Congratulations. Arlene Oberst.

It was nice to be appreciated. Of course, the promotion to vice president didn't hurt, either. Somehow, after I'd flown to Taos and helped Ranjin iron out his deal, a lot of other influential directors had gotten word that I was the business affairs attorney to talk to if you wanted to get things done right, and suddenly the studio had a lot more clout with the hot names in town. Stan Olsen nearly quit in protest when I was bumped up to vice president, but Arlene stepped in and calmed the waters by giving Stan a bigger office on a higher floor. We've barely seen each other since. I don't have time to wander the hallways, anyway; I've got a lot of work to do, each and every day of the week.

I dragged the case of champagne into my living room and changed out of my club-hopping clothes. Snoopy was sleeping on the living room rug, and I didn't want to wake him up, so I moved through the house as quietly as possible. It was nearly two-thirty by the time I'd taken off all my makeup and accessories, but I was still in a chatty mood.

Sliding back the dead bolts on the basement door, I flicked on the overhead light and tiptoed down the stairs.

"Lex?" I called. "Are you up?"

It had taken a while to find a manacle small enough to fit around her ankle without slipping off, but once I'd done that, the rest had fallen into place. Lexi yawned and sat up on her cot, stretching as she turned to sit on the bed.

"Is it morning yet?"

"Not yet," I said. Beneath my arms were a stack of magazines, familiar stock to Lexi by this point. "I just thought we could go through a few more dresses, see which ones you like."

"Sure," said Lexi. She was so much more cooperative these days. Man, does that girl have a set of lungs on her. I thought I was going to have to soundproof the soundproofing. "That sounds like fun."

I opened this month's issue of *Modern Bride* to the page I'd marked and pointed at a gorgeous Demetrios strapless gown. "They've got it in bone, too."

"What about ivory?" she asked. "You've got such beautiful skin, and it would really set off your hair."

"You think so?" I grabbed my copy of *Bridal Guide* and showed her a similar dress in a slightly darker tone. "What about this one?"

"Oh, I like that. Without all the beading."

"Really?"

"Oh yes," said Lexi, folding her legs beneath her as she reached into the pile and pulled out yet another catalog of wedding couture. "Here, now this is something you should really consider, given your figure and the way your waist tapers . . ."

We stayed up half the night, laughing and giggling over gowns and dresses, invitations and party favors. I'm in no hurry. We've got nearly eleven months to do this right. Stuart and I have given ourselves a full year to plan the wedding, but I've always believed that an early start is a good start. And when you've got talent like Lexi's on your side, you can't let it go to waste.

No doubt about it, I'm giving her an A for fashion and style. And that's a natural A. We don't grade on a curve here. Well, at least not until we get a few more students. Lorna Wilcox comes to mind as a potential candidate, as does this sassy retail clerk in the shoe department at Barneys who always makes me wait a half hour before helping me find my size. But I've got time; there's no need to rush things. Cassandra French's Finishing School for Girls is open for enrollment.

Acknowledgments

I am surrounded by women.

In my home, in my business life, in my daily trek through the world, I'm buffeted and comforted by estrogen left and right.

It's logical, I guess, that I'd eventually write a book from a woman's point of view. Hopefully I pulled it off. If not, blame my Y chromosome. If I was successful, then I owe it all to the following XX-chromosome carriers:

My wife, Sabrina, who fully accepted that while researching this book, I spent untold hours reading neon-pink-covered novels and browsing fashion websites without explanation. She keeps me honest, sane, and happy, and I couldn't ask for more.

My daughter, Bailey, who is as much a joy at four years old as I suspect she will be a terror at fourteen. Her energy and creativity are seemingly boundless, and every day I spend with her is a flurry of exhaustive joy.

My mother, Judi, who has never been convicted of any telemarketing fraud, but who *is* five-foot-one with a bob of blond hair. I've lampooned her in two books now, and she's been a great sport every time. Any trace elements of estrogen running through my own bloodstream are wholly her fault.

My agent, Barbara J. Zitwer, who probably has more faith in me than anyone other than my immediate family and isn't afraid to say so. I'm not sure who she loves more—Cassandra French or Vincent

Rubio—but it's safe to say she's my number one fan, and I can't thank her enough for that.

My editor, Cassie Jones—yes, Cassie was editing Cassie—who really understands the trials and tribulations of Ms. French, though I'm pretty sure the real Cassie has neither men in her basement nor a basement. I've had such fun working with her on this book and I hope there are more to come.

My friend Julie Shine, who vetted my legal gaffes and allowed me to snip little bits from her life, reshape them, and pop them into this book—including her two little wuzzles (yes, beware, they're real), Fred and Maggie.

My friend Laine Kontos Oberst, who acted as a fashion advisor, even though she didn't know it. Laine has the freakish ability to recall any outfit she's worn at any time of her life. You give her a date—even one twenty years back—and she'll tell you what she was wearing. Laine, any time I had a question about outfits or colors, it wasn't just for my own personal edification. I'm sure you're relieved.

Okay, to finish it off we do have one man on the list—my friend Tony Park, a compound pharmacist who I pestered with questions about chloroform and opiates and a billion other things that probably made him think about calling the cops to my house. The fact that he didn't means I know where I can go should I decide to actually become felonious one day.